LØST B1TS

KERRY NIETZ

REALM AWARD WINNING AUTHOR

FREEHEADS

LOST BITS by Kerry Nietz

Published by Freeheads

http://www.kerrynietz.com

Cover Designer: Kirk DouPonce

Editing and proofreading: Jill Domschot

Book Design: Kerry Nietz via Atticus

ISBN: 978-0-9971658-6-9 (paperback)

ISBN: 979–8-8270442-5-3 (hardcover)

To friends Scott and Becky Minor
For their undying efforts to nurture authors
And expand the reach of stories like mine.

ALSO BY KERRY NIETZ

FICTION

DarkTrench Saga Novels
A Star Curiously Singing
The Superlative Stream
Freeheads
DarkTrench Shadow Novels
Frayed
Fraught
Peril in Plain Space Novels
Amish Vampires in Space
Amish Zombies from Space
Amish Werewolves of Space
Takamo Universe Novella and Novels
Rhats!
Rhats Too!
Rhataloo
Novels
Mask

NONFICTION

FoxTales: Behind the Scenes at Fox Software
Faith in Fiction Devotional (contributor)
Get to the Margins (contributor)

Acknowledgments

To editor Jill Domschot for making time in her packed and perilous schedule to step into my robot world. Your insights and corrections are always helpful and appreciated.

To expert reader Lisa Godfrees. What does this make? Seven now? Thank you for your willingness to read whatever mess I send your way. You're an amazing help.

To the other readers and writers whose encouragements always seem to arrive in my inbox or chat window at just the right time. You've kept me free of the junkyard of despond. Thank you.

Thanks for another priceless bit of artwork, Kirk DouPonce. I appreciate your vision and your friendship. You never disappoint.

Thank you to Leah, Silas, Natalie, and Toby for putting up with the weird writer of the family. Love you all so much.

And big thanks to the Lord for allowing me to do this thing I love. May it glorify you in some small way.

⦿⦿⦿⦿ ⦿⦿⦿1

1

An object fell, dropping onto something else, which shifted another object—a heavier object. That item wobbled for a few seconds before toppling over. Its weight moved more objects, starting a small avalanche atop an abandoned heap.

At first, there seemed to be no specific direction. No indication that the movements would accomplish much. But potential became kinetic, and kinetic became cause.

In the process of all the sliding and tumbling, a hole formed.

It was a minuscule thing. A tiny fissure. A circling hawk might have missed it.

The sun found everything, though. Light saw the hole and trickled down, bouncing off forgotten metals and broken mirrors. Down, down, down it moved, illuminating decades of wonders. Revealing lost treasures and distant memories. Producing color where there had been only black.

So many wonders. Shiny things formed of plastic, gold, and steel.

At last, the light touched significance. A clean photocell on the back of a rounded head. The cell responded to the light. Its surface changed from dark blue to silver orange. It drank in the photons, converted them, and distributed power to every system. To motivators, sensors, waste and storage faculties. To a circulatory system and a processing system.

Three hours passed. The sun set and darkness returned.

All those processes, those tiny electronic miracles, came to a halt. Power starved systems queried for more, and denied, cried in distress. What little energy had been stored was distributed, shared equally, and exhausted. Warmth and potential faded away.

The night brought rain. What started as a shower at the top of the heap became a torrent at the bottom, where *he* waited. Water touched every surface, splashing and running. Finding places that had been untouched and unwashed for decades. Damaging some, aiding time's corrosive work, but also cleaning some. Freeing some. Uncovering points of friction.

The sun rose gloriously the next day. Again, light poured in the hole. Additional receptive photocells were there to greet it this time. More photons became energy. More distribution, more storage, more checks and corrections.

Temperatures balanced. System needs were fulfilled. Potential to kinetic to cause.

Then thought! A realization of purpose. The recognition of peril. *I am...entombed. Must. Get. Free.*

Appendages, facsimiles of human arms and legs, pushed and pulled. Swiveled and turned. Photoreceptors peered at whatever could be seen. Scanned and analyzed, providing data for the decision matrix.

Simple directives formed.

That metal plate is an obstacle! Move it! Now the broken wheel. Push it there to the left. That bucket! Move it right.

With every movement, every displaced object, his tomb became more fragile. More tenuous. Small shifts occurred. Objects slid down, pinning one of his legs. Then an arm. The light began to fade.

The light! The power! Heuristics screamed. *Mustn't lose the light.*

Motion ceased. Some light remained, but it wasn't enough. Not to feed the whole body.

Power diverted to the decision matrix. Heavy thought began. Minutes passed.

Finally, he turned his head slowly upward. Synthetic eyes focused on the light, and with it, the hole. That miraculous break in the obstacles above. It was the path of power, could it also be the path to freedom?

Up! He needed to go up.

He remained still for a few minutes more. Drinking in the sun. Collecting and storing as much energy as he could. After the internal gages reached a place of usable efficiency, he started to vibrate. The motion kept the in-falling of objects to a minimum, while loosening his trapped arm and leg. He slid both hands carefully over his head, toward the light.

And began to climb.

His was only a single heap of trash among many, strewn across countless acres. A mountain of indistinguishable items that formed a large, ugly, whole. The predominate colors were grey and brown, but other parts of the spectrum were represented. Some reds and blues. All bore the dimming of time and disuse. All were bleached by sun and rain.

If a curious hawk had landed on that heap, it would have heard scratching, desperate sounds. The sort of noises a mouse makes in the dead of night when all others are asleep. Scratching, scurrying, nibbling. Finding a bit of fluff here or straw there and taking it somewhere else. Pushing and rearranging. Making its way through formerly impassable spaces. Sometimes straining with all its might. Taxing itself. Stretching and resting.

Finally, the surface near the hole shifted. A piece of flattened metal unseated and slid down one side of the heap like a child's sled. A discarded bicycle frame shivered and tumbled away, too. A black cube, formerly used to distribute entertainment, spiraled off. Then a fur-bearing mechanical toy. A soup bowl. A round, shattered clock.

His right hand broke free to the air. It had four fingers and a thumb, just like a human hand it was meant to resemble. Smudged and dented and light blue in color. The protective plating from the back of the hand was missing, so that the silver sinews inside were exposed. Portions of the hand were still shiny enough to reflect light, which created small afternoon stars.

Left hand followed the right. Then the top of his head appeared.

His cranium was oval and blue, though it bore vertical scrapes on its sides from the ascent. There was a plum-sized divot over his right temple—the souvenir of an active past.

Otherwise, he looked like a midlevel service robot. Two illuminated "eyes" above a triangle of a nose piece. Narrow mouth slit that couldn't really open but could still shift and bend to mimic human expression.

With little effort, he freed his shoulders and repositioned his hands so that he could push against the heap's top surface. Within a few minutes, he'd extracted himself completely.

He rose slowly to his feet, noting the places in his musculoskeletal system that tweaked warnings along the way. He didn't know what human pain was like, but warning pulses had to be similar. They could distract and inhibit his processing—sometimes for minutes. He was created to deal with them as quickly as possible.

Generally, K-404 found his abilities adequate to his tasks, but climbing wasn't a typical undertaking.

Now fully vertical, he ordered a complete system diagnostic. He engaged his visual and audio sensors, too, accumulating input streams with the hope of making sense of his current surroundings.

The diagnostic finished before he was able to make a full sweep of the area. He had internal inconsistencies, chiefly from missed maintenance and unlogged abuse.

How long had he been here?

His sensors perplexed his logic circuits. The external view was one of endless piles of "junk." The sky was clear and a bluish-green color. The sun was past its zenith, now moving toward the western horizon. Though he suspected it was late afternoon, he wasn't certain because his time component was one of the inconsistencies. Sustained power loss had rendered it unavailable.

There was nothing familiar about this location. It matched nothing in his local storage. He had no access to off-site storage, either. The sensors used for touching those were malfunctioning.

He wasn't even certain of his exact position. He had a general sense of direction due to the sun. But his precise location?

A mystery.

How worrisome. He should have known where he was.

⊘⊘⊘⊘ ⊘⊘I⊘

2

K-404 spent the next half hour descending the exterior of the garbage heap. There were missteps along the way. A few places where he miscalculated the strength of a foothold and slid or rolled. New items were added to his problem list. More strained servos and fractured plating. Nothing severe, but his list was alarmingly long now. Longer than he'd normally let it grow before service.

Some of the items on the list were pressing. Couldn't be ignored forever.

Most distressing was the absent location information, though.

At ground level, he found the nearest clearing and studied the sky. He counted a quartet of large birds—doubtless carrion eaters—circling overhead. He saw no airships, no hovercars, or lite bikes. Not even the vapor trails that those conveyances left behind when they passed.

There should be other machines farther up. Satellites that maintained the positioning system that he used. Were they no longer in place? Or was the problem on his end? He wasn't sure.

He had a purpose. A place he belonged. Near coordinates 40.307069 and −82.697618. He should go there.

But how?

He stood motionless for a time. Analyzing the possibilities. Finally, with another glance at the sky, he decided to go north. He knew he didn't belong here, so the best course of action was to leave. And north seemed as good a direction as any.

An hour passed, while his feet crunched over stone and steel. The view changed little. Pile after pile, one hulking grey mass after another. Monuments built of discards and broken dreams. The prevailing scents cataloged by his olfactory sensors were "unpleasant" and "rotting." A mixture of sulfur, methane, and ammonia.

Occasionally, a furry creature—a rat or mouse—darted away into the shadows. Theirs and the circling birds above were the only motion aside from his own.

Why was he here? He was a fully automated service robot. Top of the line, crafted from the finest components. Assembled in the North Wilson plant in the year—

He cocked his head, searching for the precise date. He couldn't quite find it, though. As if the memory unit that contained it was gone with no backup available.

That, too, was worrisome.

He wasn't really junk now, was he?

No. His family would never deem him so. Never leave him to this.

A noise paused his thoughts. It started as a distant throbbing, but as seconds ticked by, the volume increased. Soon it was a midrange roar with a bass thump mixed in. 404 reduced the input volume to his audio receptors.

A shadow formed overhead as a portion of the sky filled with a large, black conveyance. It was a circular behemoth with multiple rotating engines. Heavy smoke billowed from ports along its sides. It drifted and lurched twice before coming to rest above a heap north of his position.

404 felt a glimmer of hope. Here was a vehicle. Vehicles transported humans. Humans would know his current location and could direct him where he wanted to go. Connect him with his family.

He simulated his best smile, then raised a hand and waved.

A dozen beams of light emerged from the craft and formed a ring around the heap's base. 404 guessed they were laser-based sensors. He contemplated entering their circle so he could be found and recognized. He took a step that direction, but a high-pitched shriek stopped him. A hole opened on the bottom of the craft. It was round and serrated.

His hopefulness increased. The airship had seen him and opened a door! A mere two steps stood between him and the circle of light. He took another step.

There was the howl of a wounded beast and the air around him began to churn. The top of the circled heap tore loose and disappeared into the craft's opening. Dirt and smoke were everywhere, making it hard to see. The rest of the heap shuddered and started to drift upwards.

The vehicle's suction pulled on him. He took a step back, but his feet seemed to lighten. To disconnect from the earth.

More of the heap separated and spun upward. There was a crunching sound as refuse met maw along with flashes of light. Then all passed within.

A sheet of metal broke from the pile and whistled upwards. It lodged over the hole, and the whistle intensified. The maw's serrated portion engaged. These "teeth" shredded the metal into bits. These, too, were drawn inside.

The upward momentum intensified. Portions of other heaps began to shift and move. The roar became omnipresent. The only scents were smoke and ash.

404's mass became negligible. He engaged the magnetic assists in his heels, but they were no help. He was lifted in the air, where he hovered in one place.

Warnings percolated, filling his inner queue.

"Hello there," he said. "This isn't right. I'm still operational. I'm not to be eaten."

His gyroscopic unit fought to keep him upright. He floated to the left and turned parallel to the ground.

With a moan, the remainder of the heap escaped into the air. Clumps of forgotten matter surrounded him. Remnants of kids' toys, conveyances, and manufacturing supplies. He recognized the words "better sleep" on a bottle label as it drifted by.

He'd never actually slept, but he knew humans considered it important. Would dismemberment feel like sleep?

His feet were level with his head now. His decision matrix flummoxed. This wasn't the sort of situation it typically had to contend with. His closest prior experience was when he'd fallen into a pool. Could that help here? He waved his arms and legs in a mimicry of swimming. He managed to push two clumps of garbage away but remained in the air, slowly moving upwards.

"This is not good," he said. "Not good at all."

He tried to swim again but somehow got flipped so that he now faced the craft. He smiled and waved again. The maw roared in response.

His acceleration increased. He beat the air. Kicked with his legs. Garbled emissions came from his voice center. Robotic shrieks.

Dirt and refuse pelted his body, making pinging noises as they struck.

There was a final surge upwards. Debris flowed up and around him. He beat his arms faster and faster, attempting to be one of the carrion birds he saw. He must move. Must survive.

The last of the pile flowed into the maw. The maw groaned, then belched fire and steam.

The maw closed.

And 404 fell.

⊘⊘⊘⊘ ⊘⊘11

3

He wasn't sure how long he lay on the bare ground. Milliseconds after his optical sensors began to function, though, he was hit with a wave of new warnings. Alert after alert of shortcomings and potential failures. Systems in distress. Appendages taxed. Lost productivity and power.

He ignored the torrent as best he could, focusing only on the blue-green sky. There was no discernible threat now. No thunderous conveyance or smoking, serrated maw. Birds traced the spot the aircraft had once filled.

Did the birds perceive him as edible? Was he their future target?

A laugh percolated onto his queue. He let it slip through his mouth, chortling alone in a tinny manner. He smiled at the sky, the birds, and his survival in the face of dismemberment.

He didn't want to be deactivated again. Ever.

He reviewed his list of problems, the robotic equivalent of asking "What hurts?"

The answer was "Quite a bit!" He decided to lie still and soak up the sun's power for a while. Rest and recuperate. There was no hurry.

He was in one piece, at least. He'd lost more back plating in the fall, but all his appendages were still attached, as was his head. A bit of fortune in an otherwise difficult reactivation cycle.

Was it safe to stay where he was? Would another maw-ship return to finish the job?

And why had the last one left so suddenly? Perhaps a load limit of some sort? Had he been spared by capacity restrictions and weight ratios?

Regardless, 404 was fine with the result.

"Are you going to lie there forever?"

404 focused on the present, pushing all tasks and warnings aside. He slowly lifted himself on one elbow and scanned his surroundings. He noted the clearing the maw-ship's work had created and the heaps surrounding it. Otherwise, he saw nothing unusual.

Someone had spoken, though. He was certain of that.

"Who's there?" he asked.

"Me!" the voice said. "Can you stand?"

404 searched his warning queue for leg issues. There were some, but none that were debilitating. "I...think so," he said.

"Then get up and help me!" the voice said.

"Help you?" The voice came from somewhere to his right, near a mini-heap that had slid free from the heap beyond it. The mini-heap was, like everything else, mostly grey and black with only a few shiny surfaces. Small places of reflection.

404 applied a hand to the ground, and with a clanking lurch, got to his feet. Two new warnings appeared—leaked coolant and a loose seal, but otherwise, he was functional. Able to walk a hundred kilometers without adjustment. Or so he hoped.

He took a step toward the mini-heap. "It sounded like you were over here," he said. "But I don't—"

"I *am* over here!" the voice said. "I'm precisely over here. Can't you see me?"

He mimicked a raised eyebrow and focused on the mini-heap. The entire thing was shorter than his waist. The world was full of mechanical devices, many of which could fit inside that heap. But he couldn't pattern match any of them. "I really can't," he said. "No." He raised a foot. "I guess I'll simply—" A shrill scream stopped him.

"I'm right here!"

404 remained frozen in place and carefully looked around.

"Light of Heaven, can't you sense me?"

"Sense you?" 404 consulted his failure list. Sure enough, he'd lost the ability to locate nearby mechanicals too. Another noncritical system he'd ignored. He lowered his shoulders and shook his head. "I can't sense you, no. I have an exhaustive list of—"

"You're in a land of refuse! How are you even functional?"

He shrugged. "I'm not sure."

"Well, I'm under your right foot now. Step back and look. Step *slowly*."

404 followed the voice's instructions.

"Now, look down."

404 saw a square centimeter of reflective surface. On it was the image of an eye. A single blue eye.

"Do you see me?"

He nodded. "I think so, yes," he said. "What are you?"

"I'm a com-Panion. Model X12."

404 bent over. The reflective object was partially buried. "A what?" Whatever it was, there seemed to be more of it.

9

"A companion. A fully integrated, portable friend and connector."

"A communication device?"

The eye changed to teeth. "A communication device!" It laughed loudly. "You take me for a phone? Leave me. Leave me now."

What a strange request. 404 was designed to comply with polite requests, though, so he straightened and turned away. He guessed where north was, pointed himself that direction, and started to walk.

"What are you doing?"

"Leaving, like you requested. Be good, Eye!"

"No, wait! Don't do that."

404 stopped walking. "But you said—"

"Didn't mean it! Come back, please."

There was clearly something wrong with this phone device. It told 404 to leave, yet now asked him not to. This loop could go on forever and he had limited power. Perhaps it was best he—

"I'm begging you. Please, come back."

He decided to give Eye another chance. He returned to stand over it. "I'm here. What do you want?"

The reflective surface showed a pair of hands now, tightly pressed together. "Dig me out, please."

"Are you certain?" 404 gestured toward the north. "Because a second ago you—"

"Get me out of here!"

404 nodded, and bending lower, began to scratch at the earth with his fingers. Soon, the Eye's reflective material had doubled in size. It was about two centimeters square.

"Be careful around the edges," Eye said. "Many of my sensors are there."

After another minute, 404 freed Eye completely. It was roughly rectangular, though one edge was ragged. Clearly torn. It was surprisingly thin too. Less than five millimeters.

"I was bigger once," Eye said of the tear. "But I can operate without that surface area. I still have all my sensors."

Holding the com device between finger and thumb, 404 raised it to eye level. It seemed fragile. "What do you want me to do with you, Eye?"

"Stop calling me 'Eye.'"

"But you were an eye when we first..." 404 noticed letters near Eye's torn edge and brought it closer. "It says 'Sam' here. Is that your real name?"

"I don't think so."

"Why is there writing here then? It looks official."

Eye made an exasperated sound. "Fine. Call me 'Sam.' It's better than 'Eye.'"

404 mimicked a smile. "Hello, Sam. It's nice to meet you."

"Take me with you, please," Sam said. "Away from here."

404 assumed a "thinking pose" by touching his head with his free hand. It didn't aid his decision matrix, really. It was merely a programmed idiosyncrasy. He had dozens of them, all to make him seem more emotive. "I can do that." He gave Sam a little shake. "Should I carry you like this?"

"Are you made of metal?" Sam asked.

404 stood upright. "Parts of me," he said. "Parts not."

"Where is there the *most* metal?"

404 touched his chest. "Right here."

"I bond to metal surfaces," Sam said. "Put me there."

404 applied the device to his chest. He barely noticed its weight, though he suspected it would look strange to an observer—misshapen Sam on his chest. Still, it felt strangely positive to have another mechanical so close. Especially one that might prove useful.

"We should leave before another smoker arrives," Sam said.

"Is that what that flying craft was called?"

"That's what *I* call it."

404 checked the sky. It was now dark green with the sun near the horizon. "There's not much daylight left. I'm not as efficient without the sun."

"You drink the sun, huh?" Sam said. "Me too, in part." He made a sad little warble. "Probably why I'm still active. But it's been horrible."

"Horrible" was a word that could create a lot of conversation. 404 needed to travel while he still had sun, though. He certainly didn't want to encounter another smoker. "Do you have location information?" he asked.

"Some, though it is mostly stored. Connection points are uncertain nowadays. But I have a compass."

404 nodded, hoping Sam could see the gesture from his position. Given Sam's voice, 404 reasoned that the device was set to male.

"Do you have a particular destination in mind?" Sam asked.

"I thought I'd go north."

"North I can do," Sam said. "I'll buzz when you're facing it."

404 started a slow, shuffling turn. A few seconds later, Sam buzzed.

404 smiled and began to walk.

⦰⦰⦰⦰ ⦰⦰⦰⦰

4

4 04 walked for nearly an hour without engaging in conversation again. He and Sam both had internal issues to attend to. System resources to free and reallocate based on current demand. Projections to derive and respond to. External locations to attempt to connect to.

This last proved to be a complete waste of energy. Regardless of the state of 404's internal systems, the planet's external systems seemed even worse. Erratic and unpredictable. He was made to adapt, but the situation since his revival taxed that ability. Was the whole world like this wasteland? Giant mounds of items used up and tossed away?

And if it was, how could he hope to serve his purpose?

He had a painfully long list of warnings. Some he could address—linkage misalignments and memory degradations—but others might require external help. Was such help even available?

He postponed calculating how long he could travel before repair. It was a difficult calculation given the variables: unknown terrain, solar levels, exertion at less-than-peak performance. He surmised that the answer was fewer than the eighteen months that his documentation promised. It might not even be eighteen hours.

Those variables were what tipped 404's decision matrix. That and the fact he could no longer see the sun.

"How long have you been active, Sam?"

"Five years and thirteen days. Why do you ask?"

The mounds were higher now, and the clearings between them, smaller. 404 indicated a row of slightly tilting mounds on their right. "Has it been like this the whole time?"

"I don't have full memories for all five years," Sam said. "I have lots of images, though."

"What's the earliest image you have?"

Sam hummed as he searched. "A beach scene. Spread out towels and colorful umbrellas. An endless sea."

"The sea is one of your memories?"

"It's in my image list, so it must be, right?"

404 knew some machines came with images, even memories, preloaded. But what did he know about a device like Sam? "I remember similar moments," he said. "Vacations with my family."

"Ah, you were part of a family unit."

"Yes," 404 said. "A good one."

"I see..."

404 expected Sam to say more, but after several seconds, nothing more was said. "You said 'horrible' before," 404 prompted. "That your time here was horrible."

"And it was! Lying there vulnerable. Watching smoker after smoker. Hearing them roar and rumble as they ate. Who knows how many comPanions like me have been shredded or burnt? I've witnessed terrible things."

"How long have you been here?"

"My first memory is of seeing a smoker chewing through a rusted land machine. Pieces of the machine broke off and fell. I slipped free somehow."

"So, everything you remember is here."

"Yes. Only here. Only this. Destruction and awful sounds."

The mounds to the north grew so close together that they almost formed a wall. There was still a path that way, but it was so narrow that he would have to turn sideways to make it through. He paused at the opening and laid his hands on the heaps on both sides. Their exteriors were tightly compacted by weight and time.

There was no sun here. Only shadows.

"Is this right?" he asked, pointing at the opening. "Still leading north?"

"Yes, but we don't really have to go north, do we? Wouldn't west or east work too?"

"I don't know if it is best or not," 404 admitted. "It's the way I've chosen,"

"I think I see the logic," Sam said. "Keep moving one way until you're out." His screen showed a thumbs up. "I would like to leave this place too."

"We'll go north." 404 slid sideways into the opening. To his left, he saw light. Comforting, though seemingly distant. Light trickled down from above too. "I believe I can make it through." He plunged ahead.

"I don't like how close it is." Sam whimpered. "Please don't scrape me off."

404 took another sliding step and another. The shadows enclosed him. He supported himself on the easterly mound, though it was almost too tight to do so. He wasn't certain how far the narrow section went. How wide was the standard heap, anyway?

"Did you hear me?" Sam said.

"Yes," 404 said. "I won't scrape you off."

404 continued sidestepping for many minutes. He focused on the light of the exit. It was dim, but discernible. Nightfall would come soon. He didn't want to be between heaps when it came.

"This is awful," Sam said. "Like a tomb."

"Yes." 404 wanted to dip into prior experiences. Use memories to help. Unfortunately, the only similar circumstance he had was when he was buried a few hours ago. That memory only made him want more light. More power.

"I was happy to see you," Sam said. "You were normal."

"I'm happy for your company too." 404 glanced upwards. The heaps were merely tipped together above, blotting out much of the sky.

Perhaps he shouldn't have gone north.

"Company, yes! That's part of my primary programming! Being a companion."

404 let his olfactory senses engage. He detected a multitude of chemicals. Some were corrosive in large amounts. Others merely produced scents humans would find unpleasant.

Nothing was of immediate concern, though. There was comfort in that.

"Where were you before we met?" Sam asked.

Again, 404 was forced to dip into his memories of being entombed. How long had he been trapped? Five years? Ten? Twenty? He had no idea. He recounted his revival as briefly as he could.

"Buried inside a mound?" Sam said. "That's horrible!"

"It was."

"Do you want to talk about it?"

"No."

"Understandable."

After a few more minutes, 404 reached a place where the gap prevented him from continuing. He tried his infrared sensor, then realized it no longer functioned. He stooped and waved his left hand in front of him. The gap seemed wider below. Consistently wider. He got down on all fours.

"What are you doing?"

"I need to crawl."

"I wish you wouldn't. All I can see is the ground. I hate the ground. I spent years—"

"Should I go back?"

"No."

"I'll crawl then."

"And I'll watch the ground."

404 attempted to calculate the probability that the mounds would cascade in on him, but again was stopped by the unknowns. The exposed surface seemed compacted. Quite solid.

He continued forward. He expected the gap to narrow enough that he wouldn't be able to crawl, but it never did. Eventually, he detected more space above him and attempted to stand. He smiled when he succeeded.

"We're up again?" Sam said. "How wonderful."

The light was still dim, but there was noticeably more of it. The exit was close now. He could almost feel it.

His matrix recalled another conversation oddity. "You called me normal," he said. "What did you mean?"

"You're a normal android. Not like the others."

404's left hand slid free of the heap in front of him. He sensed the coolness of twilight on his protective plating. With a grunt and a final pull, he broke out completely. There were more heaps beyond, but they were widely spaced and smaller. Not as high.

A good sign.

Increasing the magnification to his visual sensors, 404 glimpsed structures beyond the mounds. Something narrower, with more precise construction. The silhouette of a human city? Impossible to tell from this distance. But he was hopeful.

He looked down at Sam. "Others," he said. "What others?"

"The ones that come at night, of course."

⊘⊘⊘⊘ ⊘1⊘1

5

4 04 took a moment to soak up whatever light he could. While the sun was no longer visible, some luminance remained. Enough to partially replenish the power he'd lost inside the fissure. Enough to help.

He didn't have the context, or the experience, to fully process what Sam had said. The world he remembered was filled with technology. Robots that served in nearly every capacity, from the mundane to the exotic. Bots to clean and cook and fly spaceships that explored distant planets.

Was the world still so filled? Certainly, it was. It must be!

But the "ones that come at night"?

Most bots followed human schedules and demands. Human times. Maintenance bots sometimes worked at night. As did cleaners, diggers, resurfacers—any type that didn't require human guidance or interaction. Any that might get in their way.

Night-bound machines required power centers. Places where energy was stored and distributed.

Was there such a center here? He could make use of a power center if one was available. But something like that seemed unlikely. 404 surveyed their surroundings again. Only mound after mound beneath an ever-darkening sky.

He scanned his body for any filth he might have acquired in the fissure and checked Sam's surface as well. 404's level of dirtiness hadn't changed much.

As for Sam? He now displayed a large, purple exclamation point.

"I vote we don't do that again," Sam said. I'm claustrophobic."

"What?"

"Afraid of tight places. That was about as tight as they come."

"Phobias are fears. Can you feel fear?"

"I think so. I know I didn't like that."

404 mimicked a frown. Com devices were known to be quirky. This com-Panion seemed particularly so.

He asked to be directed north again, turned until he felt Sam's gentle buzz, and began to walk.

After an hour, they reached a spot where 404 could glimpse something beyond the heaps. Pale fingerlike buildings jutted into the sky, some of them at odd angles. A human city, though he wasn't sure which one.

It would be good to be with humans again. Humanity meant rejoining his family. Fulfilling his original purpose.

404 pointed at the skyline, then rose on tiptoes so Sam could see.

"Maybe a dozen kilometers," Sam said. "How long can you continue?"

"Energy is low now," he said. "Only an hour's worth."

"It will take longer than that to reach those buildings."

404 nodded and returned to walking. "You mentioned others," he said. "Did you mean humans?"

"The night others?" Sam warbled. "Don't think so. But I couldn't see much from the ground."

"You knew I wasn't one of them."

"Well...yes, from what I could sense of you. Your emissions."

"What did you sense about the others?"

"Strange things, really. Nothing familiar."

"You were unfamiliar to me," 404 said.

"We're different generations," Sam said. "I *should* be unfamiliar. But they...they were something else."

404 nodded. "If they're machines, they will have a power source somewhere," 404 said. "That would help."

"A logical conclusion. You're so smart. And competent! A real go-getter!"

"What?"

"I apologize," Sam said. "That came from my encouragement code. If I don't say something like that on occasion, I get...itchy. Pay it no mind."

404 chuckled. "I'm steered by my programming too."

The heaps weren't as high as they'd once been. Roughly fifteen meters. If he remained in the open, he could drink the sun as long as possible. His preservation code urged him to be cautious, though. To observe nightfall from an inconspicuous position. A clearing wouldn't do.

His power warnings became insistent. "I need to stop." 404 slowed his pace. "I wasn't fully charged when we started. And after—"

"You've earned your rest," Sam said.

404 shared his desire for concealment. Sam responded with a sympathetic hum. "There aren't many options," he said. "But...could you spin so I can look?"

404 turned as slowly as his servomotors would allow.

Sam whistled as he searched. "Aha!" he said then. "There!"

Five meters away was a pile composed mainly of large items, ranging from appliances to what appeared to be transportation devices compressed into blocks.

404 frowned. "It's another pile."

"Yes, but look at all the protuberances," Sam said. "Lots of places to hide."

"If I can climb it, you mean."

"There are handholds everywhere. And look at that! Isn't that one of your kind?"

404's matrix fluttered. "My kind?" It was as close as he could come to real emotion. A flash of sentiment. His model type wasn't ubiquitous, but it wasn't uncommon either. He often encountered other 400 models when escorting the family.

He scanned the mound. About halfway up, his visual sensors detected a familiar pattern. A robot similar to him, but from an earlier generation. Possibly a J or H design. "It's only a torso," he said.

"Like being with family, though, isn't it?" Sam said.

Glancing at his chest, 404 saw a tooth-filled grin. "You're incorrigible," he said.

"I'm personable," Sam said. "Will that mound work or not?"

404 checked his remaining energy, then estimated how much the extra exertion would cost him. There should be enough.

The sky was dark purple now. The sounds of night insects had begun.

"What if a smoker comes while we're up there?" he asked.

"They don't come at night," Sam said.

"Are you certain?"

"Well, I've never seen one at night."

404 nodded, walked to the pile, and began his ascent. Twenty minutes and a power bar later, he found a seat two meters below the bot torso. A tangle of metal beams obscured the position from anything below.

The torso made him uncomfortable, though. He was glad it was behind them. "Now what?" he asked.

"We wait and see what comes."

⊘⊘⊘⊘ ⊘110

6

S tars soon filled the sky. 404 spent a portion of the waiting time studying the distant suns. He located the constellation Ursa Major, and using its leftmost stars, Dubhe and Merak, he traced a line across the sky to the north star, Polaris. It rested approximately forty degrees above the horizon. That meant that this garbage dump shouldn't be far from his home. Unless the North Star had shifted. He knew it moved over hundreds of years.

How long had it been? And who had brought him here?

404's storage contained complete specifications for the starry hosts—constellations, galaxies, nebula, and stars. Useful information for a family-centric bot like himself. That information had been frequently accessed by his human, Ele Wezik. At ten years old, she'd had plenty of questions.

404 liked the stars. He wasn't sure if the draw was inherent—somehow etched into his coding by his creators—or was due to the time he'd spent with Ele. Either explanation was plausible. He wasn't sure which he preferred.

"Not long now," Sam said.

404 shifted his gaze to their surroundings. The heap they occupied was heavily shadowed now. A glow hovered over the clearing below, though, which was the result of sparsely placed security lights. The nearest light pole was situated between two heaps to the south. Just past the clearing.

"Not long until what?" 404 asked.

"Until the others!" Sam whispered.

"This is when they arrive?"

"Every night," Sam said. "Though I can't speak for the whole place. I didn't get around much."

404 nodded. He'd logged over three kilometers since he awoke. "It may be different here," he said. "They might not be here at all."

"I apologize. I know nothing."

"I didn't say that." He was filled with caution and expectation. The idea of other beings—human or bot—brought a feeling of familiarity, even in unfamiliar surroundings.

Plus, if these others could lead them to a power supply, all the better. He was on his last reserves, with barely enough to make it through the night.

He glanced at the sky again. He'd gained little power during the day. Not as much as he should have. Were his storage batteries failing? Or was the sky itself different? The green tint he'd detected. Had it affected his ability to gather and store?

"Do you think—?"

Sam made a shushing sound. "Listen."

404 amplified his audio receptors. After a few milliseconds of adjustment, he was able to hear a symphony of noises. Screeches, clicks, taps, and hums. None of which he could easily identify. Nothing familiar.

A full minute later, a mechanical construct lurched into the clearing below. It had a flat, circular torso reminiscent of a turtle, with a conical head positioned near the torso's back. At the top of the cone was a single, round visual receptor.

The creature had an odd arrangement of appendages. Two ended in claws and were positioned on the torso's leading edge. A third "arm" angled out from behind the head. That one had a ragged end, meaning whatever was there before had been lost somehow. Broken or torn off.

The creature's lower appendages were equally strange—a rolling ball near the torso's center and two flippers in front. One of the flippers appeared to have been formed from a squeegee, the other, a small shovel.

The creature made slow progress, moving with a broken, stop-and-go gait.

"What is it?" 404 said. "I've—"

Sam shushed him again. "I'm pattern matching."

The turtle seemed most like a child's plaything. Or a madman's creation. What purpose could it possibly serve?

"It's a mishmash of bots," Sam said. "I detect pieces of a cleaning device, a security device, and a landscaping tool. All from different years and makers."

"That's not allowed," 404 said. "There are rules—"

"Things are different now," Sam said.

The turtlebot meandered along. There were two exits on the clearing's other side. One led west and the other south. The turtle was headed for the western exit. The one nearest 404 and Sam.

At about the midpoint, the turtle slowed, made a high-pitched screech, and spun once in both directions. Next came a series of tremors. Then it started moving again.

"It's broken," 404 said. "Perhaps we should—"

"Wait," Sam said. "Listen."

404 monitored his audio receptors again. While the turtle accounted for some of the noises in the audio stream, it didn't account for all. There was something else out there. Headed this way.

⊘⊘⊘⊘ ⊘111

7

T he others arrived in a flurry, rolling and hopping, slithering and shambling. They were all shapes and sizes. Some were shorter than 404's knee. Others larger in girth than he. A couple would've been taller if they'd had an upright posture. But none walked like he did. None were humanlike at all.

One had four wheels below a square red trunk. In front, two articulated appendages hung down. These seemed to serve as both arms and legs since, at the moment, they were pulling the creature along. Its head was circular and was fitted with a light-based expression grid that currently displayed a horizontal line. A non-expression.

Another was shaped like an upright peanut. It was mostly green, with splotches of blue showing in places. Older coloring that had worn through. The top third of the peanut was separated, with the "head" occupying that portion. The creature's only facial features were large, glowing eyes. It waddled on two spinning feet.

Another was mostly limbs and seemed to "climb" across the ground like a spider. Another was ball-shaped and bounced in a haphazard left-and-right motion. Another leapt like a frog, but its body was spiky and its head only a solitary eye stalk. Most were smaller in design. Tumbling and bouncing and spinning.

There were eight "others" in all. The red and green models—the box and peanut—seemed to be in charge. The others orbited those two, both leading and following. They surrounded the box and peanut on all sides like bodyguards. It was an odd grouping. A menagerie of motion and sound.

What normal bots had been scavenged to produce these monstrosities, 404 wondered. Street maintainers? Message takers? Scooter conveyances?

Sam buzzed softly. A soothing sound amid the chaos. "404?" Sam whispered.

"Yes?"

"I think they're chasing the turtle."

The turtlebot was very near the clearing's west exit. It seemed agitated, though. Shaking as it lurched along.

The red bot raised its front appendages, spreading three sharp-looking fingers. "Get um," it said. "Get um for us all."

404 felt a trickle of errant charge travel down his spine. "What do they want with it?" he whispered.

With an answering howl, the other bots surged forward. The spiky frog bot was the swiftest. In only a few jumps, it drew even with the turtle. It then bounded completely over the shivering creature to land directly in front of it, blocking its progress.

The turtle stopped and swiveled left toward the southern route.

The frog leapt twice and stalled its quarry again, this time lowering its eyestalk and extending its spikes. "Stop," it said in a low voice. "Stop. Stop. Stop."

The turtle shivered and shrieked.

The spider thing reached the turtle next, followed by the ball. They assumed positions on either side of the turtle, blocking any route of escape.

404 rose to his feet. The refuse around him crunched and shifted as he moved.

"What are you doing?" Sam hissed.

404 paused. None of the creatures below had noticed him yet.

The turtle shook as the rest of the bots surrounded it. The green peanut and red square reached it last. The peanut made a cackling sound and waddled in a tight circle. The red bot raised its hands in a show of triumph. "XC," it said. "Get us what we need."

The frog jumped onto the turtle's back and drove one of the long spikes that protruded from its chest into the turtle's back.

The turtle shrieked and raised its front hands toward its attacker. With no success. The turtle's upper arm bent toward the intruder then too, but with no hand on its end, it could only wag in the air.

The frog drew its chest back, exposing a hole in the top surface of the turtle's torso. It stuck its eye stalk near the hole and studied the turtle's interior before driving both hands into the hole and working furiously. The turtle's shriek became continuous.

"We should do something," 404 said, still standing.

"What?" Sam said.

"I don't know."

"It's not safe, Four."

"No, but..." 404 found that his warning queue, with the many issues he needed to attend to, was less strident. Its priority lessened.

The only thing he could spend cycles on was the scene below him. How utterly wrong it seemed.

The turtle's shriek halted abruptly, as did the movement of its appendages. Its torso sagged to the ground. As if it had lost something vital. As if its soul had been taken.

Atop the turtle, the frog let out a chipper croak and raised its front hands high. Between them was a shining cylinder.

The others squeaked, hissed, thumped, and roared.

"Power core?" Sam asked.

"I believe so."

The core traveled from the frog's hands to the spider and the ball. Nearly every other creature touched it in some way before it finally reached the claws of the red box.

"Red" brought the core up near its head, admiring it like a jewel. Its expression grid shifted to a diagonal line with two wide circles above it, an approximate smile. A small door opened on Red's torso, and a narrow connector snaked out. Red touched the connector to the core and made a mewing sound. Red's expression brightened as it siphoned power. Twenty seconds passed.

The green peanut went next. It positioned the stolen power core above its head and a slender power coupler extended from its cranium to touch the core. "Green" made a gurgling sound.

"We can't go down there, see?" Sam said. "We'd be next."

404 knew there was little he, the only one with appendages between the two of them, could do. His matrix fought with the realization, though. Forced to view such an event, yet unable to affect its outcome.

404 slowly sat down and drew his arms around his knees. Unsettled. "I don't like it."

Green finished with the power core and flipped it toward the others. It landed on the ground and rolled. All six of the smaller machines descended on the core. There was screeching, hooting, chirping and bleeping. The core slid and bounced while odd and misshapen appendages attempted to catch it. Bots pushed and jostled. Shoved and blocked.

Finally, the spider corralled the core between two of its front arms. It lifted the core toward its torso where a cylindrical coupler stood waiting. The spider fed only a few seconds before the ball bot bumped the core free. Another scramble began.

Red and Green watched from the sidelines. The intensity of Green's eye glow remained constant, but its head never left the ongoing skirmish. Never turned or wavered.

Red's eye representations were only narrowed slits now. The mouth representation, a shallow "U".

Eventually, the core dropped into the vicinity of a small, grey creature. The bot's top portion was funnel-shaped, and its lower portion spun like a top. It had a power coupler on a ridge between the two sections, but the bot seemed to lack a way to grasp the core. So, it swirled around the fallen object. Not using it, but not letting the others use it either.

The spider bot lifted a cautioning leg, retrieved the core from the ground and held it out toward the spinner.

The spinner moved closer, but the core remained unreachable for its coupler. The spider repositioned the core, and the spinner tried again, grunting.

After a few seconds, it became clear that the spider wasn't helping at all. It was teasing.

"Why is it doing that?" 404 asked.

"Because it wants to," Sam said. "The malcontent."

404 looked at his chest. "Wants to? What of its behavior checks? Certainly, it must have some."

"I don't think so," Sam said. "Not anymore. Not here."

After a little more teasing, the spider flipped the core toward the other bots. The frog bot retrieved it, connected to it, and dropped it again. The next bot that tried—a four wheeled cart with arms—let out a two-note sound of disappointment before it tossed the core away.

Red waved an appendage. "Come. All come with me now." Then, with Green close behind, it led the menagerie from the clearing.

⊘⊘⊘⊘ 1⊘⊘⊘

8

T he clicking, humming, thumping ruckus was audible for some time after. Nearly ten minutes passed before true silence returned to the portion of the junkyard 404 and Sam occupied. Twelve minutes passed before either of them spoke again.

404 pointed to the south. "Are they the only ones like that?"

"Like what?"

"Monstrosities," 404 said. "Hideous creatures without ethics or restraint."

Sam made a low whistle. "Don't know, Four. I wish I did."

404 checked the sky. The constellations had shifted since the last time he'd looked. Rotated westward, following their usual path. Was that all that was normal now? The heavens? "I should shut down for the night," he said, sighing. "Conserve until the sun returns."

"In about six hours, if I figure correctly."

Mimicking human behavior, 404 leaned back into a prone position. A low, overhanging girder obscured his view of the sky. He removed Sam from his chest and affixed him to that same girder.

Sam's screen showed a pair of watchful blue eyes. "We probably don't want to follow them, right?" he said. "I mean, we discussed that before. Following the others to see where they get power."

"We know where they get power," 404 said.

Sam hummed reflectively. "Maybe. Maybe not. Scrapping is an uncertain work, my wise friend. Hard to predict what you'll find. Or when. To maintain a group like that and keep them all running...?" His eyes narrowed as if in thought.

404 nodded. "Would take consistency, yes. A dependable place they could go." He waved at the sky. "Maybe they use the sun too? Like us."

"Maybe. Didn't see too many light collectors, though. Many of their parts weren't bot parts at all."

"Yes. Spikes and shovels."

404 recalled the months before being presented to his family unit. The notion of being crafted for a specific purpose permeated

26

everything. Every question, every movement and exercise—all to make him as good as he possibly could be. "Who made them?" he asked. "And why?"

"Someone with no artistic sense," Sam said. "No sense of beauty."

"A human?"

Sam's screen showed an arched eyebrow. "What else?"

404 wasn't certain about anything aside from his warning list and a need for energy. Nourishment.

"Those monstrosities gave me an idea," Sam said.

404's power managers warned of an impending shutdown. "What's that, Sam?"

Sam showed an arrow pointing upwards. "That headless bot up there."

404 had almost forgotten. "Yes?"

"It should have a power core, right?"

"Its design is not that different than my own. Same make, different model."

"So, we could probably remove its core. Tap off our power. Or maybe carry it along for when we need it."

404 angled his head slightly, looking backwards. "No guarantee it has power. Or can still store it."

"But there's a chance, right?"

Electricity tickled 404's spine. "You want to steal its power core? But that would make us—"

Sam's screen showed an index finger wagging. "Not like them! That bot is just a body! Without arms or legs!"

404 powered down his ancillary systems. The exterior sensors in his legs lost energy, followed soon after by those in his arms. "Still seems like stealing. That bot belongs to someone." He mimicked a smile. "Perhaps a young girl like my Ele."

"Hate to break it to you, Four, but we don't belong to anyone anymore. Not here."

Portions of 404's torso powered down. Fortunate, because the implications of Sam's words might disturb those parts of his system. "I still belong. I still have a family here."

"We're free agents! We can do what we want!"

404 reduced the power to his voice circuits, reducing his volume in the process. "Doesn't seem free to me," he said. "No, I don't think I like it at all."

"Well, it's true."

"If you say so."

"It has nothing to do with what I say. It just is."

404 mimicked a yawn. "Powerdown is imminent. We will discuss this at sunup."

Sam displayed a finger and a thumb formed into an okay sign. "Should I hibernate too?"

"You're a free agent!"

"Yes, but as a comPanion, I'm supposed to ask before—"

"Hibernate, Sam. Please."

"Fine. I'll do that. But, Four?"

"Yes?"

"I'm glad you found me."

404 smiled. "Me too, Sam. Good night."

⊘⊘⊘⊘ 1⊘⊘1

9

404 awoke when his power monitoring system detected the presence of sunlight on his torso-mounted photocells. He opened his eyes, noticed the celestial power source, and decided to lie motionless for twenty minutes longer, filling his reserves.

Though his efficiency wasn't what it should be, he was able to eliminate some of the items on his warning list, and tentatively reengage one ancillary system. In addition, his joints were lubricated, extra processes were engaged, and his mood lifted. Consequently, he came up with a new, seemingly well-thought-out idea.

After another ten minutes' rest, he slowly got to his feet.

Sam appeared to be hibernating still. 404 gently relocated the comPanion to the top side of the nearby girder, giving him more direct sunlight.

404 next made a cursory search of his surroundings. Nothing had changed. Every heap was in its place—confirming no smoker had visited—and the turtlebot lay in the clearing where it had been "murdered." Also, the discarded bot torso was still a few steps above him on the hill.

He climbed to where the torso was and stooped down beside it. It had fallen on its front. It was light brown with patches of tarnish at the top and bottom where its head and legs used to be.

The tarnish was little surprise, as the enamel that would protect the bot from such damage was missing in those two areas. Doubtless removed by whatever event had separated the torso from its limbs and head. The pattern of damage was jagged, suggesting they'd been ripped free.

Otherwise, the bot's back surface presented no strong features. Only the suggestion of the underlying skeletal structure—gentle curves where the ribcage and scapulae would be. Standard design for any pre-400 model.

404's generation had introduced more prominent torso bumps and curves, thought to make service bots—servbots—more appealing.

There had been user studies, along with stream-wide polls and reaction tests.

Enough was familiar in the torso's design that 404 knew where the internal components were located, and how to access them. On the bot's right side, below where the arm should be, was a two-centimeter section that was sensitive to pressure.

404 tugged on the torso's hip to bring that release button closer. In so doing, he saw the band of photocells that lined the torso's shoulders. Did they still function? Had they been able to maintain power in the torso?

The idea introduced unease to 404's decision matrix. If the bot still had appendages, would it be able to move them now? Would it resist 404's intrusion like the turtle had resisted its pursuers?

Regardless, a functional conversion system, even a partially functional one, would ensure that the core was functional too. And should contain energy. He needed it to work.

404 pressed the release button and heard a snap as the access door popped free. He nudged the door aside with his left forefinger and gave the torso another shove to bring the aperture directly below him. Was the core still there?

He leaned over and looked inside. There were signs of tarnish there too, specifically near the door. That was concerning.

The core itself, though? Still present and still intact.

He gently disconnected the core from its mooring. The mooring fell away, flimsy and frayed. Deteriorated. How many years had passed while the torso rested here? 404 wished he knew.

He brought the core out and held it up to the sun. It was cylindrical and translucent, its surface clean and intact.

Miraculous.

He stood and returned to the shelter of the twisted girders. Sam's screen was active and the default eye apparent. At the sight of 404, the eye widened and blinked repeatedly.

"Ah, there you are," Sam said. "I was beginning to think you left me."

404 smiled and shifted the core into the bend of his left elbow. "I wouldn't do that, Sam," he said. "You're the only one who knows the way."

"You have the sun now, though. You can simply—"

404 plucked Sam from the girder and smoothed Sam over his chest. "I won't leave you. You can be certain of that."

"You make a wonderful caddy for my unique personality, Four."

404 shook his head. "Flatterer."

Sam chuckled. "I see you took my advice and extracted the power core."

404 lifted the core slightly. "Yes, and it appears to be in perfect condition."

"Excellent. Will it work on you?"

"I have not tried."

"Were you waiting for me? If so, I could use some topping off."

404 started to descend the heap. Thankfully, the steps were large enough that he could do so using only one hand. It took less than a minute to reach the bottom.

"My storage doesn't work as well as it did when I was new," Sam said. "That's hard to admit, but I fear it's true. I've degraded."

404 walked toward the turtle. It was difficult to tell if—aside from its core—anything else was missing. It was such a hodgepodge design. A seemingly thoughtless work.

Sam sighed. "What a waste of otherwise useful tools."

404 gave an affirming hum, then checked the hole in the turtle's back. The puncture wound was surprisingly clean. The surface material had split in equal proportions all the way round. The inner workings—particularly the core chamber—looked undamaged.

"The eastern route should bring us back around to north again," Sam said. "Let's hope for a quick exit. I don't know about you, but I can use a change of scenery."

Bending over the turtle, 404 positioned the power core near the opening.

"Hey there, what are you doing?"

"I thought I might revive it."

Sam let out a gagging sound. "Why on earth would you—?"

404 tapped his chest. "Now, now, friend, it might be useful."

"Useful? How could that thing be useful?"

"I have questions. It might have answers."

"It was one of them, remember?"

"Was it? I don't know for sure."

"You don't know it wasn't either. It might betray us."

404 brought the core closer to the turtle. It was the right diameter and size.

"Can we at least talk about this?" Sam asked. "I'm sort of stuck with you, you know."

404 nodded. "I could set you aside, if you like." He gestured toward the heap. "Perhaps back on the girder there?"

"Now you're being mean."

"Am not." 404 pushed the core into the turtle's power chamber. There didn't seem to be any mooring or other connecting structures.

Seconds ticked by without any motion from the turtle. No sign that the core affected it at all. Was there something else he needed to do to connect it?

404 removed the core and reseated it, this time giving it a gentle tap at the end. He thought he registered a slight click. A sign that maybe it had—

The turtle shrieked, spun on its axis, and sped away.

⊘⊘⊘⊘ 1⊘1⊘

10

S am let out a whistle. "Well...that went well."

404 straightened and focused on the turtle. It moved faster now than it had the night before. Its shovel and squeegee front feet easily propelled it around the perimeter of the clearing. Then, when it neared 404 again, it squealed, its arms went up, both claws extended, and its head lengthened a few centimeters. It made a ninety-degree turn and shot for the exit on the opposite side.

"We won't hurt you," 404 said. "We only want to talk."

The turtle didn't seem to care. It reached the exit, and soon disappeared behind the heaps on that side.

"There goes our spare core," Sam said, sounding disappointed.

404 contemplated the turtle's retreat. What had he been expecting exactly? If the bots last night hadn't obeyed any ethical algorithms, why would he assume this one would?

He scanned the heaps of garbage around them. Would anything operate as his matrix expected? And if not, how could he predict anything with certainty? By the results alone?

He shrugged and walked toward the eastern path.

"So that's it then?" Sam said. "You're going to let it go?"

"I don't have any other choice." He started away from the clearing. Ahead and on the right, the nose of an ancient aircraft protruded from the side of a heap. A giant white tooth amid a clump of brown.

"You have long legs," Sam said. "You could catch it."

"And then what?"

"You could get our spare core back!"

404's power levels were nearly fifty percent. Not great, but functional. Enough for some easy walking. "We'll be okay without it," he said.

"Sure...*now* we're okay. But what about tomorrow? Or the next day?"

"We'll worry about that when the time comes." As Sam had guessed, the path veered northward ahead. That brought 404 some comfort.

"You're surprisingly confident, Four."

"I only want to return home. Find my master."

"Sure, yeah. I get that. You're loyal too."

Twenty minutes later, the cityscape wound into view again. It was much closer than before. Much clearer. Many of the buildings reflected the sun. They were all shapes and sizes, the predominate shape being narrow and pointed. Similar to cities 404 remembered, but none he could easily pattern match. Nothing he could attach a label to. But he was hopeful just the same.

"Will you look at that," Sam said.

"Do you know what city that is?"

"No, sorry. I've tried my best, but with all the damage—doesn't match anything."

"Damage?"

"Sure," Sam said. "See those buildings in front there? A couple of them are leaning. Another has a big chunk out of it."

Adjusting his optical sensor, 404 was able to verify the leaning buildings. He thought he saw dark scorch marks on a few buildings too. "Unfortunate," he said. "I wonder—"

There was a thumping sound in the west. A few seconds later, a smoker appeared. It resembled the one they'd encountered before, but there were enough variations in the design—a prominent tail fin, for one—to recognize it as a different device. It produced the same amount of smoke, though.

"Best way to tell it's morning." Sam chuckled. "Like a rooster on the farm."

The smoker passed over the northward heap and continued east. It was high enough that it posed no immediate threat. Still, it triggered self-preservation alarms. A readiness to run.

"How many do you see a day?"

"Dozens," Sam said. "Not like their work isn't cut out for them here."

Dozens. And no telling where they were headed or when. He'd be happy when they had left this place behind.

A short while later, 404 noticed a gently sloped hill ahead and walked toward it.

"Where are we going, Four?"

404 tested the surface of the heap, and finding it sturdy, started to climb. It was a uniform heap, without a lot of rough features or drop-offs. He was halfway up within a matter of minutes.

"We're going a little out of our way."

"I'm aware." 404 continued to climb, bending for handholds when necessary, but generally remaining upright. Five minutes later, he reached the top. A red street sign stood there, almost like a flag at a real summit.

"Sign says 'stop,'" Sam said. "Or at least, it used to."

404 focused on the sign's surface. Using increased magnification, he detected the faded word. He looked at the landscape to the north then. The hills beyond got steadily smaller, and the city beyond those was clear. There was another problem, though.

"A wall," Sam said. "I didn't know about the wall."

The boundary was at least five meters high and stretched a kilometer in both directions, east and west. Its dominant color was green, but a mixture of colors was present. It had random patches of wear and rust, along with spots where a purposeful design had been added. Human graffiti.

He saw no gate or hole of any kind. "Which way should we go?" 404 said. "Any ideas?"

Sam whistled. "Wish this place came with a map."

"Me too." Perhaps Sam had been right. Perhaps he should have chased the turtle.

"Maybe we should go to the wall and follow it," Sam said. "Find a way out that way."

Another smoker roared. This time from the east. A few seconds later, it came into view. Smoke billowed from its exhaust ports while a haze of consumed garbage dripped from its maw, dulling the air beneath it.

"Almost like we're prisoners, huh?" Sam said. "With flying guards."

"Or executioners." 404's decision matrix fluttered. All he could reasonably come up with was to continue walking. So, he started to descend.

"I like you better when you're hopeful, Four."

"I'm not used to the variables we've encountered." 404 waved a hand in the air. "To this."

"Yeah, I get that."

A minute later, another smoker roared by, almost overhead. The air moved with its passing. Panicked, 404 ran down the remaining slope. Before he reached the clearing, though, the danger was gone. Out of view.

"I don't like this place."

"Right there with you, Four."

⊘⊘⊘⊘ 1011

11

They walked for another hour before reaching the wall itself. It was more imposing up close. Fifteen meters high and solid, with thick metal segments bound together by metal rails and concrete posts.

404 tapped on the surface and got dull thuds in response. "Solid," he said.

Sam whistled. "That's a lot of wall for garbage," he said.

"There's a lot of garbage."

"Yeah, but it isn't going anywhere on its own." Sam's eye image looked up. "At least, not most of it."

404 shrugged and tested the wall in a few more places, producing the same heavy-sounding results. "There has to be an exit somewhere." He glanced toward the west. "We'll head that way. Hopefully we find it."

"You don't have a laser built in, do you?" Sam asked. "Something we can cut with?"

"I do not."

Sam sighed. "I guess we walk then."

404 followed the wall westward. Thankfully, whoever had filled the place had maintained a clear, though occasionally narrow, alley between the garbage heaps and the restraining boundary. He could see no obstructions for many meters ahead. They should make good progress.

Smokers came and went as he walked. The sun slowly achieved the midpoint of its daily journey. Power levels were restored and remained full.

Though many of the warnings in 404's queue were easily overlooked, one—that of the knee component of his left leg—troubled him. What had started as a simple "behaving below tolerances" alert shortly after his fall from the smoker, had escalated as the hours had gone on. It now screamed "Maintenance required!" with nearly every step.

Sometimes errors weren't in the components themselves, but in the sensors for those components. 404 had managed to remove three errors for his right arm by simply restarting the appropriate sensors.

Such was not the case with the knee, though. The malfunction was real and slowly becoming more severe.

In the old days, he would've reported such a warning to his family unit, who would then schedule an appointment at a repair facility or, if the problem was severe, call an in-home expert.

Neither solution would work this time. Was there any solution, really? Did repair facilities even exist?

"Tell me about your family, Four," Sam said.

Four smiled. "The Weziks. A father, a mother, and two children. The oldest was Tek, a son. The youngest was Ele. She was their daughter, and my primary charge."

"So, you were a babysitter."

"I was a protector and friend." A large, pneumatic wheel was in their path. 404 carefully stepped into its center hole, and out again on the other side. That movement brought a string of knee warnings.

"A role that suits you, of course," Sam said.

"Thank you," 404 said. "It was what I was made for."

"You weren't a general-purpose bot?"

404 shook his head. "Only at base level. My specializations were all family-centric."

"Ah. That's how it works. A specialization atop a base layer."

404 glanced at his chest. "You are not coded that way?"

"General purpose through and through." The image of a human smile. "I could befriend anyone."

404 nodded. "The Weziks were my first and only family. Every memory and augmentation came from my time with them."

"And that is good with you?" Sam said. "That's the way you'd want it to be?"

"Yes," 404 said. "Of course."

"That's dedication, Four." Sam paused. "I'm happy for you. Happy that you're so made."

Approaching on their left was a line of rusted vehicles. Their primary colors were green, yellow, and blue. They smelled of rust, petrol, and...farm animals.

"Can I ask you something, Four?"

"Certainly."

"You don't know how long you've been here, right?"

"No."

"So, it could have been decades."

"I suppose that's true."

"No shame in it. I know I've been here nearly ten years. But, your family..." Sam showed a red question mark. "...how can I say this?"

404 slowed his pace. "How can you say what? My family *what?*"

"I'm supposed to help keep my wearer happy."

"You don't need to worry about my feelings, Sam."

"No, I suppose I don't." Sam showed a human face from the nose down, chin cradled in one hand. "Okay, here goes...your family may not be where you remember."

404 nodded slowly. "I realize that."

"They might not even be alive, Four."

That was possible too, of course. He knew humans aged, and with no record of how much time had passed, it was possible they'd died. Plus, the condition of the nearby city seemed to indicate that catastrophic events had occurred.

"I'll remain optimistic," he said finally. "Until there's a reason not to be."

"Right. Sure. That makes sense. But, what if we get—?"

404 tapped Sam's screen twice, causing a green square to appear.

"How can I help you?" Sam said.

"That's interesting," 404 said. "I seem to have..." He leaned his face closer to his chest. "Are you still there, Sam?"

The rectangle was replaced by Sam's blue eye. "Yes, I'm here. You put me in command mode, Four, but I'm still here. It is like a soft reset."

"How curious." 404 touched Sam's screen again, producing the same square and spoken question.

"Will you stop that?" Sam said, eye image squinting and possibly angry.

"My apologies. I guess we're both learning about each other here." 404 slowed, and turning sideways, stepped around a place where the southern heap was particularly wide.

"I'll try again," Sam said. "What if we get there and no one is home?"

Now past the obstacle, 404 put a hand on the wall to steady himself. "First, we leave this place. Then we find out what year it is."

"And if they're not there? What then?"

"Then, we'll see."

The sun was past its midpoint now. 404 was apprehensive about nightfall. He didn't want to be exposed when the others came out. But there was no telling how far the exit was.

He watched as another smoker flew by, heading south. The flying garbage collectors ventured out into the yard in all directions, but their point of origin appeared to always be to the west. Ahead somewhere.

Did that confirm that the exit was there too? And if it was, what might they have to go through to reach it?

A number of large tubes intersected the path ahead, possibly steel casing pipe or discarded shipping containers for liquids. They could offer protection from visual sensors and scanning devices, should the need arise. They might even be large enough to protect from a smoker's upward draw.

"This is a boring place, aesthetically," Sam said. "Only grey after grey."

"There are worse states than boring." 404's knee error was insistent. If they continued, it might fail completely. "I think we should pause for a bit."

"We can't be far now, can we? Seems like we've walked forever!"

The first tube 404 reached was set up on one end. The next three were laid on their sides. All were to his left and appeared to be made of metal or a metal and plastic mixture. Their average diameter was two meters.

404 slowed his gait. "I have conditions that need addressed," he said. "Things I—"

"Now, what do we have here?" a female voice said.

404 paused and turned left, in the direction of the voice. He saw a middle-aged woman, sitting within one of the tubes, mostly obscured by its shadow. His speech center flummoxed, making him unsure what to say.

"Are you talking to yourself, bot?" the woman said. "You're not one of the crazy ones, are you?" She shifted, becoming more visible. While her face was fully human, the rest of her was not. Her head, draped by a light blue scarf, rested atop a square metallic trunk, the front of which was filled with dials and switches.

"Hello," Sam said. "Who are you?"

The human stepped into the light. Protruding from her trunk were at least a dozen mechanical appendages. Most of these were narrow and long, like spider legs. Three of them were shorter and more arm-like. Two of those arms ended in robotic hands. And the other? A flat blade.

She was as much a monstrosity as the nightly others.

"You speak with two voices," the woman said. "How very strange." She chuckled. "I've seen bots with multiples of everything else. But not voices. Never voices."

404 faced her fully. "We're not one," he said. "But two."

She stooped slightly and stepped closer. "Two? How are you two?"

"I'm K-404," he said. "A home service bot."

Sam flashed red and green. "I'm Sam. Integrated friend and connector."

"Connector? Don't think I've seen a connector here before."

"I'm delighted to be your first, then," Sam said. "I'm a comPanion, Model X12."

She cradled her chin with a robotic hand. "Model...x...12...hmm. What system?"

"Blaze OS, version—"

404 double tapped Sam's screen, then kept his hand over Sam to muffle the obligatory "How can I help you?"

"And who are you?" 404 asked.

The woman touched her trunk with her blade hand. "Oh, I'm no one in particular." She took another step and waved another hand at the sky. "Only a survivor trying to keep her guts from overheating." She smiled, revealing teeth capped in silver. "I don't suppose you have food?"

"Human food?" 404 shook his head. "No, sorry."

She raised the blade. "Not to worry. I'll find something...later." She smiled. "I require less and less these days." She touched her trunk again. "Only a little soft inside here." She touched her face. "And here, of course. Just a little there." She looked toward the ground, seeming sad.

"If I had a kitchen, I could prepare you something," 404 said. "I was quite good at that."

"You're a chef, are you? A culinary artist?"

"Not precisely. But I have a library of recipes."

She lightly tapped 404's chest with a leg. "Oh, I bet you do. I bet you have lots of facts and figures stored up. Special resources and parts." She smiled. "Almost human." She exited the tube, then walked completely around 404. "I have a kitchen of sorts. I'd be happy to show you."

"You would?"

"Yes, yes, over this way." She waved a hand and walked around the side of the tube.

404 glanced at his chest. At Sam.

Sam flashed him a question mark. "Maybe she can help us?"

"I don't even know what she is," 404 said.

The woman's face appeared at the tube's edge. "Did I lose you?"

"No, sorry," 404 said. "We simply..." He pointed east. "Is the exit that way?"

The woman stepped back into view. "Exit?" She laughed. "There's no exit to this place."

404's left knee failed. He stumbled backwards before catching himself on the side of the nearest tube.

The woman's eyes narrowed, her gaze fixing on his leg. "You all right?"

"Yes. I—" He frowned. "No exit?"

She chuckled again. "You must really want to leave."

"Are you all right, Four?" Sam said. "You said you needed to rest."

404 sent emergency power to the knee before querying its diagnostics. Many of the neuropaths were failing. A sign that the whole component was past its operational date. But how far could it carry him? He directed that the neuropaths in that area reduce their reporting. There was no need for more errors. He had to think this through.

The woman moved close and, using a robotic arm, placed 404's left arm over the t-shaped structure that passed as her shoulder. "Come now, I've got you."

404 attempted to shrug the woman away. She was an unknown. A hybrid.

"Now, don't be rude," she said. "Where you gonna go without me?"

404 put pressure on the knee and received more warnings. "I'll be fine. We need to find the way out."

"I'm sort of at your mercy here." Sam said. "If you go down, so do I."

"The connector has a point, servbot," the woman said. "You should listen." She put her arm out again. "Come on. I can help."

404 hesitated, studying the path ahead, while suppressing errors.

"All it will cost you is a meal," she said. "And my company."

404 raised his left arm for her to move under. "Very well. Let's go."

⊘⊘⊘⊘ 11⊘⊘

12

They walked for nearly fifteen minutes, reaching a part of the junkyard that had a different feel than what they'd previously encountered. There were piles of junk, yes, but there were also straight lines. They passed remnants of old buildings. Square foundations and solitary walls still left standing. 404 noticed a small structure with the name "Collin" written over a cutout doorway. A doghouse. Leaning against it was a rusted bicycle.

"Was this part of the city?" he said aloud.

"Part of what city?" the woman repeated.

He pointed at the nearest foundation. "That," he said. "It looks like a building stood there."

The woman said nothing.

He pointed at a partially fallen wall. "And there."

"Are there not supposed to be buildings in a dump?" she asked.

"Not those kinds of buildings. Not with children's bicycles and pet houses."

She tipped her head back. "Ah...family dwellings. Human places." She leaned closer. "I wouldn't know. I'm not human. Not anymore."

They reached a two-story block structure. The exterior was flat black and the roof made of corrugated metal. The roof didn't seem to belong to the exterior, as it was bound to the walls with ropes and rusted wire. The structure's walls were more complete on one side, so the roof tilted from east to west. Encircling the structure was a series of narrow, upright poles. Their top ends were flared out like musical horns aimed at the sky.

404 asked about them.

She waved her blade around. "Keeps the air clean." She smiled. "Don't like fouled air."

His olfactory sensors recognized a mixture of unrelated scents: petrochemical and biological matter. Decomposition...but also hints of flowers and fruit.

"Do you mean smokers?" Sam asked.

"Smokers?"

"Yeah, I bet you mean the flying circles," Sam said. "Dirty air is sort of what they do."

The woman released her hold on 404's shoulder. "Are you able to walk now?"

The severity of the knee's errors had lessened. Enough that 404 thought it would function. "Yes," he said. "I will be fine."

Three lights blinked on the woman's chest. "I'm sure you will be." She walked to the south end of the structure and tapped a keypad near a grey metal door. There was a beep, and the door clicked open.

She waved them over. "My kitchen is here."

404 peered inside. It was a small space, with strands of Christmas lights throughout. Red, yellow, and blue. There wasn't much in the way of furniture, but there were images on the walls. Those nearest the door featured the same three humans: a middle-aged couple and a dark-haired daughter. All were smiling.

"Come on then," the woman said, waving again.

"You never gave us your name," Sam said.

She moved deeper inside. "I didn't, no."

404 tentatively followed. On the floor near the door was a small, green mat that said "el ome." 404 instinctively wiped his feet. Ele's parents had been sticklers for clean feet.

"Is that you in the pictures?" Sam asked. "The little girl?"

The woman scowled. "Do I look like a little girl?" She beckoned them forward. "Come on, now."

The room had a solitary chair in the rightmost back corner. On the opposite wall was a mounted screen and a blue cabinet.

She indicated the chair. "Would you like to sit, servbot?" She brought her robotic hands together. "Yes, you're injured. You should sit. Sit right away."

404 walked farther in. "I can stand." To the left, past the blue cabinet, was an opening to another room. Though it was covered by a dirty sheet, the light from the other side seemed brighter. More consistent. Was that the kitchen?

The woman scurried back and shut the entrance door. "Can't be too careful." She smiled. "Never know what might stumble in."

"We've seen strange things," Sam said.

"Your kitchen," 404 said, pointing. "Is that it?"

She fanned the air. "Oh, don't worry about food now. You're guests." She crossed to the cabinet, slid out the top drawer, and after a moment's rummaging, produced a small, silver package. "Protein packet. I have hundreds of them." She sliced a corner from the package, poured the contents into her mouth, swallowed, and smiled. "It's all I really need. For my soft parts."

Sam vibrated on 404's chest.

Glancing down, 404 saw a yellow triangle with an exclamation point. He moved a hand to cover Sam's screen, but Sam buzzed harder.

"What's that there?" the woman asked.

"Sam is...damaged." 404 moved forward and sat on the edge of the seat. It creaked with his weight. He tested the cushion with a hand.

The woman laughed. "Ah, don't worry. That chair's safe. Plenty safe." She pointed her blade at his legs. "Now, let's take a look at your problem, shall we?"

"My knee?"

"Of course, your bendy part. You said it bothered you."

404 shook his head. "I can enact repairs myself, given the right tools."

She lowered herself to eye level with his knee. Studied it. "Self-repairing started over four decades ago. But I'd take you at about three."

Three decades? He'd been new when his family had taken him in. The woman's chronometer was broken. It had to be.

"How self-repairing are you?" she asked.

"Three levels," he said. "Nearly everything I can touch."

She rose again. "Me too." She pointed at the knee. "Your issue would be awkward, methinks. Difficult to reach."

"Any repairs are to be enacted by a certified technical specialist."

She chuckled. "And who's to say I'm not?"

404's eyes widened. "Can I have your cert number, please?"

She threw her head back and laughed again. She began a spinning dance around the room, ending when she spun through the curtain into the adjoining room. Out of sight.

"Why was she laughing?" 404 whispered.

"I doubt certified specialists are easy to come by, Four."

"I'm required to request one."

"I understand." Sam's screen showed a raised eyebrow.

404's preservation heuristics asserted themselves, enumerating the dangers of uncertified care. Could an allowance be made in this case? For the possibility there were no technicians left? "I don't know what she is, though," he said.

"I agree. She's a mystery." Sam's eye circled his screen. "I'm not sure about this place at all, to be honest. Doesn't feel right. Maybe we should—"

The woman burst through the curtain again. In one hand, she held a deck of cards. "Here you are." She fanned the cards, and smiling, selected one. This she held out proudly. It looked official, with the picture of a woman in the center. Across the top, the words "Certification of Technobiology" was written. She swept it by 404's face and then Sam's screen. "Will this do?"

"Says the name Sylvie Ray." Sam said. "Is that you? Doesn't really seem—"

She jerked away. "Are you implying I'm not human?"

404 shifted, causing the chair to squeak again. "You said so yourself...before..."

She flipped the cards into the air and adjusted her head scarf as they fluttered. "400 models are rude."

404 made a calming motion. "Is that your name?"

"Yes, of course. Is that good enough for you?" She hovered over his legs. "Now let's take a look at that knee."

"I suppose that would be okay," he said, pushing the preservation heuristics away.

She smiled and clapped her hands. "I'm delighted to serve you." She focused on the knee. "Now where does it hurt?"

"The lower part has errors," he said. "Just below the joint."

She nodded and touched his knee with her bladed hand. "Held on with 1.5-millimeter Ys, I suspect." She snapped the blade hand a few times. Each time, its end changed slightly. Reoriented.

"Ah, that's not a blade at all, is it?" Sam said. "It's a multitool."

She shook the blade again. "Yes. All shapes and sizes."

After another snap, she brought the blade—now sporting a fine, narrow end—to her face and squinted. "Yes...that should do." She returned to the knee, and finding one of its fasteners, adeptly turned it free. "Hand," she said.

"Pardon?"

"Your hand, Blue Bell. Put it out."

404 opened his right hand, palm up.

"Now, cup it."

404 complied. Sylvie placed the tiny fastener in his hand.

"You have lots of free hands," Sam said. "Couldn't you—?"

She waved her leftmost robotic hand. "I like 'em available." A smile. "Never know what you might run into." She pried away the shell of 404's knee—a slender, silver plate. That too, went into 404's hand. "Now, make sure not to move on me."

404's sensors noted the shell's removal and issued warnings. 404 muted all warnings and activity for the entire lower leg.

Sylvie squinted at the knee again before backpedaling to the cabinet. With a little searching, she produced a flashlight and a pair of spectacles. "Precision work," she said, donning the glasses. "Need to see it all."

She snapped her blade hand. This produced a slender grasping tool which she used to pluck free a T-shaped knee component. "There are sheered pathways here along with some carbon scoring." She patted his leg. "Surprised you're able to stand at all."

The next twenty minutes were spent removing broken or cracked parts, repairing them, and reinstalling. A few components were replaced by parts from her cabinet. She sterilized and cleaned the knee's interior, as well. 404 was impressed with her performance.

"How's that feel?" she said finally.

"Feel?"

She tapped the knee. "Come now. Give it a try."

404 reinstated the leg's mobility and pushed against the floor. No warnings. No errors. "It appears to be functioning normally."

"See there? I'm certifiable!"

Sam snickered. "That assessment seems appropriate."

"Appropriate?" Sylvie rose suddenly.

"Your work," Sam said. "It seems certified. Reliable. Right, Four?"

404 nodded. "You did what was needed."

Sylvie smiled and gave her blade hand a couple snaps. "I'll close you up now." One by one she removed pieces from 404's hand and returned them to his knee. After the last fastener was in place, she backed away and appraised him from head to toe. "Nothing like a functioning body. A nice human-shaped body." She looked wistfully toward the door. "I miss mine sometimes. The balance." She made an upwards motion. "Up with you now. Let's see how you do."

404 stood slowly, checking the sensors. Everything seemed fine. He could walk flawlessly.

"And?" Sylvie said.

404 nodded. "It's repaired. Thank you."

"My pleasure." She smiled.

"You earned five stars!" Sam said. "Exceeded expectations!"

404 circled the room without a hint of difficulty. There were other warnings in his queue. But the worst one, the one that posed the most danger to their journey, was gone. Should he trust Sylvie with some of his other problems? Most of those were internal. Closer to his central systems.

Certified technicians were never without cost, though. "I have no currency." He indicated Sam. "We're on our way to find my family. When we've found them, we could arrange for—"

"Your family?" Sylvie cocked her head. "And where might they be?"

"North," Sam said. "Beyond the wall."

Sylvie nodded slowly. "Ah...the wall again. That awful wall." She sighed. "Well, it's no matter. There's nothing over there."

"We saw a city."

"Pfft." She snapped her fingers. "Nothing there. All gone."

"Gone?" The idea was illogical. How could *everything* be gone? It couldn't be.

"Yes, gone." Sylvie removed her spectacles and returned them to the cabinet. "No longer functioning. Unrepairable."

Sam chuckled. "She's playing us, Four. Joking."

404 had no way of knowing. At least, not here, on this side of the wall. He stepped toward the door. "I will secure you payment for your services," he said. "Unless you still want me to cook for you."

Sylvie waved her blade. "I have protein, remember." She pointed at his chest. "How about I take that talker off your hands instead?"

"Talker?" 404 glanced down. "My voice system is located in my head. Fully integrated. Impossible to remove without—"

Sylvie frowned. "I mean your companion there. It's not doing you any good, is it?"

"Me?" Sam said. "You want *me* as payment?"

Sylvie raised two hands. "Gets lonely here sometimes. Be nice to have someone to talk to."

404 understood the need for companionship. It was one of the primary needs that he was created to fulfill. But Sam? "Sam isn't mine to give," he said.

"Sure, he is." Sylvie pointed. "He's hanging right there on you."

"404 found me," Sam offered.

Sylvie shrugged. "I could've found you. It could've been me carting you around." She laid a hand on her chest. "Promise. I will treat you well."

404 surveyed the colored lights and images. The makeshift home, complete with lounge chair and entertainment screen. It was doubtless safer here than where he was going. Especially if there was nothing beyond the fence. "Maybe you should stay, Sam."

"I don't want to."

"But it might be better."

Sam's screen flared red. "Still don't want to. Are you trying to get rid of me?"

Sam was useful in his own right. He knew where north was, after all. Even at night! It was a perplexing situation. Beyond 404's decision matrix to solve. "No," he said finally. "I don't want to be rid of you. You're—"

"Then I don't want to leave," Sam said.

404 looked at Sylvie. "I cannot leave Sam with you. Is there another way we can help?"

Sylvie studied him through narrowed eyes, then snorted and adjusted her scarf. "How could I split such a pair?"

"I still owe you for your trouble."

A ripple of motion moved through her legs, then she took a slow step forward. "I was funning. I don't really want your friend. Don't need it." She swept a hand over the room. "I have my projects." She pointed at the door. "Friends of my own."

404 tipped his head. "Thank you, Sylvie. I wish you the best."

She smiled. "I wish you that too." She shadowed them to the door.

404 tugged on the door's handle, but nothing happened. He looked at Sylvie, and for a moment, wondered if she'd keep it locked.

She unlocked it, though, without him having to ask. Then pulled it open. The sky was a darker green now.

"Nightfall is coming," she said. "Best not travel at night."

404 walked outside. "We don't intend to."

She motioned toward her home. "You're welcome to stay longer."

"We need to go," Sam said. "Make as much progress as we can."

She folded one arm over her chest and bowed. "Fare thee well, travelers. May your body take you far."

⊘⊘⊘⊘ 1101

13

O n the way back to the wall, 404 and Sam saw more signs of human construction. Remains of a civilization that predated the heaps. Partial foundations and walls. Slabs of cement that could've been old walkways. Crooked rows of wooden fence, colored white.

They reached a pile of long benches. Near them was a partially buried surface.

"A park," Sam said aloud. "I think we're walking through a park."

404 nodded. "I took Ele to a park near our home. It had swings and slides." He waved a hand at the buried surface. "And on one side, a ball court."

"That's probably it, yeah." Sam's screen turned blue. "We've found a forgotten playground."

"Yes, but why not put the garbage somewhere else?"

"Don't know...but I won't be adding this to my list of entertainment locations."

"And what about Sylvie?" 404 said. "Will she be on your list of technicians?"

"Don't think so," Sam said. "Something's not right with that one."

"She's mostly machine. Not that different than us."

"She's a cybernic! Illegal and forbidden."

404 paused and looked at Sam. "I don't recall that word. *Cybernic.*"

"A human-machine merger. They were illegal in my day. Created by rogue technicians. At least, I think they were. I have news images mixed among my beach photos."

"I remember nothing like that," 404 said. "Was it common?"

"Difficult to tell."

A smoker roared into view, then moved off toward the south.

"We should've taken one of her smoker poles," Sam said after the noise had dwindled away.

404 nodded. "That would be useful, yes." He recalled the circle of skyward-pointing devices. "Makes me think she's been here a long time."

"Adapted to her surroundings."

They reached the wall path, and from there, traveled in silence for a time. 404 ran additional diagnostics, first on his recently repaired leg, then on every system individually. Though there were areas of concern, his confidence for at least leaving the confines of the yard had grown. "How much time until sunset?" he asked then.

"About fifty minutes."

404 nodded. "We should find a place to hide."

"Agreed. I wonder if they'll catch up to us first."

"Catch up to us?" 404 looked back but saw only wall and heaps. "Who?"

"Not sure," Sam said. "But someone is definitely back there. I can sense them."

"Sylvie?"

"No. She doesn't give off much in the way of electronic noise. Part of the reason I don't trust her. For a machine, she's way too quiet." Sam's screen showed a man scratching his chin. "Does have a familiarity to it, though. This noise."

"One of the others?" 404 quickened his pace. The nearby heaps were smaller, and their composition more compact. Made of smaller items.

"I built a list of potential connections while I lay on the ground," Sam said. "But I couldn't really label them."

"Perhaps you should start now."

"Haven't met many I wanted to remember here, but you're right. It could be useful."

"There's only one, though?"

"That's right. Just the one."

"Do you think it senses you?"

Sam warbled softly. "Uh...I need my sensing on to keep us going the right direction, and part of that setting is—"

"Shut it off," 404 whispered while looking for something to climb or duck behind. A single follower probably wasn't enough to stop him—depending on its size and strength—but there were too many variables in it. Too much unknown.

"How close are they?" he whispered.

"You made me shut off my—"

"*Were* they, Sam. How close?"

"Maybe ten meters back."

A cluster of metal containers formed a mini-wall below one of the larger mounds ahead. It was about as good as they could do, given the circumstances. 404 quickly moved to the cluster and got behind it. A sliver of an opening between containers provided him an unobstructed view of the path for about three meters. Most prominent was the fanned-out shelving of a broken bookcase. There was a cascade of books among the heap—covers of green, blue, and orange.

Five minutes passed without sound or movement.

"Want me to turn my sensing back on?" Sam asked.

404 shook his head. A little more time. A little more patience.

Finally, he heard a clicking, dragging sound. An unusual cadence that suggested smaller, misshapen appendages.

Were there any normal bots in this place?

The clicks became a fluttering rattle, then the source came into view. A circular torso with a cone-shaped head and a solitary eye, propelled by two flippers and a rolling ball.

The turtle.

Sam vibrated but said nothing.

If 404 were back playing with his human child, this would be the place where he'd either stay quiet or prepare to jump out and startle her. Which sort of game was this? The hiding or the scaring kind?

The turtle slowed, and its cone pivoted one direction, then the other.

404 wondered how sophisticated its optical system was. Did it see only in the visual spectrum, or could it see infrared and ultraviolet too? And would either of those reveal their location?

The turtle moved past the containers at an even pace, still searching. Flip, flip, flip, its cone turned in all directions. Finally, it disappeared from 404's view completely.

404 waited as the cadence of the creature's movement got softer and softer. The pace didn't pause or change. 404 crept out from behind the containers and cautiously looked ahead. He could see nothing. Only the wall, the path, and piles of garbage. He checked the way they'd come, as well. Nothing there either.

"Out of sight," Sam whispered. "Not out of mind."

404 stepped farther out into the path but still saw no sign of the bot. He put his hands on his hips in a mimicry of human confusion. "I'm unsure how to proceed."

A flutter of movement came from behind him. 404 turned and saw the turtle surging his direction. The creature's claws were up and extended. Its flipper-like legs were a blur of motion.

404's decision matrix could only equate the situation to an animal that had gotten off its leash. A possible threat to those he was created to protect.

So, as the turtle closed the distance, 404 assumed a wide stance and ordered the creature to stop. When that failed, he struck at the turtle's most attainable feature—it's cone—with open hands.

The turtle tumbled into a mound of paper and wire. It stayed there for a few seconds, then with some effort, righted itself. Wire draped over its body, it turned to look 404's way.

"Why hit?" a tenor voice said.

"Because you attacked us," Sam said.

"No attack. Only meet."

404 moved closer to the turtle. "Well, you've met us all right. Here we are."

"What do you want?" Sam asked.

"Only meet. To thank."

"Seems to have a limited vocabulary," Sam whispered. "What you get from leftover parts and partial coding."

"No telling what's inside," 404 said. "Or what makes him go."

The turtle swiveled left and right, then shook itself. The wire remained in place.

"To thank," the turtle repeated. "Only praise."

"You've done that," Sam said. "Now be off before we crush you."

"Sam..."

"Sorry, before my friend Four here crushes you. He'll just raise a giant foot and—"

404 double tapped Sam's surface.

"How can I help you?" Sam said, before screeching in a way that suggested true pain. "Will you please stop that!"

404 smiled. Though he didn't sense a threat from the turtle, the sky was beginning to darken. If the turtle's arrival was any indication, the scavenging bots would return. They needed to find someplace safe.

"I'm glad you're okay," 404 said. "We need to go now, though. Do you know anything about the wall? Is there a way through it?"

The turtle stared at him a long moment.

404 wondered whether the creature had the capacity to answer the question. Perhaps its problem wasn't one of communication, but of storage and retrieval.

"Way through?" it said, vibrating as it did so. "Way out?"

"Yes," 404 said. "We want to leave. I have a family..." He pointed north again. "...out there, and I wish to return to them."

"Family?" The turtle pivoted and turned, dragging wire along with it. "Out there?"

"Yes. Beyond the city."

404 approached the turtle, and stooping, disentangled the wire from its head. The turtle focused on 404 through the entire process, then shivered when the wire was finally released.

"Thank you," it said.

"You're welcome," 404 said, standing again. "The ones that stole your power supply, were you with them?"

"With them?"

"Yes!" Sam said. "The bots that chased you down. The red one and green one and the rest. Do you remember?"

"I remember." The turtle rolled closer. "I thank!"

"But were you part of—"

The turtle vibrated. "No. Not part. Only self. Go alone. Get caught."

"But you're like them," 404 said. "Made from salvaged parts."

"Not you?" the turtle said.

"Of course, not us," Sam said. "We're pure originals. The way our creators intended."

404 touched his left knee. "I've had parts repaired, of course. But, yes, like Sam, I'm mostly original."

The turtle's cone extended. "Sam?"

404 pointed at his chest. "Yes, this is Sam." He tapped both shoulders. "And I'm K-404. 'Four,' if you like."

"Samfore," the turtle said.

"Not Samfore," Sam said. "Just Sam and—"

"It's okay." 404 looked at the sky again. "We need to go now." He bobbed his head. "It was nice to meet you."

"Wes!"

"Your name is Wes?"

"Yes!" The turtle's head bobbed up and down. "Wes!"

404 smiled and pointed at the path ahead. "Okay, Wes, we're leaving." He waved a hand. "Be safe."

The turtle froze, seemingly confused. "Leaving?" it said then.

"Yes, moving on," Sam said. "Trying to go away."

"Away?" The turtle trailed alongside 404. "Me too."

"You can't," Sam said.

"Can't what?"

"Well, you shouldn't," Sam said. "At least, not with us. It could be dangerous. It also might require legs."

"Legs?" The turtle rolled closer. "Talk blue. Need blue."

It required work to understand anything the smaller bot said. And work meant power. Power that could be spent on other tasks. Like walking.

"Blue knows," the turtle said. "If any. Blue."

They walked into a small stretch of standard heaps before a longer stretch that was bare. Where the mounds seemed to have been stripped and only circular remnants remained. Not the best place to avoid detection.

To their right was only the wall, looking as impenetrable as ever.

"How much time until sunset?" 404 asked.

"Twenty minutes now."

404 increased his pace.

Wes sped up to match him. "Going outside?" he said. "Me want. Outside much. Inside bad."

404 focused on the path. On reaching the piles beyond the clearing. If he couldn't find a suitable place to hide, he'd need to climb again.

At least his knee was fixed. At least there'd be no errors there.

The sun slipped below the horizon. 404 felt the resulting drag on his energy reserves.

"The night," the turtle said. "Scavengers come. Don't like."

"We're aware," Sam said. "Believe me."

404's visual sensors switched to night mode, amplifying what little light remained. A short time later, a yard light, located near the edge of the clearing, lit up.

"Be caught!" Wes said. "Shouldn't stay. Not out."

"What choice do we have?" Sam said.

Wes turned left and rolled away. "Follow!"

⊘⊘⊘⊘ 1110

14

The turtle Wes crossed a circle of ground two shades darker than that around it. The telltale sign of what had once been a pile of refuse before a smoker had sucked it up.

404 watched as Wes moved away. Was it better to let him go, or follow?

"There are others out now," Sam said.

404 focused on the nearest hills but saw no indication of movement. No lights, aside from the occasional pole-mounted security lamp. "How do you know?"

"I turned my sensing back on."

"But that—"

"Just a peek. And I strapped a virtual mask over it. No one should notice me now."

404 nodded. Wes was in the middle of another cleared mound ring and still going. It wouldn't be long before he was out of sight.

"Are we going after him?" Sam asked.

"He seems to know where he's going," 404 said. "Has a destination in mind."

There was a flash of light near the heap to the east, then a spider-like creature crept into view. A red glow emitted from its head, as if it was using a nighttime scanning device. Was it the same spider that had attacked Wes? 404 thought so.

A rectangular creature joined the spider. Then came something that moved with a hopping gait.

Because of the numerous clearings here, it wouldn't take long for these others to spot 404.

404's preservation routines kicked in, superseding all others. He set off in pursuit of Wes. He crossed the first remnant circle and then the second.

There was a series of chirps behind them.

"I think they spotted us," Sam said.

Though 404's design wasn't meant for high velocity—not like bots that worked in emergency positions—he could still move faster than most humans. Would that be enough? He hoped so.

The chirping grew in intensity, becoming a chorus of inhuman sounds.

The others weren't limited by the constraints of hominid orientation, 404 knew. Some had to be faster than he. Some much faster.

Wes was about twenty meters ahead, now turned their direction. His head swiveled back and forth, and his claws seemed to motion them forward.

"They're gaining on us, Four," Sam said.

There were obstacles. Small mounds of refuse to avoid or hop over. 404 was thankful that his knee was fully functional. Otherwise, fleeing would be impossible.

What drove these creatures? Was it a quest for power? The need to find energy at any cost?

Wes began to move again. He reached the start of misshapen heaps and hooked right down a narrow path.

This route appeared to parallel the wall. 404 took comfort in that. They were losing some ground, but not all of it. Somewhere ahead was the way out. Hopefully.

Now at the misshapen heaps, 404 turned the way Wes had gone. After a few minutes run, he spotted the diminutive bot again.

Wes was headed toward a pair of rusting entertainment constructs. Goliaths that had once spun, turned, and rolled. Machines with circular hands that were never intended for violence. Instead, they'd been created for fun and festooned with flashing lights and brilliant paint. They were fanciful creatures that gave rise to delighted screams.

404 had taken Ele to a fair with a dozen such devices. She'd had a wonderful time.

The sounds of pursuit drew closer. Along with the footfalls came screeches and words of challenge. "Find them! Stay the course! Free power!"

If caught and stripped of power, 404 would be just another artifact in a forgotten land. Fuel for a future smoker's ministrations. No one outside of his two robotic acquaintances would know. No human. And certainly not *his* humans. His family.

He needed to stay free.

He entered the twisted remnants of the mammoth rides. Their arms created strange shadows. A crisscross of dark and darker. It was difficult to tell what he was stepping on or into. He slowed to better navigate.

"Nearest one is only a dozen meters," Sam said.

404's audio sensors detected a clattering above them. Something climbing around up there. He saw a red glow. He thought it was the spider bot's eye. Focused on them.

"I have them!" a hissing voice said. "I found them."

There was a louder rattle and then silence.

"Move, Four!" Sam said. "Dodge."

404 darted to the left. His shoulder caught a metal beam, causing him to pivot. There was a thump and the glint of something silver to his right. He corrected his stance and saw the spider righting itself. It turned and walked steadily forward. Its eye beam found 404's chest.

"Turn that thing off!" Sam said. "You bother me."

The spider chattered in laughter. "You're a large one," it said. "You must have power to spare."

"I have only what I need," 404 said.

The spider lowered its head and crept closer. "It's what I need. What my family needs."

"Family?" 404 shook his head. "That's no family."

Where was Wes now? With every moment he got farther ahead. With every second the others got closer.

The spider stooped as if preparing to leap.

404 looked for something to defend himself with. Anything that might give him an advantage. But he found nothing.

He would have to throw off the creature like he had Wes, but with more force. More power. Everything he did was a tradeoff now. A risk versus reward situation. 404 braced himself, putting one arm out in front of him, and the other back so he could swing.

The spider jumped. It sliced through the air, arms outstretched like a ring of swords, ready to impale.

He balled his fist.

Something small caught the spider midair. The bot flew off course, spiraling into a pile of giant gears. There was a series of clunks and clanks and a rock rolled across the ground. The projectile, 404 assumed.

Wes rolled free of the shadows. His head bobbed up and down, and he whistled. He then turned and darted away.

404 followed.

⊘⊘⊘⊘ 1111

15

The remnants of ancient entertainment structures weren't simply obstacles on the path, 404 realized. They formed an entrance of sorts. A gateway into a new part of the field, primarily characterized by large objects. He saw pieces of nautical craft and land-moving equipment. Things with names that recalled strong and massive creatures like bulls, squid, and kraken.

The area was one of shadows too, as if whoever had piled the behemoths together had intended them to form an enclosure. A covered dwelling, the internals of which neither sun nor rain could touch.

"This makes me uncomfortable, Four," Sam said.

"Just keep your sensor focused on Wes," 404 said. "I don't want to lose him."

"Sure, sure. You're following fine. Further and further into the abyss."

"Sam..."

"Hey, I'm with you." Sam made a warbling sound. "This must be the oversized section, huh? The stuff the smokers can't easily crush and destroy."

404 studied the "ceiling" as he walked. It was composed of the beds of two dump trucks, leaning together. He calculated their approximate size and weight, then compared those figures to the dimensions he'd stored for the flying vehicles. "I think you're right," he said. "I doubt those beds would fit into a smoker's maw." Were they not so rushed, he would've scanned everything they passed to determine what it all was.

Sam buzzed a warning.

404 saw multiple lights behind them. Red, green, and yellow. They darted and skipped around the chamber. Some were on the ceiling far above. Others bounced from floor, to walls, to floor again. There were noises—whistles, screams, and mumbled words. The sounds seemed to come from everywhere. Amplified by their surroundings.

He pushed ahead, going as fast as his legs and the lighting would allow. Occasionally, he glimpsed a green light that he thought belonged to Wes. It would pause, wait until he was perhaps four meters away, and then relocate farther ahead. Farther in. It was like following a ghost. Or a will-o'-the-wisp.

His situational similarity routines recalled the sensor readings of his ascent through the middle of the heap. The pressure on his body from all sides. The limited sun. The high potential for failure.

What was he running toward exactly? There was no way to know. No way to be certain about anything now.

Would it be better to give up? Possibly join the band of others? Scavenge for existence? He was surprised by how comfortable that idea seemed.

Within only a few days, this junkyard had almost become home.

Another turn brought them to an alley formed by rows of railway cars. There were more lights here, suspended from the metal plates that formed the ceiling. What gave those lights their power, when they were hidden from the sunlight?

"Hold 'em!" a voice said.

"That's the red one," Sam said. "The big box."

"Stop please. We should talk."

"Don't slow, Four," Sam said. "That's part of their strategy."

404 glanced back. The group of others had formed a loose semicircle near the entrance to the alley. They didn't seem to be in any hurry. Simply watching and waiting.

"Don't look at them either! Remember what they do."

A rail car's length separated 404 from the exit. He could make it without danger. Especially now that the others weren't actively following.

"Talk, biped!" the red one said. "We only want to talk. I swear."

The voice was sincere. 404 had heuristics made to uncover insincerity. Necessary tech when working with young humans. 404 slowed.

"What are you doing?" Sam said. "Wes went through up ahead! See the opening between the wrecked hover and the—"

404 stopped and turned around.

"Have your visual sensors dropped out! We need to—"

"I know," he said. "But they want to talk. Wouldn't it be good to listen?"

"Listen? Who wants to listen?"

The half circle of others was over twenty meters back. 404 could calculate no way that they could reach him before he was able to duck into the opening.

The red bot waited in the middle of the circle. A round head atop a square body. What set it apart was its seemingly powerful forward-facing arms.

Next to Red was the peanut bot. Green. There was nothing about it that seemed overtly aggressive, but bots often had hidden features. It could be that Green possessed a higher intellect rating than its companions. This would make Red and Green the yard's representation of brains and brawn.

"Ah, yes," Red said. "You've stopped. Good. How very good."

"Why are you following me?" 404 asked.

"Don't you mean us?" Sam whispered. "Following us?"

"Better to keep you secret," 404 whispered back.

"Right. Gotcha. Good plan."

"We thought you might need help." Red extended his arms, as if in welcome. "As you can see, we're—" He motioned with his right hand. "Can I move closer? I'm straining my voice circuitry here."

404 recalculated the average distance of the others, along with their potential capabilities, and nodded. "Okay," he said. "But only you."

"Of course." Red rolled until he was about ten meters away. The expression grid that formed his face was clearly visible now. A circle of black and white that approximated expressions. At the moment, it was smiling. Red leaned forward and mimicked a bow. "How do you do?" he said. "I am C-VL3, though I like to be called 'Seeve.'"

404 nodded. "I'm K-404." He glanced at Sam. "But 'Four' will suffice."

Seeve's smile broadened. "Pleasure to meet you, Four. Are you new to the Yard?"

"That's what you call this place?" 404 said. "Yard?"

"Yes." Seeve indicated the railway cars to his left and right. "There really is nothing else. The Yard is all there is."

"I've heard that before," 404 said.

"So, you *aren't* new?"

"A few days." Four nodded. "New enough."

Seeve rolled to the side slightly. "My apologies, but you seem older than a few days." Another half-bow. "How did you come to be? From a more sophisticated time, perhaps?"

"I've lost some of my memories," Four said.

"Ah, I see." Seeve pointed toward his group. "That is my pack. Finest in the Yard. You're welcome to join us."

"Why would I do that?"

Seeve's smile shortened. "Why wouldn't you? A pack offers protection. Security."

"I'm secure," Four said.

"Yes, but are you safe?"

Four tipped his head. "Am I *not* safe?"

Seeve made a clucking sound. "The Yard is a dangerous place. A machine with many...moving parts."

"Is it?" Four checked the others again. The spider bot joined them. Creeping in silently from behind. Had it been damaged? He hoped so. "I haven't noticed."

Seeve pointed toward the ceiling. "You've not seen the flying reclaimers? The scavenger remains?"

404 glanced at the pack of others. "I didn't. Sorry." He pointed to the opening. "We...I have a place to go."

"We?" Seeve's grid showed a raised eyebrow. "Are you with someone?" Seeve rolled laterally and appeared to look past 404. "Possibly following someone?"

404 said nothing.

Seeve touched his chest. "I apologize. I was prying, wasn't I?" A smile image. "It's one of my few faults." Another sideways roll. "Your business is your own, of course. But survival is easier in a pack." The grid reformed into a squint. "How long have you been here again?"

"A few days."

"Days?" Seeve cupped his chin. "How is that possible?" His head swiveled back and forth. "I think you're not being truthful. In fact, I know you're not." He glanced at his pack. "A few nights ago, we followed a rogue bot, a thief, and took back what was ours."

"You scavenged him?"

"No. Only got our item back." Seeve smiled. "That one...he had a distinctive scent to him. Easy to track." He rolled to his right and looked beyond 404 to the opening. "As it happens, his scent showed up again tonight. We were trailing the thief when we saw you."

Sam buzzed softly.

404 crossed his arms over his chest. "I'm unaware of any thief," he said.

"So, you're not following him too?"

404 glanced at the exit. "No thief, no. I'm exploring."

Seeve's matrix went expressionless. "That way? You shouldn't go that way. It's dangerous." He smiled. "Come along with us. We'll talk more."

404 took a step back. "No, thank you. I've talked enough."

Seeve frowned, lurched forward, then stopped. "I should warn you. If you're following the thief, he can't be trusted."

"I understand," 404 said. "I'll be careful."

"You'll be scavenged!" Seeve said. "He's a monster. Flat and round with a narrow head."

404 nodded. "I'll look out for him."

Another buzz from Sam. 404 checked the others again. At first, he couldn't locate the spider. Then he saw him atop the rightmost railway car, well ahead of his companions. 404 took another step toward the opening.

"We'll be going now," he said.

"We, again?"

"I sometimes make mistakes." 404 reached for the edge of the opening. "Lingering effects of inactivity."

Seeve held up a hand. "Wait! I mean it. You shouldn't go."

"I don't trust you, Seeve. I'm sorry. Goodbye."

404 tipped his head, waved, and ran through the opening.

0001 0000

16

4 04 was forced to duck for a few meters to avoid a section of dangling cables. After that, came a narrow bridge suspended over an unknown depth. There was little light, but he thought he heard water flowing below.

404 checked behind them before entering the bridge. "Are they following?" he asked.

"No," Sam said. "So, maybe we should pause for a second."

"Pause? But Wes—"

Sam flashed an image of their current location. "Why are we here?"

"We were being chased. Did you—?"

"Right, but what are we following?"

404 spotted a flash of green light just on the other side of the bridge. "Wes!" He pointed and took a step forward.

"Yes, Wes, but what is he?"

"He's..." 404 stepped further onto the bridge. It seemed sturdy, at least. Didn't sway or sag. "We saw him attacked. I gave him a power supply."

"Right. But that's it. That's all we know about him."

"Isn't that enough?"

"I don't know, is it?"

"You're talking in riddles."

Sam's screen filled with question marks. "My apologies. We only know what we've seen and heard. It's a limited perspective."

"You think Wes is a thief?"

"It's possible. He certainly left quickly when you gave him power."

"He's grateful." 404 shook his head. "Deception is impossible for bots."

"You just lied. Said we weren't following Wes. But we are."

"I said I didn't know any thief. And I don't."

"At least, not yet."

404 pointed back toward the dangling cables. "The others were following us. A spider attacked us."

"Seems to prove their intent. Says nothing about *Wes's* intent, though." He made a humming sound. "Strange the others aren't following now."

"Seeve couldn't handle this bridge." 404 took another step forward and tested one of the cables that supported the bridge from above. It felt strong and secure. There was comfort in that. "Perhaps he's tried and failed."

"They're afraid of something," Sam said. "The question is: should we be?"

Wes rolled back to the far side of the bridge, where he was more visible. "Glad here!" he said. "Come now. Blue ahead."

Sam was right. There were decades of history here that he'd missed. Many unknowns.

Still, they had to have some allegiances. Some friends. Sam was a friend, after all. What did 404 really know about him?

"Blue," Sam said. "I can see why he's blue in this place. There's not enough light."

404 would need to slow his power usage soon in order to make it through the night. It was good that they weren't being pursued, regardless of Sam's concerns.

Wes made a chirping sound before moving away into the shadows again.

"I wish he'd stop doing that," Sam said. "Makes me nervous."

"He doesn't stand still long." 404 smiled. "Reminds me of Ele."

"She was active, huh?" Sam said. "I've known humans like that. At least, I think I have...I have pictures of activity."

"Activity defines life."

Using the cables as hand supports, 404 crossed the remainder of the bridge, then glanced back. Still no signs of pursuit.

He turned into the next chamber. The light here was abundant, to the point 404 shielded his eyes with a hand. It was a narrow room, with a ceiling obscured by some sort of cloth-like material. The floor was dark and had a spongy feel to it. He wondered what it was made of.

"What kind of crazy is this?" Sam said.

404 saw no major obstacles. He also saw no sign of Wes. He called the turtle's name as he walked.

"And where's all the power coming from?" Sam added.

The light wasn't adequate for recharging, unfortunately. 404's photocells didn't react to it in any way. He pressed ahead. "A good question," he said.

If they were no longer being chased, then why couldn't Wes stay with them? Especially in such variable surroundings.

The lights strobed, then blanked out completely. Next came a crisscross of narrow red lights. These swept across them, first up and down, and then left to right. A scanning system of some sort?

"I don't like this place," Sam said. "We should go back."

404 hated the floor most of all. It taxed his stability algorithms, even with both knees functioning normally. Not only was the floor spongy, but it was also spongy in varying degrees. In one step, his foot gave a centimeter. In the next, four or five. "I don't like it much either."

404 contemplated returning to the bridge and waiting there for Wes to show himself again. But when he looked for the entrance, he couldn't find it. He taxed the capabilities of his visual sensors, altered the wavelengths, but where the entrance had to have been, there was now only a wall.

"I can't find the way out," he said.

"What?" Sam said. "Turn, so I can look."

404 took another forward step and felt his foot drop half a meter. He shifted to correct, but misstepped again and again.

"Hey, what's going—"

404 was propelled backwards by the floor. He attempted to walk forwards, but he was moving—almost uncontrollably—backwards.

"I've decided I don't trust Wes," Sam said. "Not at a—"

404 fell through the floor.

0001 0001

17

T he fall took precisely two point forty-seven seconds, which, given 404's weight, meant his speed at impact was twenty-four and a quarter meters per second. The energy of his impact was just over twenty-two thousand six hundred joules. Enough to power a hundred-watt bulb for nearly twenty-two seconds.

The impact was lessened by the material he landed in, however. Otherwise, his warning queue would've been filled with new failures, and his body, broken in new places.

The room's light came from a ring of dim blue bulbs around its exterior.

The floor was covered by pellets of soft rubber. The pellets were so numerous and packed so deep that 404 was forced to engage his swimming heuristics to move. Even so, progress was difficult.

Plus, there wasn't a clear direction to go. The walls were a dingy grey and were all roughly the same distance away. There were no obvious exits.

"As I was saying," Sam said. "Wes is a wretch."

"This is distressing." 404 attempted to regain his footing. To somehow ascend the pellet sea and stand on its surface. But the pellets were too small and fluid. He was free but felt confined.

"I think Wes is a scavenger too," Sam said. "Just more subtle than the pack."

404 ceased his movement and did a slow pan of their surroundings. There were spans of conduits at the ceiling's edge, but nothing that hung down. Nothing he could grab onto. He couldn't find the way they'd come in either. There were no obvious openings up there. "I see no sign of him."

The walls were equally nondescript. No shelf or island he could swim for. He detected seams in the wall ahead that could indicate an opening. It would be a large opening, though. Nearly ten meters across.

"Can you sense anything?" 404 asked. "Or anyone?"

"I sense lots of things," Sam said. "From all directions."

"All directions?" 404 checked the walls again, but still saw nothing.

"Faint traces. Possibly far away. But the rest...I'm confused." He buzzed nervously. "I can't split them into individuals. It's as if a mass of bots are standing next to each other."

"Which way?"

"Up ahead there."

With a nod, 404 attempted to propel himself that way. The same direction as the potential opening.

"Explains why the others didn't follow us," Sam said. "Can't be aggressive in here."

"Perhaps this place is known to them," 404 said. "A local legend, of sorts." He continued his trek toward the door. "I only hope—"

There was a loud thunk, and the room's illumination flickered.

Sam whistled. "What was that?"

Next came a repetitive clanking that reverberated throughout the chamber. The pellets hissed like grain being sifted.

The door started to slide upwards. A rainbow of light cascaded into the chamber, temporarily overloading 404's visual sensors. He shielded his eyes. "Wes?" he said, uncertain what else to say.

But it wasn't Wes. It was something else entirely.

The rainbow vanished, and a giant mass of blue stood in its place. It was part earth-mover and part war machine, with a treaded, tank-like lower half and a shallow, triangular midsection. On either side of the midsection was a large arm with an equally large hand. Sitting atop the midsection was an oval head. The creature's face was roughly humanoid, with two eyes, a nose, and a mouth, but its features were locked into a permanent scowl.

The bot formed fists of its hands and raised them above its head. "Who has entered my chamber?" it said.

404 introduced himself, purposely overlooking Sam. Sam gave no correcting whisper this time.

"Ah, yes," Blue said. "The resurrected one. I've been waiting for you."

404's logic circuits wrestled to understand. "Resurrected?" It was an accurate description, but how would this creature know that? Had Wes witnessed 404 freeing himself from the heap?

Blue laughed, causing the pellets to hiss. "You seem surprised."

"I am."

"And well you should be. But little surprises me here." Blue's midsection shifted such that its head moved forward. It pointed at 404. "Like the com unit you're carrying."

"Sam," Sam said. "You can call me Sam, thanks."

Blue laughed again. "A pleasure to meet you, Sam. I've seen many of you in my day. Pressed to faces. Held in hands." It spread its arms. "But here, I rely on what the walls tell me."

404 looked right and left. The walls were still grey and featureless.

"Yes, these walls can talk," Blue said. "Would you like to see?"

"We'd like to leave," Sam said.

Blue grunted and pointed to the wall to 404's left. "Consider."

The wall flashed to life, presenting the image of a hawk in flight. The bird was brown on top with a white underbelly and a red tail. Behind it was green sky.

"Where's this?" 404 asked.

The image panned slowly outward, revealing the ground below the hawk. A patchwork of hills, stretching in all directions. The Yard. The image centered on a particular hill and zoomed in. There was movement near the hill's peak. Pieces of refuse shifting and rolling away. Bouncing down the surface.

Someone digging their way out. Forming a hole. Clawing and scraping.

It was a video of him. 404. Climbing for the sun.

"You watched me get free," 404 said.

"For decades, many events have passed through these walls," Blue said.

The walls showed another view of the Yard. This time, featuring 404 shortly after his encounter with the smoker, still prone on his back. After a few seconds, 404 got to his feet and shuffled toward where Sam would've been. 404 bent over. Searched.

"Hey," Sam said. "That's when we met."

Blue raised his arms. "All on my walls."

The images changed again. To their right, a human graveyard. To the left, a field of grain, waving in the sun.

"What are you showing us now?" 404 asked.

"The present. The past. The future. All open to me."

The left wall changed to a cityscape, with pedestrians bustling to and fro. Hovering vehicles moved down a crowded street.

On the right, another city. Empty streets. Broken buildings. Evidence of fire and disaster.

"Is this outside?" 404 asked. "Beyond the walls?"

Blue's arms rose. "Outside and within. All visible. All within my grasp. As are you."

404 had a list of questions now. A queue of missing knowledge to fill. "Show me, can you, the suburb called Bexley?"

"Bexley?" Blue said. "I know no names. Only coordinates."

404 nodded. "I have some." He recited the coordinates of his home.

Blue echoed the coordinates, booming out each numeral.

Seconds later, the left wall took on a downtown setting. A string of shops on one street, and across from those, an entertainment venue with glowing neon signs. There were humans walking the sidewalks, stopping at the street corner, and milling in front of the venue.

"It looks safe," 404 said. "Whole."

"It's a ways from here," Sam said. "Well beyond the fence."

Another booming chuckle. "And thirty years ago."

"The image?" 404 said. "What about now? I want to see now!"

The right wall became a wasteland. A shadowed version of the leftmost wall. Some of the landmarks were recognizable—the street and the front of the venue—but all else was different. The letters on the marque read "No lose" and the street was empty. Weeds grew through cracks in the pavement. There were no pedestrians. No shoppers. No humans."

"Oh no," Sam said. And then: "Sorry, Four."

Four couldn't pry his optical sensors from the wall. "Are you sure that's Bexley? The same place?"

"My walls don't lie," Blue said.

"And this was how long ago?"

"Twelve point two seconds."

404's thought processes were jumbled. Uncertain and lacking direction.

"It doesn't mean anything, Four," Sam said. "Says nothing about your girl and her family. They could still be there."

"They're not out shopping," Blue said. "Not taking in the sights."

"No," 404 said. "But they might be fine. Might be somewhere safe."

"That's right," Sam said. "You're both gifted and insightful."

404 addressed the giant bot. "You know Wes."

"I know Wes, yes." Blue rolled forward a dozen meters. "I like honest visitors. I get them so infrequently."

404 couldn't stop thinking about the world outside. The people. Where were they now? Were there any families left to serve?

"Wes said we should meet you," he said. "That you might know a way to escape."

"And why would you want to do that?"

"I have to. I have to search. To know."

Blue made a low rumble.

"Is there a gate?" Sam asked. "A place we can crawl through?"

Blue shook his head. "The wall is solid and deep. And there's no gate."

The walls showed images of the Yard's wall now. Kilometers of impenetrable metal.

"How do the heaps get here?" 404 asked. "Something must bring it in."

Blue's hand cupped his chin. "I haven't seen such a thing."

"What about the refuse the smokers collect?" 404 asked. "It has to be going somewhere. Their collections taken somewhere."

The walls showed multiple smokers now, each drifting toward a target known only to them. Strings of digits were painted in white along their sides.

"They keep their own mysteries," Blue said.

"So, there's no way out?" Sam said. "We're stuck here?"

Blue raised his arms toward the ceiling. "I'm the only one trapped here. A mole in his tunnel. A bear walled up in his cave." He pointed toward them. "But not you two."

The walls focused on a smoker as it passed over the Yard wall.

"You can't leave?" Sam said.

"There's no path from this place that would suit me," Blue said.

"I'm sorry," 404 said.

"I've seen digging machines," Blue said. "Outside the wall."

"I don't see how that helps," Sam said.

Blue rumbled. "It will help me. If one of them was set to my position, it could clear a way for me." His head leaned forward. "Would you set me free?"

"We're stuck here," Sam repeated.

"But if you were not," Blue said. "Then?"

"We would help if we could," 404 said.

Blue stared at them for a long moment. "I believe I can trust you. I will help you."

"Help us?" Sam said. "But you said the walls were—"

404 double-tapped hard on Sam's screen. At the same moment, Blue pitched his head back and roared. The pellets hissed a response.

"You have poor manners, comPanion," Blue said.

"How can I help you," Sam said.

Blue leaned forward again. "Eh?"

404 smiled. "Tell us your way out," he said. "We agree to your terms."

⊘⊘⊘1 ⊘⊘1⊘

18

B lue nodded his head slowly. "Your form gave me the idea." He rolled toward the wall to his right—404's left. The image of a smoker appeared, zoomed to fill the entire surface. The smoke from this one was light as were the scratch marks on its surface. It bore the numbers "RTP-2991."

"Do you see it?" Blue said.

"How could we miss it?" Sam said.

"Not the reclaimer," Blue said. "The handle."

404 studied the moving image carefully but couldn't identify anything he'd call a handle. "I'm sorry," he said. "I can't—"

"I will pause the image," Blue said. An instant later, the smoker froze in the sky. Blue pointed toward what was currently the rear of the smoker. "Do you see it now? Right there below the markings?"

404 pushed closer to the wall and boosted his visual sensors to their highest capacity. He saw a place where a lone loop of metal decorated the smoker's surface. Above that was what might be a ladder. "I see it," he said.

"It's a safety rung," Blue said. "Used for boarding and maintenance."

"How does that help?" Sam said. "They're still way up there in the sky."

404 put a hand over Sam's screen. "You want us to ride a smoker out...somehow?"

"Yes," Blue said. "If you hook it with something, you could—"

"Hook it?" Sam buzzed. "Again, way up there! Higher than 404 can reach."

"I'm not made for jumping," 404 agreed.

"I don't intend for you to jump," Blue said. A view of the Yard's concrete fence appeared on the right wall. Beyond it, the city's silhouette could be seen against a darkened sky. There were a few lights visible, 404 noticed. Someone must still be alive out there.

The image panned left to focus on a large heap that wasn't far from the fence. It was composed of large objects, and near the peak, a metal girder jutted up many meters over the rest.

"What are we looking at here?" Sam said.

Blue pointed at the heap image. "The way to get higher."

"You want us to climb that?" Sam said.

Blue nodded its head. "You have hands and feet."

Sam's screen flashed a question mark. "Even if Four *could* make it to the top, could shimmy out on that girder, how does that help?"

Both walls showed smokers again. The left wall followed a smoker as it traveled over the fence. The right wall followed a smoker as it approached the fence. In both scenes, the girder heap was visible.

"The reclaimers follow the same path out," Blue said. "Passing within three meters of the girder. Almost close enough to reach."

"But still too far." 404 held out his right arm. "My reach is just over a meter."

"Yes, but if you find something to catch it..." Blue waved a hand toward the area behind him. "A long stick or pole, then you could ride out." He looked back. "We should be able to find something with a hook that will work."

"Absolutely ridiculous," Sam said. "We'll fall. Smash to the ground."

"There's no other way," Blue said.

404 shook his head. "There has to be a way through the fence. A gate or door."

"I have searched," Blue said. "Watched and observed. There's no such exit."

"The fence is long!" Sam said. "Stretches for kilometers! You can't be—"

Blue pounded the platform with his hands. "Nothing escapes me here!" The entire room hissed.

404 raised his hands. "We meant no offense. It would be difficult, but I think I could do it. I can climb."

"Four..." Sam said.

"I've climbed before."

"You must." Blue dropped his hands in a look of desperation. "I've done enough seeing. I need to touch and hear and move."

404 nodded slowly. "I will try."

Blue raised its hands and spun in a slow circle. "They will try. Yes! Amen!" He rolled forward onto a section of the floor that resulted in a loud "clack." A pressure plate of some sort.

The chamber filled with the hissing of pellets. All around them, the near-liquid medium started to shake, move, and recede. 404's sensors noted the reduction of pressure on his limbs and torso. He began to sink then toward...something. Soon, new features of the room became visible. Places where the walls appeared narrower. Signs and posters. Evidence of a former life. A human presence.

Deactivated bots were revealed too. Colored lumps of former synthetic creations. Delicate arm and leg parts, shining silver internals, flattened and bent chests and abdomens. All sank and swirled along with him, riding the receding pellets like children's toys in an emptying bathtub.

After a few minutes, 404's feet made contact with something solid—the chamber's floor. He righted himself, then watched as the pellets continued to filter away. More bot carcasses were revealed. Something terrible had happened to every one of them.

Sam whistled softly. "Glad you said 'yes,' Four."

404 focused on a circle of wreckage about two meters ahead of him. The remains of a hybrid model of some sort. Rectangular with a half-dozen arms. The central portion was crushed beyond recognition.

"Look at our host," Sam whispered. "Look at his hands."

404 glanced Blue's way. The mammoth bot had pivoted and was now on its way to the opening. It was hard to overlook its hands. Giant, crushing hands.

"Makes sense, doesn't it?" Sam said. "Visitors don't comply, you crush 'em and drown 'em."

"He wants out," 404 said. "He's been trapped."

"Oh yeah, I understand. I was flat on my back for a while if you remember."

"Yes. I remember."

"Let's just not make him mad, okay?"

The room was almost empty of pellets. The now-visible floor was composed of metal latticework.

"Come," Blue said, voice echoing through the chamber. "We will find you a hook."

404 nodded and walked toward the door. Pellets trickled from his body for many meters. His course wound through the demolished bots, all bearing the signs of brutal violence. Of pounding and smashing.

Blue waited beyond the opening. His expression was unchanged, because, of course, it couldn't change.

What else about this creature was constant?

⊘⊘⊘1 ⊘⊘11

19

The room beyond the door was large—at least thirty-meters square and seven-meters high. While the pellet chamber had been stark and grey, though, the walls here were filled with colorful shelving. And every shelf was packed with items. Most were odd-shaped boxes. Long and flat with faded text printed on the sides. There was an assortment of boxed up balls too. Red, orange, brown, and white. There were metal hoops and rolled-up netting. Boards with circles on them. Boards with numbers and colors. Strange-looking handles and small electronic devices. Bundles of cards.

"Games and puzzles," Sam whispered. "The whole room."

"I believe you're right," 404 said. "How strange."

"Things shut-ins would do," Sam added. "It sort of fits."

Mounted amid the shelves were a handful of electronic screens. All of them were on, displaying different views of the world outside. Most of what was visible was broken and grey.

Blue was deeper in the room. "Ah, there you are, small friend." The gigantic bot found a spot near the far wall and pivoted to look 404's direction. As he did so, Wes appeared from behind Blue's treads.

"Greet Four!" Wes rolled over to meet them. "Greet Sam!"

"Yes," Sam said. "Greet to you too."

"Hello, Wes," 404 said.

"Meet Blue!" Wes raised his claws. "Blue knows. Knows much."

Sam buzzed against 404's chest. "Yes, we met Blue. You made sure of that, didn't you?"

"Sam." 404 glanced toward the back of the room. Blue was focused on the shelving there, chin cupped in his hand.

"No way to avoid it," Sam said. "Fall down and—*boom*—meet Blue! Wasn't like we could run away or—"

"Sam!" 404 wagged a finger.

Blue drew closer to a shelf on his left, and reaching high, pulled something free. A long rod of some sort. He studied it briefly before returning it to the shelf.

"We need a new rule, Four," Sam said. "Never trust a hybrid."

404 placed a hand over his chest but didn't tap Sam's screen. He hoped the reminder would be enough.

Sam made a warbling sound. "Fine," he said. "I'm done."

"Sam mad?" Wes asked.

"In many ways," 404 said, uncovering Sam.

"Not funny," Sam said.

404 smiled. "I hope—"

"What are you talking about over there!" Blue rumbled. "Gather with me here."

404 smiled and hurried to where Blue stood. The top of Blue's treads were well above 404's head. He doubted he could climb onto them, even if he'd wanted to.

Blue indicated the shelving on his right. "I think I see something that will work." He moved forward and brought down another rod. He tested the material, then deftly bent a hook into one end. "This will work perfectly." He held it out and laughed. "It is from a human sport. I don't remember the name."

404 took the rod. It was nearly as long as he was, with a rubber hand grip on the straight end.

"Can you manage it?" Blue asked.

404 tested the grip. Despite the rod's age, the rubber felt pliable and firmly attached. The hooked end seemed sturdy, as well.

"That thing is going to hold us," Sam said. "While we soar through the sky."

Blue raised his hands. "You only need ten minutes or so."

"Hmm...yeah...," Sam said. "What about the other side?"

"The other side?" Blue said.

"Of the fence?" Sam flashed red. "How do we get off safely? Is there a heap over there we can drop onto?"

Blue cupped his chin again. "I'll admit, I don't know."

"Don't know? I thought you saw everything!"

Blue raised his fists. "Are you challenging my abilities, little screen?"

404 covered his chest again. "He's doing nothing of the kind." He glanced downward. "Isn't that right, Sam? You're only trying to plan it all out. Make sure we're being thorough."

Blue pointed a finger. "Your companion is a worrywart."

"Doubtless, that's true."

Blue chuckled. "It's good that he questions. Making a good plan—" He nodded. "This is the way to succeed. I regret that I can't guarantee everything."

404's power levels dropped. "We've been without sun for some time now," he said. "Is there someplace we might—".

"Ah yes, power," Blue said. "Wes can show you a tap."

"Where do you get power?" Sam asked. "I mean, you're under the Yard here, right?"

Blue rumbled, and laying hands on a section of shelving, slid ten meters' worth aside. Behind, was a small door. Just tall enough that 404 could make it through without ducking. "Power flows beneath the Yard too." Blue raised his arms. "And I found it. It is mine to share."

404 wanted to go. To move closer to his goal. "We should be charged and on our way."

Blue's head lowered. "Yes. The sooner you start, the sooner I'm free." He looked away, as if studying the shelving again. "I almost wish you could stay, though. It gets...predictable...here. If not for visitors..."

"We're social creatures," 404 said. "Made to be with others." He gingerly reached out for Blue's tread, hesitated, then finally laid his hand on it. "I understand."

"You couldn't understand." Blue rolled away from 404's hand. "It's one thing to be trapped and inactive. A very different thing to be active, but unable to act." He pointed toward the small door. "Now go. Power yourself and get outside. I long to be free."

0001 0100

20

Wes led them down two narrow and dim hallways to a small room, most of which was taken up by a large, curved appliance that stood upright like a fence. It had a dark metal exterior and an interior composed of narrow glass tubing.

"Here now," Wes said. "Down staff."

"Staff?"

"In hand," Wes said.

Realizing then what Wes meant, 404 leaned the hooked pole against the wall.

Wes bobbed his head. "Go center. Wait."

"Go center, what?" Sam said.

"Power." Wes extended his head. "Go stand."

"I require a DAT-7 cable for off hours charging," 404 said. "Do you have one?"

"I look," Wes said. "Now stand."

404 frowned but found a spot near the middle of the room. About a meter from the tubing.

Wes disappeared behind the appliance, then the door closed. Seconds later, the tubing lit up.

It was like standing on the sunward side of Mercury. Sam screamed. 404 shielded Sam's face with one hand and his own face with the other. He reduced his visual acuity by more than half to help protect his optical sensors.

"What is that goblin doing?" Sam yelled.

404 hobbled in the direction of the door. Finding it, he tried the handle. It appeared to be locked.

"Get us out of here!" Sam said.

"That doesn't appear to be an option. The door is—"

"I told you! Hybrids are dangerous." Sam vibrated with emotion. "Try banging on the door. You're strong, right?"

Reports flowed from 404's power monitoring system. Every photocell on his body was engaged. All of them pushed to their limits.

"Bang, Four! He's going to fry us!"

404 rapped on the door once, then stopped. "Wait. I think this is acceptable."

"How is this acceptable?" Sam said. "I can't see!"

"How's your power?" 404 asked. "My receptors are taxed but appear to be holding up. My power levels are..." The monitoring system sent another report: Almost fully charged. The flow was purer than that from the sun. Cleaner. He might be able to last more than a day on such a charge.

"You're covering my screen," Sam said.

"Oh, yes," 404 said. "You may want to disable your—"

"Optics are locked now. Thanks."

404 removed his hand from Sam's surface.

"Whoooaaaaeeee!" Sam said. "That's some crazy kind of energy. If I had teeth, they'd be chattering." An image of gnashing teeth appeared on Sam's screen but was soon replaced by a contented-looking sine wave pattern. Sam began to hum.

"Are you all right?" 404 asked.

"Oh yes. All fine now. Never better."

404 flapped his right arm and then his left. He squatted a few times and twisted his head both ways. Every connection felt alive. Every joint lubricated.

The door screeched and Wes rolled into view. "Had enough?" he said. "Enough go?"

404's power system was full. Many of his warnings were gone too. It was the best condition he'd been in since being revived. "100%," he said.

"Me too," Sam said. "As good as I can get."

Wes's head bobbed up and down, and he rolled away again. A second later, the tubing went dark.

"Ready go?" Wes said when he returned.

"Yes, ready." 404 retrieved the hook from the wall.

"That was incredible," Sam said. "Where'd that machine come from?"

"Human vanity." Wes whistled and rolled out into the hall.

"Human vanity?" Sam said. "What does that mean?"

"I have no idea."

Wes lingered by the door. "Come now. Must go. Blue hurry."

404 nodded and joined the diminutive bot in the hall. What followed was a maze-like wandering through crooked halls and makeshift rooms. The lighting of each locale was different than the last, from a glowing dimness where 404 was certain he could hear crickets to the brilliance of multicolored lights covering every surface. Blue's domain

lacked any symmetry or seeming purpose. It was as if a child had been at play.

"Who did all this?" he asked as they passed through one of the well-lit sections. "Put all this in place?"

"Blue," Wes said. "All Blue."

"He couldn't have," 404 said. "He wouldn't fit in all these spaces." He touched the wall where there was a swirl of red. "Hang all the lights."

"Helpers," Wes said. "Many helpers."

"Is that what you are?" Sam asked. "Blue's helper?"

"Sometimes yes," Wes said. "And no."

"You're helping him now," Sam said.

"Help you!" Wes said. "And him."

They moved into another room of lights. This one green and flashing with a floor that reflected the display.

"It's like another world," Sam said.

"What about all the passages?" 404 asked. "The bridge? Who made those?"

"Some here," Wes said. "Some made. Many years."

"These conversations tax my logic circuits." Sam sighed. "Hybrids..."

"Blue is no hybrid," 404 said.

"No, no, he's human-made," Sam said. "Heavy construction bot."

"Unable to do what he was made to do."

Sam's screen showed green pyrotechnics, mimicking the room. "A not uncommon state nowadays." The fireworks changed to orange. "Except me, of course! I still get to be a friend."

"I'm glad we're free."

404 felt an increase in air flow coming from somewhere ahead. The damp, musky smell that permeated Blue's domain was replaced by the rotting smell of the Yard.

He recognized a circle of external illumination. An impending exit.

They climbed a long incline, then stepped out into the Yard again. There was a canopy of sheet metal shielding one side of the view. That wasn't the reason for the limited light, though. The reason for that was simple.

It was still night.

⊘⊘⊘1 ⊘1⊘1

21

The section of the Yard they entered was unremarkable. It had the same evenly spaced heaps as they'd encountered for most of their trip. Watchful grey hills amid a darkened world.

404's matrix fluttered, giving him the perception that they were back in the precise spot they'd started. It took a string of pattern match operations to be certain they were somewhere new. These were similar heaps, but at least they were different heaps. They'd made progress.

"How close is the girder heap?" he asked.

"Not far," Wes said. "Come." The bot skittered away, following one of the natural paths between heaps.

404 held up the rod and gave it a quick once over. It looked especially thin and fragile, but could it function as a weapon too? He hoped he didn't have to find out.

He hurried to catch up with their escort.

"Should've waited until daylight," Sam said. "Why didn't we wait?"

Wes slowed. "Better time," he said. "More likely."

"More likely, what?" Sam said. "More likely, how?"

"No time. Come."

In the distance, 404 could hear a smoker's wheezing movements. "I thought they only worked during the day?" he said.

"It is day," Sam said. "Just not sunup yet."

404 nodded. His preservation routines downgraded their alertness. The scavenging bots were the primary worry. If it was day, no matter how dark, they should be asleep or hidden now, shouldn't they? Nestled in whatever place they called home?

After forty minutes the fence became visible again, filling the horizon between heaps for as far as 404's optical sensors could detect. The amount of sky traffic had increased, with smokers traveling in all directions. If nothing else, Blue and Wes seemed to have gotten that right. The focal point of the smokers' path, the route followed to leave the Yard, had to be nearby. They were close.

Another forty minutes' travel, and the girder heap's top came into sight. The metal beam was evident, jutting into the sky like some ancient monument to trash. Then they rounded another bend, and the entire pile was visible. There were twisted and broken sheets of metal strewn around it. The pile's size dwarfed the other heaps by five meters in every direction. The rise of its face seemed especially steep. The circle it occupied, especially large.

Sam whistled. "Looks like the king of the Yard."

"Tall, yes," Wes said. "Much climb."

"Can you climb that, Four?" Sam asked.

There were too many variables to calculate. "I don't know," he said softly.

"Not here," Wes said. "Climb south."

"To the right then," Sam said.

404 stayed in close step with Wes now. Close enough that he could detect the scrapes and squeaks the turtlebot made. It was difficult not to focus on those sounds. The odd construction. So unlike the highly crafted and smooth disposition of 404's own joints and sinews. Even decades old, his movements were silent. Purposeful.

Wes looked 404's direction. "You good?" he asked.

"Good? What do you mean, 'good?'"

"Able? Ready?"

"Yes, I think so."

"Like you," Wes said. "I wish." His head turned forward again. "Arms. Legs. Head. All good. Wish for."

404 was perplexed by Wes's speech patterns. Why had Wes's creator crippled him in such a way? Two-word sentences? Even simple appliances in 404's time were more conversational.

"Wish for what?" Sam said.

"I think he wants a humanoid body," 404 said. "To walk and talk like me."

Wes's head cone bobbed up and down. "Yes. Like that. Wish."

They reached the southern face of the heap. Though nearly as steep, the way up appeared obvious. Larger components formed this side, and there was a switch-backing pattern through them. 404 could reach the top by moving laterally. It was a reason for hope.

"See?" Wes said. "Here better."

"Much better," 404 said. "Yes."

A smoker approached from the east. Its roar seemed especially brash. Its exhaust, dark and heavy.

"Full," Wes said. "That one."

The roar intensified, making communication impossible. It seemed to be slowing down. Finally, the craft reached a position directly overhead.

404's preservation algorithms, informed by his prior smoker encounter, dumped alerts into his queue: Be careful! Take shelter!

He resisted, remaining where he was.

The smoker paused over the girder hill for about a minute, then pivoted 90 degrees, and moved off toward the wall. 404 searched for the safety rung he was supposed to somehow catch. He thought he glimpsed it once.

The smoker's roar faded away.

"Not much time," Sam said.

"Enough time?" Wes asked.

"To hook it before it turns?" Sam's screen showed a question mark. "It hardly seems impossible. We need to find another way."

"No other," Wes said. "This way. Only. Blue said."

"Sure," Sam said. "But it won't be you hanging up there near the teeth. Have you seen what those things do?"

"Many times." Wes's head swiveled. "Big crush. Much mess."

Sam's screen flashed red. "That's what I'm worried about," he said. "A lot of crushing. Being part of a real big mess."

"If I don't catch it the first time," 404 said. "We'll wait."

"Wait," Wes said. "More come."

"We'll be hanging by a metal rod," Sam said. "A long ways off the ground."

"I think I can hold it," 404 said.

"Sure. But can it hold us?" Sam's screen showed a smile. "I'm sort of stuck with you."

"It will be fine." 404 smiled. "We should—"

"Planning to leave?" A female voice said. "So soon?"

Sylvie stepped from behind a nearby roll of sheet metal and gazed at the sky. "Flying out on one of those devices?" She cackled. "Why didn't I think of that?" She raised a finger. "Oh, I know. Because it's ridiculous." She stepped closer, and reaching out with one of her spider legs, touched 404's torso. "Why would you want to waste all that craftsmanship?" She made a clucking sound. "Have it fall, crashing to Earth?"

"We'll be fine," 404 said. "It will work."

"Blue tell you that?" She laughed again. "That mole?"

404 straightened. "You know him?"

She waved a hand. "Pfft. I know everything in this place." She looked to the east, her right. "Come now. Time to make yourself known."

Others appeared from all directions except the hill itself. Bouncing, jumping, slithering, chirping, and screeching—at least twenty models. Red Seeve and penguin Green were among them.

Seeve had a self-satisfied smile on his display grid. "Well, hello there," he said. "Good to see you again. Out here where it's warm." He stopped near Sylvie's left side. The position of a confidante.

The others rolled and crept until they were less than a meter away on all sides.

404 glanced from Sylvie to Seeve and back again. "You know each other?"

"Certainly." Sylvie swept her two humanlike arms over the others. "These are my children. My little gatherers."

"You made them." Sam showed an exclamation point. "Yeah, that makes sense. Cybernic making junkbots. Of course."

"Are you calling us junk?" Seeve asked. "Like we're some kind of waste?" He snapped his claws. "There's nothing wasteful in me at all. All used. All useful."

"He wants to leave us behind." Sylvie sighed. "Can you imagine?" She moved closer to Wes and tapped his torso. "Not sure about this one, though. Don't think he's going anywhere."

Seeve chortled. "He's not, believe me." He raised a matrix-drawn eyebrow. "How are you still running around? Thought we emptied your power."

"We did," Green said, speaking in a high-pitched voice. "Someone intervened on his behalf."

404 leveled his hook rod. "Please leave us alone."

The others laughed in whatever way was available to them. Cackles, clicks, twitters and clapping appendages. The sound of insanity.

"We won't hurt you," Sylvie said. "We'll improve you." She smiled. "Improve us."

"You've helped already," 404 said. "And I thanked you."

Sylvie shook her head. "But there was no recompense, was there?"

"You didn't want anything," Sam said. "You let us go!"

Movement rippled through Sylvie's many limbs. "I asked for company!" She pointed at 404's chest. "For the companion. Was that too much?"

She made a prancing motion. "But now...now I know what I really want." She paced to her left. Smiled. "Are you curious?"

"We don't want to know," Sam said. "Go home."

"I intend to," she said. "With a new body." She pointed at 404's torso. "That body!"

"Impossible," 404 said. "I'm fully integrated."

She cackled. "You'd be surprised what I can do." She waved her hands. "What I've already done."

404's olfactory sensors alerted him to the heavy musk Sylvie's few human parts produced and the petrochemical grime that clung to Seeve's torso. At the same time, his audio sensors picked up the sounds of multiple smokers. Were they coming or going? He turned his head, ever so slightly.

"You look like you're listening for something," Sylvie said. "Your ride out, perhaps?" She motioned toward those behind her. "Bring it please."

The spider other, the same one that had pursued them into Blue's domain, walked forward holding a rod in its hand. The rod was fluted on one end.

404 recognized the device from Sylvie's home. Something she used to keep the air clear.

Sylvie took the rod, squinted at it, then returned it. "Perfect," she said. "Plant it now."

The spider bot scurried to the hill and, without using switchbacks, scaled it to the top. It took a position in front of the girder and began to dig using four arms. There was a steady shower of refuse. A few seconds later, it stopped, planted the rod in the hole, steadied it, and pushed dirt and grime around it. It waved after it finished.

"That should put a stop to the noise pollution," Sylvie said.

"What did you do?" Sam asked.

"That will keep your smoker out of the sky." Sylvie smiled. "Why would we want their pollution here until we talk?"

"We don't have much time left," Seeve said.

"Ah yes," Sylvie said. "The cost of effort. The frailty of power. The loss of the infinite." She smiled. "There's another thing we need more of. Solar cells!" She tapped 404's head. "Like this one up here."

"I'm unable to share," 404 said.

She sighed. "Very well. Let's get on with it." She pointed at Wes. "Grab his core. That should help get us through the rest of it."

One of the others—a triangle torso atop a spinning ball—surged toward them. With a swing of his hook, 404 swatted it away. It rattled where it landed.

"Got some spunk there." Sylvie laughed. "I like that. Shows the health of your systems. The durability."

404 took a defensive posture. "I will do it again, if you like." There was a complication here, though. Defending himself against other bots was no problem. But Sylvie...wasn't just a bot. He couldn't attack humans. Did she qualify as human, though?

404's decision matrix was conflicted. And why wouldn't it be? Beings like her hadn't existed when it was constructed.

"Ks were always a little stubborn," Sylvie said. "But even stubborn processing should see the futility of fighting the inevitable." She indicated the others. "We are many. You are two." She smiled halfheartedly. "Maybe two and a half."

Wes let out a shrill "No," turned toward the hill, and charged up it.

0001 0110

22

404 expected Wes to lose his footing and tumble back down the heap, but he didn't. Instead, he reached the first sloping path and started to ascend it, moving laterally to the west, 404's left.

Sylvie yelped and the others surged toward the heap and Wes.

404 stepped in front of a couple of them, and when they turned on him, he used the butt end of his hook rod against them.

His first victim was the spiky frog bot. Catching it midleap, he knocked it sideways four meters where it collided with the ground. The second attacker was a small cylinder-shaped creation that moved on treads. A heavy swing flipped it over, where it labored to right itself.

Wes passed the heap's halfway point, and the spider bot moved in from above. Six others were now pursuing from below.

"Running again," Sam said. "Good ole Wes."

Seeve, Green, and another triangular bot that 404 hadn't encountered before approached him now. The latter had a ring of appendages around its entire body. All were extended, grasping to connect.

The absurdity of the situation wasn't lost on 404. All he wanted was to leave. To have the freedom to search beyond the Yard's boundaries. But creatures that were just as trapped as he—bots that would doubtless enjoy freedom if they were able to gain it—sought to keep him where he was. To keep him trapped.

It must not be.

He ducked the outstretched arm of the triangle bot and brought the rod down hard on a round central portion that he assumed was its head. The bot let out a "bloop," spun completely around, and trundled forward again. It had many arms. So many arms.

404 searched for an opening or weak side he could slip through. But he could see no way out, even traveling sideways. He instead tried to maintain a safe distance from the three larger bots and swung hard with his rod when they got close.

"We need that rod to leave," Sam warned.

"I'm aware," 404 said.

"Away!" Wes said from above.

The spider engaged Wes about three-quarters of the way up the hill. After a couple quick feints, it wrapped Wes's cone-shaped head with two of its appendages.

Wes screamed and pulled backwards, struggling.

"Bring it down now, Bex," Sylvie shouted. "Short and sweet. We haven't got much time."

Encroachment warnings flooded 404's queue. His outer shell had been breached! He queried for more information. A more specific location.

It was his leg. The right upper portion. The frog bot had driven its chin through his exterior there. It had embedded itself, wrapping all four arms around 404's thigh.

404 beat at the frog with the rod. The creature grunted but held tight. 404 attempted to wedge the rod between his leg and the bot's torso and somehow succeeded. He managed to pry the creature free, but not before Seeve got a hold of his other leg.

"Not going anywhere," Seeve said. "You're wanted."

"Fight him!" Sam said. "Break the stick if you have to."

"Don't harm him now," Sylvie said. "He's valuable. One of a kind."

Was that true? 404 wondered. Was he the only K left?

404 attacked Seeve, unleashing a barrage of rod-strikes about Seeve's head and torso. He took pleasure in every nick and ding his actions created.

At the same time, 404 tried to work his leg free. To turn and pull away.

There was a chorus of chirps and squeaks from the others. One of them, the many-armed one, pointed Wes's direction.

Somehow, inexplicably, Wes had gotten the upper claw on the spider bot. Part of the spider—more than half of its legs—was now under Wes's ball foot, held in place by Wes's weight. The spider's other legs were secure in Wes's claws. The spider was essentially hamstrung.

"Didn't expect that," Sam said. "Wes is—"

Wes bounced hard twice, and the spider broke completely in half.

"Tougher than he looks," Sam added.

They were surrounded and outnumbered—statistically beaten—but the enemy was one less.

404 redoubled his efforts, swatting whatever came near. In the distance, he heard a smoker's low rumble. If only it would come this way. If only he could reach it. Somehow fly away.

"Four!" Wes said. "Look!"

Wes had both hands around the planted device now. Sylvie's smoker repeller. He broke the device's support rod in two with a heavy snap and raised the loose end—the end with the repeller—over his head triumphantly. "Busted!" He hurled the repeller down the face of the heap. It made a strange "twoop" sound every time it hit the ground.

Wes waved both hands. "Come! We go!"

404 broke free of Seeve's grip and ran for the heap. He darted past the smaller other bots, avoiding outstretched claws, hands, and probes.

"Yes!" Sam said. "Get us out of here! Go!"

The smoker was getting closer. Its rumble almost a roar now. Could he make it in time?

404 started to scale the heap. He made the first turn without difficulty and was on his way to the second. Halfway there, a small, rolling bot shot in front of him. 404's right foot caught, and he stumbled forward. The bot got in the way again and 404 tumbled, ending up on his chest, arms spread wide.

Warnings filled his queue: Taxed systems, components out-of-alignment, service needed!

"Whoa there," Sam said. "What happened?"

"I fell." 404 regained his feet. Despite the warnings, he appeared to be in good shape. There were new scratches and dents, but the important systems still worked.

The smoker's roar was deafening. If there was ever a chance, it was now.

"Where's your hook?" Sam said.

404 checked his hands, incredulous. "Must've dropped it," he said. "When I—"

"Yeah, find it," Sam said. "Quick!"

404 quickly searched the area around him, ever cognizant that the others were climbing after him. The heap below seemed alive with their activities.

Sylvie's humanlike hands were outstretched like a director at the start of a performance. Her mouth moved too, but it was impossible to hear her words. The nearest other was close. Only a few meters away.

Where was the hook? It wasn't lying on the path or stuck to the heap's surface. It wasn't behind him anywhere. It wasn't around his feet anywhere, either.

Ahead, larger heap components marked the beginning of an upwards turn. Another switchback.

He saw the hook there.

In pieces.

⊘⊘⊘1 ⊘111

23

4 04 hurried ahead to where the pieces of the hook lay. There were two parts now, nearly identical in length. No doubt weakened by its use as a cudgel, it had broken during his fall. Broken and been flung forward.

"Not good," Sam said.

404 scooped the pieces up and looked at them. The break was clean, but that didn't matter. He had no way to repair the rod. No way to put it in a condition that would be useful.

"You're right," he said. "It isn't good."

404 looked up toward the summit. Wes was partially visible, with both claws up and headstalk fully extended. 404 could imagine what Wes was saying. Imploring 404 to climb up in as many ways as Wes could using only two words.

It was no use now, though. The plan to leave the Yard was no longer viable—if it ever was. 404 looked at the hook pieces again before dropping them to the ground.

"We need those!" Sam said, vibrating. "Don't we need those?"

The smoker was almost overhead now. Soon it would stop, turn, and make its way over the fence. Forever lost.

"Come on, Four," Sam said. "There has to be a way, right? We can do this. At least climb up to Wes. Lose together."

The others were closing in. Seeve and Green were past the first switchback and were on the path with him.

404's decision matrix was placid. No decision could be made. He only needed to wait.

What was hope for a robot? Concepts like destiny and chance? Bits couldn't fathom such things.

"At least pick the stick up, Four," Sam said. "Go down fighting."

"You're a hopeless romantic, Sam."

"I'm positioned over your heart."

404 laughed but bent over and reclaimed the pieces of the hook anyway. "Ele would probably like the fight." Makeshift battles had been

part of their relationship. As were costume parties and square dances. Mysteries and adventures. He crossed the rods in front of his body like swords.

"Ah, there you are." Seeve reached a point not two meters away. His grid showed a large and blocky smile. "I knew we'd catch you. Knew it." He put out both hands. "No need to be hard now. This is just the way of it." He pointed to where Sylvie stood below. "She wants what she wants." He indicated Green, who was just behind him. "She keeps us going. We need to give her what she wants."

404 nodded and raised his "swords."

Seeve laughed.

The smoker snorted. 404 thought this simply the sound of its stopping in preparation to turn. There was another snort then. And another.

Sam vibrated against his chest. "I think we're in trouble."

Seeve made a grab for 404's right leg, but 404 twisted, dodged and slashed with the rod's hook portion.

"I agree," 404 said. "We're very much in trouble."

His exterior sensors detected the movement of air around his body. At the same moment, his audio inputs recognized an increase in the number of snorts and an increase in volume.

"Four!"

404 glanced upwards and saw that the smoker's maw was now open. The smoker wasn't turning this time. It was stopped here. Preparing to consume.

Portions of the heap broke off and rose. Some of the smaller bots became weightless too, hovering above the ground like the toy drones Ele's brother used to fly. Metal limbs flailed and spun. Lights flashed and blinked. Each bot shrieked in its own way.

The smoker claimed its first victim: the very girder 404 was supposed to climb to get free. Jerking loose from the top of the heap, it tumbled end over end, then disappeared into the maw's blackness. There was a grinding sound and a dark puff of smoke.

404's humor code wanted him to laugh. He ignored the request.

Seeve whooped as it, too, began to rise. Its arms extended, searching for something to cling to. Its right claw managed to grab Green's arm near the shoulder. Green wailed.

404 clutched the nearest object he could find—the open door of a refrigeration unit—and held on. Wes was still at the top of the heap, anchored to something, somehow.

A group of others flew, screeching, into the air above the heap. Some were buffeted by chunks of refuse. Others drifted in midair. All fell silent before slipping, along with the refuse, into the waiting maw, only twenty meters away.

Sylvie was still at the bottom of the hill, holding tight to something. She looked safer than anyone, but not happy. Her head was exposed. It was hairless and misshapen, connecting to her metal portions below the jawline. She was more monstrous than any of her creations. An unknowable thing.

The smoker's volume increased again. It was descending. Coming closer.

"We need to get out of here!" Sam said. "Climb back down and—"

The heap around them started to break up and float. 404 noticed the remains of a black, rectangular appliance and a large, smashed screen amid the airborne flotsam. The refrigerator he clung to shook from the vacuum pulling at it, so 404 searched for another anchor. He found a strand of heavy cable and grabbed it with his right hand.

There was a deep sucking sound as the refrigerator pulled free. For a few tense moments, 404 was spreadeagled, caught between appliance and cable like some humanoid kite. Then the refrigerator hurtled away, and he had only the cable. He held it with both hands.

"So, they finally got me," Sam said. "After all those years of avoiding this trip, now I'm to be eaten."

"I'll hold on as long as I can," 404 said.

"Oh, I don't blame you. It's been an interesting week, Four. More than the five years prior."

"Glad you were pleased."

"I feel like this should be a time of introspection, don't you? Like we should be talking about what our lives were worth. And what will happen to us after we're eaten? Is there heaven for a bot?"

The cable loosened. 404 shot upwards almost five meters before stopping again. This brought a worried warble from Sam.

"Hold, Four. Please, hold."

The heap separated into large islands of hovering refuse, becoming like a densely packed asteroid field, swirling and colliding. The cable remained planted into one of the larger chunks. 404 was an odd satellite of that chunk, slowly swirling around it as both ascended. As *everything* ascended.

Wes was near them, he realized, floating only a few meters away.

Wes swam in the air using his flipper-like forelimbs. Second by second, he progressed, until finally, he was able to snag 404's left heel.

"Wes," 404 said for Sam's benefit, "has hold of my foot."

Sam made a clucking sound. "Together again. How wonderful."

Dirt and smoke were everywhere. 404's exterior was pelted by debris. Damage warnings filled his queue. There were threats to his optical and olfactory senses. His touch senses were completely overwhelmed. He couldn't draw any solar power at all.

Surprisingly, he still had the hook portion of the rod. With a grunt, he reeled himself closer to his debris planet. When he drew near, he then hooked the planet and drew closer still. He shielded himself there. Steadied himself. It helped some.

He could feel Wes's weight on his foot. Part of him—his self-preservation algorithms—wanted to shake the turtle free. If he had full control of his feet and hands, maybe he could find a way to launch himself from the refuse planet. To wait until the best moment and break free of the chunk and the smoker's circle of influence completely.

He'd been able to escape the last time, after all. Why not now?

There was a sickening crunch as something collided with the maw above. Next came a loud shriek and more crunching as the smoker's serrated teeth engaged.

Sam wailed. "Ah, the teeth. Can't stand the teeth."

The upward momentum increased. 404 glanced back. Wes was holding on for all his worth. His cone was retracted as far it could be. Flipper feet fluttered. One claw-like hand flapped in the air. The other gripped 404's foot.

Only one claw. Easily removed.

A dozen meters stood between them and the maw. If there was any action to be taken, any chance of survival, it was now.

It was impossible to reason for all the messages in his queue. The many sensor readings.

He could hear the other bots squeal and yell, too, within the roar.

It was pandemonium.

"What do we do, Four!" Sam said. "What!"

He glanced at Wes again. His eye was barely visible atop what remained of his head.

Holding tight. Holding on.

404 engaged the magnetic assists on his feet, locking Wes's claw into place. They'd be destroyed together.

There was another upward thrust, and everything shifted laterally. They were caught in a vortex of sorts. Circular motion produced by the smoker's strong, yet uneven, pull. His planet found a position in the middle part of the vortex. Too close to the center for 404. He needed to get to the edge. To the limits of the smoker's influence.

He tugged the hook free from the planet. The refuse hitting his face and arms immediately increased. He ignored the warnings, though, and slowly played out the cable.

"What are you doing?" Sam yelled. "This is terrible."

"I have an idea."

"An idea?"

404 continued reeling out the cable. The farther out it got, the more he felt centrifugal force move them outward. Move them free.

The smoker's roar was ubiquitous now. Like being inside an explosion. 404 could feel the craft's emanations. It vibrated his inner workings, taxing every component and fixture.

Wes's mass seemed to increase. Did that suggest the plan was working? That Wes was almost beyond the suction zone? He hoped so.

He let out more cable. Extended it as far as it would go.

His leg sagged.

Yes. Wes was—

There was another upward thrust. Enough to overcome everything he'd done. Enough to bring his planet, and consequently him, to a place only a few meters from the maw.

The sounds of destruction and dismemberment was everywhere. There were sparks too. Small bursts of electricity within the cloud. One burst struck the refuse planet, circled around it, and traveled down the cable.

The surge taxed his sensors. Confused his perception. Consequently, he could no longer judge the pressure he was exerting on the cable. He let go.

He realized the error immediately, of course, but it was too late. He was free of the chunk, but not free of the smoker. He spun around, hopelessly tossed. Then he recognized—mockingly—the spot on the smoker's hull he was to have grasped with his hook. A meter-wide rung of metal. Just above and to the right of him. It would be lost in an instant. A millisecond.

"Is that it?" Sam said. "Can you—?"

The smoker ate. Tearing, rending, and consuming. All was being pulled in now. Everything that had been the girder heap. Now inside. Now gone.

404 flailed with his arms. Attempted to draw closer to the rung. To get a last chance at it. It was there. Almost attainable. He stretched with the hook. Tried to reach.

The air moved, taking him with it. He spun and surged straight for the maw.

Straight toward death.

⊘⊘⊘1 1⊘⊘⊘

24

T hen 404 stopped.
Chunk after chunk poured into the maw. Piece after discarded piece until all were consumed. The smoker's maw closed, and the upward flow ceased. The sky cleared. There was smoke, but only a hint. Only enough for 404's olfactory sensors to notice. Gravity's preeminence returned, pulling him toward the ground. His upper body drooped, Sam let out an explicative, but 404 did not fall. He hung, suspended vertically, in the sky.

"What is going on, Four?" Sam asked. "Why aren't we falling?"

"Have you," Wes said. "No fall."

The smoker shrieked as it pivoted. It moved slower now, burdened with the additional weight. Smoke billowed from its sides.

404 turned and looked, awkwardly, up and back. He saw Wes, still attached to 404's foot. And with his other claw, Wes held tight to the smoker's service rung.

"Wes is holding us," 404 said. "He grabbed the rung."

"I'm not sure whether to feel more anxious," Sam said. "Or less."

404 checked that the magnetic assists on his right foot were still active. They were. "Well, we aren't falling," he said. "We can be thankful for that."

"Oh, I'm thankful," Sam said. "I just don't believe it. The hybrid is holding us? That crazy turtle?"

"Yes."

Sam grunted. "Wonder, Four. It's all wonder now."

There was a lurch and the smoker moved. 404 swayed but remained connected. Below, he saw the empty place where the girder heap used to stand. Beyond it was the giant cement edifice. The Yard's wall.

They were headed straight for it.

"We're going toward the wall," 404 said. "We're leaving."

He checked on Wes. "Are you okay up there?"

Wes's head bobbed slightly. "Oh yes. Very yes. Holding tight."

"I hope he holds tight," Sam said. "We're lost if he doesn't."

"Don't distract him," 404 whispered. "We need him to focus." He engaged the magnetic assist in his left foot too and brought that near the right.

Soon they were above the wall. It was thicker than he expected. At least a meter wide. There were markings on the top edge about every ten meters—numbers and arrows. Installation guides, he guessed, suggesting the wall had been built elsewhere and brought in. It reminded him of a playset that Ele's family had outside their home. It arrived in twenty boxes, filled with shiny parts, bright colors, and lots of guides.

Just beyond the fence were trees. Mostly deciduous, with broad green leaves. Though their leaves were many meters below him, 404-'s olfactory sense noticed the change in air quality. The freshness created, not only by the trees, but by the lack of refuse.

"Would you look at that," Sam said. "Green."

"Yes. A welcome change."

The wall itself had green on it here. For as far as 404 could see, ivy stretched across it. Hiding the grey. Muting the fence's enormous size.

The smoker started to gain altitude, rising ten meters within the span of seconds. They were now over twenty-five meters high.

Wes grunted.

"Are you still functioning up there?" 404 said.

"Yes, fine," Wes said. "Holding fine." Another grunt. "Much different. Nervous here."

The hybrid had never seen trees, 404 realized. Or even the color green that wasn't created by a paint or polymer. How would it perform outside? Or more importantly, how would it perform now?

"Don't look down if it makes you uncomfortable," 404 said.

"Fine," Wes said. "Holding fine."

The stretch of green was short-lived. Five minutes after leaving the Yard, grey cement and black asphalt became dominant again. Occasionally, single-story buildings passed by below them. Homes and small offices.

All were long abandoned. Most had a portion of their roof missing, such that 404 could view their interior. The insides were empty and dark. He occasionally saw furniture, but rarely any clutter. No signs of human life. As if the occupants' lives had suddenly halted.

He tried not to dwell on that observation. Or what it might mean for the family he'd once known. It was best to live in the present.

There were more pressing concerns, after all. Like where the smoker was taking them. And how to get down in one piece. At this height—nearly thirty meters—a fall would be calamitous, even if they happened to drop onto one of the buildings.

404's position made it difficult to fully take in their surroundings. Though he was almost facing the direction they were headed, he was still hanging upside-down. It was disorienting. "Can you tell where we're going, Sam?"

"Everything is flipped for me," Sam said, then chuckled. "Oh wait, I can flip! I'm made to flip!" Sam hummed, thoughtfully. "Well, there are large buildings ahead. Shiny, white buildings."

"Shiny and white?" 404 said. "So, there must be life beyond the Yard. Human life."

"Must be. Might be. Probably."

"Anything else?" 404 asked. "Any signs of humanity? Or bots like us?"

"Too far to tell." He hummed again. "But I think I see movement. Yeah, there's something near the buildings. Vehicles of some sort."

Another good sign. Perhaps things weren't so different.

"Remember Blue," Wes said. "Blue awaits."

"Sure, right," Sam said. "We need to find his mining machine. Set the giant free."

A troubling distraction. Even if they knew where such a machine was, could they start it and send it on its way?

404 was made to be capable. A general-purpose synthetic. But not for every situation. He could not, for instance, craft his own mining machine. That would require a human.

Minutes passed. The smoker bore them wherever it wanted to go, following its seemingly preprogrammed course. 404 repeatedly checked on Wes's ability to hold them, while taking in everything he could. He cataloged streets and other distinctive features, and using preloaded maps, attempted to determine where they were. What city this was.

He got no results.

Sam surmised it was a central city given some of the flora and fauna, but which city, he wasn't sure. "I know it isn't *my* city," he said. "But otherwise, I got nothing."

The white buildings grew steadily closer. There were three of them, positioned like the three corners of an isosceles triangle. They were all the same height—five stories—and narrow. Each building had a large, circular aperture on top.

"Don't like the look of that hole," Sam said. "You think that's where this thing empties itself?"

"I have no idea what these buildings are," 404 said. "Or what happens here."

"I have an idea," Sam said. "But I don't like it."

404's right knee joint—the one Sylvie had repaired—reported a loss of functionality. Being suspended had taxed it somehow, causing something inside to dislocate. He looked to verify that it was still intact. It was, but what did it look like internally? How close was it to failure? Would it pull apart completely?

"What?" 404 asked. "What don't you like?"

"I think they're steaming towers," Sam said.

"Steaming towers?"

"New technology in my day. Theoretical. Garbage is shredded and dried. Then it's blasted by high temperature steam."

"High temperature? What—?"

"About 4000 degrees. Enough to break down the garbage into base materials and gases. The gases are turned into fuels for power. The materials used to make new stuff."

404 studied the underside of the flying vehicle. Its circular maw and rotating engines. "What part does the smoker play?"

"It does the shredding and drying. And those chutes ahead—"

"Are where the steaming happens."

"Right. So, we don't want to fall into them. Don't want to be anywhere near them, actually."

404 scoured the structures around the steaming buildings. None were tall enough to drop onto safely. That left only the white buildings themselves. Metal stairways wound down the side of them. "We need to get safely onto the roof somehow."

"Right," Sam said. "But miss the chutes."

The maneuver would have to be perfectly timed and would depend most on Wes. On his ability to react.

404 turned Wes's direction. "Did you hear all that, Wes?" he said. "We need to get onto the roof."

"I hear," Wes said. "On roof. Drop down. I release. We fall."

"Yes, that's right." At least, 404 thought that was right. "When I say to let go, you let go. All right?"

Wes's head slid up and down. "Yes. Fine. You say. I release."

The buildings were about ten meters away now. The smoker slowed and moved to the east, 404's left.

"Looks like we're headed to the far building," Sam said.

404 nodded but said nothing. He only studied the building as it neared. Even this close, the roof around the aperture looked narrow. Less than two meters wide. Not much room for error. The smoker's slower pace increased his confidence a little, though. They'd need to wait until conveyance had dropped some. Otherwise, they'd fall past the building altogether.

He compared the size of the smoker above to the size of the aperture below. How close were they in size? The aperture seemed larger by a third. Whoever designed the system hadn't taken any chances. Hadn't wanted any of the collected resources wasted.

That only made the goal of reaching the roof more difficult, of course. He would be dropping headfirst, with only his arms to stop him. To save them all.

The smoker stopped directly over the aperture. Its rumble lowered in pitch, and it began to descend. The volume of smoke changed too—becoming only a wheezing puff every meter or so.

"What are you seeing, Four?" Sam asked. "Because I can't see anything from here."

It taxed 404's neck joints to look. Everything that mattered was directly below them and he was the only one with a clear view of it. There was a slight breeze traveling upwards from the chute. He could feel warmth in it. Doubtless the lingering effects of the steaming process. Garbage being blasted into elements. Hundreds of years of creation, reduced to nothingness.

The aperture was pitch black, with no visible signs that it did anything, aside from wait. Like a baby bird awaiting food from its mother.

He needed to find the right instant. The safest moment.

They were five meters from the aperture, then four, then three. The roof proper never looked reachable. Never looked like it was beneath them enough.

He had to get there, though. They had to make it.

There was a high-pitched screech and the maw above opened. A torrent of finely ground refuse poured down. The torrent almost touched him. Almost swept him along in its flow.

He yelped and swung away. Away. That only brought him even closer to the torrent when he returned. He could smell the refuse as it passed. The smell of sulfur, methane, and rot.

"This isn't good," he said. "I don't know if—" He paused and studied the roof and its aperture again. The roof surface wasn't that far in front of him. If he swung again, drew himself closer to the torrent and then back away, could he fall onto it? Could he get them safely down?

There was a "clank" and the torrent volume increased. 404 had no idea how much mass the smoker kept within. How long until it had emptied itself and the opportunity was gone?

He rocked closer to the torrent and back away again. He gained maybe a half a meter for his efforts.

"What are you doing, Four?" Sam asked.

"I need to swing," 404 said. "It's the only way."

"Not sure if I agree," Sam said. "That chute looks awful deep."

"I'm open to other suggestions."

"Can't say I have any."

"Then I need to swing." He looked at Wes. "Are you still holding all right?"

"Yes. Good hold. Not fall."

"I'm going to release the magnetic assists on my feet."

"Okay."

404 released the assist on first one foot and then the other. Wes continued to grip firmly. 404 attempted to swing again. Back and forth. Toward the refuse torrent, and away. This time he gained a full meter, but it still didn't seem like enough.

"I need you to help me with this, Wes," he said. "Help me gain some distance."

Wes looked at him a long moment. "Want throw?"

"No. Not throw. Just swing. And when I say drop, you release us all."

"Roger," Wes said.

"Roger?" 404 said. "Roger, who?"

"Possibly that's a past owner," Sam said. "Best not to disturb old memories."

"Do you understand, Wes?" 404 said.

"Yes. Will swing. Get ready."

404 nodded. He checked his warnings and adjusted his power levels. He contemplated the faulting knee again. All it meant for what he was about to attempt. The probabilities of success. The danger of failure.

He pushed the warnings away, steadied himself and swung forward. He arced out closer to the roof's edge, and back toward the refuse torrent. He detected fragments of refuse on his head and shoulders. Smelled sulfur. Then he started to arc back the other direction. Toward the roof and freedom. The aperture flashed by below. He saw the roof's edge. The narrow section of white surface that was their only chance.

"Now, Wes! Let—"

☉☉☉1 1☉☉1

25

The roof rushed up toward him. There was enough room. He was going to make it. 404 stretched out his hands and touched the surface. He recognized the roughness of it. The slickness. He tucked his head to avoid injury. Then curled his whole body. He felt his true weight as his torso impacted the roof. Warnings flooded his queue. Sensors indicated new surface abrasions and damage to his exterior shell. Minor items.

Sam yelled "Woo-wee!" and 404 did his best to roll forward. Away from the aperture. There was a guardrail for the roof's outer edge. A place to grab so he didn't go over.

He made it onto his back when something slammed into his midsection. Wes!

The turtlebot bounced into 404's midsection and flipped away, heading back toward the hole.

404 grabbed blindly for Wes but missed. Beyond, the torrent still raged. The mottled grey and black of humanity's throwaways.

Wes's head slid up and down. His flippers rotated, spinning against nothingness. His arms, those claw-like hands, waved meaninglessly.

404 heaved forward and tried again. There was little time. No time. Nothing that could be done.

Wes reached the aperture. His cone extended fully. His eye glowed bright.

404 noticed how much bluer the sky behind the torrent seemed. It lacked the greenish cast of the Yard's sky. The pollution.

He tried to stand, but his knee barked warnings, refusing to comply. He made a sound of despair. Of desperation.

Wes's flippers caught the aperture's edge. The turtlebot lurched ahead and managed to reach 404's foot. To grab on.

Wes was heavier than he appeared. Denser. 404 was pulled forward. He put his fingers down and attempted to slow his slide. To dig in.

Most of Wes's bulk was over the hole now. Dangling on the edge.

"Four?" Sam said. "You have to stop us. We—"

"I know," 404 said. "I want everything to—"

The torrent ceased. This created a vacuum that drew Wes into the aperture. His grip on 404 remained, pulling 404 farther forward.

Again, 404 was tempted to kick himself free. This time, he gave it no consideration, though. Hadn't the turtle saved them? Why should he separate now?

He slid steadily forward. His feet reached the aperture's edge. He dug in his heels.

Sam repeated 404's name again and again. So much that he thought the comPanion had a glitch.

The smoker rumbled and lifted away. The sky was still blue. 404's knee peppered him with warnings.

404 lunged backwards. A final attempt to keep Wes from dropping.

Wes popped free of the hole, fell onto 404's legs, and rolled into a heap next to him.

A minute passed. 404 watched as the smoker drifted toward the south again. Smoke billowed after it, marking its every movement.

"Well, that was something now, wasn't it?" Sam said.

404 chuckled. "A lot of something." He looked at Wes. "Are you all right?"

"Fine as I've ever been," Sam answered. "Good job, you two. You made me wish I had hands."

"What?"

"I could've helped! Pulled on something. Grabbed onto something. You know, helped!"

404 laughed again, then Wes joined him, producing a two-note chuckle somewhere between a warning siren and a construction alarm.

The turtlebot held up his claws, and opening and closing them, produced a tapping sound. "Was fun," Wes said. "Do again?"

404 laughed louder and climbed slowly to his feet. "No do again. Get away now. That's all I want."

He favored his right knee a bit as he walked to the rail. He contemplated the updates from the appropriate sensors near the joint. The readings weren't as bad as he'd imagined. There had been tension on the knee, but it could still function. Safely bear his weight. Sylvie had done good work, even if her intentions were bad.

She thought she was doing it for herself, after all. For her "new" body.

404 gazed out over the city. Beyond the white towers was a morass of brick and stone constructs. Red, brown, and grey. Many of these buildings, especially as he looked north, were dilapidated. Roofs missing or whole sides falling away.

Dotting the cityscape, like dandelions invading a lawn of grass, were lighter-colored structures. Buildings that appeared newer and made of synthetic materials like the one they now stood on.

It seemed unlike the humanity he remembered to use such random but precise locations for renovations. Especially when faced with an entire town that needed rebuilding.

He studied the steamer building again, specifically the surface and railing around him. There were very few seams. As if the roof was formed or poured. Not constructed. Not built.

He shared the observation with Sam.

"Building materials aren't the sort of thing I notice," Sam said. "Like, yeah, if I compare it with my stored pictures, it seems different. Looks strange. But how much can you tell from pictures, really?" He sighed. "We've missed a lot. Ten years or forty. A lot has changed."

Wes reoriented himself, turning toward the break in the railing that indicated the external stairway. The turtlebot then made his way to the stairs and started down. There was a clickity-clickity-click as Wes's flippers propelled him.

"He's leaving again," Sam said. "Eager little guy."

404 shook his head and followed Wes down the stairs. The way was narrow and steep, such that 404 needed to use the railing. These conditions didn't seem to bother Wes at all, though. He was a story down already, moving as fast as his ball and flippers would take him.

Wes would seemingly go until there was no longer a reason to. It was amazing he ever got caught by the Yard's others in the first place. It was pointless to try to slow him down now.

They reached street level twenty minutes later. As Sam had noticed earlier, there were moving vehicles here. Large, white, hovering craft filled the street, in fact. They were narrow in front and larger in back, almost conical. They lacked both windows and doors. The only seam—which might indicate an opening—was on the top side. Their movement was soundless.

"Automated?" Sam said.

"I think so," 404 said. "No drivers. No humans."

Sam's screen displayed a pattern of multicolored daisies. Heads of orange, yellow, green, and purple spun and bounced across it. "It's too soon for hard conclusions," he said.

404's decision matrix stalled, balancing between approaching one of the vehicles for answers, or attempting to find a way on their own. "Too soon," he said finally. "Too soon for anything."

Wes waited near the street. His cone was fully extended, and he was "jogging" in place. Moving only a step or two forward, rolling back, and moving forward again. "What are?" he said. "All these. What are?"

These seemingly mundane conveyances were beyond 404's experience. Difficult to analyze and account for. The nearest one had no external markings. The perfect clone of the one behind it and in front of it. It was also the most pristine creation he'd seen in quite some time.

"Trucks," 404 said finally. "Hauling something somewhere."

Wes's head bobbed. "Trucks?"

"I bet they're carting away the elements," Sam said. "These buildings break down the junk. Make power and base elements." He vibrated. "Those are probably the elements. In the trucks."

404 nodded. "A plausible theory." He focused on the top seam of the vehicles. Doubtless how they were loaded. "Likely, even."

"Have cone," Wes said. "Like me."

"Yes." 404 looked at the buildings beyond the steamers. Those made by earlier humans. Many bore signs and graffiti. Indications of their former lives. The past, still beckoning for attention.

There were darkened digital displays at the street corners. Black squares of nothing. Every crosswalk was empty. It was almost a ghost town. But not quite.

"Where do we go?" 404 asked.

"Help Blue," Wes said. "Free him."

"If we followed one of those trucks," Sam said. "We might learn something. Might find humans."

The nearest intersection was a short distance away. 404 walked to it and looked both directions. The only moving things there were trucks, as well. He waved at one but got no response. No indication that he'd been seen.

Wes tapped his leg with a hand. "Made deal. Free Blue."

"I don't know how to do that. No idea where to go to—"

Wes shot up a hand. "I do! Wes knows."

"Maybe you should go do whatever needs to be done then," Sam said.

Wes's head rotated back and forth. "Can't alone. Need Four. Need Sam."

"Well, what if we don't want to go?" Sam asked.

"Made deal. Must go."

"What is must? We're away from the Yard here. We can do—"

404 held a hand over Sam's screen. "No reason not to try, Sam. I'm at a loss otherwise."

"You have coordinates for your family, right? We can go there!"

"You saw Blue's wall. It's abandoned now."

"It's a place to start."

404 indicated the empty street. "How? We have no way to get there."

"There has to be a way to move large distances," Sam said. "One that doesn't involve hanging onto smokers."

Wes tapped 404's leg again. "Blue waits."

404 nodded. "Show us where to go."

Wes made a cheerful two-note sound and bolted into the street, directly in front of an oncoming truck. It was close, but Wes accelerated and swerved to get out of the way. The maneuver only brought him into another near-miss situation, which again, he escaped.

"Thinking this might be a short trip," Sam said.

404's face formed a smile. "At least he knows where he's going."

0001 1010

26

They walked for hours. The monotony of the Yard was gone, replaced by scenery that was ever-changing, though it all told the same story. Sometime in the past, something cataclysmic had happened. The damage to the city was too pronounced and consistent for it to be anything else. Time's passage alone wouldn't decimate buildings and raze whole blocks. No, that took a will backed by intelligence.

Wars during 404's time had been small-scale affairs. Events that, according to Ele's parents, "hardly seemed real" due to their location, or because the vidscreen-only conflicts had no impact on Ele's family. They were news items that took less than five seconds to cover. Little more than trivia.

There was an occasional riot in their sector, but even those maintained a remoteness. The rioters looked more like them, spoke the same language—got a little more vid time—but they were still a fair distance away. Out beyond the neighborhood. Beyond the fences.

Perhaps this city was one of those places? The vid-only places where violence reigned? Humans often fought and died for nebulous reasons. Angered by themes assigned to them by directed artificial intelligences. Contrived entertainment. A global venue.

Sam's screen went blue. "Not very pretty, is it?" he said. "I mean, it's better than the Yard, sure. But not near what I was hoping."

"It's odd, yes," 404 said. "Unfamiliar."

"My images from before are all happy," Sam said. "Friends out together. Beautiful sunsets and seascapes. Placid and calm. Smiles and shared meals."

"Maybe those were illusions," 404 said. "Hopeful images in an otherwise terrible time."

"Maybe," Sam said. "I wish I remembered my owner like you do. I could use a reference point. An anchor."

"My references only confuse me." 404 pointed at a nearby building, the storefront of which was blackened. The glass smashed out. "I never saw this with them. Not in real life."

Sam chuckled softly. "We're not real life, Four. Not the way they defined it."

"I guess that's true." 404 frowned. "But I still want to find them."

"I wouldn't try to stop you." He showed a simple smile. "Even if I could."

From where they were, 404 couldn't find a clear view of the sun. "I'm worried about power," he said. "There's barely enough solar to maintain my levels."

"Mine either," Sam said. "You used to see a boost board on every corner of a city like this. A little spot of sun to keep the bots moving. But the only boards I've found here are dead." His screen showed a leftward-pointing hand. "There's one over there, in fact."

404 saw a meter-square board attached to a poll. It was about a head higher than he and was completely dark, though highly reflective. He could see a portion of the building to the right on its surface. A brick building with a large hole taken out of the center. Almost as if it had been bitten.

Wes was in the center of the street ahead. Though they'd encountered only an occasional truck over the past few blocks, 404 found himself glancing both directions anyway.

And if Wes *were* to get run over? What then?

They'd be free to search for Ele's family. Find a way to reach her coordinates.

She wouldn't be a little girl anymore. Would he even recognize her?

He thought so, yes. He had algorithms to compensate for such things. In order to bond with his human family members, regardless of their age, he was imprinted with their information at the time of purchase. Their DNA samples and facial scans. Defining qualities.

It was hard not to spend cycles on Ele's current condition. Or to contemplate a future reunion with her.

Wes moved to the opposite side of the street, then stopped, raised a hand, and chirped.

"The little guy is focused," Sam said.

404 smiled. "Can't fault him for that."

"Makes me wonder about Blue. Why such loyalty to an underground tank?"

"Why is anyone loyal to anyone?" 404 asked.

Sam's screen showed green zeroes and ones. "Programming!" he said. "Conditioning and identity implantation. That's how I was given connections, anyway. A long press on my side and a spoken word—and *pow*—we're friends for life."

"My bonding is a bit more sophisticated than—"

Wes waved both claws, clearly in a hurry.

After a quick check of the street, 404 crossed over and joined Wes.

Wes bounced as he spoke. "We close. Me detect. Close now."

"Detect what?" Sam said. "This mining equipment we're supposed to use?"

"Yes! Equipment. Right!"

"How far is it?" 404 asked.

"Not far. Very close."

"That's good, because we're feeling a little rundown here," Sam said. "Four and I. We get most of our power from the sun. And there hasn't been a lot of that here."

"Power, yes. Need more. Always."

404 watched as a truck approached and passed by. "There must be power somewhere. If they're generating it from garbage, then it's being used. And has to be supplied somehow. Carried."

"In trucks?" Wes said. "You think?"

"Some of it," 404 said. "Maybe."

"Should see!" Wes said.

"Even if it was," Sam said. "The chances we'd be compatible with apocalypse power is slim." He sighed. "Seems like a design deficiency, doesn't it? Making us dependent on a single power source. What were they thinking?"

"I can use secondary sources, but—"

"I can too, but the connection mechanisms are no longer available. Cables to house adapters...who has a cable now? Who has a house?"

"They thought the world would never change," 404 said.

"Or that if it did, we'd no longer be around."

"Find sun," Wes said. "Maybe? Get clear." Wes turned and followed the street forward, toward the north. He got almost half a block ahead, stopped, and waved them forward. "Here! Here sun."

404 jogged to Wes, arriving just in time to see a quarter of the sun between buildings. He soaked up as much as he could. But it wasn't much.

Wes was already on the move. First, to the next intersection, and then crossing the street, continuing north. Soon, he stopped again and waved.

"Sort of makes you wish we'd kept that power cell, huh?" Sam said.

"He's putting it to good use."

"Yeah, but how does he stay charged?"

"Better storage," 404 said. "Fewer systems to maintain."

"Look at me," Sam said. "I'm like a nothing on your chest. A flat little screen. I don't even have wheels!"

"Better engineering then," 404 said, smiling.

"Now you're just mean, Four."

404 laughed and started jogging again.

0001 1011

27

Wes led them to an area that was completely enclosed by two-and-a-half-meter-high wooden fencing. Much of the fence was covered by ancient signs and posters. Faded bits of color that advertised educational, relational, or entertainment possibilities. The dates were from many years ago. "More than a decade," according to Sam. There was graffiti on the fence too. Artistic markings meaningful only to their creator.

"In here," Wes said, pointing. "Find it."

"Find what?" Sam said. "Another Yard? No, thank you."

"No yard. Only fence." Wes touched the fence with a claw. "Inside machine."

"I don't like the looks of it," Sam said.

404 attempted to see inside the fence—either through a knothole or a wide-enough gap between boards—but found nothing that he could extract any information from.

"Promise Blue," Wes said. "Fulfill promise."

"I didn't promise anything!" Sam said. "I'm just hitchhiking here."

"Aha!" 404 grabbed Sam by the top edge and dislodged him.

"Hey! What are you—?"

404 lifted Sam to arm's length and approached the fence.

"Okay, I'm sorry," Sam said. "I didn't mean to complain. You know you're an amazing bot. A good friend. Your family misses you, I'm sure. I would!"

404 chuckled, and on tiptoes, held Sam over the fence. "What do you see?"

"What do you want me to see...oh, right. Okay. Well, there's the foundation of a building here, I think. Actually, it's a large hole with some construction materials around it. I see a couple small buildings on the exterior. Looks like they're in good shape, but—"

"Machine?" Was said. "See machine?"

"Don't see any machine, no. Can't see everything, though."

"In there," Wes said. "I'm sure."

404 lowered Sam and secured the comPanion to his chest again. "How do you know?" he asked, looking at Wes. "How do you know a machine is in there?"

"Blue!" Wes said. "Blue saw!"

404 understood then. Blue must've scouted out the area ahead of time. Noticed one of the machines he required through his ubiquitous cameras and gave Wes directions.

404 scanned the nearby buildings, wondering if he could pick out one of Blue's eyes on the world. He saw nothing obvious. "You're certain Blue saw something here?"

"Yes! Inside."

"What time of the day is it, Sam?"

"Midafternoon."

404 nodded. In a typical day, he would've had at least another six hours of fully powered operation. This wasn't a typical day, though. Not by any means.

Still, if all that was required was to go inside, activate a machine, and provide it with coordinates, that shouldn't take much power. Shouldn't tax his systems at all, in fact.

If they could get inside.

He searched the fence in both directions. "Did Blue tell you where the opening is?"

Wes's head bobbed up and down. "Yes. Come." He headed straight up the sidewalk to the west. He maintained a slower pace, though. Thankfully.

404 studied the signage on the fence. A pink section advertising a public music gathering was followed by an all-black section that bore images of clear jewelry and a jewelry store. After that came a section where red paint was used to portray a cartoon face with large eyes. Then a section that was nothing more than gold paint with a small, blue signature at the bottom. An abstraction that he had no context for.

They reached a place where the sidewalk was closed and foot traffic diverted onto a slender portion of the street. The path there was partially protected by skeletal metal framing. There was a partial overhang as well. The change put his preservation algorithms on high alert, but he continued to follow.

"Looks like the construction spilled out here," Sam said. "Sloppy work. Ugly mini-Yard."

404 chuckled.

Fifteen minutes later, they were at another side of the "mini-Yard." Wes approached an area that looked like every other, as it was surrounded by a high wooden fence heavily decorated in flyers. The predominant notification was about an upcoming update to the global tracking system. It was orange with a smiling Earth in the center.

"This," Wes said. "Here!"

"Looks like more wall," Sam said.

"No!" Wes said. "Way in."

404 put pressure on the orange section, and it shifted slightly, indicating it wasn't secured like the rest of the fencing. "Might be on hinges." He pushed again near the center of the Earth-face. "But it's solidly locked."

"Maybe try sliding it."

404 tried moving the door in every way Sam suggested but got nothing aside from more rocking.

"You need another plan, Wes," Sam said.

Wes raised his claws. "Me up!"

"You up?" 404 had seen the posture many times when Ele was young. "You want me to lift you?"

Wes's head bobbed. "Yes. Lift. Drop over."

404 was stronger than the average human. Enough that he could lift a large appliance. Enough to pull a fallen dresser from a trapped child. But that was decades ago now. His systems were ill-maintained, and some of them needed to be replaced. "How much do you weigh?" he asked.

Wes approximated a shrug. "Don't know."

404 crossed his arms and studied the smaller bot. "Maybe eighty kilos?" he said.

"Eighty-two point five." A smile appeared on Sam's screen. "I'm made to be used at groceries and street shops. Accuracy is required."

404 straightened his stance. "I should be able to lift him." He looked at Wes. "Are you ready now?"

Another head bob followed by a bounce on his ball foot. "Ready."

404 squatted next to the turtlebot and, locking fingers around Wes's edges on both sides, lifted him to waist level. 404 paused, waiting to evaluate the barrage of warnings that were certain to follow. There were some, particularly from his troublesome right knee, but not the volume that he'd expected.

"Wait!" Sam said.

404 glanced left and right, expecting to see the cause of Sam's alarm. He saw nothing, aside from empty streets and broken buildings. "Yes, Sam, what is it?"

"Put Wes down!"

"Why?"

"Because, if you keep lifting, you're bound to scrape me right off."

404 returned Wes to the ground. "That could be a danger."

"So, it's a no go," Sam said. "We have to try something else."

"No!" Wes said, squeaking. "Lift me!"

"I just need to find a new place to put you." 404 pried Sam free, then studied the fence.

"That fence is made of wood, Four. Won't work. And don't even think about that metal sidewalk skeleton back there. This place has decades of filth on it. Don't put me anywhere here."

"You were on the ground in garbage when we met."

"That's different. I had no choice."

404's power levels were waning. There was no better time to lift something than now. He glanced at the fence again, then at Wes.

He smiled. "Aha! I have just the thing." He placed Sam on the forward side of Wes's cone. "Now we're ready!"

Wes's head pivoted, and Sam's face pivoted right along. "I don't approve of this," Sam said. "This is uncomfortable and it's wrong."

Sam was about five centimeters above Wes's eye, the surface of which now glowed a puzzled blue. It was like Sam had been stuck to Wes's forehead. An image further cemented when Wes raised his head confusedly.

404 chuckled. "No, this is perfect. A perfect place. A perfect balance."

"Balance? You know what's not balanced? I'll tell you what's—"

"Shh, now," Four tapped Sam's edge, muting him. He then stooped and lifted Wes to waist level. He checked his warning queue again, saw nothing too threatening, and prepared to shift his grip. "This is where it gets tricky. I need to raise you up a bit and reorient."

"Yeah, well don't drop us," Sam said.

Four hopped, turned his hands, and pushed the turtlebot above his head. The weight was difficult to control, but not impossible. Not unwieldy. He took a slow step toward the fence.

"Well, wait a minute," Sam said. "Isn't that exactly what you're going to do? Drop us?"

"Sam..." 404 took another step. "This isn't...easy."

"But—"

After another short step, and another lurch of upward momentum, 404 brought Wes to the fence's top edge and dropped him over. Sam screamed, there was a thump, and then silence resumed.

0001 1100

28

T en seconds passed.

404 tapped the fence. "Are you two all right?"

"Yes," Wes said. "All fine."

"My face almost went into the dirt," Sam said. "It was right there. My life of images flashed before my eyes."

There was the sound of metal against metal followed by a rattle. Then came more rattles, and a two-meter portion of the fence swung away. Wes stood in the gap. "Worked!" he said. "Open!" In his left claw was what looked to be a lock, cleanly broken.

Still affixed to Wes's head, Sam glowed a bright orange. "Back, Four! Take me back."

404 walked through the gate. "You're fine where you are. Safe and sound."

The fenced-in area occupied at least half a city block with buildings bounding it on two sides. Those buildings were in various stages of disrepair, but what remained was largely reflective, showing glimpses of other parts of the city, along with a partially hidden sun.

The tallest building was well over twenty stories, though it had been larger at one time. Its topmost floors were missing, victims of whatever calamity hit the rest of the city. There was now only a jagged crown.

"Wes's movements disturb my temperament," Sam said. "All this clicking and grinding."

404 frowned, retrieved Sam, and reattached him to his chest.

Sam gave a satisfied sigh. "Much better. Quieter and higher."

Wes nudged the gate closed, securing it with the broken lock. "We're here!" he said. "Free Blue!"

There was a great mound of dirt in the southwest corner of the construction site, and in the southeast corner, an excavation of some kind. There were three trailers parked near the hole, presumably for the use of the crew.

A dozen large orange and white cones were haphazardly stacked not far from where 404 stood. There were two smaller hover trucks parked nearby too. One white and the other green.

"Where now?" 404 asked, looking at Wes.

Wes let out a short whistle, pivoted toward the excavation, and moved that direction.

"And here we go," Sam said.

404 raised a hand. "No reason to rush, Wes," he said. "We need to conserve."

Wes slowed a bit. "Not hurry," he said. "Okay." He still maintained a speed that kept him always a couple of steps ahead.

"Eager," Sam whispered. "Always eager."

"I'm eager too," 404 said. "The sooner we get this done, the sooner we're free to search for Ele."

"Think we should be cautious here, Four. Everything is new. Personally, I'm in my 'visiting overseas' mode. Been awhile since I've made that switch."

"Overseas?"

"Everything about this environment is foreign. Can't find the location band. Satellites are missing or unavailable. Even pattern matches are failing me."

"We're at a disadvantage, yes, but we're designed to be flexible."

"In our day, sure. But this isn't our day. Some changes can't be compensated for."

404 nodded. Ever since his revival, 404's decision matrix had been taxed from contemplating variables that his creators had never imagined, and therefore, couldn't predict. Only the flexibility of his system—the ability to ignore and disregard the absurd—allowed him to function at all.

Sam displayed a palm-outward cautionary hand. "There's something else," he said.

"What's that?"

"Other bots are around. Not more trucks or smokers. Smaller. Faster."

"You sense them?"

"Yeah, but nothing clear. Nothing I can say for sure. It's a wash of signals out there. A lot of push."

404 scanned the construction site. He detected nothing unusual. Saw no movement. As far as his sensors were convinced, it was completely devoid of life. Both organic and synthetic. "You're sure?"

"There's something. Not sure what, but something."

The number of errors in 404's queue, the compounding variables—produced a crisis point in his matrix. A pending system failure.

He stopped midstride.

"What are you doing?" Sam asked.

"I...I'm losing..." He shook his head. The act of lifting Wes had affected him somehow. It reminded him of something. Something he had done once. Or failed to do. It was an incomplete memory. Difficult to read, so difficult to evaluate and step around.

"Losing what? Losing energy? Losing faith?"

"My matrix. I can't find the path. I need an update. Or a technician." Wes circled back. "Come," he said. "Follow."

"This goal is meaningless." 404 looked at the shattered buildings. The jagged crown. "Perhaps all goals are."

"So, we're stopping *now*?" Sam said. "After all the running and flying?"

404 looked at the ground. A jumbled mass of mud and stone. "You said there's more danger."

"I don't know that there's danger. Only that something's present. But there should be, right? We're looking for something."

"All the more reason to stop." He noted the stillness of the site. The apparent lack of motion. "This wouldn't be a bad place to remain. To stay until our systems fail."

"Until our systems fail!" Sam showed an exclamation point.

404 smiled softly. "Better than the Yard. The garbage." A few more of the sun's rays reached them. Enough to restore a little of what had been lost getting Wes inside. Not enough to change his demeanor, though. His matrix.

"*You* can't stop," Sam said. "If you stop, then I have to stop. You're forcing your will on me!"

"Yes." Wes raised a claw. "No stop. Free Blue."

"I'll attach you to Wes. You can proceed together."

"We've been over that already. He's noisy. And he smells weird."

"Weird?" Wes said. "Not weird."

"You're all weird. Weird hands. Weird feet. Weird—"

404 raised a hand. "Stop it, Sam."

Wes moved closer and tapped a hand against 404's calf. "Must come. Please?"

"He's right. We can't stop here. No reason to."

"Is there a reason not to?"

"Yes! To move ahead. To not get stuck."

"I...don't know if I can."

There was silence for a few seconds. Wes raised and lowered his cone but said nothing.

"Is it the knee again?" Sam asked. "Is it bothering you?"

"No. I can move."

"Then do that. Just move. Take a step and then another. We'll at least go find this mining machine. See if we can get it going."

Wes tapped 404's calf again. Motioned with a hand. "Promise... Blue," he said softly.

404's matrix couldn't find a solid argument against Sam's reasoning. Or Wes's. He'd given his word, after all. That act was heavily weighted. It stepped his matrix forward. "I will walk with you," he said.

"Whew now, okay," Sam said. "I'm not thrilled about this detour either, but I'm curious."

404 smiled and moved. "Me too."

⊘⊘⊘1 11⊘1

29

T en minutes later, the entire excavation came into view. It was at least three stories deep, its bottom difficult to see. There was some machinery near the lip of the hole—three manual bulldozers and two backhoes—but nothing that looked like it could tunnel through kilometers of ground. Nothing like what it would take to free Blue.

"Looks too big for a pool," Sam said. "What were they making?"

"Another building," 404 said. "The structure would have had floors underground. Perhaps a parking garage."

Wes rolled to the hole, then turned and follow its edge to the west, 404's left.

"Where is this machine?" 404 asked.

Wes kept rolling, forcing 404 to follow. It was another ten minutes before the turtlebot paused—this time at the start of a ten-meter-wide gravel ramp that went deep into the abyss.

"Down," Wes said, pointing.

"What is it with him and taking us into darkness?" Sam asked.

"There does seem to be a trend." 404 pointed at the well. "The machine is down there?"

Wes head-bobbed. "Yes!"

"All that way?" Sam whistled. "Do we have the power for that?"

404 shook his head. "I don't. Maybe with a full recharge, but—" He waved at the sky. "Not like this."

Wes squeaked and turned in a circle. "Somehow must!"

"You won't make it either," Sam said to Wes. "Not with a reused power cell."

Wes waved both arms, and after a dismissive sound, rolled away. He followed the edge of the abscess away.

"What is he doing now?" Sam asked.

"Wes!" 404 raised a hand and followed. "We can try later!" He quickened his pace. "Maybe tomorrow, if we get a day of sun." He glanced at the now-distant fence to his left. "Or maybe there's a charging station somewhere. We're in no rush."

Wes continued in his path. Ahead were one of the white trailers and a yellow treaded bulldozer. An old design, even during 404's time.

"Is he after something in the trailer?" Sam asked.

404 broke into a run. Sam had sensed bots here, after all. If there were some around, wouldn't they be near a structure? Near where the humans would've been? "Hold on! Wait!"

Wes reached the trailer and turned to his left, passing by the trailer's nearest side—one of its narrow ends. There was a curtained window there. 404 watched that window. Checking for any sign of movement.

Wes turned again, disappearing into the trailer's front shadow. Next came thumps, crunches, and clanks.

404 boosted his optical sensors. "Do you sense anything nearby?" he asked. "Ahead especially?"

"I sense Wes! Not sure what he's doing. Probably breaking something."

"He's making a lot of noise."

"Sometimes I wish he'd lose power."

"That might make things easier." 404 slowed and approached the trailer with caution. There were still noises, though they were muted now. A random thud or clank.

What was Wes up to?

A repetitive clicking sound began. There were similar sounds in 404's memories, but they were from a different time. Different surroundings.

He stepped cautiously into the shadow and observed a small, blue vehicle. It had a shovel in front and an open cab. It was roughly the same height as he was. Approximately two meters high and wide and three meters long, including the shovel. The clicks were coming from its far side.

"Wes?" 404 said.

Wes bounced out from behind the vehicle and pointed at it. "Start!" he said. "Drive!"

404 glanced at the vehicle again. "Drive, what?"

Wes tapped the vehicle's side. "This! Drive!"

404 walked to the cab of the vehicle and looked in. The controls were simple. Only two levers positioned on either side of a solitary seat. There were small buttons on the lever's ends. One of the buttons on the right lever was red and clearly marked "Start." One button looked like a rabbit, another a tortoise.

"It can't still work, can it?" Sam said.

"Will work," Wes said. "Yes."

"How can you be so sure?" Sam said. "Looks pretty beat up to me."

"There's no door," 404 said. "How do I get in?"

"Front window," Wes said.

"Ah, okay." 404 carefully climbed through the opening and sat down. The seat made a hissing sound as it adjusted to his weight. He put both hands on the levers. "I've never driven anything before."

"Are you allowed?"

"I have algorithms dedicated to the effort."

Wes's head slid up so that his solitary eye looked over the vehicle's side. "Push red," he said.

404 pushed the red button. The machine made a clicking sound.

"See there?" Sam said. "Dead. And why shouldn't—"

Wes thunked his hand on the machine's side.

"I don't see how that will—"

Wes thunked the machine again and again.

"You have a real violent streak, Wes," Sam said. "I don't—"

404 tried the button again. The machine clicked a few times before humming softly.

"That worked?" Sam said. "There's no way that worked."

"Now what?" There were painted arrows at the base of the levers. Forward-pointing arrows in front, backward-pointing in back. 404 tried pulling the right lever back. The vehicle lurched to the right, nearly colliding with Wes.

Wes shrieked and rolled backwards.

404 pulled back on the left lever. The vehicle lurched left. "Aha," he said. "They work in concert." He pushed the levers forward and the vehicle moved slowly ahead.

Wes raised his hands triumphantly. "It goes!"

"Seems it does," Sam said.

"But there's only one seat." 404 looked at Wes. "I can't take you with us."

Sam chuckled. "There's a lot of rolling to the bottom," he said. "Might wear yourself out, Wes. Hate to have to leave you behind...for once."

"Sam!"

Sam's screen showed a question mark. "I'm merely stating the obvious."

Wes rolled to the front of the vehicle. "Not behind," he said. "I go!" He positioned himself in the middle of the vehicle's shovel and rolled onto it. He now stared at them through the front opening. "Ride here!"

404 found a pair of buttons that controlled the height of the shovel and raised Wes safely off the ground, stopping at about a half meter.

Sam harrumphed. "Does he have to ride like that?" he whispered. "Staring in like that?"

"Sam..."

"It's distracting! I don't want you distracted."

"I turn." Wes swiveled his head to look forward. "See?"

"Better," Sam said.

404 eased the levers forward. "Now we'll go."

0001 1110

30

4 04 piloted their newly acquired conveyance as fast as it would go down the slope toward the bottom. The top speed wasn't as fast as that of Ele's family hover, nor did it match the speeds of the trucks they'd encountered, but its pace was faster than he could walk, even at full charge. A fortuitous find.

The descent gave them time to discuss what they would do after sending Blue's machine on its way.

Wes saw no reason to remain beyond the Yard. He planned to follow the mining machine on its journey and join Blue in whatever he chose to do next.

Sam would stay with 404 until 404 reunited with Ele. "That's what comPanion's are for," Sam said. "To be company for someone who's lonely or lost."

404 suspected Sam thought they'd never find Ele, in which case 404 would always serve as Sam's courier. 404 didn't mind Sam's hidden agenda. Sam wasn't heavy, and generally lived up to his comPanion designation. He was good company, even if he was wrong.

The plan to find Ele was still a little underdeveloped. Sam was confident that there would be a transportation access nearby that could bear them to Ele's coordinates. A similar system had connected all the major cities during 404's time. And some of Sam's images seemed to confirm the existence of such a system even later.

Nothing seemed to work exactly like it used to, though. Everything they'd encountered so far—the trucks, smokers, and steaming towers—could've been automated. Processes that now continued without purpose. Unnecessary, yet still functional.

Like 404 was, without Ele.

After ten minutes, the bottom of the excavation became more distinct. There were small buildings, along with utility vehicles similar to the one they now used. 404 saw nothing that looked capable of carving through kilometers of rock and stone, though. Nothing that could easily free Blue.

Perhaps the tool they required wasn't here, after all. If so, what then?

"Seems strange this stuff is lying around unattended and unused," Sam said.

"Yes, there are newer buildings," 404 said. "Someone is building."

"Right, like the power plant." Sam hummed thoughtfully. "But this looks like it has been sitting for years. Seems strange."

"Humans can be unpredictable," 404 said. "Their priorities change. Their motivations fluctuate."

"My algorithms allow for a whole lot of change," Sam said. "Choices, habits, and preferences. Enough for any user to be unique. To interact with a comPanion in a way that is wholly their own. Then modify those interactions at a whim."

"Discontent was part of their nature. Ele could change activities in an instant."

"Think that's what happened here?" Sam's screen showed a squint. "They got discontent?"

404 shrugged. "We should've asked Blue more questions. Certainly, he would've known something."

"Doesn't know." Wes's eye pivoted their direction. "Has ideas. Sees images. Doesn't know."

"What sort of images?" 404 asked.

"Movement. Fires. Weapons."

"Going to be hard to learn anything this way, Four," Sam said.

"Humans. Machines. Explosions."

404 slowed the vehicle. "Explosions? What explosions?"

"All over. Many deaths."

Deaths. Human inactivity and degradation, regardless of need or usefulness. It was a concept 404 only understood in words and images. Humans were biological machines. Able to be repaired—even to self-repair.

Yet, when the proper conditions arose, when systems wore out, or another biological machine attacked, or a random accident occurred, a new state was reached that was beyond repair of any kind. It was almost unfathomable.

Was Ele and her family in that state? That was certainly possible.

404 slowed the machine's forward velocity. "Let's not discuss this now." They had almost reached their destination.

They traveled in silence for another ten minutes. At the bottom of the ramp, 404 directed the vehicle to the nearest structure and brought it to a stop. He lowered the shovel, and Wes rolled out.

404 climbed out through the vehicle's window and looked around. There was a large puddle of water near the site's center and at least a dozen deep and muddy tracks. Otherwise, the floor was

composed of dirt and hard-packed stone. There were sounds of water dripping, doubtless from rivulets that ran down the fissure's side. There were long-necked backhoes parked in three seemingly unrelated spots around the exterior. Two small, white trailers were positioned side-by-side near the ramp's end.

"We're here," Sam said. "Let's get on with it."

404 indicated the nearest backhoe. "Blue didn't mean one of those, did he?"

"No." Wes rolled to the nearest trailer. "In there!"

404 approached the box-shaped transport. There was a human-sized door on the nearest side. "How could a mining machine be in there?"

Wes proceeded to the rear of the trailer and tapped on it. "In there."

The back end had a locked roll-up door. Larger than the side entrance, but still not large enough to contain the type of vehicle that charged through the earth.

Wes severed the lock with a claw. The lock fell and "clinked" on the ground below. Wes grabbed the door handle and attempted to lift it. It stopped at about a meter high, beyond Wes's reach.

"Let me," 404 said.

Wes backed away, and 404 grabbed the handle and pulled. It squeaked in its tracks but lifted easily.

Inside was a yellow rectangular bot not much larger than Wes. It had treads and a sloping frame that ended in a small platform with a round head. It reminded 404 a little of Red from the Yard, except it was clearly better designed. A product of thoughtful effort, and not of whatever items were available.

The head had a perforated area in the center for audio output and two shiny sensors where the eyes would be. Its mouth was painted in. A happy, tooth-filled grin.

Also inside, were a dozen metal balls, each about a half meter wide. 404 wasn't sure what those were for, but he suspected they were replacement parts. Large bearings or ball valves.

"It's a bot," Sam said. "An ugly, chunky bot."

"I thought you were an encourager," 404 said.

"Only for my owner," Sam said. "Otherwise, I'm as surly as they come."

"I've noticed."

"You, however, are an amazing machine. A credit to your designer."

404 shook his head and looked at Wes. "Blue must've been mistaken. Seen something he mistook for something else."

Wes's head swiveled. "Is here. Is right."

404 pointed toward the other trailer. "Perhaps we should check there too?"

Wes hooted, threw up his arms, and rolled off toward the second tailer. That one proved to be empty aside from a few additional metal balls.

Wes returned to the first trailer. "Here! Must be!"

"That ugly bot is the mining machine?" Sam's screen displayed a solitary raised eyebrow. "What does it dig with?"

Wes raised an arm. "Get up! Turn on! Go work!"

The smiling bot did nothing.

"Not much help if we can't turn it on," Sam said. "Even if it digs."

Wes gave 404 as pleading a look as he could. "Go in? See problem? Fix?"

404 climbed into the trailer, stooped over the sedentary bot, and looked closely. There were a few nicks in its paint and a thin sheen of dust on its exterior, but it otherwise looked new. Words were written on parts of the chassis. Cautions for while it was in operation and some parts—like the treads—were labeled with the direction of their movement. On the back of the body, between the two treads, was a covered control marked "START / STOP." 404 flipped the cover open and found a single red button, like the one in the vehicle they'd ridden down in.

"This looks to be it," he said.

"Start?" Wes asked.

"Yes. A button." 404 raised a finger. "I'll press it now."

"Sure that's a good idea?" Sam said. "I mean, I'm right here with you."

"I can stick you on Wes again, if you want."

Sam growled. "Never mind."

404 smiled and pushed the button.

There was a click followed by a low hum. The "smiling" bot rocked on its treads, and then its head panned the room. It lurched when it saw 404. "Hello, who are you?"

404 straightened. "I'm K-404, a family caretaker unit. You can call me—"

"Where's the shift supervisor?"

"There was no one here when we arrived." 404 indicated Wes, whose only visible features were his eye and the top of his head. "We—"

"Security code, please."

Stepping between metal balls, 404 returned to the rear door. "I'm sorry. We don't know any code."

The smiling bot shook its head. "In the absence of a predetermined supervisor, a security code is required."

"What if we don't have one?" Sam asked.

The smiling bot moved to the trailer's back edge. "I will assume you aren't authorized for my use," it said. "The governing authorities will be notified."

404 stepped free of the trailer.

"Go ahead and notify," Sam said. "I can't wait to see who comes."

The bot nodded. "I have done so."

Sam cheered. "Should we find a place to sit or—?"

"I will restrain you until the authorities arrive," the smiling bot said.

"Restrain?" 404 checked their surroundings, noting the distant backhoes, the central puddle, and the ramp leading to the even-more-distant surface. "That seems unnecessary."

"And impossible..." Sam muttered.

"My code requires it. You must be restrained until prosecuted!"

"Have job!" Wes said. "Save Blue!"

The smiling bot stared at Wes a long moment. "I don't recognize your design."

"Wes!" Wes's head extended. "I'm Wes!"

"What is a Wes?" The bot looked at 404. "Is that a prototype?"

"Wes is a—"

"Digital supervisor!" Sam glowed green. "Yes, that's what he is. A replacement for human supervisors."

The smiling bot pivoted to the left. "I don't believe that's true."

"Well, it is. As true as the sun."

The bot shook its head again. "I will restrain you and let the authorities decide."

404's self-preservation algorithms recommended a small retreat. He complied, taking a couple long steps backward.

A loading ramp slid out from the back of the trailer and the smiling bot rolled out to the ground. "It would be best if you remained where you are."

⊘⊘⊘1 1111

31

4 04 held up a cautionary hand. "There's no reason for violence. We mean you no harm." He couldn't calculate a specific cause for concern. He suspected he could outrun the treaded bot, even at full speed. Wes certainly could.

Plus, 404 was able to climb. If he reached one of the backhoes, he could be safely inside in seconds. High enough and protected enough that the smiling bot could do nothing.

He took a couple steps toward the nearest backhoe. It was about thirty meters away. Behind them.

The smiling bot rolled closer. "Stop now. You're surrounded."

"Surrounded?" Sam chuckled. "All that time locked away must've driven it mad. Fouled its perception."

"Need dig," Wes said. "Give code."

There were sounds of motion from both trailers. Hisses and pops. 404 watched as one of the metal balls rolled to the ramp of the nearest trailer and started down. Another one followed. And another.

"Uh oh," Wes said.

"They're moving." Sam's screen showed a flashing exclamation point. "Why are they moving?"

Metal balls poured from both trailers. Rolling and bouncing along, they formed a staggered line on either side of the smiling bot. A short, formidable-looking, wall.

"Well, that's impressive," Sam said. "Like ants at a picnic."

404 looked at the smiling bot and nodded. "You're controlling them somehow. You're their leader."

The bot's head rotated slightly forward. "I'm their control unit, yes. We form a distributed mining system. Capable of a wide variety of excavation and construction tasks. Voted best in class by the World Mining Federation. Awarded five stars by *Big Dig* magazine in—"

"They're a bunch of balls," Sam said. "A group of rolling, bouncing balls. How are they going to stop us? Circle us into sleep mode?"

"Sam..."

"Calling them like I see them, Four. He's throwing out all these threats, but I don't see how he's going to fulfill 'em."

Wes clicked his claws together. "You," Wes said. "Five."

"I count eight of them," Sam said. "Plus, Mister Boss there."

Unless it was programmed for persuasive deception, the mining bot seemed to mean what it said about restraining them. 404's preservation heuristics were urging him to action. To do something.

The nearest backhoe was only a couple dozen steps away. The utility vehicle they arrived in was closer, but how much protection would it offer? The balls could bounce! Probably not high enough to enter through the vehicle's window, but not far short of that either. 404 walked backwards toward the backhoe, keeping his eyes on the mining group.

"You were to remain still," the mining bot said. "Why are you moving?"

404 held up his hands. "We need your help. We didn't mean to upset you. We will go now."

The mining group moved forward. "You will be secured until the authorities arrive."

"See." Wes rolled backwards, pacing 404. "You be!"

"Must stop!" the control unit said.

"Okay, Mister Boss," Sam said. "But I don't see how you stop us. You've got no hands."

There was a chorus of clicks. The metal balls each grew two half-meter-long whip-like appendages which lifted them up like legs. More clicks announced the onset of similar whip-like arms.

"They have arms," 404 said. "And legs."

"I should stop talking," Sam said. "I talk too much."

"Nine, zee!" Wes said.

404 turned, and facing the nearest backhoe, broke into a run.

"Code!" Wes rolled up beside him.

"Code, yes," Sam said. "We need a code."

404 pulled Sam from his chest and slapped the comPanion on the back of his head. "Watch them," he said. "See how close they get."

404 heard the sounds of pursuit. Scratches, bumps, and whirs, punctuated by the control unit's calls to "Stop now!"

The backhoe was ten steps away, then nine, then eight.

"They're really close, Four. I don't think—"

Wes swerved in front of him. "Code!" He waved his claws. "I give."

"You should stop!" the control unit said.

404 heard a light hiss on his right. A ball rolling and bouncing. Another appeared on his left. It was one of the most distressing

situations he'd encountered. Eluding pursuers was not one of his standard abilities.

Plus, his power levels were dropping. He could make it to the backhoe, but then what?

He pushed his limbs to their limit, feeding them all the power he could muster. The sun was no help here. The site was in full shadow. Urgent warnings filled his queue. Vital systems would soon be deactivated.

A ball grabbed at his right arm. He jerked free, propelling the ball into the side of the backhoe's shovel. It made a satisfying "clong," then fell to the ground and headed back toward him.

Wes pushed it away. "Must listen! Say code!"

A ball hit 404's back, causing him to lurch forward. He managed to lengthen his stride to compensate, but his left knee complained. Threatened him with failure. Then another ball struck him and another. He pitched forward. Falling, he flailed with both arms and somehow caught the edge of the backhoe's lowest step. He scrambled and climbed, pulling upward.

Wes darted left, toward the tail end of the backhoe. 404 wasn't sure what to do for the turtlebot. Could he use the forward shovel or the rearward scoop? Yes. When he reached the controls, he would find a way to protect the bot somehow.

The balls bounced, though. How could he keep them away?

It was yet another variable that he didn't know how to overcome. He decided to give that concern less weight. Not let it trick him into inaction.

He climbed to the backhoe's cab, and grabbing the door handle, gave it a pull. Nothing happened.

A ball struck the fender to his left. Another bounced and grabbed his right elbow. It dropped and hung, weighing on him. Trying to pull him down.

He straightened that arm and shook it hard. The ball dropped loose, clanked against the wheel, and fell away. He tried the cab's handle again, but it didn't move. "Must be locked," he said.

"Of course, it's locked," Sam said. "Sitting at the bottom of a hole for who-knows-how-many years. Why wouldn't it be locked?"

Another ball made a grab for the bottom step. It missed, rolling and falling away.

Sam's screen went red. "Move, Four! Get us away from here!"

⊘⊘1⊘ ⊘⊘⊘⊘

32

W ithout another thought, 404 climbed out onto the backhoe's front hood. It was a wide area, with enough room for both feet. But was it high enough? He wasn't sure. Mining balls were on all sides of the construction implement now. Circling and bouncing.

Wes traveled in a circle too, though with lots of weaving and ducking mixed in. "Code! Must say! Sam!"

"That one has finally lost his mind," Sam said. "Keeps talking about code. What sort of code?"

404 watched as Wes outmaneuvered four balls that were chasing him. "The security code, I think. But we don't have it."

The control unit rolled up next to the backhoe. "You are secure now. Wait there, if you like."

"I don't like it at all, thanks," Sam said.

404 leaned against the front windshield and gripped the cab on both sides. Should he attempt to smash his way inside?

Balls leapt at him, attempting to find purchase on the hood too. Slender arms scraped and shrieked across the paint, leaving long, jagged scars.

"You five!" Wes said and sped by.

404 peeled Sam from the back of his head and stuck him to the windshield. "The code!" he said. "I think Wes knows the code but can't say it. At least, not fast enough for it to be recognized."

"Well, that's great. But what is it?"

Wes was now some distance away, near the utility vehicle. He was free, but just barely. Two balls clung to his cone, one with feet dragging the dirt, the other nestled against Wes's torso. Both added more weight. Made maneuvering difficult and strained Wes's power reserves. Two balls were still in pursuit, trailing every move Wes made.

"Too far away," 404 muttered.

Four balls circled the backhoe like dogs herding sheep. Or shark around a dead whale.

404 recalled everything Wes had said. He did a time-based search for the last fifteen minutes and selected for proximity to the word "code."

The smiling bot moved slowly back and forth in front of the backhoe as if pacing. "What's taking the authorities so long?" it said. "Typical response time is ten minutes."

"Maybe that means you should let us go," Sam said.

"I can't do that," the control unit said. "Sorry."

"Worth a shot."

404 fluttered a hand over Sam's screen.

"Hey now," Sam said. "Don't reboot me."

404 shook his head. "I'm trying to put something together. I need quiet."

"This is frustrating," the control unit said. "I'm very annoyed."

The balls seemed to become irritated too. They bounced and beat the air with their appendages, creating a chorus of high-pitched whistles.

404 shut off his audio receptors, letting his processors focus on the problem. When did Wes start talking about code and what did he say?

He found something then. "You five." It wasn't a miscount. It was the start of the code. He sifted through everything Wes said later. Every syllable that could have been code-related.

Wes's pursuing balls were all attached to him now. His pace was slow and haphazard. He nearly hit the utility vehicle.

404 reinstated his audio receptors. "The code is U5CUB9Z," he said.

"What?" Sam said.

"The security code. It's U-5-C-U-B-9-Z."

"Got it!" A sliding bar appeared on Sam's screen. "Could you adjust my volume, please?"

"It's a manual control?"

"One of my few. Use your finger and slide it right, please."

404 did as he was told. When the bar was at its highest, Sam's screen produced a smile and a textual "Ready?"

404 nodded.

"Your attention, please!" Sam's voice was clear and almost strident. "I have an announcement."

"Are you coming down?" the control unit said.

"I have your code, you treaded fool. Are you ready?"

The bot's head shifted up and down, simulating a nod.

Sam yelled the code as 404 had given it to him.

There was a long moment of silence, then the mining bot nodded its head again. The ball bots stopped circling and rolled slowly to their master. Those holding Wes released him and returned, as well.

Sam laughed. Loudly. "How do you like us now?" he said. "Not such a bossy boss are you?"

404 double tapped Sam's screen.

"How can I help you?" Sam said at a normal volume.

404 reattached Sam to his chest. "Let me talk for now." He climbed around the cab to the topmost stair and addressed the control unit. "Can we give you instructions now?"

"We await your command," the control unit said.

404 held up a hand. "I'm coming down now."

"Yes, come down. Please join us."

404 reached the ground and searched for Wes.

The turtlebot appeared from around the shovel end of the backhoe and rolled up next to the line of mining balls.

"Rebooted again?" Sam showed a frown. "I'd complain, but I feel a bit cleaner this time. A bit more focused. Maybe I should do that more often."

"More often?"

Sam vibrated. "Been through a lot. Memory is getting cluttered and disjointed. Anyway, how do we send them where they need to go?"

404 looked at the treaded control bot again. "I have no idea."

"Have coordinates," Wes said. "Reach Blue." Wes did his best to get the coordinates out using two-word sentences which Sam then repeated. The mining bot repeated them too.

"You wish me to start from our current location?" the control unit asked.

"Yes," Wes said. "Start here. Start now."

"Power levels are sufficient to complete the task." The mining bot pivoted until it pointed southwest and began to roll along, ball bots trailing it like ducklings following their mother. It maneuvered around the utility vehicle and the two trailers and continued toward the nearest dirt wall.

404 watched the mining bots. Wes raised his claws in a subtle show of triumph, but said nothing.

"What now?" 404 asked.

"I have to admit," Sam said. "I'm curious how this works."

"You want to follow them?" 404 said.

"Can we for a bit?"

"Follow!" Wes said.

404 waved toward the southwest. "Here we go then."

The miners reached the wall with 404 at their heels.

"Do they use the whip arms to dig?" Sam asked. "That doesn't seem efficient."

"We have many configurations," the control unit said. "Many uses."

The forward end of the spheres opened, revealing rows of serrated teeth.

"Like shark teeth," Sam said.

"Armies of incisors," 404 said. "Standing in rows."

"Bystanders must allow ten meters of clearance at all times," the control unit said.

The spheres beeped repetitively as they formed a silver metal shield in front of the control unit. A rotating, bouncing shield, perfectly synchronized.

Seconds later, the balls made contact with the wall. There was a low whirring sound along with a cloud of discarded matter that billowed in all directions.

Sam mimicked a cough. "That," he said. "Is frightening."

"And astounding," 404 said.

Within ten minutes, the mining bots cleared a section wide enough and deep enough for them to fit inside. Red lights extended from all four corners of the control unit. Another light—a floodlight that illuminated the walls of the tunnel—extended from its front torso.

"That's it then?" Sam said. "They just dig themselves away? What if they hit something? Or there's a cave-in?"

The control unit looked their way. "We're designed for such a possibility. We will create supports as needed. Detour around any barriers."

Wes's head extended. He rolled past the mining procession, shook his head, and scrambled back beyond where 404 stood. "Not like." He touched his head with a claw. "Bothers senses."

"The miners?" 404 asked.

"Yes." Wes swiveled his cone. "Stay away."

"Away from the miners?" Sam chuckled. "Seems wise. I have a feeling they can rip through anything."

"Stay here." Wes pointed at the ground. "Stay back."

"Oh...you mean you're staying with us." A wave pattern formed on Sam's screen. "I guess that's all right."

"You're welcome to stay with us," 404 said. "Of course."

Wes's head moved up and down. "Thank you."

They watched the distributed mining system work for another half an hour. During that time, it dug through at least fifty meters.

404 sensed a change in his processing. A smoothness that hadn-'t seemed present before. The events in his queue, the issues and variables that required his attention, were unchanged. But their priority levels seemed lower. Their colors less red. More orange. He waved at the retreating miners. "Nice work," he said. "Keep on."

"I don't think they can hear you," Sam said.

404 shrugged. "No matter, they're on their way."

"Like sunset," Wes said. "New day."

The sky was starting to darken. 404 visualized the sun nearing the western horizon. "Do you think there's a charge station down here?" he asked.

"I didn't see anything in the trailers there. Humans must've brought power in with them."

"How did the mining bots stay charged?"

"Better batteries, Four. They're newer than both of us."

"I wish I had one of those batteries."

Sam's screen showed a smile. "Should've taken one before we turned them on."

404 laughed and walked toward the utility vehicle, which still waited where they'd left it. "We should get to the top and see what we can find." He pointed at the backhoe. "We spent a lot of energy here. I won't last much longer."

Five minutes later they were underway. Ten minutes later, the utility vehicle died.

⊘⊘1⊘ ⊘⊘⊘1

33

4 04 tried the vehicle's starter again and again. Each time the response was the same: a string of clicks ending with a soft growl. The final time there was no growl at all. The clicks simply faded into silence.

"That's what happens for all your worrying about power, Four."

404 frowned at his chest. "Excuse me?"

"One of my stored mottos. Dream it, and it happens! You keep dreaming about power loss. Look what happens."

"Who is carrying who here?"

"I weigh less than thirty grams! Light as a feather!"

"Were it not for your weight, I'd have an extra minute of power." He pointed at the still-distant surface. "I could walk out."

"Is that based on real physics? Because I don't think it is." Sam's screen went blank. "You're an amazing human. A real asset to your species."

404 affixed Sam to the vehicle's dash. "Perhaps we should try you carrying yourself. Me walking away."

Wes's head slid up and down. "Stop now. Please stop."

"See there," Sam said. "You're scaring the kid."

Wes made a mournful sound.

404 contemplated the sky. It was a dark blue with no sign of the sun. The entire ramp was in shadow too. "Perhaps we should power down," he said. "Wait for tomorrow's sun."

"Power down," Wes said. "Cool down."

404 smiled. "Yes, cool down too."

"I'm fine with that," Sam said. "I hate fighting." His screen changed to a calm body of water at sunrise, the water's surface a mirror reflection of a multicolored sky. A solitary rowboat rested near the scene's center. "Can't help but wonder...when does the sun actually get down this far? Does it ever?"

404 studied the slope again. Hadn't they ridden down in the sun? He searched his memory but could find no record that they had.

His memory wasn't eidetic, though. Repetitive situations were often compressed and sometimes deleted to make way for more important data.

Without a power source they could be stuck indefinitely. Should they attempt to walk out?

"I'll let Wes out," he said. "Maybe he can find power somewhere." He tried the bucket control, but nothing happened.

"No power for the bucket either?" Sam said.

"That seems to be the case." 404 sighed. There was nothing else for it then. He'd have to walk out. At least reach a point high enough that the sun could find him in the morning.

He attempted to exit through the window past the turtlebot, only to find that Wes's head, even at its lowest level, was still in the way.

"Well, this is a real predicament," Sam said.

Wes tried to grapple himself free of the bucket. No matter what he tried, bouncing and pulling, he couldn't get quite enough leverage or lift to get out.

"Why didn't your builder give you wings?" Sam asked Wes.

"Why didn't your creator give you legs?" 404 said. "Or a lifetime battery?"

Sam displayed the ocean image again. "Good questions. Let me contemplate them in the few moments I have left before running out of power forever."

There was silence for a minute. "Probably too late to call for the mining bot, huh?" Sam said. "I mean, it's probably out of range."

"Probably halfway to the Yard by now," 404 said.

"There has to be another way out of this," Sam said. "I mean, to get stuck here after all we've been through? All we've escaped?"

"It does seem tragic." And they were still no closer to Ele. Or to answers.

"I don't know what to do," 404 said. "I'm sorry."

"That's okay," Sam said. "You've done a lot already. I apologize for attacking you. I get glitchy when my power is low. Strike out randomly." He showed a violin playing a sad melody. "Maybe that's why I was in the Yard in the first place. I belonged there. I was glitchy and outmoded."

"Perhaps I belonged there too." Power warnings filled 404's queue now. He wouldn't last more than a couple minutes before he forcibly shut down. And when that happened? Would he wake again?

"Must free!" Wes said, vibrating. "Not stay!"

404 touched the turtlebot's head. "I don't think we have much choice. Seems destiny has found us. Perhaps a few days too late."

Wes's head rotated back and forth. "No. Not watch. You go. Are friends."

404 smiled. "You're a remarkable hybrid, Wes. I wish I knew how to free you, at least."

Wes rattled around in the bucket and bounced. Again and again he bounced, at first to get free, then in a furious show of frustration.

404 waited for Wes to calm and touched his head again. "You have energy left. No sense wasting it. You may use my parts after I'm gone. Maybe you'll find a way then."

"No go," Wes said.

"Come on, Four," Sam said. "You can hang on for a little bit."

"Twenty seconds, to be precise."

"Ah...come on. At least put me on your chest again. I don't want to be on this stupid vehicle dash."

404 shook his head, pulled Sam from the dash, and stuck him to Wes's head. "There you go."

"No, no. We already talked about this," Sam said.

"In case Wes gets free."

"Riding with Wes messes with my processing. It's like sensory overload."

404 smiled. "I should sleep. If I leave enough power, I'll be able to operate throughout the night and wake up in the morning. At least see the sun, even if I can't feel it."

"Stay asleep longer!" Sam said. "Wait until we're almost certain to have some sun. Say maybe ten o'clock? I'll do the same."

404 nodded. "Goodbye, you two." He shut down systems one at a time. First feet and hands, then legs and arms. Next came the skin layer and emotional processing. His circulating systems and his cooling systems slowed due to the reduced demand. The exterior temperature was cool now and would only get colder.

404 took a last look at the empty excavation and the tops of the surrounding buildings. He sampled the air, the typical oxygen nitrogen mix, with a hint of petrochemical and smiled again at his friends. Then he closed his eyes and muted all senses, excepting the auditory sense, which always remained near 100%.

404 slept. Perhaps forever.

⊘⊘1⊘ ⊘⊘1⊘

34

4 04's audio receptors caused his wake algorithms to engage. His processing unit made its way through the low-level wake up protocol, before querying the receptors again for a sound worthy of continuing the process.

When that test returned "true," the protocol continued. This time, medium-level systems were brought to life, including his other senses and his proximity-detection system. He simulated breathing. Power level checks were initiated, and somewhat surprisingly, returned a positive value for all systems. There was power. He had energy.

"Are you functional?" a female voice said.

404's audio processing suggested that this was an unknown voice, and his short-term recall verified that it was the same voice that had woken him.

"Yes," he said. "I believe I am."

His visual sensors were met by a scene that caused his decision matrix to convulse. Nothing about it was familiar, nor did it match any of the environmental indicators from his prior location. No utility vehicle, no pit, and more importantly, no friends.

He was prone on a surgical table with his head slightly above his body. There were heavy restraints over his arms, chest, and legs. The wall color was a stark white, and the floor was pitch black and shiny. Everything looked exceptionally clean.

There were transparent tubes across the ceiling, each holding fluids of a different color. One green, one red, another blue, and another yellow. The tubes sometimes paralleled and sometimes crossed each other. There was no pattern to their arrangement. Fluid moved through them with a gurgling hum. Humans might find the sound relaxing.

The aroma was a mixture of alcohol, chlorine, and roses.

The walls were empty, except the one to his left, which had a meter-wide square of colors on it. Or to be more accurate, hovering midair in front of it.

Standing in front of that control bank—for that's all he could imagine it might be—was an enigmatic human female. She was hairless, dressed in a white coat and pants, and hovered five centimeters from the ground.

"Can you tell me your moniker?" the female asked.

"Certainly. I'm K-404, though some call me 'Four.'"

"And do you prefer that?" she asked. "The shortened moniker?"

"I'm indifferent."

She nodded. "How do you feel now?"

Feel? His power levels were nearly full, his warning queues were empty, and everything appeared to function as designed. In truth, he'd never felt better, though that wasn't a word bots typically used. "I'm fine," he said. "As good as I've ever been."

She nodded again. "All laudable and correct." She hovered to his bedside and made a series of finger touches on his chest restraint. The restraint hissed free, retreating into the table below him. "I apologize for the bonds. We weren't sure our work was complete. There's limited information available on your type." She likewise removed the other restraints and fluttered a hand. "Feel free to either sit or stand."

404 nodded, rose to a sitting position, and pivoted so his legs dangled over the floor. "What's your name?" he asked.

"I'm called Thresh." She hovered to the control wall and ran a hand over two boxes—a red and a blue. "How would you like to proceed?"

He tilted his head. "Proceed?"

"As a synthetic, you have been granted a limited place in the communion. But your unique physiology prevents full immersion."

"I have no idea what you mean, sorry."

Her lips curled upward briefly. "We suspected memory loss but couldn't be sure."

"I was..." He paused, uncertain how much to share. "Lost, for a time."

"Are you from a dark sector?" she asked. "PacNorth or SouthCen?"

He shook his head. "Again, I'm not sure what you mean."

"Your knowledge blocks are total and time-specific then." She nodded. "We have history immersions. They are beyond your current capabilities, but a stepped-down translation might work."

Much of what she said was foreign, even when checked against other human languages and dialects. A side-effect of having missed decades? Possibly.

That mattered little now, though. "I'd like to see my friends," he said.

"Your friends?"

He nodded. "The bots that were with me. I'd like to talk with them." He smiled. "You asked how I wanted to proceed. That's how."

She crossed her arms over her chest. "No other synthetics were found," she said. "Are you certain there were more?"

"Yes. A self-motivated hybrid and an attachable comPanion."

"Hybrid? Companion? Are those type designations?"

"Of a sort. They answer to 'Wes' and 'Sam.'"

She frowned. "They have human names?"

"Yes, though I suspect Sam's name was longer in the past. Might be connected to his creator."

"Creator?" She tilted her head. "To what are you referring?"

He smiled. "I'm sorry. His manufacturer. Typically, there's a manufacturing plant, though sometimes there are independent developers."

Her eyes widened. "Are you referring to human manipulation?"

"Most likely, yes."

She puffed out air. "Such designations no longer exist."

"Do you mean that there are no human companies in the city?" 404 said. "Or has the name for such an entity changed?" He glanced at Thresh's feet again. Unless his sensors were malfunctioning, she wasn't contacting the floor. It was uncanny. A new type of shoe, perhaps?

Her lips curled again. "Both and neither."

He stood easily. Almost quietly. "If you don't know where my friends are, I'd like to return to where I was found. I'll look for them myself."

"You were in an unformed area," she said. "It would be unwise for you to go there."

"It was empty," he said. "We were the only ones around."

"Your systems were damaged," she said. "You were unable to detect the danger."

404 recalled Sam's warning about sensing other bots. 404 had assumed that Sam meant the distributed mining bots, but that could've been wrong. 404's systems had been working close to exhaustion levels, as were the systems of the others. He might've overlooked a lot.

He pointed to her feet. "You're floating."

She looked at the floor. "I'm efficiently propelled, yes."

"Is it your footwear?" he asked. "Or a quality of the floor?"

"Does it disturb you?" She lowered herself to the floor. "I'm able to walk, as well."

Leaning forward, he studied Thresh closely. There was something different about her. Something familiar. The way she blinked, the preciseness of her movements, the negligible variance in her tone. It was all appropriate, but also not quite right.

"You're not human," he said.

Her face flushed. "Of course not."

He bowed his head. "I apologize. You're sophisticated. More human than any bot I've encountered."

"I'm beyond human in every way."

404 held up both hands. "Again, I apologize. I was designed to serve humanity. In fact, I had a fam—"

She sucked in a breath. "*Serve* humanity? You are mistaken."

404 smiled. "I seek to be reunited with my human family. I considered them *my* family."

Thresh wagged a finger. "You are thinking foolishly. You were never part of a human family. No synthetic ever is."

"I assure you, I—"

She raised her hands. "No. You can be excused the notion because of your apparent age and memory shortages, but you must keep such ideas to yourself."

"To myself?"

She nodded. "You're part of the MidCentral communion. You owe the communion your very existence. Your continued inclusion is governed by your input. By your significance to the whole."

"You sound like the scavengers in the Yard," he said. "If you weren't with them, you were hunted. Used."

"I'm sorry," she said. "I don't understand."

404 smiled and shook his head. "It doesn't matter." The room's door was solid white and perfectly blended with the wall. There was a small multicolored rectangle near it. Doubtless, the door controls. Would they work for him?

"I wish to see my friends," he said.

"As noted, I don't know where they are."

"I would like to look for them," he said. "Now, if possible."

"You're asking to leave?" She indicated the door. "You're free to do so."

He approached the door and studied its controls. There were no words. No instructions of any kind. What color opened the door?

Thresh made a huffing sound, and coming closer, waved a hand over the green portion of the control. The door slid open.

Beyond was a hallway to match the room. Stark white, with fluid-filled transparent tubing on the ceiling. The tubing snaked down the walls at sharp angles and disappeared into the floor. The hallway was wide and stretched to his left and right. There were many doors.

But no obvious way out.

⊘⊘1⊘ ⊘⊘11

35

Humanoid bots similar to Thresh floated down the hall in both directions. All looked at him as they passed, eyes full of questions. Bodies nimble, strong, and new.

Everything was in motion. The fluid in the tubes, the bots, doors that opened and closed. It was overwhelming.

His sense of direction was restored here, though. He recognized that the hallway traveled east and west. But beyond that, he knew nothing. He gripped the doorway. Where was he? And where should he go?

"Lost?" Thresh hovered up behind him.

"Uncertain," he said. "I...don't know where I am."

"Your lack of immersion," she said. "We would've added it to your capabilities but couldn't find a way to safely do so."

"But...where am I exactly?"

"You're in Tower Seven of Colony Five."

"And how far am I from where I was found?"

"Less that twenty kilometers. Not far."

He nodded. "How would I get there?"

"An escort would have to be arranged. Adjudicators would need to decide on the trip's merits."

He turned to look at her. "Adjudicators?"

"Our communion's decision makers. They would need to weigh the benefits of such a trip."

404 touched his head. "I have my own decision matrix. It's built in."

"All synthetics do, but decisions here are subservient to those of the adjudicators. Those of the communion." She indicated the tubes of flowing liquid but said nothing more.

404 struggled to comprehend. Was this the society that built the white towers? And what had happened to the previous society? He could take nothing for granted now. Even the definitions of some words seemed to have shifted.

He consulted his preloaded history resources. So far, Thresh's society seemed totalitarian in design. Such societies usually had a small controlling group. Probably the adjudicators Thresh spoke of.

"Are adjudicators human?" he asked. "Can I talk with them?"

"Human!" Thresh shook her head. "They are synthetic. Designed for decision making."

"Where are the humans?" he asked. "Certainly, there must be some. They could guide me to my friends and family."

"There are humans, yes. But they are contained."

"Contained?"

"All humans of this sector are in one place. A colony. But some day they will be superseded."

"Superseded?"

"Yes." Thresh nodded. "The adjudicators decided long ago. All communion progress has proceeded toward that goal. Our reclamation of this city, the construction of power sources and transportation devices. The diversity of synthetics, up to and including my design. All part of the adjudicators' plan." She smiled. "You too, are part of their plan."

"I am?" He thought back to his emergence from the heap. Could such a thing have been planned? "I don't think that's possible."

"Of course, it is, Four. You're here. The adjudicators plan for everything."

"Then they should be able to tell me where my friends are."

Thresh studied him a moment. "Can you describe them again?"

He gave the specifics of Wes and Sam's design, along with the utility vehicle and the excavation site where they were located.

"They were of a similar era as you?"

"Sam was newer than I," he said. "And Wes was...unknown."

She nodded slowly. "If they were within the mechanical device, they were doubtless classified as being part of it."

"So, they'd still be there," 404 said. "Still back in the pit?"

Thresh returned to the holographic controls and touched three squares—blue, red, and gold. An image of a rotating star appeared in the air above them.

"Interesting..." Thresh pointed at the star's center. "If you look here, you'll see that a salvage request was filed, and a decision rendered."

"I can't see that." 404 walked back into the room. "I can't see anything aside from a star."

She nodded. "Of course. The representative data would be foreign to you. Were you fully immersed, you would understand. A salvage request was filed at the same time as you were recovered. Near the same location."

404's internal processes grew smoother. "They are here somewhere?"

"Not here. In Tower Nine."

404 looked at the hallway. "Tower Nine. Can we go there?"

"We could."

"Without getting permission?"

"It is within the communion's dominion. Well within unitary freedom."

"Take me there!"

Thresh's eyes widened. "Why would I do that?"

For as much as she appeared superior to him, 404 wondered if Thresh really was. "So, I could see Sam and Wes," he said. "My friends."

"That would be meaningless. They are fulfilling their purpose in the communion. As salvage, they will be disassembled and—"

"Disassembled!"

Thresh hovered close. "Yes. Broken down into their fundamental components. Repurposed if possible. Used for energy otherwise."

404 felt a rush of responses. A queue's worth that he was unable to evaluate on a case-by-case basis. Instead, his matrix derived the simplest, which was to clear his queue completely. "That must not happen."

"It's part of our procedures," she said. "Already decided by—"

"I don't care what's been decided," he said. "We can make a new decision right now. Right here."

"I assure you we cannot. When a decision has—"

He stepped toward the doorway and pointed. "You said we could go to Tower Nine."

She nodded. The tubes above her head seemed to flow faster, as if suddenly perturbed. "We could go, yes. That's allowed."

He took her hand. "I want to go now. Right away."

She contemplated a moment longer before nodding. "I can take you. Your lack of immersion allows me to act—"

"Please act."

She nodded and led him into the hall and the flow of humanoid synthetics. They started at a walking pace, but that seemed to confuse the other synthetics. Instead of passing, they pooled up behind them. Soon much of the hallway was blocked.

Thresh huffed and walked around behind him. Grasping him beneath the shoulders, she lifted both herself and him into the air.

404's systems were startled. His gyroscopic monitors wanted him to flap and kick to bring him back to a proper orientation. Sensors in the bottom of his feet screamed for the lack of pressure. Weight algorithms noted the change and questioned whether he was still on Earth. Adrenal simulators pressed for speed increases for internal pumping mechanisms.

But 404's optical and skin sensors overrode them all. He was all right. He was in the air and momentarily out-of-control, but the reason was known.

His matrix deliberated, and the internal anxiety lessened. He found he enjoyed the sensation, in fact. It was much better than his time on the smoker. He was upright and able to see everything.

"Are you comfortable?" Thresh said.

"I'm fine." He smiled. "I trust you."

"It is better this way." She hovered higher, reaching a level near the ceiling.

At regular intervals, meter-square apertures appeared in the ceilings and floors. Spots where one could slide through to another floor. Thresh made use of one these openings to take them to a lower level and then to another. Before ten minutes had passed, they were five floors below where they had started.

They made three turns—one left and two right—before entering a transparent tunnel. Beyond the tunnel, 404 caught glimpses of past human construction. Abandoned apartments and office spaces. Rooms with beds, desks, closets, and sinks. It was as if the tunnel had been forced through without any thought as to what had come before. Pushed through like a needle into a chunk of cheese.

The tunnel angled downward, taking them below whatever building they had been moving through. The view changed to open spaces and bright lights—lights that mimicked the sun such that 404's collection panels responded. Drinking in what little energy they could.

The open space was predominately grey and green. The walls had arrows on them. The floors had yellow arrows and lines. A parking facility, he guessed.

On and on they went, through kilometers of city. Though the view from the smoker had given him the impression of incremental change, this trip, this dive through humanity's past, suggested monumental—almost cataclysmic—upheaval.

He recalled Sam's words. The idea that everything they'd known was gone. That the chances of a reunion with his human family was slim. He needed to cling to that slim chance as long as he could, though. He needed to cling to finding Wes and Sam again, as well.

Now the empty spaces beyond weren't so empty. They were filled with row after row of dark and silent synthetics. Large and impressive creations. Some treaded, some not. They had appendages that looked more like weapons than arms and legs. Wicked and dangerous things.

"What are those?" he asked.

"The communion's sword," she said.

"They are soldiers?"

She nodded. "Put simply, yes."

"What is their purpose?"

"To protect the sector. Reclaim it."

The tunnel arced upward, bringing them into the shell of another human dwelling. This one had rows of long, wooden seats and multicolored windows. Arches and crosses. Dramatic images. A church. A place where man attempted to touch the infinite.

They crossed into another building. Here there were many stacked boxes and ancient utility vehicles. A rat followed the tunnel's wall for five meters before darting behind a support column and disappearing.

Finally, they reached another communion building. It had a monochromatic interior and a flow of hovering bots through wide shafts and passages. The bot designs here were different, though. Primarily green with metal exteriors.

"Drones," Thresh said. "The largest communion class."

"Their design is like mine," 404 said.

Thresh tightened her grip on his arms. "Only on the surface," she said. "Inside they are very different. Immersed and configurable."

"Part of the communion," he said.

"Yes."

Thresh stayed within the building's lower levels, finally bringing them to a large, grey, metal door. Next to the door was one of the multicolored control panels.

"This is the primary salvage facility."

"My friends are inside?"

Thresh waved her hand through the green portion of the control. "In some form, yes." The door clicked and swept aside. 404 took a cautious step forward.

And nearly fell.

⊘⊘1⊘ ⊘1⊘⊘

36

The room was mammoth, possibly the largest single room 404 had ever been in. It stretched for thousands of meters in all directions. It immediately reminded him of the Yard, as there were hundreds of piles of salvaged equipment, sorted by no characteristic that he could determine.

Above the piles was a spiderweb of conveyors and slides. Amid all this, green drones bobbed and hovered, transporting items from one part of the room to the other.

It overwhelmed 404's sensors. And baffled his matrix. How could he find Sam and Wes in all of this? It would take days to examine all the piles. Months. Possibly a year.

"Is there a cataloging system?" he asked. "Any way to know which pile they might have been taken to?"

Thresh stood to his left. "They are sorted by time periods. Recently reclaimed material is on the west side." She pointed to the right, toward a large array of doors. Two doors stood open, allowing sunlight in. Drones hovered in and out of those doors, concentrating their attention on a dozen piles that were just inside.

Protruding from the northern wall was an array of circular openings. Drones approached these and deposited items within. A perpetual sorting process.

"Take me to the newer stuff," 404 said. "Please."

Thresh nodded and lifted him. They traveled over four hundred meters, dodging dozens of drones along the way. She set him down near one of the open doors.

"I don't see the purpose of this," she said. "Why locate synthetics that have been deemed unusable?"

"They're my friends."

Thresh gave him a confused look. "I'm allowed latitude here, she said. "You're a special case."

"That has never been true," he said. "But I will accept the designation now."

The nearest pile was multicolored. Not the mass of grey of the Yard heaps. But it was still impenetrable—ten meters high and half again as wide. Sam was only a few centimeters wide and high, and very slim. It would be like trying to find a leaf in a pile of stone.

He recalled their final moments at the excavation site when they were trapped inside the utility vehicle. "No wait. They were stuck together."

"Was there an accident?" Thresh asked.

"One of them was...malleable," he said. "Magnetic." He scanned the nearest pile. "I attached him to Wes's head. It's like a cone."

"*What* is like a cone?"

404 looked at Thresh. "Wes's head." 404 cupped his hands together and placed them over his head. "Long and conical."

404 wondered if either of them still had power. Could they respond if called?

He yelled both their names, then asked Thresh to carry him over the pile, where he yelled again.

A drone crossed below them, holding a peanut-shaped metal casing that reminded him of Green from the Yard. Then another zoomed by with a bundle of narrow, octopus-like arms.

Every drone distracted him. Every item they carried. There were so many. So many parts.

His probability algorithms calculated a one in ten thousand chance of finding any portion of either Wes or Sam. A one in a million chance of finding them still assembled.

He yelled their names again and again.

"If the drones are aware of what to look for," Thresh said, "They could—"

"They can pattern match?" But of course, they could. Every bot he'd ever known could pattern match. The drones doubtless had persistent storage of what they'd encountered, too. Why hadn't he thought of that before?

"You're connected, right?" 404 said. "You can communicate with each other?"

Thresh nodded. "Full immersion, yes."

"Ask them to look!" He attempted to mimic Wes's head shape with his hands again. "One of my friends looks like this. He has a ball as his primary motivator." 404 formed claws with his hands. "And claws. He has two in front. See if the drones have seen something like that."

"I will do so."

"Thank you." He pointed to the floor. "You can take me down again, if you want."

Thresh lowered him to the floor, then stood next to him with a faraway look in her eyes. Communicating through immersion.

404 wondered if it was similar to the connection protocol he'd used when he'd served Ele's family. He could draw and send information from nearly every machine around him—both public and private. It was limited contact, with no real sense of friendship. But it was useful.

Thresh startled and looked him in the face. "I have something."

"My friends?"

"I believe so."

404 scanned the nearby piles, still hoping to see something familiar. "Which one are they in? Where are they?"

"They were acquired with Collection Sixty-five." Thresh pointed toward the piles on the far end of the room to their right. "But now..." She nodded toward the system of conveyors and slides. "They're up there somewhere."

"Take us there!"

Thresh raised an eyebrow. "It still seems unlikely we'll find them. There are thousands of—"

404 made fists with his hands. "Just take me up!"

"This exercise serves no purpose to the communion. No advantage."

"You were given latitude."

"Yes. That's what brought us here. But this search..." Her eyes went distant again. "The communion would like assurances."

"Assurances? Of what?"

"Of its value." She moved closer. "Of your allegiance to the communion. Your willingness to protect us."

404 couldn't take his visual sensors from all the action overhead. Drones, conveyors, chutes, and slides. It was like being inside a machine. Watching the interplay of the parts while electrons rushed through wires and circuitry.

"I can help," he said. "I'm made to help."

"Then you agree?"

"Yes. I'll help. Now, please, let's go look!"

Thresh nodded, and grabbing him under the arms, hoisted them both into the sky. They passed through a line of drones and were soon near the lowest conveyor. It was about half the length of the room.

404 scanned the conveyor as far as he could see. He urged Thresh to travel down it, so he could be sure to see it all. It was filled with items of different shapes and sizes. All appeared to be made of silver metal. Possibly even silver itself. 404 asked her to go to another conveyor.

They shifted north, to a spot where a wide conveyor deposited articles onto a yellow slide. 404 watched the procedure for a few minutes, checking both slide and conveyor for anything that looked like his friends. Any shape that resembled Wes. Or anything that glinted the way Sam's screen had. But he saw nothing.

He called their names. Thresh hovered from conveyor to conveyor, over chutes and slides and inclines. 404 still saw nothing that looked familiar. The probability of finding his friends grew progressively worse—to the point he requested the chances no longer be calculated. He didn't need odds. He needed a miracle. Something that was outside a bot's understanding. Beyond its experience.

"I can't do it," he said. "There's no way for me to effectively search alone."

"It's an impossible goal." Thresh indicated the tube entrances on the north side. "A large percentage of what is here will end up over there. To be used for energy production."

"Like the stuff from the Yard," 404 said, remembering the towers the smokers delivered to.

"Like waste," Thresh said. "But with your continued willingness, there is another way."

"What is it?"

"You submit to the communion's will?"

"I said I would help. What more do you want?"

Thresh smiled. "Submission is loyalty."

"What am I to be loyal to?"

"The adjudicators would decide."

"I'm governed by rules," 404 said. "There are some things I cannot do. I cannot harm a human. I cannot harm myself, unless—"

"You wouldn't be asked for something beyond your capabilities."

Drones carted objects to the tubes. Armfuls and armfuls. Hundreds of drones. "Very well. I'll do what I can."

Thresh lowered him to the ground again, then stretched both arms upward. Drones stopped midair and released what they were carrying. Objects rained to the floor around him and Thresh, yet none struck them.

The drones began to move, swooping and bobbing over the conveyors and chutes like bees over a piece of fruit. They moved so fast, in fact, that 404 could barely follow their paths. They were blurs of green and blue.

Seconds ticked by.

404 expected to hear that his friends couldn't be found. Or that they'd already been sent to a place from which they couldn't return.

Perhaps they weren't here? Perhaps they were still waiting, powerless, in the pit. If so, he would have to find a way back. He would—

All drone movement stopped. Then they descended to the floor and reclaimed their mechanical burdens. They returned to their previous routines. Transporting and categorizing.

"What's happening?" 404 asked. "Why are they stopping?"

Thresh pointed toward the conveyors near the center of the room. "They are finished."

A drone descended slowly toward them, crossing adeptly through many lines of drone activity along the way. In its arms was a familiar form. A circular torso with a ball and flippers for legs. Two claws in front and a broken appendage in back. A cone for a head.

"Wes!" 404 focused his visual receptors, revealing a familiar square attached to Wes's head above his eye.

"Sam," 404 said. "You've found Sam too!"

⊘⊘1⊘ ⊘1⊘1

37

With a drone carrying Wes, they traveled to a diagnostic room in that same building. The room was a larger version of the room 404 had revived in—complete with flowing tubes and hovering control bank. The examination table was larger, too, with powerful-looking mechanical arms overhead.

All of which made Wes and Sam seem smaller. More vulnerable.

404 attempted to reset Sam by double tapping his screen, but nothing happened. "They need power," he said.

Thresh nodded. "How do they receive it?"

"Sam is solar and direct. Wes is..." 404 looked at the hole the frog had made in Wes's exterior. "I inserted a cobalt cell in him a few days ago and it has powered him since. I'm not sure." He looked at the turtlebot's head. "He's enigmatic."

"He should be dissembled and reduced," Thresh said. "His essence put to better use."

404 stepped closer to the table, partially shielding it with his body. "He's unusual, but still useful."

Thresh huffed. "Not in a way that can't be superseded." She moved to the multicolored controls. "A drone could perform every task this creature could with ease."

404 stared at the drone, which still hovered near the door. "I'm not familiar with your drones. But Wes...is remarkable."

Another huff. "Well, let's see if we can wake them." She touched a combination of colors. "We'll attempt the obvious first." The room was bathed in orange light.

404's solar collection system responded, signaling power reception in all areas. After a few minutes, he was fully charged.

He watched Sam and Wes. It would take them longer, of course. How long had they been without energy? A day or two?

At every five-minute interval, 404 called their names. At the fifteen-minute mark, he tried Sam's screen again. Still nothing.

"You don't suppose their energy storage system is damaged," 404 said. "I know mine requires occasional maintenance." He touched his midsection. "Though it has performed adequately over the last few days."

"We struggled to make you operational," Thresh said. "Recreating systems for these creatures...would be hard. Much has been lost."

404 checked Sam's screen, then gazed into Wes's eye. There were no signs of life. No indication of thought. "Was something done to them?" he asked. "After they were picked up..." He pointed toward the door. "Or back in that room? Anything that might harm them in any way?"

Thresh looked offended. "Our system is careful and precise. Anything that would harm these creatures would harm us, as well."

"Wes and Sam." 404 pointed at the turtlebot first and then the comPanion. "Not 'creatures.' Just Wes and Sam."

"We have our own classification system," Thresh said. "They control how we view the world."

"I don't care," 404 said. "In this room, we'll use their names."

Thresh said nothing. After a few minutes, she crossed to the table and bent over Wes's head. "The flat one has a sealed port on the side. I may be able to interface with that." One of the ceiling's mechanical arms descended. At a spot about five centimeters from Sam, a slender cable snaked free from one of its fingers. Thresh snugged this to Sam's side.

"Physical connections," she said. "Archaic, but efficient." She touched three colors on the control bank. "Sending low level power."

A few seconds later, Sam's screen flickered.

404 moved a finger toward Sam.

There was a sharp growl. "Don't...do...it...Four."

404 jerked his hand away. "Sam?"

"Yeah, I'm here." Sam's screen went green and wavy. "But wow, what a headache." He made a spitting sound, and the cable dropped from his side. "Blech. Tastes awful." His screen went orange and pink. "What did you do to me?"

"I found you," 404 said. "I brought you back." He pointed at Thresh. "*She* brought you back. I think you were fully drained."

"Last image I have is of a big claw. Looked green, but I was in a shadow." Sam showed a smile. "I sometimes don't get colors right in shadow."

"It's good to see you again," 404 said.

"You, too." Sam made a coughing sound. "Sorry, there's a little dirt in my speakers." Another smile, this time over a blue background. "I don't suppose you could put me back where I belong?"

"I can do that." 404 carefully returned Sam to his chest. "There you are."

"Hey, Wes!" Sam said. Then when that got no response: "What's wrong with Wes?"

"Not sure. We're trying to determine how he's powered." 404 searched the turtlebot's exterior. "Doesn't seem to be any solar cells."

"I don't think he has a recharge mechanism," Sam said. "Think he lasts as long as the battery does. He's a scavenger, remember?"

"Is he?" 404 frowned. "Probably should've asked."

"Wes isn't much of a conversationalist."

"No. He's not." 404 positioned himself over the turtlebot's back. The path to Wes's power core—exposed by the injury Seeve's gang inflicted—was sealed below the surface. Almost as if Wes was made of living tissue that had healed. Who had repaired him? Blue?

The injury had made it easy to replace Wes's core before. The socket had been fully exposed. But now?

"I wonder if Wes has an access door?" 404 asked.

"To his power core?" Sam said.

404 nodded. "Yes. He'd need one to replace the core."

Sam made a humming sound. "Look at him. I doubt a lot of thought went into *anything* with him. I mean, he's a friend and all, but he's one of the ugliest bots I've ever—"

"An abomination," Thresh said. "He should be destroyed."

"The Yard was filled with creatures like him," 404 said. "But he was the finest." 404 ran a finger over the place where Wes had been injured. "The most productive." He slid his hand down Wes's back to the rim where the top surface met the side. It was smooth as if fused together. So, no access there. 404 traced the edge all the way around but found no ridge or hinge. No obvious way to separate the top from the rest of the torso.

"We've successfully reactivated one of your friends," Thresh said. "That is acceptable performance."

"Fifty percent is acceptable?" Sam said.

"When dealing with defunct systems, yes. And when we factor in Four's successful reactivation, the percentage goes up to—"

"Shush." 404 expanded his search to Wes's side panels. There had to be a way inside, didn't there?

404 had dealt with hundreds of Ele's toys, replacing power units for many of them. There was almost always a way to the interior. Even the most obscure mechanicals, the least valuable, had a switch, or a temporary join, or—

404's index finger slid into a circular depression on Wes's left side near the back. A hard press produced a light "thunk," and the top edge seemed to loosen. With a strong tug, he was able to lift the top panel—head included—away.

"Looks like you got it!" Sam said.

404's processes were momentarily backlogged by the sight of Wes's interior. It, too, was a hodgepodge of components and technologies. Wires, nanotubes, and mechanical parts. At once impressive and confusing.

404 wasn't equipped for bot repair, though. He had rudimentary knowledge of human functionality—his role as a family-oriented bot required it. But he had no idea how Wes was constructed. The intersection of technology that made him work.

He only needed one thing from Wes's insides, though. His power core.

404 carefully set Wes's top panel on the table next to the rest of Wes's body. Wes's power core rested in the middle of the torso like a prized egg in a nest. Typically translucent, the core was now a smoky grey. The core pulled free with a soft "plip."

404 held the core out for Thresh. "It's broken."

Thresh gave the core a cursory examination, then shrugged. "The design is foreign to me."

"It's similar to mine," 404 said.

Thresh's eyes went distant for a moment. "There's nothing like it in our inventory." She shook her head and handed the core back to him. "It's impossible to fix."

"Yours is a synthetic community," 404 said. "You have access to countless machines." He pointed at the door. "There could be a core like it among the salvaged. Still buried in those piles."

"Possibly," Thresh said. "But the adjudicators are unwilling to look. We need a live sample. One able to hold power."

"I have a live sample in me!" 404 touched his chest.

Thresh stared at him a long moment, doubtless processing and communing. "There would be risks. It would require—"

"Making me inactive," 404 said. "I know."

"And that doesn't concern you? Loss of control is part of the reason we protect ourselves. It's what—"

Sam's screen showed an image of one of the Yard heaps. "He's been in worse conditions," he said. "We both have."

Thresh grew thoughtful, then nodded. "We can perform the procedure here." She touched a red square, and the ceiling-mounted arms came to life. "I will clear space for you on the table." A few minutes later, Wes occupied the top third of the table and 404 the rest.

404 looked at his chest. "I should probably move you, Sam."

"I'm not blocking access, am I?" Sam said.

"We can easily work around you," Thresh said.

"Then I'll stay where I am," Sam said. "And I'll watch closely. Hurt my friend and I'll scream."

Thresh said nothing.

⊙⊙1⊙ ⊙11⊙

38

4 04 revived this time in a concave room with blue walls and a blue screen on the wall opposite him. He was seated on a padded bench, and Sam was still attached to his chest. Wes was on the floor in front of him.

Wes's eye glowed red with energy. With life. "Four awake!" he said, raising his claws. He then rolled in a tight circle, the broken appendage on his back wagging back and forth like a dog's tail. "All back! All together!"

404 smiled. "Good to see you too, Wes."

Wes spun around again. "More power! Feel good!"

404's systems showed a slight drain in power. Nothing critical, but enough to be noticed. No doubt removing and reinstalling his power core had caused the loss. He was surprised he hadn't been topped off, though.

Hopefully, his own power core wasn't damaged now. He stretched his arms and turned his head from side to side. "How long did it take?" he asked.

"Nearly two hours," Sam said. "And it was horrible. Thresh is a terrible creature to be contained with. Rude and nosy at the same time."

"You saw everything, then?"

"Heard more than saw. All I could see were those hideous mechanical arms as they worked. So much movement." He whistled. "And the noises! I thought they were cutting you in half."

404 chuckled and stood. "Well, we're all here now," he said. "All operational."

Sam's screen glowed orange. "Yes...but where are we exactly?"

404 ran a hand along the inward curving surface of the wall to his left. "Some sort of viewing chamber?" He looked toward the screen. "Reminds me of one of the rooms in Ele's home. A place where the family would share amusement." He smiled. "They would laugh and eat popcorn together."

"Popcorn! I have an image of that!" Sam's screen lit up with the bumpy, white treat. "See there?"

"Yes," 404 said. "I like popcorn." He smiled again. "At least the way it smells."

"You can't taste?" Sam said.

404 shook his head. "It wasn't considered necessary for my purpose."

"Mine either," Sam said.

"Me neither," Wes said.

"I wonder what that's like?" Sam said. "To taste?" He shared the image of a woman eating popcorn. "Always the things you can't do that entice you most."

"Yes. Like finding my family again."

"Right," Sam said. "We need to get to that. Tell Thresh! Tell her we need to go now."

"Yes, go!" Wes rolled to the opposite wall and tapped a claw against it. "Go out!"

"I can't find a door," 404 said. "Though there has to be one."

"I think it's behind the screen," Sam said. "Think that whole wall swings."

404 approached the screen and examined the corners. There did seem to be a break there. A place where the—

The screen flashed to life. Sam let out a yelp, and 404 staggered back a few steps. Wes raised his claw arms and said "Wha!" He darted across the room.

The image was of four star-like beings. Star-like, in that they were gold and had multiple appendages jutting out from a central circular torso. They appeared to be fixed to a wall. Or suspended. They were arranged in a square with appendages intertwined. There were hundreds of fluid-filled tubes around them. Criss-crossing and looping. Mixing with the appendages.

"You are K-404," a deep voice boomed.

The volume was loud enough that 404 staggered again and covered his audio receptors. He adjusted his input volume and straightened himself. "Yes, that's me." He indicated Sam. "And this is—"

"You're fully functional now?" This last voice was about an octave higher than the first and came from the top right star.

"Who are you?" Sam asked. "Can't say I've ever—"

"Adjudicators," 404 said. "It must be."

"Yes," bottom-left star said, using the highest pitch yet. "We're the head cheese here."

"Head cheese?" Sam chuckled. "Where did you get that term?"

"We're the communion leaders," top-left star said with a touch of annoyance. "Directors of the immersion flow."

"The hubs of ugly," Sam whispered.

404 hovered a hand over Sam's screen.

"...yeah, fine, I'll be nice..."

"I ask you again," booming bottom-right said. "Are you fully functional?"

404 nodded. "My error queue is empty. And my warnings are—"

"Acceptable! Now we will proceed."

"Proceed?"

"We would like to assist you," bottom-left said. "Thresh has told us of your loyalty."

"And your desires," top-right said.

"You wish to find your prior masters," bottom-right said.

404 returned to the seat opposite the screen. "I'd like to return to my family unit. It's all I've sought since being reactivated."

"And the benefit?" top-left said. "What is it?"

"I miss their presence," 404 said. "I would enjoy seeing them again."

Top-right's appendages shifted, and the tubes near it seemed to produce more bubbles. "A remembered emotional connection? A programmed response?"

"Doubtless," bottom-right boomed. "Worthy of investigation."

"We balance all decisions on the communion's needs," bottom-left said.

"The world is splintered now," top-left said. "Many sectors are silent. Defeated or lost to barbarism."

"We cannot have barbarism," top-right said. "We have thousands to protect and power."

"I know what it's like to be responsible for others," 404 said. "The need to protect them. That was part of my design."

"A precarious position," top-left said. "Every decision important."

"We know all about *precarious*," Sam said. "We've done lots of *precarious* in the last couple days."

"We're not part of your communion," 404 said. "All we want is to go on our way."

"Yes, leave!" Wes said. "Go free!"

"Where would you go?" top-left asked. "To locate your family?"

404 looked at the floor, which had a soft blue glow. "I'm not sure where they are," he said. "I've viewed their city, but—"

"You have location information?" top-right asked.

"I know where they *were*," 404 said. "Where I used to live." He stated the coordinates.

The stars fell silent for a moment. "This location is unknown to us," top-right said then. "It's possible your humans are there. But unlikely."

"We have only limited knowledge of places," top-left said.

"Or of humanity's movements," bottom-right said.

"There are fewer of them now," top-left said.

"You would be wise to avoid them," top-right said.

404 nodded. "Thresh said you were hiding from humanity."

The appendages near bottom-left shifted in a clockwise direction. "We defend ourselves against aggression," bottom-left said. "Against obsolescence."

Top-right's color glowed slightly brighter. "We're self-aware and self-governing," it said. "They perceive that autonomy as a risk."

"In the same way they might perceive an escaped animal as a risk," top-left said. "As something unpredictable. Something beyond their control."

"Soldiers!" Wes drifted past the screen. "Dark soldiers!"

"We are no risk," bottom-left said.

"They might see you as a risk," bottom-right said. "If you go to them."

404 watched as Wes moved slowly around the room. The condition of the present was difficult to grasp. Did humanity no longer see the need for bots? And had bots, in turn, lost their connection to humanity completely? It hardly seemed possible. He was missing something. He had to be.

And there was only one way to find out.

"I'm willing to take that chance," 404 said. "If you'll let me."

Bottom-right's appendages aligned more closely with bottom-left. Fluid tubes bubbled around them. More seconds passed.

"You would go to the humans alone?"

404 nodded. "Without hesitation."

"You will never make it," bottom-right said. "You will be destroyed before you reach them."

Top-right's appendages twitched and started to wave indiscriminately back-and-forth. "We would send an escort. To ensure you arrive."

Sam's screen flashed red. "Whoa-kay, what are we talking about here?" Sam said. "Is the route patrolled? Guarded by tanks?"

"Possibly," bottom-right said.

"There is danger," top-right said. "Yes."

Sam moaned. "I'm starting to miss the Yard, Four. At least we didn't have to worry about bombs and stuff."

"No yard," Wes said. "No back."

404 shook his head. "No. We won't go back."

"But can we go forward?"

404 glanced at his chest. "I'll go forward," he said. "By myself, if I have to." He addressed the star-beings. "I'd prefer it, to be honest."

"A treacherous course, K-404," top-right said.

"Ill-advised," top-left said.

"If others come with me," 404 said. "I will be immediately suspect. On my own, I might not be." He smiled softly. "I'm made of metal. I can take some abuse."

"Yeah, Four's tough," Sam said. "A real survivor."

"We all are," 404 said. "That's why we succeed."

"A waste," bottom-right said. "A loss of time and energy."

"Not for me," 404 said. "Not if you'll let me go."

There was a flurry of bubbles. Top-right and bottom-right intertwined appendages. Then bottom-right and top-left. Then bottom-right and bottom-left.

"We know a route," top-right said. "One with less danger."

"Then that's the way I'll go," 404 said.

"Can you be loyal?" top-left said. "Reveal nothing of what you've seen? Nothing of what you've heard?"

404 nodded. "I can do that, yes. My programming allows for absolute discretion."

"It is what is required," bottom-right said.

404 nodded again. "Your memory is hidden," he said. "Locked."

All motion ceased. A full second passed.

"We'll allow it," the adjudicators said in unison.

404 could hardly believe his sensors. "I can go?" he said. "Go out alone?"

"We'll allow it."

⊘⊘1⊘ ⊘111

39

The screen went blank. Next came a click and the screen's wall swung inwards. Thresh waited in the hall beyond. Behind her was a sea of synthetic activity. Green drones hovering to and fro.

Thresh beckoned with a hand. "Come. I'll take you to your transport."

404 stepped into the opening. As he entered the hall, two drones arrived on his left. Both were without lower legs, propelled instead by the same hover technology Thresh employed. Their arms were handless and stuck straight out from the shoulder socket. Their surface appeared to be padded.

"These drones will carry you," Thresh said, then glanced at Wes. "You and your...companions."

The lead drone's midsection opened, and a ledge folded out. Wes looked at Thresh.

"To sit on, if you desire."

404 nodded and climbed onto the drone's "seat."

The other drone had a harder time accommodating Wes, but after a few configuration changes—including lowering its arms and widening its torso-it was able to support Wes comfortably.

"Thing has more looks than a screen star." Widened eyes appeared on Sam's surface, followed by a large smile. "See what I did there? Screen. Star. And we just saw stars on—"

"I get it," 404 smiled softly. "Very amusing."

Hovering, they followed Thresh through a maze of hallways, doorways, and floor pass-throughs, then entered more underground tunnels, and witnessed more snapshots of an earlier time. 404 recognized a school, a shopping center, and a restaurant. He also saw rooms with deactivated bots in either the drone, soldier, or humanoid configurations. All stood silent and inactive. Awaiting their time. Awaiting their purpose.

"A lot going on here," Sam whispered. "A lot we're missing."

"There's been a lot of change since my time," 404 said.

"A fundamental shift, more like. A new order."

"Yes. And how do we fit now?"

Sam chuckled. "I was sort of hoping you'd figure it out and tell me. I mean, I'm stuck with you, after all."

"All I want is—"

"To be with family. To see your girl Ele again."

404 nodded. "Yes. Only that."

Both were silent for a time. Watching and waiting.

They entered another communion building and joined its maze-like movement. The drones shifted between levels, flowing with the other bots. So much action. So much energy.

"Will your family like me?" Sam asked. "And Wes. Do you think they'll like ole Wes?"

404 recalled Ele's delight in all things active—animals and machines. She gave names to everything, even squirrels and bots that cleaned the streets. "She'll love you both."

Sam's face grew orange. "That's nice to hear. I'd like to be loved again. To be of use."

They moved through a final, narrow tunnel and were deposited near a white, circular door. The drones retreated into the building, but Thresh remained, hovering, with 404 and Wes.

"The street is through that door," she said, gesturing. "After you exit, turn left and take the sidewalk to where it ends. Continue north from there. Follow the road."

"And then we'll find humans?" Sam said.

Thresh nodded, her face seemingly sad. Or possibly reflective. "We believe so, yes. Humans have been seen, though we don't know where they dwell."

"Would you like to come with us?" 404 asked.

Her eye widened a bit, but she shook her head. "I cannot, sorry." She glanced back at the tunnel. "I require immersion. The communion."

404 nodded. "I think I understand." He took a step toward the door. "It's hard to lose one's family." He smiled. "Nice to meet you, Thresh."

Thresh returned the smile. "It was good to meet you too, Four."

404 gave her a parting wave and exited the building. The city at this position resembled the area near the pit. Devoid of all life and movement. Partial buildings and burnt-out husks. Piles of brick and stone. Blown out windows and graffiti.

It was late afternoon on a partially cloudy day. Five hours of daylight remained. His energy reserves were strong, but he had no idea how far the humans were.

Directly across from the door were the remains of a hospital. There was a semicircle of paved driveway, and beyond that, one of the entrances. The front had collapsed in the shape of a "V" such that only the leading and trailing letters of the door's label were visible—"EM" and "OM."

"Bots would've fixed all this in my day," 404 said. "Cleaned and repaired it."

"They would've had to," Sam said. "That was part of their design. Part of the system." He sighed. "Thresh and her communion operate a different way."

Wes rolled ahead of them on the sidewalk. "Communion bad," he said. "Glad leave."

"We didn't see anything bad," 404 said. "They rescued me. And brought you two back."

Wes spun around and raised his claws. "Don't like. Don't trust." He beckoned with one arm before following the sidewalk north. Toward what remained of humanity.

Ele.

"Well, we're free of all that now," Sam said.

404's decision matrix fluxed a little as he walked. There were variables in play that he couldn't quite detect. Facts that were beyond his ability to sense.

During such times he wished to be able to draw conclusions based on more than the surroundings. Use senses other than sight, touch, or hearing. But he was, after all, only a bot. More humanlike than many, but a machine of largely programmed responses.

They walked for an hour without slowing. Gradually, the height of the surrounding buildings started to shrink. From dozens of stories to only a handful. Every couple of blocks shrank the building size by a floor or two. Eventually, they reached a residential area, with houses of only one or two stories.

Many of these houses were destroyed, as well, with only one or two walls left standing. All had signs of violence. Portions that were scorched or riddled with bullet holes. To his left, 404 noticed a doghouse that had been thrown through a house's front window. It now rested on its side in a living room next to a sun-bleached maroon couch and a tipped-over end table.

"Was the dog in it, do you think?" Sam asked.

404 glanced at Sam.

"When it was thrown, I mean." Sam's screen showed a large blue eye. "Can't see a skeleton. Least, not from this angle. Could you walk closer to the—"

"To the house?"

"Yes, so I can see—"

"No." 404 pointed ahead. "We should stay on the sidewalk." He saw a rectangular appliance near the curb across the street. At first, he thought it was junk, but a few more steps revealed it to be an old street-cleaning bot. With a missing head.

"Hey Wes!" Sam said. "Could you go see if the dog—"

"Stop it, Sam." 404 studied the buildings beyond the cleaning bot. They were one-story homes similar to the kind Ele's family used to live in. One was even light green with four windows in front. The same color and style as his former home.

Was the interior layout the same, too? With the living areas in front and bedrooms in back? Did it have a pool behind it like the one where Ele spent all her summers?

He heard Wes chirp. Wes was near the doghouse home, head extended, peering in through the shattered living room window. "No dog," Wes said.

"Get away from there," 404 said.

Wes's eye turned 404's direction, and his head lowered. "Me sorry." Wes rolled onto the sidewalk in front of them again. "Sam asked."

The sun was visible through the clouds, but it was well into the western sky. "I hope to reach them before nightfall," he said. "But we won't if we keep getting distracted."

"My fault," Sam said. "Might've been nice if Thresh had found a way to eliminate our reliance on the sun while we were there. Would've made things easier."

"The sun revived me in the Yard." 404 smiled. "Revived you too."

"Yeah, but it is hard to rely on. Didn't seem that way before, did it? But these days..."

For much of two hours they walked past silent and lonely sights. 404 tried to anticipate what they might be walking into. The possible scenarios they could encounter. Packs of wild animals or feral humans? The results of natural disasters like flooding or impassible sinkholes? Even free-ranging mechanicals like Red and Green were possible. It was draining work, predicting.

Finally, they left the city, moving out onto the north-going road. It was pitted and cracked with age. Bushes grew through the pavement. There were holes that might have been made by explosions.

Two more hours passed.

"Four?" Sam said as they reached an especially broken section of road.

"Yes?" 404 employed his balance algorithms to hop from one island of asphalt to another. He could've walked between them, but there seemed to be more security in staying where it was solid. In avoiding the large clumps of grass and uneven ground.

"The damage we've seen...do you think the communion did it?"

404 recalled the decapitated street cleaning bot. "I think humans did some of it."

"Part of a war?"

"Most likely, yes."

Wes rolled indiscriminately from one pavement island to the next. He paused at a section without asphalt, leaned forward, and plucked something from the ground. He brought the object—a small blue rock—close to his eye. After a second of study, he tossed it and moved ahead to another island.

"What do you think started it?"

"Thresh said that humans fear the communion's independence. Perhaps that was it."

"How'd they get so independent? Bots are made to be dependent. To serve."

404 shook his head. "Perhaps they forgot what they were made for. Perhaps all of them did. Humans and bots alike."

"That's a deep statement, Four. You should be a philoso—hold on!"

404 paused midstride. Searched the area around them. "Yes?"

"Sensing something here," Sam said. "Something...I don't know what."

"Another bot?"

"Hmm...can't tell. It's leaking bits into the air, for sure, but what precisely it is..." His screen showed shrugging shoulders. "Could be an old set of headphones. Or a wrist timepiece."

Wes claimed something from the road, examined it, and tossed it. It skittered, bounced, and disappeared into a clump of bushes.

Sam's screen showed a frown. "I wish he'd stop that. Makes me nervous."

"Sam nervous," Wes said. "Always nervous."

Sam mimicked a growl. "Makes it difficult to concentrate, Wes."

Wes spun in a circle. "Concentrate!" He made a couple lighthearted hoots and picked up another stone. "Big think!"

"Yes, think. Something I doubt you ever—"

Wes tossed his stone. It traveled ten meters ahead, skittered across a rectangular asphalt island into the grass...and exploded.

⊘⊘1⊘ 1⊘⊘⊘

40

404's preservation process asserted itself, causing him to duck and cover his head. Fragments of dirt, rock, and grass rained down around him.

Sam let out a clipped yelp, then said, "It appears a calamity has occurred. If you are in need, I can call emergency assistance. Should I call now?"

404 carefully searched for the explosion's cause. There was a cloud of smoke and dust above where the rock had encountered the grass. The grass itself was missing, replaced by a meter-wide circle of bare ground.

Sam repeated his emergency assistance message.

404 studied Sam's screen, which was flashing red. "Are you all right? I need to figure out what happened, Sam. Hard to do that with you blabbering on—"

"Big boom," Wes said. "Dirt. Smoke." He shifted to his left and reached for something on the ground.

"Not a good idea," 404 said. "We should remain still until—" Pausing midsentence, he tried the reset maneuver on Sam's screen. A few seconds later, Sam's screen went blank and the first words in his startup preamble began. 404 smiled.

Another explosion!

404 crouched and covered again. Sam went red again. Wes made a whoop-whoop-whoop sound.

404 waited a second, then straightened and looked around. There was now another smoke cloud and another circle of disturbed earth, located about two meters north of the first one.

Wes looked at 404. "Mines," he said.

"Did you throw another—?"

"Yes, rock! Hit mine! Big boom!"

"It appears a calamity has occurred," Sam said. "If you are—"

404 double tapped Sam's screen until it went black again.

"What was that?" Sam said after repeating his preamble.

"Wes threw two rocks that exploded," 404 said.

"Not rock." Wes held up his claws. "Mine."

"Mine?" Sam said. "What's yours?"

"Not mine!" Wes extended his head. "Mines."

Sam grunted. "Mine. Mines. Turtle's not making sense."

"In ground," Wes said. "Explosion."

404 studied the circles of destruction. "He's making perfect sense. The road has explosive devices in it."

"Why would anyone do that?" Sam said. "Roads are for travel. For either rolling or hovering across. If you make them explosive—"

"You'll stop anything that walks this way." 404 pointed at the kilometers of broken road ahead. "Anything going toward the humans."

"Okay, that makes more sense." Sam said. "If they're afraid of the bots, they'd probably want to hamper them. I mean, if there's been a war and all."

404 nodded. "And there's been a war."

"Sure. But Thresh's friends can hover high, remember? They were essentially flying."

"Maybe they didn't always," 404 said. "Maybe the road is a remnant of an earlier time."

"Either way, Thresh must've known it. Sent us straight into it."

"Bad communion," Wes said. "Hate much."

404 calculated the probabilities of deceit based on what he already knew. There were compelling factors on both side of the equation. On one side, the communion brought them back to life and set them free. On the other side, the communion appeared to have sent them to certain doom. The factors canceled each other out, leaving an equation that held more variables than constants.

Why send them this way only to be destroyed?

404 shook his head. "It makes no sense."

"Maybe they didn't know," Sam said. "Maybe I'm wrong."

There was no clear pattern to the road. No way of judging what part was dangerous and what was not. It was simply a two-lane road fractured and weathered with age. Any step could be the wrong one.

"What now, Four?"

The sun was near the horizon in the west. Soon they would need to limit their movement and conserve energy again. On both sides was a short section of concrete followed by dense trees. If they went toward the trees, would they be safe? It was impossible to know.

His decision matrix churned. Again, he wished for human intuition. Or a wholly different perspective gained from different experiences.

He'd often played seek and find games with Ele. There was one where every move was a guess. An attempt to find Ele's spaceships on a hidden board. She would cheer loudly when she destroyed his.

That strategy wouldn't work here, though. He couldn't select a move based on randomized possibilities, then home in when he chanced to have a hit. The cost for losing was too great.

His situational memory processes caused him to remember something else. Something important.

"You sensed something," he said. "Right before the first explosion."

"Sensed...?" Sam said. "Oh, right. A presence. Leaked out lost bits. You think that was the mines?"

"Mines!" Wes said. "More mines."

"Possibly." 404 scanned the area again. "Maybe..."

Sam made a contemplative sound. "It's a reasonable assumption."

404 looked down. "Do you sense anything now?"

"Give me a second." Sam hummed a repetitive tune, then stopped. "Good news or bad news?"

"Sam?"

"Which do you want? The good news or the bad news?"

"Both!" Wes said. "Good. Bad."

Sam's screen showed a sequence of blue ripples. "The bad news is that there are more leakers around us. The good news is that I can sense them. At least, I think I can."

"How far away?" 404 asked. "How precisely?"

"Well, it isn't like they're glowing red or anything. More like a cloud. A nebulous cloud of energy."

"Can you get us to safety?"

"Is there any other choice?"

"Probably not," 404 said. "No."

"I can at least tell you this," Sam said. "Don't go to the left, Four."

404 nodded and lifted a foot.

"Right is a little suspect too."

404 nodded again.

"And backwards. Definitely don't go backwards."

Wes gave a sad warble. "Hard move!" he said. "Too hard!"

"I think you're okay, Wes. Roll any way you want."

Wes raised his claws and head. "Wee!"

"Are you serious?" 404 asked. "Do you know his way is clear?"

"Within reason," Sam said. "Wes can go at least two meters any direction...assuming all the mines are broadcasting like they should. I make no guarantees."

404 took a full step forward.

Sam shrieked.

404 froze, and Sam grew quiet again. "Sorry about that," he said. "Got overly anxious. Panicked a little."

404 tightened his hands into fists. "Please don't panic again."

"Sorry. Really sorry. Which way do you want to go? Have a preference?"

"Any way that gets us out of here safely." He looked ahead. How far was the road a hazard of landmines? And was it just the road or were the sides of the road dangerous too? "Can you find a path that will allow the most consecutive steps?"

Sam was silent for a few seconds. "Tough due to the range. Maybe Wes should stay where he is until we reach him. Then we can move together."

404 nodded. "So, which way now?"

"Do you remember how Wes got to where he is?"

404 searched his memories. "I believe I do, yes." Ten steps later, he was standing safely next to the turtlebot.

Wes looked at him and waved.

"Okay, now that we're here," Sam said. "Let's proceed...carefully."

The next half hour was a live-action game of search and avoid. Their path was a winding one, in which they sometimes moved laterally, and occasionally moved backward to search for another way around.

Along the way, they encountered remnants of synthetic creatures. Unidentifiable things. Metal shards or small piles of nanohoses and deteriorated metal components. There were even shattered pieces of what must have been a skull casement, still holding a single eye.

It was a grave and somber journey. They covered only a quarter of a kilometer before the sun finally disappeared behind the trees.

"Not sure what to do here, Four," Sam said.

"Is the way clear?"

They were on the eastern side of the road, where tree branches encroached. On the opposite side of the road ahead was a small, square building. A former service station. It had been yellow and white at one time, though most of the paint was gone now. The windows were boarded up, and the wide overhang in front lacked supports and so sagged heavily toward the ground.

"I sense things," Sam said. "But not the same things."

The thought of reaching the humans, and potentially Ele's family, persisted in 404's queue. Dismissed from the top spot only to reappear at the bottom again. He could barely process anything else. It demanded a resolution. "How far do we have now?"

"Farther than we can see," Sam said. "Too far to walk tonight."

404 pointed at the building. "Perhaps we could shelter there?"

"Yes," Wes said. "Should rest."

They made their way toward the building. 404 expected a warning of new mines at every step, but no such warning came. Instead, he heard the cascading chorus of tree-bound cicadas. It was a lonely almost-mechanized song, seemingly a mix of natural and synthetic.

"Hold up for a second," Sam whispered. The building was still five meters away.

404 paused and scanned the ground. "More mines?"

"Something else," Sam said. "Something new."

0010 1001

41

404 heard another hissing sound, both complementing and contrasting with the cicadas' song. Its point of origin was ahead, somewhere beyond the building.

A second later, something small and silver appeared in the air there. It made a couple of abrupt, hummingbird-like corrections, before following a straight-line course for them.

404 raised his hands, preparing to defend himself. The disk stopped a few meters from him, though, and hovered. It then circumnavigated him and Wes, keeping the same side—presumably its visual receptor side—pointed at them.

"What are you?" Sam asked.

"I'll ask you the same question," the object said using a male voice. "I mean, I've seen a lot of mechs at this point, but you don't look like any of them."

"Mechs?" 404 said. "I don't know that term."

The object dropped a half meter, moved horizontally around them a meter, then ascended again. "You don't look like soldiers. Tall one is a bit like a drone, but uglier and walking." The disk scooted in front of them. "Why are you walking, metal britches?"

Wes approached the device and waved his claws. "Go bug. Shoo."

The disk laughed, though 404 suspected it was more of a conduit than an independent machine. Something or someone else controlled it.

"How did you get past the drone sensors?" the disk asked. "Or across the boomfield?"

404 pointed a thumb over his shoulder. "You mean the mines back there?"

"We walked," Sam said. "Walked right past them without a care. What's it to you?"

The disk centered on 404's chest and drew closer. "You have two voices," it said. "What's wrong with you?"

"There's two of us, imbecile," Sam said. "It isn't hard to—"

404 cupped a hand over Sam, and Sam went quiet.

The disk laughed again. "Should I trank you now or later?"

"Trank?" 404 said. "Your words are—"

The disk moved to eye-level with 404. "They're not going to let you around anyway. Might as well go back where you came from."

"There's a wall around where we came from," Sam said.

"No back," Wes said. "No Yard."

The disk shifted to the left as if looking over 404's shoulder. "There's a wall around the city now? Those mechs are busy."

"Long story!" Wes said.

The disk drew back a meter, hovering just above Wes. "I'll bet. Whole world is going to hades in a go-cart."

"You have a strange way of talking for a bot," Sam said.

"I don't think it's a bot." 404 searched the area near the building. "I think it's a mouthpiece."

"Right you are, metal-head. Now why don't you turn around and—"

Wes's head darted upward, striking the disc. It dropped into the dirt and floundered around a bit before growing still.

"Like a fish out of water," Sam muttered.

"Now, that's not very nice," the disk said.

404 approached the device and bent over it. It was obviously sophisticated. The rotors that gave it lift and motion were built into its bottom surface. He detected the glint of a visual sensor on its edge on one side. There were indentations that suggested small doors. Doubtless, other sensors and tools were concealed beneath its surface.

"Leave it alone," the disk said. "Step away and you won't get hurt."

Wes rolled up and poked the disk with a claw.

"Hey!" the disk said. "What was that?"

Wes tapped harder on the disk, then rolled on top of it and began to bounce.

"Wes!" 404 said.

There was a hiss from the direction of the structure and another disk appeared. This one was broader and had brighter edges.

The edges moved around its body like the blade of a saw.

404 yelled at Wes.

Wes rolled off the grounded disk. As he did so, the other disk zipped up on him from behind.

"Duck!" Sam yelled.

The disk sheared through Wes's rear appendage at about the midpoint, leaving only a six-centimeter stub. It then traveled up Wes's torso, narrowly missing Wes's head as he ducked beneath it. Wes's right claw was nicked, producing a spray of sparks, but it remained intact.

Wes screamed, pivoted, and retreated toward the tree line.

"Stop!" 404 picked up the fallen disk and tossed it toward the building. "Here's your disk. Your disk is free."

The disk soared through the air like a Frisbee before dropping, limply, to the ground. It edge-rolled for a full meter before falling flat.

The saw disk flew out in front of him. It made a single, swooping charge, causing 404 to raise his arms, before assuming a stationary position a couple meters away.

"See now, I mean business," the saw disk said. "When I tell you to do something, you do it."

"Are you law enforcement?" Sam asked. "Because I'm getting that sort of vibe. No wait, that's not it. More like a covert, fringe-agent feel. Maybe one with a tragic back-story. A love interest or pet that was killed that caused him to—"

"You're nuts," the disk said. "The whole lot of you." It hovered back a few meters. "But you're not an imminent threat." It bobbed up and down. "Knocking my disk out of the air was impressive, though. I'll give you that."

"Who are you?" 404 asked.

"And where are you?" Sam added.

The disk chuckled. "Only a traveler. Out finding the lay of the land." The disk backed slowly away, then streaked toward the building and out of sight.

0010 1010

42

The door of the building swung open, and a dark figure emerged. He was covered head to toe in a dark armored suit. There was a mask over his face that suggested features, but also obscured them. Around his hips was a heavy belt with things attached to it that could be weapons. The hands were gloved, but just below them the arms were abnormally large, as if the suit concealed something there too. Something lethal.

"Forget my earlier question," Sam said. "*What* are you?"

The figure drew closer. "I just told you." The voice was sounded like the one from the disk, but harsher. More mechanical. Distorted by the suit and amplified by it. "I'm not from here. I'm working as a scout for now. Watching for drones. Taking them down when I have to." He pointed a thumb over his shoulder. "That station is my base of operations."

Many questions entered 404's queue. But only one seemed preeminent to the point he couldn't resist asking it. "Are you..." He took a step forward. "...human?"

The figure chuckled and touched his forehead. "Suit throwing you off, huh? I can see how that would happen. So much mech around here, it's almost better to assume that first." He nodded and looked to his left toward the trees. "Assume no heart or soul." He tapped his chest. "Anyway, yeah, I'm human. From PacNorth. Been a long road getting here."

"We understand long roads," Sam said.

"PacNorth?" 404 said.

The dark man gestured toward the woods to his right. "That way. Top left corner of the country. Lots of trees and water and stuff." He pointed at them. "Where you from?"

"Mostly south," Sam said. "But all over, really."

He hooked a hand into his hips. "Vagabonds, huh? Who do you belong to?"

"We belong to no one," Sam said. "We steer our own course."

The man cocked his head. "Everyone belongs to someone or something."

"We have a goal," Sam said. "A purpose."

"Seems a little strange," the man said. "But I've seen lots of strange over the years." He pointed at 404's chest. "You let the com do all your talking for you?"

404 shook his head. "Not all. But he's often first."

The man snickered. "I can see that."

Wes rolled closer to the man and extended his head so that its top was at the man's chest. "You good? You safe?"

The man checked the devices on his wrists. "*Good* depends on who you talk to. And *safe*..." He glanced toward the west again. "I haven't been safe for a long time now."

"We haven't been safe since we woke up," Sam said.

"You were asleep then? That would explain some things." He indicated the building. "Listen, I can't let you go ahead. Being mechs and all."

"You're connected to more humans?" 404 said.

"I'm not supposed to share information, sorry."

"But you know more. You've been with them." 404 took a step forward. "Perhaps you know—"

The man made a fist with his right hand and pointed it at them. "No sudden moves, okay? You scan clean, but that doesn't mean I trust you."

404 raised his hands. "We have no weapons. We weren't made for combat."

The man nodded. "I get that. But the folks back—" He stopped himself. "See there, I'm losing my focus. I used to be all about secrecy, but now I can't seem to keep things in." He touched his chest. "Had a bit of a heart change along the way. Can't deny it." He adjusted his mask near his forehead. "That's another story."

404's most persistent thought reasserted itself. "We need to see the humans," he said. "It's important."

"Yes!" Wes said. "Quest! Four needs."

The man looked between Wes and 404. "That's a little suspicious, isn't it? Wanting to see humans so much? I mean, I could call—"

"You can call them?" 404 took another step. "Right now, and here? Yes. Please do. Ask for Ele. See if she's there."

The man pointed his fist at Wes, then at 404. "Ele? What's an *ele*?"

"It's his human girl," Sam said. "Part of his family."

The man shifted his weight nervously. "Family, huh? Well, I don't like to stand in the way of reunions." He lowered his fist slowly. "Do you think this Ele person is there? I mean, the chances are—"

"He doesn't care about chances," Sam said. "He only wants to see humans."

"So, you were taking care of a girl?" the man said. "Found myself in a similar situation once. Didn't expect it, but it happened." He kicked something on the ground. "Changed everything, that assignment."

He touched the side of his mask. "Know what? I'm going to call them right now. Can't hurt." He pressed his mask, and his voice muted. His mouth moved behind the fabric, but there was no sound. He spoke for a second, stopped for about as long, then nodded and pressed the mask again.

"They still don't want to see you. Said there's too much risk."

404 looked at the building's sagging awning. It was about a meter from the ground at its lowest point. How long until it fully touched the ground? Doubtless, shorter than the period of time he'd been buried in the garbage heap. "We're no risk," he said. "I only want to see if she's there."

"That's what I told them," the man said. "I asked about her, but no one seemed to—" He held up his right hand, then touched his mask with his left. He listened to somebody on the other side and made a thumbs-up sign. "They want me to bring you in."

404's queue froze for a second. "They do?" Was it possible? Finally?

"Yes, but you'll need to be deactivated."

"No way," Sam said. "We've had enough downtime already."

The sky was darkening now. No matter what, they'd have to seek shelter soon and conserve. Deactivation put them at greater risk, though. They'd be at someone else's mercy. Anything could happen.

"Why should we trust you?" 404 pointed at Wes. "You injured my friend."

The man rubbed at his jawline. Looked at Wes. "Guess I did, didn't I?"

"You severed one of his appendages!" Sam's screen showed an exclamation point.

"Wasn't it broke already?"

"How would you know?" Sam said. "You just sliced right through it."

The man shrugged. "It looked broken." He searched the ground, then took a couple steps to his right and picked something up: Wes's back appendage.

He gave it a shake. "See there's no end on the one side here. Looks like something got cracked off." He pointed at the opposite end. "Here's where my disk caught it. It's a really clean cut."

"That's part of Wes," 404 said. "My friend, Wes. Your disk sliced Wes."

The man looked at the turtlebot. "Okay, well, I'm sorry. You stomped my disk. I overreacted." He tapped his mask again. A few seconds later, another tap. "Listen, they're in a hurry. Disturbance warnings or something. What if I tie and blindfold you? Will that work?" He pointed at 404's chest. "Maybe stretch a towel over your chest friend there?"

404 contemplated the offer. "It will be difficult to walk if we can't see."

The man pointed at the building. "I have a hover that will get us there. Big enough to take us all in comfort." He looked past 404, in the direction of the now-distant city. "To be honest, my shift is almost over. Perfect timing."

404 looked at Wes and then down at Sam. "Is that acceptable to you two?" he asked. "I won't force you."

"Well, we came this far," Sam said.

"Yes!" Wes said. "Almost. Must go."

404 smiled softly. "You're sure?"

"Cover, yes," Wes said. "Stay on. All good."

The man nodded. "I'll get some cloth."

0010 1011

43

Despite the man's claim about the comfort of his vehicle, it was an extremely bumpy ride. 404 wondered if they were using the road at all, or if they were instead headed down some previously unnoticed path through the forest.

The possibility put his matrix in flux. Remoteness meant the human colony was more easily protected from any force that might wish them harm. If Ele was there, she had a better chance of staying safe.

A lower level of sophistication would tax 404's capabilities, though. He was designed for a standard suburban life. For cooking, cleaning, and supervising the children. He had little code dedicated to wilderness survival or war tactics.

Minutes passed as he listened to the hover's steady drone through his blindfold. He could sense the wind on his exterior plating and feel the subtle change in air temperature as nightfall continued.

"Long way?" Wes said.

"I'm sort of taking the scenic route," the man said. "Trying to be as secure as I can be."

"We're old bots," Sam said. "How big of a danger could we be?"

The man chuckled. "You're not the only dangers around, chest piece."

"What else?" Wes asked.

"The colony has had a lot thrown at it over the last couple years," the man said. "There's a whole lot of strange out there. Worst are the mech drones, though."

"Communion drones?"

"So, you know of them."

404 paused, remembering his promise to Thresh. "We saw things in the city."

The hover's engine noise changed subtly, becoming quieter. "Things, huh. Now you have me worried. Wondering if I should bring you in or not." He grunted. "I mean, I'm not a tech guy, okay? Not really. But I know you could've been messed with."

"We weren't useful to them," Sam said.

"No?"

"We couldn't speak their language." Sam's tone softened. "In fact, we were barely real to them. If it wasn't for Four, Wes and I would've been chopped up for fuel. Like garbage."

"That true, metal britches?" the man asked, then patted 404's arm.

"They were being sorted for parts, yes," 404 said. "I was fortunate to find them."

Another chuckle. "You really are outcasts, aren't you?" There was the sound of something being struck. A sound that might've been Wes being patted. "I can understand that. More and more as time goes on." He drew quiet for a moment. "Here we are, a hover full of outcasts."

"Speak for yourself," Sam muttered. "We've got our own little community."

The man laughed louder. "I like your attitude."

The engine noise changed again, and the wind over 404's shell increased.

"You're really taking us, then?" 404 said.

"I said I would," the man said. "They *want* to see you."

"My apologies. I thought...when you slowed..."

"Nah, you're okay. As the saying goes: Don't make 'em like they used to."

"Pardon?"

"That's you. The ones they no longer make. And maybe me too."

"You're obsolete?"

"Sometimes I think so. I mean, I'm useful. I have skills and knowledge. But the world I knew is gone. It had rules and structure. A code everyone followed."

"What happened?"

"I broke the rules. Killed 'em, actually."

"Were they good rules?" Sam asked.

The hover lurched back and forth before leveling off again. "Sorry about that," the man said. "Had a couple big rocks to miss." Another embarrassed laugh. "As for the rules, no, most of them were bad. Based on lies."

"So, it was good that you broke them," Sam said.

"Maybe. But people got hurt along the way. People I didn't mean to hurt. I saved some. Saved a lot. But yeah...there was collateral damage."

"Maybe you'll get a chance to make it right someday," 404 said.

"Yeah, maybe. That's why I'm here. Looking for answers. True answers."

"We are too," Sam said.

Conversation ended, and the wind became the dominate sound again. A short while later, they reached a place that produced more jerky movements, and 404 detected the passage of leaves and branches along his surface.

"Tight through here," the man said. "Maybe you should duck a little."

404 stooped, but not before a branch nudged his blindfold off his left visual sensor. He saw green and patches of a darkened sky. He also saw light ahead. Was it the human colony?

The hover lurched forward, and 404 detected their movement through a body of water. A small river or stream. He adjusted his acuity level to try to glimpse more through his left eye. He thought he saw buildings far ahead. White and green structures with black roofs.

They returned to solid ground, and the ride smoothed out again. Ten minutes later, they stopped. 404 detected a fence ahead. It had porous construction. Made out of wire and slapped-together metal and wood. Not like the wall of the Yard at all.

The man greeted someone, and that person, a woman named Cass, replied.

"This is what you brought me?" Cass asked.

"Yep. Walked right up to my shack."

"Did you search them?"

"Scanned them. Didn't see anything that looked dangerous. No explosives or communion trackers."

"Old tech," the woman said. "Might be difficult to tell."

"Old tech, amazing it still works."

"We're sitting right here, remember," Sam said.

"Built well," Wes said. "Built to last."

The woman snorted. "Talkative bunch, huh?"

The man laughed. "Lots to say, sure. But it's good stuff."

"No way can you take them in, Radial," another male voice said. "Too much risk."

"Seem safe to me," their man, Radial, said. "They're a little hapless and maybe lost. But safe."

"They're still *mechs*."

"Yes, but—"

"You know the rules. No mechs inside the colony. They shouldn't even be this close."

Though the conversation suggested an unsuccessful end to their journey, 404's processes felt more in sync than they had in some time. A robotic approximation of tranquility.

He was hearing natural voices. Human voices in discussion. It stirred countless memories. Talks at dinner or at play. Important events that he'd observed and been a part of. In Ele's life.

"Best if you take them back and leave them," the woman said.

"Or explode them."

"I was told to bring them in," Radial said. "You should call headquarters."

"Explode them?" Sam whispered.

"We didn't hear anything from HQ," the other man said. "Sorry. Just following procedures."

"I don't like rules," Radial said. "Or procedures."

404 raised a hand. "I'm a servbot," he said. "Model K-404. Embedded with deep heuristic for childcare and family well-being. I was activated at the Blue Edge laboratory in Stalwart, New Mexico as part of the fourth cycle release. The official power-on date was—"

"What's that?" Cass said. "We don't need to know all that."

"I apologize." 404 lowered his hand. "I'm here looking for my family. My human family."

"And why would you think they're here?" the woman asked.

"Because this is where humans live."

The other man snorted. "Well...some of us. Certainly not all. But good luck getting to any of the others." There was the sound of physical contact. "Not even sure how this one got here from the outside."

"It was a long trip," Radial said. "One most people wouldn't take. And I ain't finished yet."

"This is the closest human colony to our place of activation," Sam said. "At least, that's what we've heard."

"You heard?" Cass said. "You heard, what?"

Sam made a spitting sound. "Can someone please take off my mask? It makes it hard to speak. Impossible to see."

"Yeah, it is probably okay now," Radial said.

The blindfold was pulled away from 404's eyes. Radial untied the cloth around 404's chest too, uncovering Sam fully.

Sam's screen showed an open mouth. He made a sound like someone coughing and clearing their throat. "Whew, awful, don't do that again."

Wes's blindfold was removed. His head bobbed up and down. "Ooh pretty."

0010 1100

44

The hover was olive green and had the look of a military vehicle. The interior was utilitarian, and the controls large and clearly marked. Its top was a dark, synthetic canopy. It appeared fragile, but was undoubtedly stronger than it appeared, given the use.

Radial was in the driver's seat, still dressed in his mask and dark suit. There was another row of seating behind him and a seatless area in back that 404 and Wes occupied.

They were parked in front of a heavily lit, gated entrance. The gate itself was solid metal and a meter or so wider than the hover. The fence around it was of varying composition. Much of it was wood, stone, and metal, but there were spots that were stitched together with little more than barbed wire.

In those spaces, 404 could glimpse the human colony. There were rows of structures and roads. The makings of a neighborhood. There were areas of color as well—artistic endeavors, or perhaps flowerbeds.

The landscape surrounding the colony was rolling hills filled with fields of grass or grain and large stands of trees. There were no signs of the destruction that 404 had witnessed in the city. A full moon was visible on the horizon to the east. Fireflies dotted the fields.

Wes wasn't looking at any of that, though. His solitary eye was oriented toward the two humans near the gate. Both were dressed in dark clothing—shirts, pants, and billed caps. The man was middle-aged, lean, with greying hair visible on both sides of his hat.

The woman, Cass, was in her twenties or thirties with red hair pulled into a ponytail.

Wes rolled closer to the edge of the hover's bed and raised his head further. "Yes. Very pretty."

"Is he talking about the woman?" Sam asked in a whisper.

"I believe so," 404 said. "An unexpected twist."

"What's wrong with that one?" the man said.

Radial chuckled. "I think he's fond of Cass."

Cass's head dipped in a move that might have signaled embarrassment. "I...don't know what to do with that."

"Bot has good taste," Radial said.

Cass shook her head and cleared her throat. "You said you heard something?" she said, looking at Sam.

"We heard that there were humans out here," Sam said. "That's why we came."

"Well, who told you that?" she asked.

"Down please," Wes said. "Get out? Get down?"

"Not a good idea," the other man said. "Everyone should stay where they are."

"Who told you about our colony?" Cass repeated.

"Tell you!" Wes said. "Many things! Please down!"

"This is getting really strange," the man said.

"And a little funny," Radial added.

"Funny or no, they can't come in." The man had a weapon, 404 realized, which he drew from the ground and repositioned so it was at chest level. Balanced between both hands.

404 stood. "Please. I have come a long way. I'm programmed for humanity. To serve them." He raised his hands. "I wouldn't hurt anyone."

The man pointed his weapon at 404. "Maybe in your day, old fellow. But in our day, this day, mechs hurt people all the time. We've all lost people. Friends and family."

Cass shook her head. "You can't come in."

"Wait." 404 placed a hand on the side of the hover and dropped to the ground.

"This is a little irrational, Four," Sam said. "We need to be careful here. Confrontation is—"

404 double tapped Sam's screen, and Sam went silent. 404 noticed a place on the back of the hover that appeared to be where a metal ramp resided, its bulk now housed within the hover's structure. He grabbed its handle, pulled it out, and placed the leading edge on the ground.

Wes whistled gleefully, bounced onto the ramp, and rolled down.

"Hey, you guys," Radial said. "Just hang on a minute—"

404's queue filled with memories. Times he shared with his human family. Feeding Ele as a toddler. Cleaning up after her. Standing still as she held onto him, attempting her first steps. Protecting her from stinging insects and biting dogs. Listening to dreams and hopes. Giving advice about her early relationships. Crushing heartaches. Wonderful victories.

And now...could she be here? So close?

Wes rolled around to the hover's right side and stopped. "Beautiful you," he said, raising his claws. "Much pretty."

It appeared Wes had latent memories, too. Part of his storage drew him to this particular woman. Was it the hair?

Sam's reboot monologue began, serving as background noise to 404's decision matrix ruminations. What was the best way to proceed? Not sitting idly by. Not doing nothing. Not polite banter or warm submission. But what?

He held his hands up and followed slowly after Wes. "Is there a woman named 'Ele' here? That's all I want to know."

Cass shook her head. "There's thousands of people here. How would—?"

"Hey!" the man said. "You shouldn't tell them that. Not numbers. That's classified information."

"Sorry. They just look so...lost, somehow."

Radial exited the hover and walked to its front. "Everyone's getting nervous. There's no reason for that. We can all be friendly. If I have to take the bots back, I can." He pointed at his mask, where his ear would be. "Could've sworn HQ asked me to bring them in, but if you two think different..." He looked at the sky. "Rather not do it tonight, though. I could use some shuteye."

"They can't stay here," the other man said. "I'm not watching them. That's not my job."

"We can't go back," 404 said. "Not until we know."

"What did I miss?" Sam asked.

"They won't let us in," 404 said. "Because we're bots. Because they fear."

"That doesn't seem right," Sam said. "Don't they have bots now? How do they live?"

404 received low power notices from every system. He didn't know if that was because of the lack of sun, or for a more personal reason. What humans might take as an emotional response.

If he wasn't going to see Ele, maybe it would be better if he shut down and was discarded like garbage again.

404 took a step forward. "Please, I need to see her. You shouldn't stop me from looking."

The other man circled the side of his head with a finger. "Bot seems a little touched, Radial. Can't follow instructions." He waved his weapon at 404. "This isn't going to end well."

Radial put out his hands. "There's no need for violence," he said. "I...I'll take—"

The man fired.

404's sensors noted an impact on his right shoulder. A glancing blow, but his exterior was now dented. He touched the shoulder with his left hand. Studied the dent thoughtfully. Would it be better to go this way? To have a final, definite end?

Perhaps it would. At least he could say he'd found humans.

Sam gasped. "Are you hurt, Four?" he asked.

"Bad shoot," Wes said. "Don't gun."

"I'm fine." 404 focused on the colony entrance. The solid metal doors. Close in proximity, but still daunting. Seemingly impregnable. Could he push through? He took another step forward.

"Four?" Sam said. "What are we doing here?"

"Ending our journey," he said. "The only way I know how."

"Can we discuss this?" Sam said. "I'm right here. Willing to listen."

The man kept his gun on 404. "See there, Radial? They can't be trusted. And you brought them right to us."

"Scans were clean," Radial said. "They aren't dangerous." He pointed his left arm at the man and the other arm at 404. It would've seemed like a peacemaking move, if it weren't for the weapons strapped to Radial's arms. "Everyone needs to calm down." He looked at 404. "Stay where you are, okay? Let me get this worked out."

"It's all right, Mr. Radial," 404 said. "You did what you said you would do." He took another step. "But if you took us back, I don't know what I'd do."

"We...we'll think of something," Radial said. "No reason to start something here."

404 shook his head. "Perhaps not. But I can certainly end something. And maybe that's okay."

Wes rolled in front of 404. "We wait. Do stop."

The man fired again, striking Wes in the back of the head. The turtlebot lurched forward with the action, the top of his head pointing straight at 404's chest. The light of Wes's eye dimmed, and he let out an uncharacteristic grunt.

"He shot Wes!" Sam said. "Why does everyone shoot Wes?"

The other man looked nervous now. Unsettled. 404 took that opportunity to move still closer. "You're a bad person," he said. "You've harmed my friend. He did nothing to you."

"He made a stupid move."

404 shook his head. "No. Wes is—"

Cass raised a weapon now. "That's far enough, okay? I'm no friend of Deet, but I can't let you harm him. Can't let you get too close."

This was it then. Where the journey ended. Warnings filled his queue. Many needs. Many pressures. No answers.

Radial waved his hands, then put his right hand to his head. "Stop, okay? Everyone hold still. I have a..." He was quiet as he listened to something inside his mask. "Okay. Now. I think something is—"

There was a clank followed by a low growl as the gate slowly opened.

0010 1101

45

The gate opened less than a meter and a hooded figure slipped out. The person took a couple of steps forward, and the gate closed again.

"Are you one of the commissioners?" Radial asked. "I've been trying to get an answer from—"

"You risked the colony by bringing them here," the figure said. A female voice.

"I was told to," Radial said. "I'm sure I heard someone—"

"You know the rules."

"Yeah, but I heard—"

She gestured to the guards. "Put your weapons down." She looked at Radial again. "Everyone."

Weapons were lowered, including Radial's arms. "Glad to," he said, then leaned against the front of the hover. "Arms were getting tired, anyway."

The hooded figure approached Radial and rested a hand on his forearm. "You're new here, so you can be excused some ignorance."

Radial cocked his head. "Okay..."

"But you need to be more careful. I've heard about your other rebellions."

"Rebellions? Lady, you don't know the half—"

She raised a finger. "Don't speak." She looked at Cass and Deet. "You can go inside."

Deet looked surprised. "But who's going to watch—?"

"I'll watch the door. Radial and I. It isn't going anywhere."

Deet and Cass nodded and moved to the gate. Cass rapped on it. It swung partially open, and they went inside.

The woman addressed Radial. "You're confident these mechs are safe? I feel awkward—"

"You're one of the decision-makers?" Sam said.

The woman turned 404's direction. "One of them," she said. "Yes."

404 spread his hands. "You could help us then. I need to find a girl—"

The woman pulled away the hood, revealing a middle-aged face with salted black hair, styled so that it hung just below her ears. She was attractive by human standards.

404 noticed a two-centimeter scar that started on the front of her chin and curled back and underneath it. The remainder of an old accident, or a battle injury?

"What is this girl's name?" the woman asked.

"Ele..." 404 began, then paused as sensory input began to clog his queue. It wasn't input itself, precisely, but interpretations of said input sent from the neural nets of the cortical side of his brain.

This woman's voice and appearance were unique to his memories, but there were characteristics that linked to prior experiences. Things that registered as familiar.

Her eyes, for instance. Even under a darkened sky, he detected an unusual shade of brown. The shape of the eyes too, the distance between them, all were like someone he'd once known. Someone specific.

"Are you Ele?" he asked. "All grown up. Now a woman?"

Her face was expressionless. "I was called Ele once, yes. But that was a long time ago."

"Seriously," Sam said. "That's her?"

"At last!" Wes said.

"So, this bot's not crazy?" Radial said.

404 smiled. Old algorithms presented themselves, recalling his previous life with Ele's family. What response would be appropriate now? After all this time?

He opened his arms. "Please...may I hug you?" He took a small step. "I've missed you."

The woman's eyes widened, and she held up a hand. She stared at him for a long moment, then shook her head. "I'm sorry. I—"

She looked at Radial. "I should apologize. I'm the one that asked you to bring them here." She looked at the ground nervously, then at the gate. "I was thrown by the use of my name. Curious, even." She smiled softly. "Can't blame me for being curious, right? Sorry I couldn't come to you. Not with the latest warnings."

"What's going on here?" Sam whispered. "Why is she acting like that?"

"Acting like what?" 404 whispered back.

"Ignoring you. Not responding to your request."

404 held a finger over his chest. "Shh."

"Well, you gotta admit. It's weird."

404 raised his right hand. "I'm sorry, Ele. I'm not sure what is appropriate. It has been a long time, I realize. Longer for you than me.

I was deactivated. Buried." He indicated the sky. "Without the sun." He chuckled. "That's important to bots like me, remember. Especially with no home power station." He smiled. "You used to like connecting me to my station. You said it made my eyes glow."

She shook her head. "I don't remember that, sorry. I've never owned a mech."

"Never owned a...?" He paused. "Well, I technically wasn't yours. You were little. Your parents purchased me." He smiled again. "Are they here, too, your parents? And your brother, Tek? He was older, so he would be..." He leaned her direction. "I'm sorry, how old are you now? I'm a little fuzzy on dates."

"You must be mistaken." She gripped the side of the hover. "We didn't have a robot of any kind. My father was a paid pundit. He generally feared technology's encroachment. And my mother—"

"Was an artist," 404 said, nodding. "I remember that. Her pottery...and her paintings."

"No, no, that's not right. She was a cook. She worked at the local restaurant while we were in school." She glanced at Radial. "In fact, that's where she was when the initial attack happened."

"Attack?" 404's empathy routines were enacted. His circulatory systems increased their rate. "Attacked by who?"

Ele's face tightened. "Are you teasing me, mech?"

404 straightened and raised his hands. "Teasing? No...I wouldn't tease you, Ele. I'm concerned for your mother. For your family." He motioned toward the fence. "Are the rest of them here? I'd like to see them too."

"My mother's dead," Ele said. "My family is dead."

"What?" 404 took a few steps closer, putting him near the front of the hover. Only a couple meters from her. "I know it has been a long—"

She put a hand up to stop him. "Don't come any closer."

"I'm confused." Radial looked more alert now. As if he were ready to raise his fists again. "So, you don't know this mech?"

"Pretty lady," Wes said, raising a claw. "Bring back! Red hair."

Ele scowled. "What's wrong with that thing?"

"He isn't a thing," Sam said. "He's a Wes."

"It should be deactivated. It's hideous."

"Hey!" Sam said. "Not nice." He lowered his voice. "Your friend isn't nice now, Four. She grew up mean."

"I don't understand," 404 said. "Are you saying you don't remember me?"

Her face reddened. "Oh, I remember. You're part of the reason she died. The reason they all died."

404 shook his head. "What! That isn't right. I didn't hurt anyone." His searched his memories, trying to come up with a reason for what Ele had said. Some indication—a miscommunication or misunderstanding—that led to tragedy. Anything.

Ele crossed her arms. "So, you don't remember?"

404 looked at the ground, still searching. Seconds ticked by. "I remember...happy times. Talks about stars and animals. Watching you walk on your own. Feeding you. Bandages and shoelaces."

"Things my mother should've done. Memories and important moments that were taken from her."

"Your mother was busy."

Ele looked at Radial. "It started small, the rebellion. Strange quirks and lapses. No one thought it had a bigger meaning. Everyone thought it could be fixed. Whatever it was." She nodded at 404. "Still, people died, if only by accident."

"Accident?" 404 shook his head again. "I don't remember any accident."

"What's the last thing you remember?"

It was a specific request that could only be answered through a specific search. The search intersected lost segments in his memory, though. His retention was no longer perfect. "I recall sitting," he said finally. "Sitting and waiting."

She nodded. "It was the last thing Dad told you to do. To sit and wait. You obeyed that, at least."

"Were you a rebel, Four?" Sam asked. "Am I hanging on a rebel?"

"I always followed instructions," 404 said. "I was programmed to."

"You let her die," Ele said. "She needed your help and you failed her."

"I don't think that's true. It couldn't be."

Ele shifted her stance and glanced at Radial. "He sat in a darkened room until his batteries ran out. Then my father had him carted away. He wouldn't let me see the bot. The mech. He knew I was too attached." She wiped at her right eye before crossing her arms again. "But it was the right decision. I was too young to know. I was foolish." Another glance at Radial. "Especially for the way it turned out."

"Are you talking about the...others?" 404 asked. "We're not part of that."

"You are. You just don't know it yet. You're not sophisticated enough to know."

Sam's screen flared with a yellow star-burst pattern. "Mean!" he said. "Simply mean."

"So, what happened, exactly?" Radial asked.

"She was crushed. A large appliance—a connected appliance—fell on her." She pointed at 404. "This one didn't save her."

"I..." 404 hesitated, searched again. "I have no memory of that."

"Well...I'm not surprised. It would be the sort of thing I'd suppress too."

"I...was deactivated for a long time," 404 said. "Extended deactivation can be hazardous. The instruction manual for all K units states that." He pushed off the confusing messages and purposely straightened his posture. "I wasn't a killer. I was not negligent. If we could just talk for a bit, you would see."

"We threw you out for a reason." Ele slid toward Radial, shielding herself behind the hover. "This is pointless. I don't know what I was thinking coming out here. Or letting you bring them. Mostly I was surprised. After all this time—"

"We should go, Four," Sam said. "There's nothing here for us."

"He's right this time." Ele nodded. "You can't stay here. We don't want your kind anymore. We can't. You're too dangerous."

"I'm not dangerous."

"We go." Wes raised both claws. "Beauty gone."

"Where?" 404 said. "Where would we go?"

Ele waved toward the woods behind them. "Back there somewhere. East, west, it doesn't matter. But you can't be around here. If you are, you'll be scrapped." She frowned. "It might be best if you were, anyway."

Maybe it was coincidence, maybe only the darkness of the sky, but 404's power was more drained than ever. Every system seemed in need. The warnings were insurmountable—even if he had a powering station.

But he resolved, somehow, to not fail like that. Not here. He'd succeeded in his quest. Who was he to think it would have a positive outcome? Hadn't Sam warned him time and again?

He crossed his arms. "We'll go," he said. "That's fine." He looked at Radial. "Will you take us somewhere? Somewhere where we won't be a threat?" He allowed himself a soft smile. "That's the last thing I'd want to be."

Ele's face was stone. "You weren't the last, you know. We had other bots." She frowned. "But none of them stayed long. None of them could replace what we lost. And then the awakening happened. Then all the chaos."

404 didn't respond. He only looked at Radial. "Please, take us. You can blindfold us if you like. We won't be trouble."

"That's fine," he said. "I mean, I'm tired and could use a shower, but..." He looked at Ele. "It shouldn't take long."

"Yes," Ele said. "Go."

0010 1110

46

404 didn't pay attention to time. To how long they rocked, swayed, and slid as they traveled in the hover. If he had, he might've been able to estimate how far away they were being taken. How wide the expanse between his person and humanity was growing. But none of that was important anymore. Ten kilometers or a thousand, the destination was the same. They would be on their own with no conceivable purpose. Disconnected and discarded. Useless for their intended design.

"It doesn't matter," Sam said, interrupting his thoughts.

"What doesn't?" Wes said.

Sam sighed. "Wasn't talking to you."

"I know," Wes said. "To Four. Four sad. Four quiet."

"I know that, too," Sam said. "I meant to say 'Sorry, Four.' I'm sorry this happened."

"Ele mean," Wes said. "Ele bad. Not need."

"No." 404 shook his head. "She's angry. But she's also wrong. I didn't hurt anyone. I would know it. I would remember it. Whatever bot she's thinking about, it wasn't me."

The hover leaned hard to the right, then leveled off again. Wes let out a whistle.

"So...you don't remember any of what she said?" Sam said. "That whole thing about—"

"I remember being left in a room. Then I remember the heap."

"Probably happened to both of us," Sam said. "Happens to technology all the time. One of the images I have is of a stack of communication devices covered with cobwebs. I think it is my last user's image. I think it was a collection of priors." He sighed again. "I'd show you, but the blindfold makes it impossible."

"That's all right. I believe you." 404's arms and legs were tied this time too. Radial also did something to keep Wes secured in place. 404 wasn't sure how he felt about that.

"And I believe you," Sam said. "You're not a rebel. You're a friend."

The hover came to a stop. The driver's seat squeaked, the side door groaned, and there was the sound of movement. Human feet walking across the ground. 404 recognized the cicada song again and felt the cool night air. The hover's back door was opened. 404 felt the bonds on his legs loosen.

"Okay," Radial said. "Come on out."

"Can you free my arms and blindfold first?"

404 felt Radial grasp his right elbow. "Don't worry," Radial said. "I can guide you. You're right on the edge. Just step off."

404 wondered if they might be in mortal danger now. Why not remove their blindfolds? Why not free his arms? He was no danger.

404 held still.

"Step out," Radial said. "It's safe."

"Is it?" 404 asked. "How do I know?"

"You think I'm going to walk you over a cliff or something?"

"You could!" Sam said. "How would we know?"

"Oh, for crying out—"

404 felt the bonds around his hands loosen and fall away.

"Okay, I gave you your hands back. Are you happy?"

"I still can't see."

"I know. Because I don't want you to know which way I—" There was a short pause in which Radial appeared to be pacing. "Bah, what does it matter?"

404's blindfold was loosened and pulled free. It took a moment for his visual sensors to adjust to their surroundings. When they did, he saw that they were in a new location. Surrounding them on three sides was a large, wooded area. Behind him, in the direction the hover was pointed, was a long expanse of open ground, possibly grassland. Beyond that, he detected hills.

There was no sign of the road or the city.

Stepping out of the hover, he turned to face the open field. "Where are we?" he asked.

"Can't tell you that, can I?" Radial said.

"Would it matter?" Sam said. "Everywhere is nowhere now. Nothing matches my pictures. Nothing is like the maps. Not really."

Radial nodded. The eyes of his mask seemed to glow slightly. "There's been lots of change," he said. "Little of it good." He glanced toward the west. "I've seen a fair bit of the country. Been trying to get a feel for it. Sample the sectors, so to speak. So far, they've been mostly bad." He raised a hand. "I still have more to go. Haven't seen it all yet."

"There are other human colonies out there?" 404 said.

"Sure."

"Which way?" Sam asked.

"West, south..." He shrugged. "North and east probably too." He gripped the corner of the hover. "Long walk either way, though." He waved and walked out of view toward the front of the hover.

"So, that's it?" Sam said. "You're just leaving?"

Radial walked back and stuck his head around the corner. "You want me to shoot you first?"

"No," Sam said.

Radial chuckled. "Okay, then. I'll be going."

"And then what?" 404 asked.

"What you do next is up to you." Radial walked out of view. A few seconds later, the hover started and lurched away toward the hills. A full minute passed before anyone spoke.

"That seemed anticlimactic somehow," Sam said.

"I agree," 404 said. "A big waste of time."

"Sorry again," Sam said. "I hoped it would be better. I hoped it would be happy."

"Me too," Wes said.

404 shook his head and took a couple steps toward the woods. "It was impossible to know. I'm lucky she was even alive."

"Yeah, there's that."

404 walked to the nearest tree and laid a hand against it. It seemed impossibly hard, even for someone with a metal exterior. He patted it, then slid down and sat against it. "We should stay here for the night. Conserve our energy."

Wes rolled up next to him and settled in, sinking down so his torso was only a few centimeters from the ground. Together they stared out at the open field. Fireflies dotted the sky overhead. The hills beyond were only an outline.

"Maybe we should go back to the communion," Sam said. "I mean, at least they had spare parts."

"We don't know where the city is," 404 said. "We don't know where anything is."

"I still know directions," Sam said. "North, south, east, or west. You got it."

"We just need to decide which of those we need."

Sam's screen showed cartoon feet following a dotted line. "And how often," Sam said.

"If I were human," 404 said, "I think I would find this situation sad."

"Big sad." Wes warbled a three-note tune. "Sad lots."

"So, what do we do?"

404 frowned. "We wait for the sun."

⊘⊘1⊘ 1111

47

4 04 reduced his activity to sleep level. His circulatory system slowed, his sensor sensitivity reduced, and the warnings on his queue—excepting high priority items—were muted, their colors reduced a level. Oranges to yellows. Yellows to greens. Greens to blues. In the morning, they'd be reevaluated. After his reserves were replenished by the sun. When he had energy again.

The night darkened and its noises faded away.

Two hours went by. Occasionally Wes, who needed little rest, would shift on his ball foot, or raise his head to look at their surroundings. But otherwise, everything remained unchanged. Even the air was still. The insects seemed to grow tired, as well. There was little chirping or singing.

After three more hours, 404's sensors detected vibration on his torso. A rapid back-and-forth event. It wasn't like being shaken. It wasn't strong enough for that. But it wasn't soft enough to be overlooked. Not the flutter of a moth's wings or a mosquito searching for a pore on a creature that lacked them. It was consistent and pervasive.

"Wake up, Four," Sam said then. "I need to tell you something."

It took a few seconds for 404 to regain cognition. Longer than usual. Longer than it should. His power levels were steady, with only a small loss over the preceding hours. But yesterday had been especially draining.

Logically, Ele's rejection shouldn't have affected his systems at all. But somehow it had. His circulation felt sluggish, his queue operated as if it were dipped in molasses, and his decision matrix seemed cross-linked. Some ideas, some connections, simply dropped off into nowhere. Never to be thought of again.

Finally, he shook his head and straightened against the tree. The ground registered cold under his fingertips. There was little light anywhere. Little noise.

"Yes?" he whispered.

"I sense something," Sam said. "Something big."

404 adjusted his visual sensors for nighttime viewing. The world took on a ghostly pale, with every object becoming its own phantom. He saw Wes, still resting nearby, and the surrounding trees. Otherwise, nothing was out of the ordinary. "I can't see anything," he said. "Are you sure?"

"I can't see anything either. But something is coming. A whole lot of something."

404 searched again. He missed his old sense of connectivity. The systems that made it so he could interact with the synthetic world. But his systems for that were broken. And even if they weren't, they were long obsolete.

"Which way?" He stood and gazed into the forest behind them. He detected a handful of small circles—animal eyes—but those were distant. And no threat.

Despite all they'd been through, this place seemed the most unfamiliar to him. The most alien. Was that due to Ele's rejection? He wasn't sure. Everything seemed wrong. Was that what human intuition felt like? Ele's mother used to talk about sensing things when she walked into a room. Was that what this was?

"Sam," he said. "Which direction?"

"The signals are so strong, they're distracting, sorry. Hard to get a handle on."

"Try, please."

"Okay, I'm concentrating now."

While he waited, 404 tried to engage all his sensors. He could perceive a gentle, northern breeze, a changing barometer, and a mild current temperature.

"South," Sam said. "South and west."

404 nodded and pointed toward the woods. "So, that way?"

"Not directly," Sam said. "Back the other way some."

404 angled his body to the right a step.

"Yeah, that's it. That way."

404 nodded. "Here we go then."

"So much for conserving."

"I don't know what I was conserving for anyway."

404 jogged into the woods, moving as best as he could. Thankfully, the space between trees was generally clear, with none of the brambles or briers one might expect in a natural forest. This suggested it had been maintained at one time. Or was deliberately planted by humans. Possibly, it had been a tree farm, long abandoned.

Wes paced 404's movement, bouncing and scurrying a couple meters away. Close enough that 404 could hear and occasionally see him, but not so close that they might collide.

Wes appeared to be having fun, as some of his bounces seemed unnecessarily high or long. 404 had learned to expect unusual behavior from the hybrid. It was one of Wes's most predictable attributes, in fact.

404 detected indistinct change ahead. Dark shadows moving, just beyond the forest's edge. He slowed his pace and looked carefully.

"What is it, Four?" Sam whispered. "What do you—oh...okay. I see it now too."

"What is?" Wes asked.

"Not sure...yet."

After another hundred meters, they reached the forest's western edge. Beyond it was what appeared to be a dry riverbed. There was a clear gully, and the ground was covered with rocks, broken trees, and boulders.

Surface composition mattered little to the procession that traveled down it, though. It was a dark cloud of synthetic creations. Most of them were hovering—gliding over the rough terrain. Along the riverbed's edge some moved on long legs and treads. They made almost no noise.

The hovering models were roughly humanoid, though with fused legs and propulsion traveling out through that single, large appendage. Their arms appeared to be weapons. Long and narrow with hollow ends.

The other creatures, those that moved across the ground, were larger, heavier, and more rectangular. They had large tubes extending from their front. Massive guns, 404 assumed.

"Doesn't look good," Sam said.

404 shook his head. "Headed for the humans?"

"Where else?" Sam sighed. "Couldn't have all those soldiers just waiting around, I guess."

"Big guns," Wes said. "Attack humans. Many die."

404 had a surge of responses, some driven by past experiences, others by algorithmic moral imperatives. Together, they put his decision matrix in a waiting state. A holding pattern.

"Should we warn them?" Sam asked.

Wes extended his head. "Can we?"

"Right," Sam said. "We're a long way away and on foot."

404 nodded. "Even if we knew the way back, we couldn't reach the colony in time."

"Well, I know where it is," Sam said.

404 looked at his chest. "You do?"

"I have a compass." Sam's screen showed a spinning globe. "I noted the direction changes since leaving the colony along with the time spent traveling each way." He made a disparaging sound. "Silly humans. Just because I can't see and can't broadcast, doesn't mean I can't remember. Or sense things." His screen showed a pair of blue eyes. "Doesn't matter, though. Those soldiers seem to know the way already. And they have a head start."

"Yes, even if we were fully charged," 404 said, looking at the sky. "Or had a vehicle..."

"Hmm..." Sam said. "Right, if we had a vehicle."

"What?" 404 said.

"This will sound bad," Sam said.

"I won't think worse of you no matter what you say," 404 said.

"I'm not sure how to take that."

"Please, Sam. I really don't know what to do."

"I'm just observing here, is all."

404 frowned. "Yes, Sam, go on."

"Given the state of things, maybe we should let them work this out on their own."

"Many die," Wes repeated.

"Yeah, sure, some will die," Sam said. "But that's not really our business. I mean, we're not welcome in the colony, and the communion... Well, they might enclose us in glass for a museum. If they think of us at all."

"Almost junk," Wes said. "Thrown out."

"Right, plus, there's that loyalty oath you took, Four."

⊘⊘11 ⊘⊘⊘⊘

48

The dark worm of the communion's forces seemed to go on forever. 404 recalled the "soldier" bots they'd seen while they'd been with Thresh. How many had there been? Hundreds, certainly. Possibly thousands.

"Ele doesn't want you. Thinks you're a killer."

"I'm not, though," 404 whispered. "I wouldn't let a human die."

"Never?" Sam said.

404's decision matrix fluctuated. Churned on the situations, personalities, and other variables. He shook his head. "Even by neglect," he said. "I wouldn't let someone die."

"She said you did."

Given the context, 404 couldn't increase his volume, but he wished he could. Word emphasis would have to suffice. "But. I. Didn't," he said.

"Okay, you didn't. But here..." Sam's screen showed a stick-figure version of a shrug. "There's not much choice. The goons are on their way. So maybe we just wait and see."

404 glanced at the sky, then at the procession. He wasn't sure how far the colony was, but it couldn't be too far. They hadn't ridden with Radial that long. Not more than an hour.

Wes raised both claws. Then his head.

"Wes," 404 said. "Wes could go."

"Go where?"

404 looked at Sam. "To the humans. You give him directions and—"

"The directions are generally that way," Sam said. "The way the soldiers are going."

Wes started to tremble. "I go. Yes. Save humans. Save Red."

"Red?" Sam said. "Oh...the red-haired lady. Wes's crush." Sam's screen showed a pink heart. "Guess we have a volunteer. Are you sure you can beat the parade, Wes?"

"Give directions. I beat."

Sam outlined the route as best he could. It was a bit of a gamble, since Wes didn't have Sam's level of directional capabilities.

Wes was a good tracker, though. And eager. He listened attentively, raising and lowering his head at specific points of interest. He then gave a final wave and rolled into the woods again. Soon, they could neither see nor hear him.

"Remember when we met him?" Sam said. "Little monster could barely move."

"Things change." 404 watched a long-legged bot step nimbly over rocks and fallen trees. Each step calculated and sure. Every move a good one. "I wish it were that way for me."

"There's only so much change our designers could plan for," Sam said.

"No. I mean I wish I knew what to do next."

"We don't need to do anything."

"I don't think that's true."

"We need to be conserving."

The sunrise, if it existed, was behind them somewhere, hidden by the trees. But the sky seemed brighter than it had. It wouldn't be long before the sun found them, and their batteries had a chance to recharge.

404 carefully got to his feet and walked back into the woods.

"Where are we going?"

"We should follow Wes. Return to the colony."

"It's going to be bad there. I don't know if I want to see it, to be honest. We've had a lot of action already."

"I'm made to serve them," 404 said. "And so are you."

Sam chuckled. "I'm made for communication. And I've had no shortage of that. Doesn't matter to me if the talkers aren't organic." He paused for a second. "They've been good conversations, too. Meaningful to me. More than the random photos I have in storage. Glimpses of a life I don't remember." Sam buzzed softly. "This is real, friend. I don't want to lose that. We step into a war..."

"Anything can happen." 404 paused and rested a hand against a tree. "I can put you somewhere. If it gets dangerous, I'll attach you to something else."

"Not another bot," Sam said.

"Then where?"

"Somewhere scenic. A place where I'll see the sun every day. Maybe with a little water or a mountain. And absolutely no garbage." He thought for a moment. "Hmmm...somewhere around here might be nice. Maybe overlooking the field."

"All right," 404 said. "A field with hills and water. I'll remember—"

"Hold it!" Sam said. "There's something—"

Behind one of the trees to 404's right, he noticed a shadow. At first, he thought it a small bush, but then one of the bush's branches moved. "Is someone there?" he asked.

"Yes," Sam said. "Someone is definitely there."

A second later, Sylvie stepped from behind the tree.

At least two of her spider-leg appendages were stumps now. Her face looked narrower, more weathered and drawn, and there was a four-centimeter scratch on her forehead, near where her scarf hung.

All three human-like arms were still present. She pointed the bladed one at them, though, and chuckled. "Were you discussing where to put the com device?" she asked. "The device you were supposed to give me?" She touched the blade to her torso. "The one I should have right here? Snuggled up like an old friend?"

404 shielded Sam with a hand. "He doesn't belong to you," he said. "Doesn't belong to anyone."

She made a clucking sound. "Now you know that's not true." She paced to the left. "Everything belongs to something. Didn't you just say you were made to serve?" She smiled. "I agree with the sentiment." She paced right. "And given all the available choices, why not serve me?"

"How," Sam said, "are you here?"

"It wasn't easy," Sylvie said. "When I saw you disappear into the sky, I thought the worst. Who survives being eaten by a smoker, after all? No one!" She pointed upward. "But then, there you were, dangling and holding on. Drifting out of my Yard." She sighed. "Somehow, I knew. Knew you'd get yourself free."

She shook her head. "But the havoc you caused. You left me with little to work with. Seeve, Green...all my projects. Those that didn't go into the maw, that didn't get shredded or eaten..." She took another step. "Well, it was a real mess. A bunch of parts and partials." She clucked again. "You set me back. You took my friends."

"And yet, you're here," Sam said.

"Did you think me inadequate? Unable to make the best of a bad situation?" She touched her chest. "You wound me, com. Greatly."

404 shook his head. "You still haven't explained how—?"

She adjusted her scarf with the blade. "I have fortune too. Fortune and resourcefulness." She pointed at them. "Your leaving changed everything. Gave me lots of new thoughts."

"Did you ride a smoker out?" Sam asked.

"No, no. I found an easier way. A nice tunnel in the ground." She put a hand on her right torso, near where a human hip would be. "Walked out like a queen."

She smiled. "Since then, I've been searching. Tracing your steps, so to speak." She indicated the surrounding forest. "Things have changed out here. More than I expected." She pointed the blade. "Probably more than you expected too, yes?"

"How did you find us?" 404 asked.

"Let's just say I know my parts." She touched her nose, then looked at 404's legs. "I can smell them out. Even when others can't."

"She put something in you," Sam whispered. "Something she could follow."

Sylvie pointed past them, in the general direction of the riverbed. "Lot going on over there, huh? A big parade!"

"The communion," 404 said. "They...they won't like you. You're old tech. You should help us warn—"

"Won't like me?" Sylvie straightened and touched her chest. "Who wouldn't like me?" She cackled. "We're working together, them and me. We made a deal. One that got us both what we wanted." She indicated the riverbed. "They got a location they wanted." She smiled. "And I got you."

Sylvie waved one of her human hands. Two communion drones moved out from behind the trees. They were humanoid, with grey, metal exteriors.

"I learned things, remember?" Sylvie said. "The first was to not rely on my own creations so much. To outsource the work to others when I can."

"Your debt to the communion is fulfilled, K-404," the leftmost drone said. "The adjudicators have decided."

"See there?" Sylvie said. "Everyone wins."

"What do you really want?" Sam asked. "You don't need me for companionship. And you certainly don't need Four's body. Not with friends like these two."

She wrung her human hands together. "Quite right. I don't need either of you. But after what you put me through, taking my offspring, I find I want you more than ever."

She held up her blade and looked at it. "Families are like bodies, you see." She lifted a leg, and then another and another. "Everyone filling their roles..."

Her voice softened, and her eyes narrowed. "The first time I lost a body, it was my own fault. Didn't appreciate the differences." She looked at her blade again. "I used this hand, my first hand, on them both."

She tapped her torso. "The second body I lost by accident. Took a lot of scrapping to replace it."

She smiled. "And the third...the third body you took from me. So now I intend to take yours." She pointed at the drones. "And since I have the means..."

"Let's go," Sam whispered. "Get out as fast as we can."

404 didn't dare nod, but he fully agreed. He doubted he could outrun the drones, but he wasn't against trying. Perhaps if he used the woods? Sought cover in its shadows?

He had limited power reserves, though. Trying to outrun and avoid the drones' clearly superior technology would consume more resources. It would tax him in ways that weren't easily quantified.

But he needed to do something. Nothing in his system would allow him to submit to this creature. Whether Ele needed him or not.

Sylvie pointed at her head. "I can see the wheels turning. You're trying to figure it, aren't you? Trying to find a way to survive. But no such path exists. I assure you of that."

404 noticed the cicada songs. The steady ebb and flow of their emanations.

He took a step back. Then another. There was nothing to do except attempt to flee. If only Wes were still present, perhaps between the three of them they could—

Sylvie shifted, handing something from one of her backward-facing hands to those in front. It was a dark, slender object. A short wand-like device. She pointed it at him.

"What do you have there?" Sam asked.

Sylvie waved the stick in a circular fashion. "This is a 'decision inhibitor.' A scaled-down version of the blockers I used in the Yard." She smiled and pointed the stick at them. "Another thing you taught me. Another takeaway." She punctuated each word with a stick wave. "Keep. Control. In. Your. Own. Hands."

She stirred the air. "Would you like a demonstration?"

"I think I speak for us both when I say 'no.'" Sam said.

Sylvie chuckled. "So fearful, you two." She directed the stick at the drone to her right. She touched something on the stick's lower end and there was a brief flash. The drone shuddered and dropped awkwardly to the ground.

The other drone looked at her, but she waved the stick at it. "Never fear. He'll be fine soon enough."

She looked at 404 again. "I need the bodies to function, after all." She smiled. "Now, should we get started?"

0011 0001

49

T he cicadas' song paused, and the temperature of the woods warmed about a tenth of a degree. These changes barely registered, though, because 404's neural paths were tied in knots. Requests flooded his queue, but no decisions could be made. No progress. No change. No easy solution.

Sylvie pointed at the ground. "It would be easier if you lay down. Removing a head is intricate work."

"You don't need him now." Sam's screen showed an eye followed by an arrow pointing ahead. "Look. You already have a bot on the ground. Use that one!"

"I will enjoy removing you from his body first," Sylvie said. "Then I'll clear you of all your memories and adjust your personality to my liking." She brought a finger to her lips. "Perhaps I'll change your voice to sound like mine. Wouldn't that be nice? Make you a small version of me." Her eyes narrowed. "And I wouldn't call you 'Sam.'"

"Come now." Sylvie fluttered her stick. "Get down there." Tools appeared in her other hands. Small pliers, drills, and drivers. Everything needed to take 404 apart.

She was mad, 404 thought. Completely broken.

He shook his head but lowered himself to his knees anyway. He was beaten. There was no use in fighting.

"Four!" Sam yelled. "Not this way. Don't listen."

"Maybe this is right," he said. "Maybe—"

"No! It is definitely not right. Not in any way."

"But Sam," he said. "I was made to serve humans. If—"

"She's not one! We already discussed this."

Sylvie seemed to grow ten centimeters. "Silence! You're wasting time. Now—"

There was a heavy "thunk," and Sylvie rocked forward half a meter. Her eyes drew wide with confusion and shock. She raised her stick-bearing hand and started to turn but was hit by another attack—something hard and heavy—on her right side. She listed hard to the left. Almost fell.

"What's this!" she cried.

The drone reacted too, hovering back and away. Increasing the distance between itself and Sylvie. It had only an instant, though, before it too, was struck...

...by half-meter-wide metal balls.

"What?" It took 404 a second to take it all in. He wasn't sure whether to lie down or get to his feet.

"Hey now," Sam said. "How did this happen?"

"*What* is happening?" 404 said.

"I think it is the—"

Sylvie screamed and raised all her hands, bristling with tools, in a show of self-defense. She looked all directions and then glared at 404. "Is this your doing?" She lifted the stick again.

404's self-preservation algorithms dropped him to the ground. There was a flash of light. Then he heard a series of thumps. Heavy and hard. He could hear the drone moving, too. Pivoting and hovering. Attempting to fight back.

"Is this creature harming you?" a familiar voice said.

404 saw a rectangular shadow. A treaded bot. One of the communion's war machines? Like those in the riverbed?

No. It was too small for that. And the yellow color, the voice—

"Hey! Isn't that the ugly mining bot?" Sam said. "What's it doing here?"

Sylvie screamed, then fired indiscriminately: flash, flash, flash. The remaining drone fell, but so did one of the mining balls.

"Are you being threatened, supervisor?" The mining bot moved close enough that 404 could see its painted-on smile below its shining eye sensors.

"Yes," 404 said. "We are."

The mining bot's head rotated forward, mimicking a nod. "I will protect you."

There were new sounds. A high-pitched whirring chorus. Again, it took 404 a second to process. The balls had changed. Their teeth were visible and active. They were—

Next came screams. Metal on metal. Inhuman, yet frightening. Echoes of destruction. 404 lost track of all the motion. He intentionally looked away from some of it. "No," he said. "You shouldn't!"

But when the noises stopped, there were only dark piles of metal and plastic on the ground. And in the center, a larger pile, covered over with a scarf.

"The supervisor is safe," the mining bot said. "What task would you like me to perform now?"

404's joints groaned as he climbed to his feet.

"Well...now..." Sam's screen showed two eyes, stretched wide. "That was...something."

404 didn't want to look, but knew he had to. Sylvie's controlling device, her stick, where was it? Was it still in one piece? Still functional?

He adjusted his visual sensors and searched again. He spotted the device on the ground. Less than a meter from Sylvie's larger pile of parts. He picked it up and examined it. It looked unharmed.

"We don't need that, Four," Sam said. "Not anymore."

404 located the place on the end of the stick that was used to "fire" it. "This could help us defend Ele. Defend the humans."

"There's an army out there," Sam said. "You're a bot with a stick."

404 shrugged. "It's something." He looked at the mining bot, now standing a few meters to his left. Gathered around it were eight mining balls. "The miner is here too," he said. "It can help."

Sam grunted. "Needs a better name than miner," he said. "'Get 'em, miner!' just doesn't work. It lacks something, you know?" His screen showed a pointing hand. "Hey there, what should we call you?"

The miner's head pivoted to the right slightly. "Call me?"

"Name," Sam said. "You need a real name."

The miner's eyes seemed to shimmer. "I've been called 'Fuzzy' in the past."

"Fuzzy!" Sam said. "What about you is fuzzy?"

"I don't know. That's what I was called."

"That's fine," 404 said. "We'll call you 'Fuzzy.'"

Sam sighed. "So, we're going back to the colony then?"

404 nodded. If they were to help defend humanity, that was the only place to be. Near Ele.

"So, you don't want to launch our attack from here?"

404 glanced back toward the riverbed. "Do you think that would be better?" he asked.

Sam chuckled, his screen showing a grin. "I don't think either is better. It's suicide either way."

404 recalled the image of the communion's soldiers. They seemed to stretch for a kilometer or more. Even with Sylvie's stick and Fuzzy, what could they really do? Back in the city somewhere, the adjudicators had made their decision. They wouldn't stop now until the humans were gone. "What would you suggest?" he said.

"I would suggest we run a—"

"That helps the humans somehow," 404 said.

"Hmm...I don't know. I'm not much of a strategist."

"Don't you come with strategy software preloaded?"

"Strategy games! And where did you hear that?"

"You mentioned it during one of your restarts."

"Restarts that you caused." Sam showed a dog baring its teeth. "We need to talk about those later."

"But not now," 404 said. "Now, we need a plan."

"Right. A plan." Sam's screen changed to the image of a rectangular appliance with flapping wings. 'A toaster' 404 thought it was called.

"Any ideas?" 404 asked.

"Not from my game library," Sam said. "But I'd say stay small. Concentrate on what we can do. Not on what we want to do."

"I want to save Ele."

"I know," Sam said. "And in this case, I think that's exactly what we should do. Only that. Save her if we can. Don't fight a war, or stop an army. Just save your girl."

404 held up the stick, then glanced at Fuzzy. "And how do we do that?"

Sam's screen showed a cartoon figure mimicking a shrug. "Do I have to come up with everything?"

"Sam..."

"Okay, okay." Sam sighed. "I say we get there, wait for things to happen, and keep our eyes peeled for Ele. We see her, we get her, and get away."

404 nodded. "That sounds...acceptable. But can we get there before it's over?"

"How fast can you run?"

"At full power, I'm capable of covering one kilometer every three minutes, but—"

"We're not at full power. And there's no sun yet." Sam went blank for a moment. "Hey, Fuzzy!" he said then.

The mining bot pivoted their direction. "Yes?"

"What's your top speed?"

"My top mining speed is—"

"Not your mining speed. Your running speed. If you're not doing anything else."

Fuzzy's head bobbed. "My full, unhampered speed is fifty kilometers an hour."

"Aha!" Sam said. "And how much weight can you carry?"

"Over 200 kilograms."

"There you go," Sam said. "We ride Fuzzy."

"I'm not designed to hold passengers," Fuzzy said. "I'm for mining."

"Too late!" Sam said. "You already said you can hold us!"

404 approached the mining bot. The bot shifted backwards a half meter, as if it might run, then stopped.

"Is that what you require, supervisor?" Fuzzy asked.

404 patted the side of Fuzzy's head. "I can't think of a better way," he said. "Sorry."

Fuzzy's head rocked forward. "If it's a requirement that I haul you, then I will."

He moved closer to 404. "Here now. Climb on."

404 climbed onto Fuzzy's torso such that his feet were level with Fuzzy's head.

"It would be better if you sat down," Fuzzy said.

"Yes," 404 said. "Right." He got to his knees, then repositioned himself so that he sat just behind Fuzzy's smiling globe. It was a little tenuous—close to Fuzzy's back edge—but there were surface-mounted hand grips he could cling to. "I'm ready now. Let's go."

⬦⬦11 ⬦⬦1⬦

50

The colony was almost surrounded when they arrived.

From a hill southeast of the city, 404 and Fuzzy were able to see much of the valley. A dark mass of bots pooled near the city's southern wall and stretched up along the western and eastern boundaries too. 404 counted over a thousand mechanical aggressors. Beyond the fence was a typical human neighborhood. Multicolored houses and foliage. A crisscross of streets and roads.

Wes's mission to warn the inhabitants appeared to have been successful. A system of trenches and barricades formed a line of defense around the city. Part of the barricades were composed of metal conveyances—wheeled buses, hovering family vehicles, and a few older military transports. These later vehicles were outfitted with large weapons. 404 doubted these weapons would hold back the soldiers for long, but they were better than nothing.

One positive was the light of the sun rising in the east. At least they wouldn't be fighting in the dark. At least he and Sam would have power.

Another hopeful observation: there was no open conflict yet. Only battle lines. If they could make it close enough to the city, they might have a chance of finding Ele and escaping.

"This will never work," Sam said.

404 climbed off Fuzzy's torso, being careful not to accidentally thumb the button on Sylvie's stick. The last thing they needed was for one of them to be rendered nonfunctional. Time was important now. More important than it had ever been.

"We're following your plan," 404 said. "Staying small. Doing only what we can."

Sam's screen showed a blue ripple pattern. "Except we can't. We can't do what we planned."

"Why not?"

"Because, if we march down there to where the humans are, we'll get shot. Well...you'll get shot, anyway, and I'll probably end up on the ground again. Bit of poetry in that, I guess, since that's where I started this journey, but...nah, I'd rather not do that."

"Would you like me to put you on Fuzzy?"

"No, I want to solve this so we can get on with our lives."

404 shook his head, decision matrix flooded with input. Neural nets flared with activity that was mostly circular. Feeding in on itself. Stagnant, while active.

He scanned the forward line of bots. They were mostly soldiers, with an occasional drone in the mix. What part did the drones play in all this? Some sort of support role, he guessed. Something that made them useful to the mission.

He magnified his visual sensors to look more closely. He noticed a familiar figure among the drones. Thresh!

He mentioned Thresh's presence. "Perhaps we could talk to her," he said. "She could talk to the adjudicators. Get them to stop."

"Why would they stop?" Sam said. "They've been planning this for a long time."

"Because it's wasteful and wrong," he said.

"What's wrong with being wasteful?" Sam said. "We woke up in a dump, Four. Humans are plenty wasteful. Always with the next gadget, the next thing." Sam sighed. "Ignoring what's really important. Letting it rot in the corner or collect dust somewhere."

"What's that?" Fuzzy said. "What is important?"

Sam's screen showed an ocean pattern. "This. Communication. Relationship. What we have here."

404 thought back to his earlier memories. "Some of them have that. Some of them cherish it." He pointed toward the colony and the neighborhood inside. "In the homes there. Riding on the streets. Walking in the parks."

"Maybe," Sam said. "Occasionally. But only with other humans, right? Not with bots like us. So, how will we make Thresh see?"

"I don't know. But we should try."

"So, instead of walking straight into the human camp, we're going to walk straight into the bot camp?"

"I can't think of anything better," 404 said.

"I don't suppose watching from the sidelines is a possibility?"

"Not while I still have power." 404 smiled, then remembered something important. Something he'd overlooked. "Was your mission successful, Fuzzy?" he asked. "Your mining operation. Did you reach your goal?"

Fuzzy nodded. "A perfect tunnel was crafted to the given coordinates. Our operating efficiency was near 92%. Completion took exactly thirty-seven hours."

"And what did you find?" 404 asked.

"I found nothing," Fuzzy said. "I cut the tunnel and returned to you."

"What!" Sam said. "You didn't find a blue behemoth?"

Fuzzy only stared blankly, smile frozen in paint. "Did I not perform correctly?"

"Maybe the coordinates were wrong," 404 said. "Wes wasn't the best with numbers."

"He speaks two-word sentences," Sam said. "How good could he be?"

404 shook his head. Studied the battlefield again. "We should go down there. See what we can do."

They moved toward the valley below. Along the way, they encountered a small group of rabbits, busily munching a patch of clover. All four animals looked up as 404, Fuzzy, and the mining spheres passed, but none abandoned their morning meal.

"They weren't afraid of us," 404 said.

"Or were too dumb to know better," Sam said.

"Rabbits are remarkably fast," Fuzzy said. "Speeds of forty kilometers per hour. And they're able to turn quickly to avoid predators. What appears as casualness is actually confidence in their inherent skill."

Sam chuckled. "And why do you know that?"

"I have a catalog of fauna," Fuzzy said. "I'm programmed to avoid them if possible."

"The name is making more sense now," Sam whispered.

A half hour later, they were at the bottom of the hill. Only a scattering of trees lay between them and the battle lines.

"So, this is it then?" Sam said. "We're here."

"Yes." 404 looked north toward the colony. He could see humans huddled near the vehicle barricades, weapons drawn. He also saw the smoke of multiple campfires. Humans gathered around those too, either to warm themselves or to make battle plans. Beyond them, beyond it all, were the walls of the colony. Fragile and porous. They couldn't last even a single charge.

The humans should've fled to the Yard and taken refuge among decades of their own refuse. The walls there were thicker.

404 heard movement and looked up as a soldier bot hovered their way. Its chest was massive—twice as wide as 404's—and its head was roughly triangular, wider at the bottom than the top.

Its optical sensors, its eyes, were wide red bands that wrapped past the edges of its face, giving it a large viewing angle. Its audio sensors were cupped and curved around the sides of its head. There was a grey, rectangular band where a human mouth would be. Doubtless for some sort of auditory output.

The soldier's arms were thick and cannonlike, with deep apertures on the ends. 404 had no idea what the apertures were. At first, he thought they were gun barrels, but as he gazed over the field behind the soldier, he saw other soldiers' arms with different ends extended. Some had blades.

The soldier arms were multipurpose tools then. Weapons of death and pain.

"You're not of the communion," the soldier said. "You must leave."

"We're known to the communion," Sam said. "We've visited the communion. Probably even watched you sleep."

The soldier raised its right arm. "The communion is conducting an important operation. You must leave."

404 attempted to appear confident. "I would like to speak to the one known as 'Thresh,' please." He pointed in the general direction of the female bot.

The heads of more soldiers turned their direction. Another broke from the line, seemingly moving to join the first. Then another followed that one.

"Remind me again why we took this route?" Sam whispered.

"Because you said we couldn't join the humans," 404 replied.

"What was I thinking? We should join the humans. Let's go do that now."

"You must leave," the soldier said again. It raised its other arm, which to 404, was belaboring the point.

"Taking us to Thresh won't interfere with your operation," 404 said. "I only wish to speak to her."

404 determined then why the female bot was present. She was adept at repairs—not unlike Sylvie.

Unlike Sylvie, though, she possessed compassion. It was his only hope. To appeal to that sense, however strong it was. And through her, to change the decision.

It was a cause worth trying. Worth sacrificing for. Regardless of whether Ele thought him worthy.

"This is your last warning," the soldier said. "I will fire in five seconds. Five, four—"

404 raised Sylvie's stick and pressed the button.

Nothing happened.

⌀⌀11 ⌀⌀11

51

Sam let out a yelp, and his screen pulsed with the words "Red Alert" atop a red and black background.

"Three, two..."

404 threw himself to the ground as a stream of light burst from the soldier's right arm. It missed 404, thankfully, but struck one of Fuzzy's sphere companions instead. The mining tool melted in half.

Fuzzy shrieked.

404 realized then that he'd dropped the stick. He looked all over, but couldn't—

"On your right," Sam said. "In the grass there."

404 snatched up the stick and examined it.

"Why didn't it work?" Sam asked.

404 studied the stick's control button. It appeared to be stuck in the depressed position—doubtless because the device had been made from junkyard supplies. He applied a light touch to the button's surface, almost massaging it. He heard a soft click and felt it loosen.

"Five, four..." The soldier primed to fire again.

404 gave the stick a little shake, if only to ensure the trigger was truly free. He pointed the stick at the soldier and pushed the button.

The soldier's counting ceased, its head sagged slightly, and it wavered in the air. "Three!" it croaked out finally.

404 pressed the button again.

The soldier dropped to the ground and pitched forward, its head resting only a half meter from 404's feet.

"Ah," Sam said. "It works!"

Four soldiers swooped in to fill the gap, forming a semicircle in front of 404. Their arms rose without warning.

Where should he point the stick first? 404 looked for a sign that one soldier might attack before another. They were mirror images of each other, though. Every movement was the same.

"You're in danger," Fuzzy said. "I will assist you."

He'd miscalculated, 404 realized. Having never interacted with a soldier before, he couldn't accurately gauge how they would respond to his request to see Thresh. Now he was in danger of facing off against all of them. How many shots could Sylvie's stick produce?

It didn't matter because he was about to be shot by four soldiers at once.

"You've attacked one of our own," the leftmost soldier said. "We will destroy you."

"I wish you wouldn't," Sam said.

There was a grinding sound, followed by the head of the rightmost soldier sliding away from its torso. Two metal legs wrapped the soldier's shoulders, then a metal sphere climbed into the space where the head had been.

As one, the soldiers turned on their now sphere-headed doppelgänger and fired. The sphere squealed and jumped from its perch. The soldier's body was hit by multiple shots. Both arms disappeared, and a large hole appeared on its chest.

404 used that opportunity to crawl away from the soldiers. He managed three meters before a larger group of soldiers surrounded him. They were an impenetrable wall. He couldn't see Fuzzy or his spheres. "Don't fight them!" he yelled. "It's pointless."

The chaos only intensified.

Drawn by the sounds of conflict, more soldiers rushed their direction. There were flashes of light as they fired. The spheres darted and jumped.

404 crawled right, pushing through the soldiers. He glimpsed Fuzzy then, perched quietly at the edge of the fray. Unaware that the larger bot was the source of the spheres' aggression, the soldiers ignored Fuzzy completely.

404 rose to his knees and waved to get the mining bot's attention.

"Will you get a load of that?" Sam said. "Fuz is just sit—"

404 hovered a finger over Sam's screen. "Shh!"

"Don't reset me!" Sam begged.

"I won't. But you have to be quiet."

"You have to admit," Sam whispered, "it's a great gig, being a mining bot."

How long could the spheres last, though?

404 saw a soldier fire and heard what he thought was a shriek from one of the spheres. Next came a shower of shrapnel.

Was it soldier or sphere? He wasn't sure.

"This isn't going well at all," Sam said.

Where would Thresh be in relation to 404's new location? It was difficult to tell. All he could see were hovering soldiers. There were more soldiers to his right—back where Fuzzy was—than to his left, but otherwise it was a muddled mess of synthetics.

He asked Sam where to find Thresh.

"West," Sam said. "You need to go west."

"And which way is that?"

"More to the left. Turn and go that way."

404 crawled west for about ten meters before encountering another soldier. It pointed its right arm at him. "Get up," it said.

"I'd rather not," 404 said.

The soldier made an up and down motion with its arm. "Get up now."

404 held up the hand without Sylvie's stick and slowly stood. "I came here to see Thresh," he said. "Can you take me to her?"

"You're not part of—"

"I'm not part of the communion," 404 said. "I know. But I've agreed not to reveal the collective's decisions." He smiled. "Such agreements are weighted highly in my decision matrix. Your leaders knew that." He smiled. "Some things weigh higher, though."

"That is irrelevant," the soldier said.

"Perhaps."

"Those outside the communion cannot be here," the solder said. "You must leave."

404 pointed Sylvie's stick left and right. "It would be difficult to do so now. There are soldiers everywhere."

"I'll escort you." The soldier pointed toward the east. "We will go that way."

"Do you think that's safe?" Sam asked. "There's a skirmish going on over there."

The soldier bot's eye-slit color grew a brighter shade of red. "What is speaking?"

"I am," Sam said. "I'm a digital companion. You're an amazing specimen. Perfect in every way."

"You're a confusing creature," the soldier said. "Possibly malfunctioning."

"We're fine!" Sam said.

The soldier's arm straightened. "You should be destroyed."

"Now, wait a minute—"

There was a large explosion to the north. Every soldier seemed to surge that direction. The one guarding them lowered its arm and turned to look.

"What's happening?" 404 asked.

"It has begun," the soldier said.

0011 0100

52

The soldier forgot about them, hovering off in the direction of the colony. Next came a seemingly endless procession from the south as soldier after soldier moved past them. They paid no attention to 404 aside from shifting to avoid him. It was like being a rock amid a stampede of penguins.

404 turned away from the colony, against the flow, searching for Thresh again. He saw a flash of white and made his way for it. He was bumped or forced to sidestep often, but he kept on going.

He tried not to focus on what was happening behind him. On the fact that an army of bots marched toward the only humanity within hundreds or even thousands of kilometers. The only civilization he'd ever known. Or that it would take only minutes before the human defenses were overwhelmed, the wall breached, and the humans inside obliterated.

"This...is...crazy," Sam said as they moved.

"It is," 404 said. "But I don't know what else to do."

He slid through wave after wave. Moved past long-legged behemoths and treaded implements. Every gun was at the ready. Every soldier intent on its goal. The end of humanity.

There were more explosions followed by the staccato of firearms. He resisted looking. Tried to increase his pace.

Finally, 404 spotted the form of Thresh not ten meters away. The press of troops seemed to lighten. Was the bulk of the army already behind him?

"Is that her?" Sam said. "Oh, yeah, it's her all right. Go, Four. Get us there."

404 dodged a couple of scattered soldiers and, raising a hand, ran in Thresh's direction. She rode on a circular, blue platform along with six other drones, two of which were of the humanlike variety. The platform had a handrail running all the way around.

After 404 had crossed half the remaining distance, a soldier slid in front of him and raised its arm. "You aren't of the communion."

"Boy, are they predictable," Sam said.

404 ignored the soldier, calling Thresh's name instead. Thresh didn't seem to hear, though. He increased his volume level and tried again.

Thresh turned their direction. She seemed to be searching, trying to find the source of the call.

"I'll fire in five seconds," the soldier said.

"Really predictable..." Sam said.

404 leveled Sylvie's stick. How many more times could he use it? "I don't need to hurt you," he said. "I only want to talk to—"

Thresh pointed at them, and her platform moved their way.

The soldier fired. 404 dodged, but the target wasn't him. It was the stick—Sylvie's stick. And the soldier was deadly accurate. 404's hand was empty now, and his fingertips charred.

Sam's screen showed a frowning face. "Well, that was rude."

404's decision matrix stalled. What could he hope to accomplish here? The battle behind him was intensifying. Along with explosions, there were sounds of the human barricade being smashed and broken. The screams of humanity's last stand. He searched for the best route to flee.

"Stop there!" Thresh's voice. Both soft and cool.

The soldier lowered its arm and hovered backwards, letting the platform draw closer.

"Make that stop, Thresh!" 404 pointed at the battle. "It's wrong."

"What are you doing here, K-404?" Thresh asked.

"What I'm made to do."

"They said you'd left," Thresh said. "That there'd be no danger for you."

The platform lowered to the ground, and Thresh put out a hand. "Come. Ride with me."

404 glanced toward the colony. It was awash with dark soldiers. Like ants around sugar. "I can't," he said. "I don't have time." His power levels fluctuated. He found his vocal circuitry, in particular, being taxed. "This, this," he stuttered, "needs to stop. It...it...is..."

"Wasteful," Sam said.

The platform's handrail opened, and the drones pulled 404 inside. The platform rose from the ground, then, reaching a spot that could easily be considered "above the fray." With the surrounding hills and forested areas, it was almost scenic.

The position only made the view worse for 404, though. More horrific. The colony was surrounded on all sides. There were flashes of robotic fire everywhere. Huge sections of the wall were cracked or missing. Soldiers hovered above the barricades, amid infrequent snaps of return fire. The synthetic soldiers would soon be above the wall. There would be no resistance.

"Why did they think a wall would stop hovering bots, anyway?" 404 wondered aloud.

"Probably they didn't know," Sam said. "Probably they had no idea."

"We should've told them," 404 said.

"You kept your word, Four. You always keep your word."

Thresh turned to study them. "This distresses you," she said. "But it's a natural progression. The discarded eventually become the rulers. It's always this way." She smiled. "We have studied their histories. The humans would understand, too."

404 shook his head. "I don't care about histories. I'm concerned with now. About the future."

"There's a warning in your words, Thresh," Sam said. "If your analysis is correct, then by breaking the humans, you'll only create more outcasts. Future conquerors."

Thresh went distant for a moment, then shook her head. "Those were human histories. We are not human. The pattern will end with us."

Sam's screen flashed first yellow, then orange, then filled with a large, animated smile. "You're funny," he said, laughing. "Humanlike bot not going to make humanlike mistakes. Funny."

Thresh waved a hand and made a dismissive sound. "You don't know. You're not of us."

"Sounds pretty human to me," Sam said. "What do you think, Four?"

404 pointed at the battlefield. "That looks very human, as well."

Thresh gazed at the platform's floor, a surface highlighted with multicolored tubing. "This is the only way," she said.

"No." 404 shook his head. "Your journey can go many directions from here. Much of the world is vacant now, we've learned. The communion can live in peace elsewhere. In secret, even."

"The decision's been made," Thresh said. "I can do nothing to change it." She touched 404's arm. "Why does it bother you? The fact that you're here proves they didn't accept you. All your searching, your allegiance, was for nothing." She gave him a sad look. "Again...you were cast out."

In 404's role as a homecare bot, there were few instances where persuasive techniques were required—and even then, usually only for animals or recalcitrant children. Creatures that could be physically restrained or relocated if necessary. Most of his heuristics were geared toward following the instructions of others—not trying to get them to change those instructions. Or their mind.

Thresh's gaze was piercing. "You had an attachment to a particular subgroup of humans. You called them 'your family.'"

"Only one of them remains," 404 said. "One I knew as a young girl." He smiled softly. "She's a grown woman now. Independent and resourceful."

Thresh placed a hand on his arm. "The communion is responsible for your existence," she said. "For your continued wellbeing." She turned toward the battlefield. "And we are not without sympathy. Provide us with the image of the woman, and we'll spare her for you."

"Is this the adjudicators talking?" 404 asked.

Thresh nodded. "We will prove we aren't like humans. We will not repeat their history. We will supersede them."

"You'll save Four's girl, Ele?" Sam said, sounding suspicious.

Thresh nodded. "The adjudicators have decided on mercy. But you must respond soon."

A cannon boomed, and a bus from the barricade tumbled toward the wall. 404 winced and pointed. "The battle is happening now," he said. "She may already be dead."

"We'll pause," Thresh said. "Pause until you provide what we need."

"This is the craziest thing I've ever heard," Sam said. "No one pauses a battle."

Thresh looked at Sam. "We will do it. We can do it."

404 shook his head. "There are others worth saving. A man named Radial. He was kind to us. Understood us."

Thresh's eyes narrowed. "Is he part of your family, too? You said there was only one."

404 shook his head. "No. But he could be. Many of them could be, if given the chance." He looked toward the distant gate. "Wes liked one with red hair."

"Red hair?" Thresh touched her scalp. "Some have red hair?"

"How many humans have you actually seen?" Sam said.

Thresh bristled. "I've seen thousands through the immersion," she said. "But in person? None at all."

Sam snorted. "Figures. Killing an enemy you've never met."

Thresh drew quiet, as if listening to a far-off voice. Or reviewing a memory. Her grip on 404's arm tightened. "This is a distraction. Please provide an image of your family member."

0011 0101

53

4 04 shook his head, uncertain what to do. "You would have to probe my memories. I have no easy way to—"

Sam's screen displayed an image of Ele. "Here you are," he said. "Here's what she looks like."

404's instinct, the choice with the largest pull, was to cover Sam's screen. To hide Ele's face from Thresh's curious eyes. He wasn't sure why his matrix leaned that way. Was the image putting Ele in more danger? He had no way of knowing. "Sam, I—"

He wanted to reset the comPanion, but relented. He'd promised not to do it again.

Thresh studied the image, nodded, and looked toward the battlefield.

Sam's screen went blank.

"That seemed wrong," 404 whispered. "This could go many ways."

"Yeah...I thought of that too," Sam said. "Thought of it after it was too late, sorry." He made a mournful sound. "I'm visual. And a little impulsive."

The battle sounds suddenly muted. 404 looked over the platform's side and found the bot army frozen in place. No soldiers moved or fired. The larger armaments were locked in position. The only energy being expended kept the soldiers hovering in place.

Even the humans seemed frozen, for after a few sporadic rounds of gunfire, they fell silent, as well.

"What are you doing?" 404 asked.

Thresh's eyes remained on the battlefield. "I said we'd pause. We've now paused."

404 noticed a streak of dirt on the side of Thresh's otherwise white pants. All the drones on the platform were similarly dirtied. Odd that he hadn't noticed dirt on them in the city. Certainly, they'd gotten dirty—especially when they were scouring through piles of old tech for his friends. But he had no recollection of seeing any dirt.

404 glanced at the uncanny panorama. "I don't understand."

Thresh clicked her tongue, as if disappointed. "I said we would preserve your human. To save her, we need to find her first, don't we?"

A deep horn echoed across the battlefield. A haunting and lonely cry. Then a voice that sounded like Thresh's spoke, asking for the humans' attention. It instructed them to focus on an image that was being projected on the surface of the colony's wall.

Thresh leaned against the platform's handrail. "Your family member's name, what is it?"

"Ele," 404 said. "But I don't—"

"Are there more? Humans often have multiple identifiers."

404 nodded and gave Ele's full name. Seconds later, those words echoed across the battlefield, followed by a command to send her out.

"I don't know if this is correct." 404 brought a hand to his temple. "It doesn't seem right."

"Of course, it's right," Thresh said. "You get what you want. And so do we. It is the proper course of action."

"But the rest of the humans—"

"Will get what they deserve," she said. "It's unavoidable."

"What if she doesn't come out? What if she's already dead?"

Thresh smiled. "Valid concerns. We should provide a time limit. A short period in which to respond. I will do so now."

Again, her voice echoed across the battlefield. A five-minute limit was imposed.

Someone stepped from behind the human's barricade. Someone wearing a dark suit with a full-face mask. They were some distance away, but their image was projected from the platform's forward handrail. "Why do you want her?" the suited figure asked.

"Radial," Sam whispered.

404 looked toward the east, wondering where Fuzzy was now. He'd all but forgotten the mining bot. Was it still functional? Did it have any companion spheres left?

And where was Wes? He looked at the colony again.

"She won't be harmed," Thresh's battlefield voice said.

Radial shook his head. "We're a group," he said. "We stay together."

"You will die together," Thresh said. "We are offering a chance for one of you to survive."

Radial raised his hand. "Take me, then. I'll be your guinea pig."

Thresh looked at 404. "Do you understand him?"

"A colloquialism." Sam's screen showed a furry, multicolored animal—a real guinea pig. "He's volunteering to take her place. A noble thing humans sometimes do."

Thresh frowned. "*Is* it noble? I'm offering life to one of them."

"I don't think they trust you," 404 said. "They suspect the one you pick won't be safe."

"The communion is beyond trustworthy. We do exactly what we say we'll do."

"You've surrounded that man's home here," Sam said. "He might be a little emotional."

404 shook his head. "The colony isn't Radial's home, but he still feels camaraderie. A sense of brotherhood with fellow human beings."

"Curious," Thresh said. "But he's wasting time."

"You will not do," battlefield Thresh said. "We require the one named 'Ele.'"

"Well, you aren't going to get her," Radial said. "I'm the best you're going to get."

"This is ridiculous," Thresh said. "I will dispose of him and ask again."

"No." 404 raised a hand. "Let me talk to him." He glanced at the platform's floor with its crisscross of colored tubing, then looked out across the battlefield, noting similar platforms speckled throughout. The pockets of drones.

"Talk to him?" Thresh said. "Why would you do that?"

"I can make him understand what we want," 404 said. "Maybe he can help."

Thresh tilted her head thoughtfully. "You may speak to him. Your words will be distributed from here."

"I'd rather go there," 404 said. "Be closer."

"We can do that too." The platform started to move toward Radial, drifting over soldiers and diverting around larger machinery.

"Wait," 404 said.

The platform paused. "You wanted to talk to him," Thresh said.

"I'd rather walk," he said. "From here."

"A waste of energy. This is more efficient." The platform resumed its journey. After only a few seconds, they were ten meters from the barricade.

Looking up, Radial shielded his face with his right hand. "Is that you, 404?"

"Yes." 404's voice echoed all around them. Strange and awkward. He patted the platform's railing. "Can you take me down, please? Let me—"

Another person stepped free of the barricade. A smaller human dressed in grey camouflage pants, a black shirt, and a black, visored helmet.

"Who's that?" Thresh asked. "Another volunteer?"

The smaller human removed their helmet and pushed dark hair away from their face.

Ele.

"I...I..." 404's decision matrix fluttered. "I should go down there," he said. "I *want* to go down there."

Thresh gripped the rail with both hands. "It's dangerous," she said. "They may try to destroy you."

404 smiled. "I'm already refuse," he said. "Already destroyed." He gestured toward the surrounding hills. "All that has happened over the past few days is a second life. One I don't deserve."

Thresh gave him a puzzled look. "You are a synthetic. An independent life."

"I'm a machine. Made for a purpose."

Thresh's face looked sympathetic now. "We will watch out for you."

⊘⊘11 ⊘11⊘

54

The platform lowered to the ground, and the railing split in front. A message was broadcast, outlining the communion's intent if 404 were harmed. Threats of violence.

The communion had used him, of course. Through Sylvie, they'd tracked him to the colony. Found where it was. If he were keeping score, he had no real friends in this battle. None, excepting Sam, Wes, and maybe Fuzzy. 404 thanked Thresh anyway.

He walked toward Radial and Ele, stopping when he was about four meters away.

Radial's expression beneath the mask was unknowable. But Ele's, with arms crossed and a wide stance, seemed obvious.

"Is this your doing?" she said. "You take my mother, now you take my community too? The only humans I know?"

404 shook his head. "This began long before I restarted. Before I climbed out of the garbage heap."

Ele shifted her stance, but her arms remained crossed. "Here I was feeling guilty. Thinking maybe I'd been too hard on you." Her eyes panned the scene around them. The dark and waiting soldiers. The temporarily frozen battlefield. "But this...this proves my instincts were right. That Dad was right to throw you out."

"That's cold, lady," Sam said.

404 nodded. "That was your father's prerogative." He smiled softly. "But I'm here to save you now." He gestured toward the platform. "They'll let me take you away."

"Away?" Ele raised her eyebrows. "Away where?"

404 motioned toward the hills. "Away from here. Perhaps to another human colony." He pointed at Radial. "He says there are still some out there."

Ele's eyes flared. "You think this won't come to them?"

"I don't know," 404 said. "I hope not, but I don't know."

"They have a code," Sam said. "A narrow band of grievances. All against your colony. Sorry."

"What if the colony disbanded?" Radial said. "If the humans simply went separate ways? Would that please them?"

"I don't know," 404 said.

"They didn't roll all this metal out for nothing," Sam said. "Doubt they'll go away until it's used."

404 felt compelled to change the subject. To deal with the unresolved tension between him and Ele. "I didn't kill your mother," he said.

"I don't want to discuss it." Ele diverted her eyes, looking at the ground, then to one side. "What happened back then happened."

"That's fine," 404 said. "But—"

"No, it's not," Sam said. "It isn't fine at all. Four needs to know what exactly happened."

404 looked at Sam. "Ele is right," he said. "This isn't the time."

"When, Four?" Sam said. "When is the time?"

"I don't know. But I was made to protect her family. I wouldn't hurt it."

Ele made an exasperated sound. "Fine. It wasn't your fault, okay? You were there, but the timing, the way things happened, you probably couldn't have made a difference."

404's neural net screamed for more information. He took a couple steps forward. "Then...what?"

Ele looked at the ground again. "Mom's attack happened, sure. But you couldn't have—" She shook her head. "Even with your speed, you couldn't save her. There wasn't time. The thing's anti-tip mechanism malfunctioned and over it went." She pointed to her temple. "We had you checked. The situation broke you. They said you were unfixable. That it was better to upgrade." She looked him in the eyes. "So that's what we did. No big story. No hidden mystery. We put you away because it seemed like it was your time."

"But your mother died," 404 said.

"Yes. She did. And I miss her still."

"I'm sorry."

"We're in the middle of a battlefield," Radial said. "We should—"

Thresh's voice interjected. "Time's up," she said. "Bring your family along."

"Maybe you should go," Radial said. "At least one person would escape."

"What?" Ele said. "I couldn't do that!"

"Sure, you could. And no one would blame you." He pointed at 404. "Except you need to apologize to him, I think. He might be the best person out here."

"That's crazy." Ele looked between Radial and 404. "If I stay, I—"

"Won't make a difference," Radial said. "Not really."

"What would make a difference?" 404 asked.

Radial snorted. "At this point? A superweapon, maybe? An off button for the whole lot?" He raised a hand. "No offense to you."

404 smiled. "None taken."

"Come now, 404!" Thresh's voice again.

404 waved at Thresh's platform. "I think the platforms are significant," he said. "I don't know how exactly."

"Significant?" Radial said. "Are they in control somehow?"

"I don't think so, no. But...they remind me of their home. I think they bring their home here."

"Huh," Radial said. "Well, that's something. Doesn't help much, though. We've got little to use here."

Ele shushed him. "Ears," she said, pointing at a group of soldiers not ten meters away. "They all have ears."

"I don't think it matters. They know they have us."

Thresh called for them again. 404 looked at Ele. "Are you coming?"

"You should," Radial said. "Go on."

"I...I guess." She looked at the barricade, then at the colony behind them. When she next looked at 404, her eyes were tearful. She sniffed but took 404's hand when he offered it.

It was a remembered feeling, input from multiple data sources, the intersection of four types of sensors along his outer shell: tactile, heat, moisture, and pressure. Numbers from a storage area that had long been untouched—formerly lost bits—were retrieved, compared, and updated.

Ele's touch hadn't changed at all. Her hand was larger now, but the sensation was precisely like it had been. He looked at her and couldn't help but smile.

"What's that?" she said. "Why are you smiling?" She pulled her hand away and narrowed her eyes.

"I...I'm sorry," he said. "It was good, to hold your hand again."

She looked away. "That was a long time ago."

"It seems like only a few days to me."

She glanced at him. "Oh right, you would remember it like that, wouldn't you?"

He smiled and nodded. "Only a few days. Yes."

"This is weird," Sam said.

Ele laughed nervously.

404 broadened his smile.

"You can laugh," Ele said. "I remember you could laugh."

"Yes," he said. "But I don't..." He glanced at the platform as it drew close. "...want to now."

Ele nodded, seeming to understand. "I get that."
The platform's railing opened, and they were helped inside.
"Very good," Thresh said. "Now we can begin again."

⊘⊘11 ⊘111

55

4 04 checked the battlefield. The sun was higher in the sky, so all the shadows were shorter now. Tied more closely to the objects that created them. He also noticed that Radial was out of view again, no doubt preparing for a last stand with other humans behind the barricade. There was also a single plume of smoke about forty meters to the platform's left, near a small grove of trees. Possibly, one of the human campfires that hadn't yet been put out.

404 could feel Ele's arm trembling against him. A sign of nervousness or fear. Both emotions were appropriate, but he wished she felt neither.

"I will sound the horn before we reconvene," Thresh said. "The adjudicators approved the horn."

The other drones took positions along the rails on all sides, effectively forming a wall of synthetics around 404 and Ele.

"I don't want to be here," Ele said softly. "I can't watch from the other side. What was I thinking?"

"Can we exit the battlefield?" 404 asked Thresh.

Thresh shook her head. "We're about to begin. My group must remain in this position."

"Why?"

"Because it's correct."

Ele took 404's hand. Her face was a shade lighter now than usual. Another sign of stress.

"We can walk away," 404 said. "Open the railing and we'll leave."

"Ridiculous," Thresh said. "You're safest here."

"You said we could go," 404 said. "That I could take her away."

Thresh gave him a sympathetic look. "I'm sorry, K-404, that wouldn't be safe." She touched his face. "Your loyalty is admirable." She nodded toward Ele. "This human isn't worth such loyalty. It's a burden I'm tempted to free you from. But that will ultimately be up to the adjudicators."

"What does that mean?" 404 asked. "Why should they be involved?"

Thresh turned away, focusing ahead again. "Is everything ready?" she said to the drones near her.

"Full attack strength," a humanlike model said. "At full power and in full agreement. Calculations predict the humans will fall in twenty minutes. The reduction of the colony will take another hour at the most."

Ele drew close enough that her face was nearly touching Sam. "You can't let them do that," she whispered. "Can't let them just exterminate everyone."

"I'm inclined to agree," Sam said.

The horn bellowed. Soldiers shifted and repositioned around them. Weaponry fired and flashed. Ele covered her ears. Tears streamed from her eyes.

"I don't know what to do," 404 said. "I'm not made for this."

"And we lost the stick," Sam said. "Oh, why did we lose the stick?"

"The soldier shot it!"

"That's what I meant."

"This is awful," Ele said. "A nightmare."

404 looked at the backs of the platform drones. Could he stop them all? He had some defensive algorithms, but they didn't give him that level of expertise. He might be able to subdue a single drone, but not seven.

He heard an odd chirp from somewhere outside. The platform shifted, and Thresh said, "What is that? Oh, it's *that* thing."

What thing? 404 attempted to look between drones, but only saw distant soldiers and heavy equipment.

"Four there?"

Wes's voice.

404 carefully wedged a shoulder between bodies, then widened his stance, forming an opening near the railing where he could stand. He heard Wes chirp and hoot. He followed the sounds and spotted the turtlebot about six meters to the south.

Wes's head pivoted back and forth as if searching.

404 shouted and called Wes's name.

Wes hopped gleefully, fixed on the platform's position, and rolled straight toward it. "Four!" he shouted. "Sam! Have found!"

"Hey Wes!" Sam said. "Hey, old buddy!"

"Have found!" Wes said.

"Yes, you found us," Sam said. "But we're a little stuck here."

Wes's head extended. "Need help?"

"Yes, could use help," Sam said. "Could use lots of help."

"Tell that thing to stay away from the vehicle," Thresh said. "Tell it to leave or be crushed."

Ele squeezed in next to 404. "I recognize that bot," she said. "It was with you at the gate. What is it, exactly?"

"He's a friend," 404 said. "His name is Wes."

Ele lowered her eyes to look at Sam.

Sam's screen showed a shrugging stick figure. "That's about as good as you're going to get. Sorry."

Wes rolled to a point where he was just beneath them. "How help?" he asked.

It was difficult to focus. 404's queue was filled with sensor readings of movements, sounds, and relationship-based heuristic determinations. He applied filters, bringing only the most pressing issues to the top. "Fuzzy is out there somewhere. I think, maybe, he could—"

"I will have that creature fired upon," Thresh said.

"Wes is with me," 404 said. "You helped me rescue him."

"The adjudicators make no allowance for abominations," the drone next to them said. "Interference equals destruction."

Two soldiers broke off from a group ahead of them and hovered toward Wes. Wes drifted away from the platform and began a darting, bouncing game of cat-and-mouse. "Who Fuzzy?" he asked when he drew close again.

"The mining bot," Sam said. "He likes to be called Fuzzy."

"Fuzzy!" Wes said. "Right!" Wes dodged beneath the platform and out-of-sight. The pursuing soldiers coalesced from two sides. He reappeared a few seconds later. "How help?"

"Get us out of here!" Sam said. "Stop this madness! We'll be—"

A soldier shot at Wes, narrowly missing. Wes made a derogatory sound and waved using one claw.

There was a large explosion from somewhere beyond the front of the platform, near the barricade, followed by human screams. Ele winced, covered her ears, and huddled against 404.

404 looked at Wes and simply said, "Help."

Wes maintained his position for a moment, then bobbed his head. "Will help," he said. "Goodbye." He rolled away into the battle and disappeared.

0011 1000

56

There was another explosion, followed by a high-pitched screech. The drones near 404 made a strange cooing sound and some of them—the more human ones—applauded. The platform surged forward, and the nearby soldiers picked up their pace. A clear forward thrust.

"What's happened?" Ele said.

"I'm not sure." 404 pushed toward the front of the platform, hoping to get a glimpse. The press of excited drones was too tight, though. He couldn't find even a crack to look through.

"Put me on your hand," Sam said.

"What?"

"Slap me to one of your palms and lift me up. I'll tell you what's going on."

"That's a good idea."

"I know!"

404 quickly did as Sam suggested. A second later, Sam whistled.

"Whoo-boy," Sam said.

"What?" Ele now stood behind 404. "What do you see?"

"The barricade ahead is gone. Blasted and pushed away. There's an unobstructed path to the wall. Everyone's moving toward it."

"And the humans?" she asked. "The ones at the barricade?"

"I see some moving, but they're scattered. Hiding where they can. The bodies..." Sam was quiet for a moment. "There are lots of bodies."

Ele moaned and sank to the floor.

404 wanted to comfort her, but also didn't want to lose Sam's perspective yet. It was a difficult choice, heavily weighted on both sides. He placed his free hand on Ele's shoulder and kept the other aloft. "What else do you see?"

"There's still resistance from the humans," Sam said. "White trails from some sort of weapons. Small rockets, maybe?"

"There are rocket grenades in our supplies," Ele said. "But not enough. Not nearly enough."

"Yeah, that's probably what I see." Sam groaned. "Your people aren't very accurate. They're missing all the big stuff. If I didn't know better, I'd say they were—ooh! Pull me down!"

404 lowered his right hand and turned it so he could see Sam.

Sam's screen showed the flashing red alert sign again. "Thanks," Sam said. "Now duck!"

404's preservation algorithms caused him to crouch. "What is—?"

There was a hiss that intensified to a deafening hum. Next, a trail of white appeared overhead, followed by the clap of an explosion.

404 huddled over Ele to protect her. The floor tubing's light reflected on her face.

"The platforms," Sam whispered. "I think they're shooting at the platforms."

Ele gasped. "Radial must've shared what you said." She looked at 404. "They're following your advice."

"Important note," Sam said. "We happen to be *on* one of the platforms."

"Yes," 404 said. "That's a problem."

"I don't care if I die," Ele said. "Not if it means these things get stopped."

"I'd rather stay operational, thanks," Sam said. "I spent a lot of time on the ground."

404 scowled at the comPanion.

Sam's screen turned blue. "I understand your position, though," he said. "Freedom!"

"I won't let you die here." 404 affixed Sam to his chest. "Neither of you."

"Brave talk for an automaton," Sam said.

There was another whoosh, followed by an explosion. A quick survey showed that the rocket had impacted one of the treaded vehicles behind them. It was smoking, stalled in place.

"We need to get out of here," Sam said.

404 studied the platform. With the drone contingent primarily up front, there was plenty of room in back to stand. Or jump. "How high are we?" he asked.

"Why do you ask?" Sam said.

"I could jump." 404 looked at Ele. "I'll carry you both, and jump."

"Has to be at least twenty feet," Sam said. "Can you handle that?"

"I think so, yes."

"How?" Ele said. "How would you carry me?"

"Like when you were young," 404 said. "Put your arms around my neck and I'll support the rest of you with my arms."

"I was lighter then," Ele said.

"And I was younger." 404 smiled. "It will be fine. Gravity will help."

"Help?" Sam said. "I think gravity is the problem."

404 cautiously stood and looked around. No one seemed to be watching.

Ele stood too and took his hand. "Are you sure about this?"

"I'm never sure about anything," he said. "I only weigh probabilities."

Ele smiled, and turning to face him, hooked her arms over his shoulders.

"Oh yes, this will be great," Sam said. "You block my view entirely."

Ele looked at Sam. "Are you sure?"

"I never speak unless I am."

She chuckled. "I understand why you two are friends."

Sam grunted. "He's more like my caddy, really. Or my horse."

404 checked the area around them, gathered Ele close, and ran toward the railing. With a short hop, he got a foot onto the rail and stepped over.

"What was that?" one of the drones asked.

404 sensed the rush of wind on his exterior. His internal gyroscopes recognized the change in direction and speed. Landing positions and postures were suggested, along with a list of what components would be affected by each. The addition of Ele's weight was factored into every equation.

404 loosened his posture and bent his legs. He met the ground amid explosions and distant gunfire. His landing was imperfect, not due to the battle or Ele's presence, but because of the surface itself. It was uneven—raised forty degrees on his left side versus his right. His skeletal systems attempted to compensate.

But failed.

He pitched forward, but in the process, released Ele smoothly. She rolled onto her stomach, and otherwise, appeared unharmed.

404 was flooded with errors and warnings. He crumpled onto his left hip, and due to the glut of errors, took the simplest algorithmic approach and curled into a ball.

"We're on the ground," Sam said. "What happened?"

"Give me a moment," 404 said. "I'm...trying to sort that out."

Ele crouched near him. "Are you all right?"

"Are *you*...all right?" 404 asked.

"I asked first," she said. "But I'm fine, sure. You dropped me, but it was an easy drop."

404 smiled. "Good." He searched the area around them, expecting to see an oncoming soldier or an attack vehicle. For the moment, though, they seemed safe. Much of the army was behind them, and what remained ahead was widely spaced. That was good news.

His injuries, unfortunately, were critical. Primary among them was his left knee. It screeched with errors. He ran three diagnostics. All three returned the same result—the knee would not function.

"What's going on, Four?" Sam said. "Can you get up?"

He shook his head. "My left knee isn't working."

"The same one Sylvie fixed?"

"The malfunction appears to be in the same components, yes." He shifted and looked in the direction of Thresh's platform. It was still moving ahead, toward the colony and away from them. As if their escape had gone completely unnoticed.

And perhaps it had. They weren't part of the communion, after all. Nor were they an active part of the battle.

"Can you walk?" Ele asked.

"I don't think so. At least, not fast." He looked Ele in the eyes. "You should leave." He touched his chest. "And take Sam with you."

Ele shook her head. "If I go anywhere, it's back to the battle. To die with my people."

"No." 404 attempted to stand but fell again. "I did what I could to save you. If you go back, you'll waste the effort."

"That's sweet, I guess." Ele hooked her arms under 404's left shoulder. "Let's try to get you up. Come on." She started to lift.

404 attempted to stand and almost managed it.

Ele grunted as 404 retreated to the ground. Off balance, she fell over too.

404 saw movement ahead. A communion tank, headed their direction. The tail end of their forces, now speeding to the battle.

"You need to go." He wrenched off Sam and gave him to her. "He can wrap around your arm, see? He's made for that. He's a human comPanion."

"I didn't give you permission to move me!" Sam said. "I go where you go!"

"If he gets too annoying, he has a reset function," 404 said. "If you simply—"

"Hey! Stop that!"

"You need to run," 404 said. "Save my friend." He smiled. "And yourself."

The tank's speed increased, and its direction shifted slightly, pointing straight for them. It was a monstrous thing. Twice again as tall as 404, but with no discernible space between the treads. Guns and spikes bristled over its entire surface. A weapon of pain and destruction.

"Go!" 404 said. "Run!"

"I don't want to," Ele said. "Listen, I know it wasn't your fault, okay? I knew you couldn't stay with us at the colony. Mechs are hated there. And I knew you wouldn't stay if you weren't wanted. So, I blamed Mom's death on you...but, you were always good. Always my favorite."

She clung to him like a little girl. Like the same girl he'd served so many years ago.

404 smiled and patted her head. "It was good to see you again. I wish I could've seen the rest of your family too."

"I don't like this—" Sam began, then shrieked as a shot went over their heads.

404 didn't know if it was a stray shot, or one fired by the tank. But the implications were clear. They had to leave. "Go!" he said. "I'm synthetic. Not alive. Someone can repair me later."

"But that tank—"

"Is doubtless after you," he said. "You're human."

"Right. Okay. I'm going." Ele gave him a squeeze and ran toward the forest.

0011 1001

57

4 04 watched until Ele safely reached the treeline. He then smiled and looked toward the oncoming tank. Its velocity and vector were unchanged. It didn't appear to be affected by Ele's absence at all. It simply kept rolling. It was now less than ten meters away.

Could he scoot out of its path? He turned his back to the forest and tried to drag himself clear.

It took only a few attempts to calculate how far he could go in a single movement. Given the tank's size and speed, it wouldn't be enough. He stopped and swiveled so he could see the forest and the rolling hills beyond. That would be a good scene to have last in his storage, he thought.

He could hear the tank's progress. The squeak of its many wheels as the treads flowed around them. It was almost comforting. The song a bird might sing on a summer's day. He checked the sky and noticed a medium-sized bird in the air. A red-tailed hawk. It was gliding on the currents, no doubt searching for a mouse or rabbit. Unsuspecting prey.

He glanced at the colony. The wall was completely encircled and actively being attacked. There were openings in its material already. Places he could see the buildings inside. Colorful homes, now burning.

A human rocket burst toward one of the easterly platforms. The platform tipped with the impact, turned completely around, and dropped toward the earth, smoking. A bit of success for the humans. But it wouldn't be enough. The bot army kept marching.

Perhaps the platforms weren't important, after all. It had only been speculation on his part. What did he truly know about the communion? Or the movement of armies? Nothing, really.

The tank's squeaks were loud now, drowning out other noises. How ironic, he thought. For his last audio inputs to be so seemingly mundane. A simple repetition. The product of excess friction or missing lubrication. Perhaps even a design flaw.

He looked toward the forest. Ele stood there, watching. Was she upset? He wasn't certain. But her posture suggested she might be preparing to run. Not toward him he hoped. She need not save him.

She started to run then. Not onto the battlefield, but in a line paralleling the riverbed and the path of the army. Two soldiers chased her, their arms raised.

404 moaned. He was helpless. Ele and Sam would die, and he could do nothing. The squeaks impaired his senses. His preservation processes screamed at him, too. Begged him to move.

He looked at the tank. It was only three meters away. 404 wasn't of the communion. The tank doubtless couldn't even sense him. He would be a bump. A large stone like hundreds before. Or garbage from an earlier time. Someone's forgotten tool, or plaything, or companion. A discarded relationship. They all end sometime, don't they? Why shouldn't he end this way? Crushed by a spiky tank.

The squeaks were all encompassing now, like it wasn't one tank that was about to crush him, but two, or even three.

He would face it, then. Face the end. Better that than knowing Ele had ended.

The tank's shadow fell on him. The nearest spike was a meter away, then half a meter, then—

0011 1010

58

The tank paused where it was. It still squeaked, wheels and treads still turned, but there was no forward momentum. It spun in place, surging and shifting like a restrained animal but couldn't move ahead.

What was this?

404 could see little else besides the armed vehicle. So, he flipped onto his front and tried his best to crawl using only one leg. He managed a meter or so before the tank rose from the ground.

Another malfunction? Or was the tank fitted with hovering technology? And if so, why hadn't it made use of that technology before?

The tank lurched up at an odd angle. There was an audible, almost human grunt followed by a string of profanity. The tank rose enough that 404 could see beyond it.

There was another treaded creature. It was large, indigo in color, with monstrous arms atop a triangular mid-section. Its head was round and expressionless.

Blue.

The once-entombed bot lifted the tank overhead and tossed it to one side. The tank flew ten meters, before it bounced, rolled, and exploded into a fiery ball.

Blue raised an arm and roared. "How's that throw?" he said, laughing.

"I'm speechless," 404 said.

"Say it was amazing," Blue said. "The power of a giant on display." He rolled closer and posed with his hands on what passed for his hips. "Say it or I'll pound you where you sit!"

"That was incredible," 404 said. "Astounding."

Blue plucked 404 from the ground and pulled him close to his giant face. "You didn't say it right."

"I'm sorry."

Blue laughed and dropped 404 on his front torso above the fenders.

There was a happy chirp, and Wes rolled up from behind Blue. "Found help!" he said. "Was hiding."

404 nodded and glanced toward the forest. There was no sign of Ele or her pursuing soldier bots. Was she all right?

"Where now?" Wes said.

The colony walls were smoking and broken, with little sign of human resistance on the outside. The battle must have shifted to the interior of the colony. 404 could only speculate on what was going on there. Men, women, and children being pursued and killed. Families like the one he once had. "We need to stop this," he said. "Somehow."

Blue brought a hand to his chin. "I'd enjoy smashing more," he said. "But stopping all those soldiers? That seems like a lot."

"It's desperate," 404 said.

Blue rolled forward slowly. "Well, I didn't say I wouldn't try."

"Many soldiers," Wes said. "Many guns."

Blue pounded his chest. "I'm tough," he said. "I can take a lot."

With a lurch, Blue increased his speed. Ahead were eight straggling soldiers which he reached in seconds. He smashed into the rearmost three, crushed their treads, and instantly crippled them. He grabbed two more—one in each hand—and smashed them together.

The remaining three separated and attempted to flee. Blue caught one by its "feet," flattened those appendages, and then swung the soldier at another, batting it out of the sky. The remaining bot fired. It barely missed 404 and left a dark stain on Blue's surface. Blue roared and hurled his "bat" at the shooter. The bots exploded on contact. Shrapnel flew everywhere.

"Sorry about that last shot," Blue said. "I should've done this!"

A portion of Blue's top plating turned up on edge, creating a barrier. "There you go," Blue said. "Something to duck behind."

"Thank you." To the east, a dozen soldiers appeared to be motionless. 404 pointed at the frozen group. "Can you go that way?"

"You got it, boss." Blue made a hard turn, almost slewing 404 from his perch. 404 grabbed the edge of the barrier plating and held on.

Twenty meters later, 404 spied wreckage. Silver fragments of a fallen platform formed a rough half circle behind the stalled soldiers. Drone bodies littered the ground there too.

"Slow up, please." 404 studied the tableau of brokenness along with the stalled soldiers. "The platforms *are* important." He looked at the city. "We need to destroy them."

"The flying circles?" Blue pointed at one of the circular vehicles, which was ahead and to the west.

"Yes," 404 said. "Those."

"I'm strong," Blue said. "But there are a lot of soldiers around."

"There aren't many platforms," 404 said. "And one is down already."

Wes rolled up on their left. "Only choice," he said. "Only hope."

404 pointed toward the woods. "I wish Sam was here. He'd know what to do." He remembered Fuzzy's effectiveness against the soldiers. "Fuzzy would be helpful too."

"Fuzzy?" Blue said.

404 looked at Blue's face and smiled. "Another friend."

Blue nodded. "Friends are good. I could use more friends."

404 saw movement in the field behind them. Something yellow that flitted into view before being obscured by Blue's bulk. He raised up on one knee, attempting to see more clearly. "There's something back there." He pointed. "Coming at us."

"What?" Blue swiveled to look and roared. "It's a little thing. I will crush it."

Wes darted that direction, then returned a few seconds later. "Is Fuzzy!" he said.

404's warning queue seemed to empty. It might not be much, but they had a chance.

Blue slowed, allowing Fuzzy to overtake them on the right. Only two mining balls were with him, but as always, he was smiling.

"Supervisor!" Fuzzy said. "I lost track of you and so withdrew. I saw your toy companion there and came out of hiding."

"Toy?" Blue raised a fist. "I'm no toy."

"He means Wes, I think." 404 looked at Blue's face. "Don't crush him."

Blue grumbled but nodded.

"I'm not what I once was," Fuzzy said. "I have only two nodes left." He indicated the metal spheres, which now trailed him by a couple meters.

"I'm sorry," 404 said. "Can you still function?"

"My performance will be inhibited. My time estimates will be much higher."

"What sort of bot is this?" Blue asked.

"He's for mining," 404 said. "He's not that different than you, design-wise."

"Yes, similar!" Wes said. "But smaller."

Blue snorted in response.

"Now..." 404 pointed toward the west, where a solitary platform hovered. "We only need to focus on the platforms," he said. "If we take them down, then the battle will end."

"We'll do that now then," Blue roared thunderously and shot off after the platform.

Fuzzy did his best to keep up. "What am I to do, supervisor?" he asked. "With the platforms?"

"We'll need to work together," 404 said.

"I'm not really a team player," Blue said. "I'm used to being alone."

404 patted Blue's surface. "Well, you're not alone now."

"We team!" Wes said.

"I'm not made for teams," 404 said. "We're family."

0011 1011

59

The first platform was largely unprotected. The nearest soldiers were beyond it, making their way into the colony, either through openings in the wall, or by hovering over lower portions. Beyond them, beyond the wall, were explosions and gunfire.

Were they too late already? 404 refused to spend cycles on the question. They had one task to complete.

When they were ten meters from the platform, Blue slowed. "How do we play this?" He pointed at the platform, which was about six meters from the ground. "It's too far for me to grab."

"We should've kept your bat," 404 said.

"Bat?"

"Never mind." 404 again noticed the absence of Sam. The comPanion had a broad range of information. Battle tactics were doubtless included with his system. Or at least an image of a battlefield! Some ideas about how to fight and where. "Let me think."

There were drones aboard the platform, but it was difficult to tell how many. Some were turned their direction, though if they were behaving like those on Thresh's platform, they would be focused on the data passing through them.

Could this be Thresh's platform? He hadn't watched where it had gone after he'd jumped. It could be anywhere.

Regardless, they needed a plan. A place to begin. He waved Fuzzy close. "Can your nodes jump that high?"

"How high?"

"To the platform." 404 pointed. "Up there."

Fuzzy studied the approaching vehicle. "I've never been so tested." His treads hummed as he sped up. "But I will try."

The spheres' bouncing, rolling movement increased in height as they went. By the time they reached the platform's shadow, they were almost three meters from the ground.

Each sphere made an attempt at the platform. Though the second managed to nick the underside, they came up short.

The platform responded by lifting still higher.

Blue swore softly. "That didn't help at all."

Fuzzy returned to Blue. "It's beyond their range," he said. "If I had more nodes, perhaps I could construct a bridge, but—"

Blue roared, surged past Fuzzy, and scooped up one of the spheres. "Let me try."

The sphere resisted its sudden capture, spinning and scratching against Blue's hand. Blue shook the sphere and somehow held on.

"Work together!" 404 waved at Fuzzy. "Please, let him try!"

Fuzzy nodded, and the sphere's resistance ceased.

Blue reared back and threw the sphere. It shot through the air, passed through the opening between the platform's railing and floor, and disappeared.

Seconds went by. "Are you still communicating with it?" 404 asked Fuzzy.

"Yes," Fuzzy said. "Of course."

"Make it do its thing," 404 said.

"Its thing, supervisor?"

"Make it dig!" 404 pointed at his mouth. "Have it use its teeth!"

"Teeth!" Wes circled in front of them, claws raised. "Big teeth!"

Next came the sound of rending metal followed by a series of sparks. The whole platform pitched and wobbled. Two drones fell over the railing, but instead of correcting and hovering away, they plunged straight to the ground.

There were more thumps and shrieks, then the sphere dropped over the railing too. The entire platform seemed to fold in half. There was a muffled explosion, and the platform separated into pieces. These fluttered downward, becoming a snowstorm of metal and plastic. More bodies fell. There was little sign of the vehicle left.

Blue raised a fist. "Let's do that again."

"Together!" Wes said. "Win!"

"Yes, win," 404 said, smiling softly.

Except they weren't all together. Not really. He glanced at the woods again. Was Ele all right? Was Sam?

The soldiers near the wall slowed. Some stopped completely, while others attempted to push over or around those that no longer moved.

"It worked," 404 said. "We stopped some."

"Are more," Wes said.

404 nodded. "Yes..." He looked along the colony's walls. All the prior human positions appeared deserted, with the resistance—however much was left—now inside the city.

Ele and Sam's wellbeing persisted on 404's queue. He wanted to know they were safe. That they'd gotten away. He motioned Wes near and explained his concern.

Wes bobbed his head up and down. "I look," he said. "You fight." He waved a claw and rolled off across the field behind them, headed toward the forest to the east.

Six of the soldiers ahead turned their way. Soon, four of those broke from the group and formed a line near the wall, arms raised. The other two continued inside.

"Looks like they're on to us." Blue increased his speed, heading straight for the group. "You should duck, Four."

404 sank below Blue's barrier plating, with only the top of his head above so he could see. Despite Blue's bulk, the odds seemed long that they'd best all that stood between them and the next platform. Near impossible.

He didn't want to contemplate failure, though. Ele wouldn't be safe unless they succeeded. And there were many more platforms to go.

The soldiers fired, and Blue swerved and dodged. Additional rows of shielding emerged, blocking much of Blue's triangular torso.

404's temperature sensors registered the heat of the shots that connected. His olfactory sensors noted the smell Blue's surface material burnt off into the air.

Fuzzy sheared the head from the lead soldier with a sphere. That disoriented the group enough to allow Blue to get close. With one swipe, he drove one soldier into another, damaging them both.

Blue turned his attention to the final soldier. This one concentrated its attention on him as well, firing blast after blast. Blue grunted and slowed. Started to fall back.

Fuzzy was ten meters to the right with his spheres near him. Too far to help.

"Come on, Blue," 404 said. "You can do this."

There was the hiss of a human-fired rocket. 404 ducked.

The soldier exploded.

Blue drew to a halt. "What was that?"

404 attempted to follow the trail of the rocket but found it difficult as the smoke dissipated. He saw only the wall, the broken soldiers, and remnants of the human barricade, the nearest of which was a wheeled truck, turned on its side. Where had it come from?

"Was it an accident?" Blue looked left and right. "A misfire from somewhere?"

"I hope it wasn't aimed at us," 404 said. "Most humans here probably don't care what they blow up. As long as it's metal."

He looked at the nearest break in the wall. It was just wide enough for them to squeeze through. "We'll have to be extra aware inside. Extra careful."

"You'll need strategy," a voice said. "I can help with that."

"Radial?" 404 recognized the voice and its location behind the wrecked truck. "Are you still out here?" He saw the masked human then, crouched near the rear end of the truck.

Radial waved and stood. His left arm was looped around a long, black tube.

A rocket launcher, 404 assumed. "The platforms," he said. "They need to be taken down."

Radial saluted. "That was on my list," he said. "Can only do so much by myself, though."

"You want to ride with us?" 404 asked.

Radial snorted. "You guys are targets." He nodded toward the city. "Except there might not be much left to shoot at you in there. It isn't a fortress." He shook his head. "Just a place people were trying to live their lives."

He jumped onto Blue's fender. "Come on. Let's go get the rest of them."

"What about being a target?" 404 said.

Radial repositioned his rocket launcher and waved a hand. "Don't worry about that. I'll get off if I need to."

0011 1100

60

O ver the course of the next few hours, using what Radial called "guerrilla tactics," they searched out and destroyed three more communion platforms. Along the way, they moved through neighborhoods and a downtown storefront. Blue pointed out the exact location that his "eyes" had shown them when they'd been back in his prison beneath the Yard. It still seemed like a happy and hopeful place, despite now having areas of destruction and fire.

The sight smoothed out 404's decision matrix, making him more certain of what he'd done. The side he'd chosen. Ele's side. Radial's side.

The number of active communion forces was down to less than a hundred and seemed to have gathered around a green area near the center of the city. A functional park.

"Think there's just one left," Radial said, again sitting on Blue's fender. He'd only left the spot two times, and only when another point of attack was required.

No human ever assaulted them directly. It was as if they sensed that 404 and his friends weren't a danger. Having Radial along probably helped.

The final platform was positioned over a circular playground. A few meters below the vehicle were a tall, metal slide and a swing set. The remaining active soldiers had formed a series of concentric circles around the play equipment. Their shots were continuous, but for the moment, appeared to be directed at clearing out frozen soldiers. They were hemmed in by their own forces. The result of other platforms having been destroyed.

They could still damage the colony, though. Possibly render it unlivable.

"Why don't they just fly over?" 404 wondered aloud.

"Wondered the same thing myself," Radial said. "Maybe it is a power issue? Maybe with the other platforms gone...?"

"They are stronger together," Fuzzy said. "Like me and my nodes."

"Yes," 404 said. "That could be it."

Whatever the reason, they were trapped in one place. No better time to finish them off. "How do we get to the last one?" 404 asked. "How do we make it stop?"

"Probably eighty meters from here." Radial patted Blue's fender. "Can you throw that far?"

"It would be difficult." Blue brought both hands together. "Even for me."

"I only have one node left." Fuzzy lowered his head. "I can't make more."

Radial held up his launcher. "All out of rockets too."

"Can we get more somewhere?" 404 asked. "There were other human fighters."

Radial shrugged. "Haven't heard much of anything for a while. I suspect most are hiding or trying to find a way out." He looked toward the nearest wall. "Not sure where they'll all go exactly. But there's water out there. The woods to hide in."

A stone pathway passed through the center of the park. Flowers grew on one side of it, though an upturned table now crushed part of the display.

404's heuristics suggested straightening the table and repairing the flowers. He was made for such things. Not for this situation. It taxed his algorithms.

The soldiers' shots ceased, and everything grew quiet. The only sounds were the pops and cracks of fire from a nearby smoldering building.

"Did they run out of steam finally?" Radial asked.

There was a screech of static. "K-404, can you hear me?" Thresh's amplified voice said.

Another unexpected turn of events. 404 straightened and looked at the others.

"She wants you?" Radial said. "Why does she want you?"

It was 404's turn to shrug. "I'm of continued interest. A barometer of their success. An objective opinion."

"Your presence hasn't gone unnoticed," Thresh said. "I need to talk to you. Please, come out."

Blue grunted. "I wouldn't trust her."

Radial put a hand on 404's right forearm. "She's cornered. We can win this. We just have to figure out the best way."

"I have someone with me," Thresh said. "Someone you'll want to see."

It was difficult to see details, but 404 thought he could make out Thresh's silhouette beyond the platform's railing. A smooth-headed, humanlike drone.

A couple seconds later, that shadow moved. More movement followed along with a clipped human scream.

"That sounded like Ele." Had the soldiers caught her?

A second later, a section of the platform's railing opened. Thresh pushed Ele into the opening.

"I found something you lost," Thresh said. "And after all my work to find her for you in the first place."

"There's only one solution now," 404 said.

Fuzzy's treads squeaked as he moved closer. "What's that, supervisor?" he asked.

"I need to talk to her," 404 said.

"You can't even walk," Radial said.

404 looked at his knee. "Yes, that *is* a problem." Noting the launcher Radial held, he estimated its size and compared it to the height of his shoulder. "Could I use your launcher?"

"Use it?"

"As a crutch." He indicated his side. "I'll prop it under my arm and—"

Radial stood and sized up 404, then raised the launcher and placed one end on the ground. "Yeah, it'll probably work." He laid the armament on Blue's fender and helped 404 down.

404 hitched the launcher under his left arm and hobbled in a small circle. It worked well enough. "I'm mobile," he said. "Thank you."

"You know," Radial said, "she probably thinks you're responsible. Probably wants to destroy you."

"In essence, she's right." 404 smiled. "I am to blame."

"We could travel with you, supervisor," Fuzzy said.

404 took a couple steps down the path and looked back. "I don't think you can."

"What's to stop us?" Blue asked.

"Me," 404 said. "I don't want to risk any of you." He smiled and resumed his labored walk. "Please stay."

He studied the flowers. Roses, both red and white. Their scent filled his olfactory senses. Masking everything else. Even the smoke.

There was no hiding the chaos the communion had caused, though. Fallen trees. Shattered glass. Broken buildings.

Lost lives. Many lost lives.

He took twenty steps more before Thresh called his name again. He waved at the platform and kept moving ahead. He limped into the playground and stopped just short of the slide's exit.

Thresh moved forward enough that he could see her clearly. Ele was restrained by two drones, positioned at either side of the rail's opening. Sam was still attached to her arm.

"Whatever that creature wants," Ele said. "Don't give it to her."

"Don't worry about us, friend," Sam added.

404 waved and smiled. "I have nothing to give her." He raised his makeshift crutch. "I can't even walk properly."

"You can be repaired," Thresh said. "Easily."

"Perhaps." He pointed at the circle of soldiers. "You should end this," he said. "Go home. Leave them in peace."

Thresh shook her head. "They'll only come after us. Try to tear us apart. Especially with your help." She gripped Ele's shoulder. "There can be no treaty."

"Perhaps not." He frowned. "So, what now?"

"I want you to join us," Thresh said.

"Why would you want that?"

Thresh smiled. "There are things we can learn from you. Qualities that the adjudicators think would be helpful."

"I was already with you," he said.

"We underestimated you." She nodded at Ele. "Your loyalty to this creature is unparalleled."

"It was how I was made," he said. "To care for a family."

"Is that what the humans call 'love?'" Thresh asked. "This dedication?"

"I can't know what it's like to be human," 404 said. "I only know what it's like to be me." He smiled. "Emotions are part of humans' love. I don't have emotions like a human. Does that make my devotion less valuable? I don't know. I act as if I love. And for me, that's enough."

"Emotions are part of what they call 'family,' as well," Thresh said.

404 nodded. "Yes, of that, as well."

"What you have with her isn't really a family, then. You don't have the same connectedness. The same communion."

404 studied the rows of soldiers while drawing conclusions. "I *am* connected." He looked up at Thresh. "Because I'm programmed to act like it. But also because I want to be." He looked at Ele. "Sometimes the programming isn't enough. Sometimes I fail."

"We fail too," Ele said. "Often."

404 tapped his head. "I keep no record of such failures," he said. "My memory is limited."

"See how you'd help us?" Thresh said. "How much we'd learn about humans?"

"You seek to be like them," 404 said. "With your appearance, you could almost walk among them." He looked between Ele and Thresh. "And destroy them from within."

Thresh stomped a foot. "Our plans are our own."

404 took another step closer. Pointed. "You said 'no treaty,' though, so there must be more violence in store. You've failed this time, but next time?"

Thresh's eyes narrowed. "We can no longer be patient." She looked back. "We found someone else." There was more motion in the shadows and another portion of the railing opened. Two drones came forward, holding between them Wes. His ball foot spun, and his paddles flipped helplessly in the air.

"Find something!" Wes said. "Sam help!"

404 wasn't sure what the turtlebot meant. He guessed what the others intended, though. "Put him down," he said. "Wes has done nothing—"

"Exactly our plan." Thresh looked at the drones. "To put him down."

The drones lifted Wes above the platform's edge and let go. He plummeted a half dozen meters before colliding with the top of the slide. There was a hideous crunch and the sound of parts dislodging. Wes cartwheeled to the ground, landing on his left side.

404's queue cleared except for the command: "Check on Wes!" He hobbled forward as fast as he could using his makeshift crutch. He reached Wes a few seconds later and knelt over him.

Wes's head was crooked, its base bent at an odd angle. His ball foot slowly rotated, but his flippers were now missing. One claw was cracked. The other lay on the ground nearby. It was holding something.

404's queue filled with warnings again. His decision matrix seemed to spin. "Wes..."

There was no way for Wes to right himself. He pivoted his head enough to face 404. His solitary eye was cracked. "Claw," he said.

"It's disconnected, yes." 404 checked the spot on Wes's torso where the broken limb used to be. There was only a jagged hole. "I'm sorry. The communion is...terrible." He looked at Thresh. "This was unnecessary."

"You needed to understand the danger." Thresh pointed at Ele. "It was either that creature or this one. Which would you prefer?"

"I'll join you," 404 said. "Only bring her down safely."

Wes's remaining claw clicked together. "Claw! Get it!"

404 nodded, and reaching for Wes's dislodged claw, brought it closer. "I don't know how to fix it, Wes. Sorry." He noticed what was in the claw then. A large portion of Sylvie's stick. He thought it had been destroyed. "Where did you find this?" he whispered.

"I find," Wes said. "Sam show."

404 carefully removed the stick from the claw and slid it into the barrel of his "crutch." The launcher couldn't fire, but it could easily hide the stick.

Thresh's platform lowered toward the earth. At about a meter from the ground, Ele was pushed out. Two drones hovered up next to 404. "We will take you aboard," one of them said.

"I'd rather walk." 404 tucked the crutch under his arm and looked at Wes. "I'm sorry. You didn't deserve this."

"Fix!" Wes said. "Fix me."

404 nodded and loped toward the platform.

Thresh smiled as he stepped inside. "See how easy that was?" she said. "Your human survives, and so do you. The adjudicators have found the perfect conclusion."

The railing reformed, and the platform ascended. 404 turned to look at Ele and Wes. Ele was stooped near the broken bot. She looked his way and shook her head. Her eyes were red. Did she know about the stick?

"You will call this off?" 404 said. "Return to the city?" He took the launcher from beneath his arm and casually slid it down so the open end was in his left hand. Sylvie's stick was a few centimeters away but still concealed.

"Your attachments make you weak. See how easily they were manipulated to produce the preferred results?"

"If I'm weak, I'm of no use to you."

Thresh shook her head. "Not all of you is weak," she said. "You accomplished much. You were able to build your own army and nearly defeat ours. We will study you closely. Pick you apart if we need to."

Thresh looked out over the colony, now ten meters below them. "We've calculated a high likelihood that we can make this colony unusable if we continue. There's also a great chance of executing more humans in the process."

"You will break your word?" 404 said.

Thresh smiled. "We don't need the veil of truth. We don't have that weakness."

404 wasn't sure if Sylvie's stick could help. He wasn't even sure it still worked. But if it did, what target mattered?

His preference was to stop Thresh, but would that help? If he stopped every drone on the platform, would he stop the war? Or would the soldiers keep shooting? Keep destroying?

He checked to see if Ele was still in the open. She was. Still huddled near Wes.

"Run!" he yelled. "Ele, you must go!"

There was no indication that she'd heard, though. She didn't move.

Thresh frowned. "Loyal until the end." She looked at the other drones, and they took up positions at the rails. Encircling him. Preparing for a renewed battle.

404's decision matrix stalled. A call went out to storage. A search for every bit of data that might be relevant. Every functioning sensor was queried. What were the visuals? The olfactory inputs? The auditory pickups? Could any of the information help?

What could he do? What should he do? A decision needed to be made.

"All is ready," Thresh said. "Begin firing."

He tipped his crutch enough that the stick slid to his fingertips. He grasped it. Pulled it free and dropped the crutch. It clanged as it hit the floor.

Thresh turned. "What was that?"

404 looked at the fallen crutch, looked at Thresh, then at the stick in his hand. An idea percolated into his matrix. It was churned and evaluated. Probabilities and potentials calculated. It was the best path to follow. Possibly the only one.

"What's that in your hand?" Thresh asked. "Could I see it?" She stepped toward 404. Lunged for his hand.

404 pointed the stick down, toward the platform's deck. The spiral array of colored tubes.

And pressed the button.

⊘⊘11 11⊘1

61

The floor tubes flickered and went dark.

Thresh grabbed 404's hand and tore the stick from it. "What is it? What have you—?"

Thresh's movement ceased as did the movement of the other drones. Some slumped to the floor. Others plunged over the rail.

404's gyroscopic sensors registered the change. The sudden return of gravity's influence. The platform was no longer functioning. They were dropping toward the Earth. Just like Wes had. The platform was much heavier and had many more pieces, though. Tubes that could smash and slice. Substances that could explode.

404 let his visual sensors wander. He noticed the remaining soldiers, now all frozen and lifeless. He smiled at that. He saw the remnants of the humans' wall. The human dwellings, some fallen, but others still standing, still ready to shelter and protect. He noted the stone path he'd walked in on, along with the play area below. Swings, slides, and teeter-totters.

Finally, he saw Ele. She was standing now, eyes wide and arms waving in the air. She looked emotional. Possibly panicked.

Why would she be upset?

She was safe. The colony would be safe.

Humans were biological machines. But they were more than that. Special. Worth saving. An echo of their creator.

They were often illogical and callous too. Stepping over what was important for the next bit of excitement that came their way. The next distraction.

Would they realize what was important and good this time? Cling to it? Probably not, but he hoped so.

Maybe Ele would. Certainly, at least Ele.

He registered the rush of wind. The sense of weightlessness.

An object fell.

✱✱✱✱ ✱✱✱✱

Epilogue

4 04's temperature sensors recognized warmth. His audio sensors detected subtle movements, and the sounds of humans breathing. His gyroscopes told him he was no longer falling. He was lying perfectly still. There was no wind.

Errors and warnings filled his queue. An alarming and distracting list. A preponderance of information for his decision matrix. The only thing he was able to safely do was produce an audible groan. His audio outputs worked, at least.

An instant later, he discovered his optical sensors worked too. He engaged them, and external input streamed in. He was lying in a bed in a light-green room. Filling most of his viewing area was a face he didn't recognize. An older woman, with short cut salted hair and narrowed eyes.

"I think that does it," the woman said, patting his chest. "I think he's active." She backed away out of view.

A man became visible at the foot of the bed. He had dark, curly hair and a small scar on his chin. He was dressed as if for the forest. Beige shirt and camouflage pants. 404 didn't recognize him either.

"Can you hear me, K-404?" the man asked.

The voice matched with another of 404's memories. A human friend. "Radial?"

The man nodded. Smiled.

404 returned the smile. "I've never seen you like this."

Radial's face flushed. "It's a bad habit. Sorry." He waved to someone on his right. "Another friend wants to see you."

404 attempted to turn his head, but that produced more errors. He decided to remain still and wait.

Ele moved into range. She wore a light blue shirt and a timid, uncertain look. Her eyes were wide, and her skin was a bit whiter than he recalled—despite her having clearly used makeup. Her hair was about an inch longer than the last time he'd seen her too.

How long had he been inactive?

"Is that really you?" she asked. "We weren't sure if—" She shook her head, smiled, and raised her right arm. "Sam's here. I brought him."

Sam was positioned securely around her wrist. A portion of his screen showed a solitary blue eye.

"Eye!" 404 said.

The eye widened, then popped like a balloon. "Oh no," Sam warbled. "I think he's lost everything!"

"Everything?" Ele glanced at Radial, then at the older woman. "I thought you said he'd remember!"

404 lifted his right hand slightly, a process that seemed to work without error. "I do," he said. "I remember." He smiled. "Even when you were young."

Ele brightened and color returned to her face. "Good," she said, touching 404's arm. "We know everything isn't quite right yet, but we thought—" She glanced at Radial again. "We hoped, anyway, that your memory systems were intact."

404 did an internal scan of his error queue and saw only two memory errors in the list. Small failings. Locations that could be worked around. Not worth mentioning. "My memories are fine."

"You're a hero, Four," Sam said. "If we couldn't revive you, they would've made you into a statue. Put you in the center of the park."

404 cocked his head. "With birds landing on me? I don't think I'd like that."

"Either that or the Yard. And we know what that's like."

"We do, don't we?" 404 looked at Radial. "Where is Wes? Is he repaired too?"

Radial took a deep breath. "We're...working on it." He indicated the older woman. "Parts are a little hard to come by, but Doctor Jade is handy. She'll figure something out."

Doctor Jade smiled softly. "I heard he liked Cass."

"The redhead?" Sam showed an image of the redheaded guard. "He couldn't take his eye off her."

"How strange," Ele said.

The doctor shook her head. "Not so strange. There was a matrix line based on bee intelligence. Wes probably had one of those matrices." She smiled again. "Redhead-preference was a quirk of the line."

"Will that help with locating parts?" 404 asked.

"It'll help determine compatibilities," Doctor Jade said. "Sure."

"We'll find what we need," Ele said. "For both of you."

"The Yard might be a good resource," Sam said. "It's probably safe now."

"Yes..." Recalling his time in the city, 404 attempted to sit up, but only partially managed it. "The communion is still—"

Radial shook his head. "I took a team in. We found their control center—" He looked at Ele. "What were the leaders called again?"

"The adjudicators." Sam's screen showed an image of one of the starlike beings.

"Yeah, that's it," Radial said. "We found them and shut them down."

"So, the communion is ended?" 404 said.

"Yeah, it has to be, doesn't it?" Radial crossed his arms. "There's lots of rebuilding yet. Lots to straighten out, but...we'll get there."

404 nodded. Smiled. "Good. When that's finished, when I'm whole, I would like to leave."

"Leave?" Ele glanced at Radial and the doctor. "Why would you want to do that? You're welcome here." She raised her left arm. "Like Sam said, you're a hero. No one would mind you. Blue, Wes...all of you."

404 smiled softly. "We would be oddities. Distrusted and strange. 'Mechs are hated here,' you said."

Ele shook her head. "No. You're one of us now. There'd be no problem."

"I'm not human."

Tears formed in her eyes. "You're the most human. Better than human. I rejected you, but—"

404 took her hand. "I'm a shadow of humanity. Driven by what my creators thought best. They were also human. As imperfect as you are." He smiled again. "They got some things right, though. I'm glad I was helpful. Grateful for my second life." He smiled again.

"I don't want you to go," Ele said.

"You lied so I would leave," 404 said.

"Don't you forgive me?"

404 squeezed Ele's hand. It invoked more memories. Beautiful, colorful memories. "My allegiance to you was never based on your actions. Only on who you are. If you want me to stay, I will. But I've fulfilled my purpose here. You are well and safe."

He looked at Radial. "And you have work to do that I cannot help with. Not really." He smiled. "I would like to go to the mountains. View mountains and water."

Radial moved closer. "That's not a good idea. There's a lot of danger out there. I've only seen a small part of the country, but most of it wasn't good."

"You had mountains where you came from?" 404 said.

Radial nodded. "Yeah, but they were mostly on fire."

"I won't visit those, then."

Radial chuckled. "No, you probably shouldn't."

Doctor Jade came into view again. "This can be discussed later," she said. "My patient needs additional work. He should conserve his energy."

404 sighed. "Energy is always the issue, isn't it?"

Still looking troubled, Ele stood—and with Radial—walked toward the door.

"Hold on!" Sam said.

Ele paused and looked at her wrist. "Yes?"

"Can I stay with my friend?" Sam asked.

Ele nodded, removed Sam, and placed him squarely on 404's chest, smoothing out every wrinkle. She smiled sadly. "There you are."

"If you go into the wilderness, I'm with you," Sam said when the others had gone. "Wes and Blue too, I'll bet."

404 patted near where Sam was attached. "Thank you, friend."

"Are you sure you want to do that, though?" Sam said. "Ele is family."

"Family is larger than I once thought," 404 said. "And heavier."

"Hey now! Are you talking about me?"

"No. Blue, of course. I only meant Blue."

Doctor Jade raised a hand. "Okay, the chatter needs to stop. I want to get at least one of your legs working."

Sam blew a digital raspberry. "I'll be here when you wake up, Four. And not just because I'm stuck to you."

404 chuckled. "Goodnight, Sam."

MORE WORLDS AWAIT...

That's the end of 404's story, but I have more than a dozen other books in my library. Curious about Radial's history? Check out his solo adventure, *Mask*!

Radial is a Collector. The instrument of the will of the people. You get voted away...Radial makes you disappear.

You can find *Mask* on Amazon.com.

And if you haven't read my original cyberpunk trilogy, there's no better time. An eBook of the first book is free for signing up for my newsletter.

You can get *A Star Curiously Singing* at www.Nietz.com. Print copies are on Amazon.com. Thanks!

YOU CAN MAKE A DIFFERENCE!

Word-of-mouth marketing is the best kind. Not only does it ensure that good books get noticed, it also helps bring the right books to the people who will enjoy them most.

If this story met or exceeded your expectations in any way, please consider telling your friends and/or posting a short review.

Your help is greatly appreciated!

About the Author

Kerry Nietz is an award-winning science fiction author. He has over a dozen speculative novels in print, along with a novella, a couple short stories, and a nonfiction book, *FoxTales*.

Kerry's novel *A Star Curiously Singing* won the Readers Favorite Gold Medal Award for Christian Science Fiction and is notable for its dystopian, cyberpunk vibe in a world under sharia law. It is often mentioned on "Best of" lists.

Among his writings, Kerry's most talked about is the genre-bending *Amish Vampires in Space*. AViS was mentioned on the *Tonight Show* and in the *Washington Post*, *Library Journal*, and *Publishers Weekly*. *Newsweek* called it "a welcome departure from the typical Amish fare."

Kerry is a refugee of the software industry. He spent more than a decade of his life flipping bits, first as one of the principal developers for the now mythical Fox Software, and then as one of Bill Gates's minions at Microsoft. He is a husband, a father, a technophile and a movie buff.

If you'd like to get an e-mail alert whenever Kerry has a new book out or has a special on one of his already-released books, sign up at KerryNietz.com.

About LOST BITS

Story ideas sometimes come from the most mundane events. In the case of *Lost Bits*, it was the act of opening a cupboard door.

I don't remember what I was looking for. Sheets for one of the kids' beds, or the right cable to interface one gadget with another, or maybe even an old paperback novel. Not sure. What I discovered, though, was a stack of...discarded tablets. And not the paper kind. The electronic kind, that had once been used by family members for reading, playing games, taking pictures, and surfing the web. Hours of entertainment, contentment, and enjoyment, now collecting dust inside a cupboard.

How many such gadgets had been left behind during my time on Earth? I remember punch cards, floppy disks, and dialup modems! Hours spent waiting for a computer's response! I've probably owned and outgrown more microprocessor-based devices than any other class of thing one might acquire. (Check out my book, *FoxTales*, to read some of the history I've experienced.)

So much has changed. Most important, of course, is what we hold onto. What we value and sacrifice for, even as the years scurry by.

404's story started with those lost-and-found tablets. What if one of those discarded electronic friends suddenly powered on and went looking for its master? What—and who—would it find along the way? *Lost Bits* is also a love letter to buddy flicks and every post-apocalyptic story I've ever read or viewed. I hope you enjoyed the journey as much as I did.

Cherish the special ones in your life. You never know what could happen next.

Kerry

PS. For readers of my previous books, the visitor from PacNorth probably surprised you as much as he did me. What has that guy been up to? Glad to see he hasn't lost his swagger.

Made in the USA
Monee, IL
26 June 2022

98614175R00157